ONE SUMMER IN VENICE

NICKY PELLEGRINO

ISIS
LARGE
PRINT

First published in Great Britain 2015
by
Orion Books
an imprint of The Orion Publishing Group Ltd.

First Isis Edition
published 2017
by arrangement with
The Orion Publishing Group Ltd.
An Hachette UK Company

A catalogue record for this book is available
from the British Library.

ISBN 978–1–78541–342–1 (hb)
ISBN 978–1–78541–348–3 (pb)

Published by
F. A. Thorpe (Publishing)
Anstey, Leicestershire

Set by Words & Graphics Ltd.
Anstey, Leicestershire
Printed and bound in Great Britain by
T. J. International Ltd., Padstow, Cornwall

This book is printed on acid-free paper

Life isn't about finding yourself.
Life is about creating yourself.

George Bernard Shaw

This isn't a mid-life crisis, OK? For a start, I'm not old enough to have one of those. I'm calling it a happiness experiment. I've stolen an entire summer from my life, and by the time it's over, I plan to leave this place with a list in my hand.

I live by my lists. At home there is one stuck to the fridge with a magnet; at work one is pinned to the wall. Both are full of things I have to do and stuff that needs attention. Now I'm going to write another.

The ten things that make me happy, that's all I want to know. How difficult can it be? They may be small things — a cup of tea in bed, a day without rain — or bigger ones. It's still the beginning, so how can I know?

These are the questions I keep asking myself: am I missing out? Is there another life I ought to be leading? Did I fall into the one I have for all the wrong reasons? I want to find out now before the years slip by and it's too late for me to change.

Am I scared? Yes, a little. An experiment like this isn't for the faint-hearted. Much safer to bump along with the life you have than walk away from it; far more acceptable, too.

It's fair to say no one is very impressed with me right now. I'm sure my husband thinks I'm being selfish, my sister that I've lost my mind, my daughter that I've deserted her. Perhaps all of them are right. But the thing is, it's only one summer, here in a city where no one knows me; one stolen summer.

What do I want from my life? I want to be happier. Don't you?

CHAPTER
ONE

Looking back, I can see I was living life through gritted teeth. I had been for ages.

That's not the person I am; just ask anyone. I'm the girl who turns up the music at parties. The noisy, laughing one you want to hang out with. At least that's who I used to be.

Something changed me. Not growing older, not motherhood, not working such long hours — or, I don't know, maybe all those things. It was as if I'd started shrinking, curling up inside myself, growing still and silent. Outwardly I must have looked the same; even acted it. Certainly no one seemed to notice.

"Addolorata Martinelli, you have a dream life," my friends often said. They envied me, I guess. There were the single women who thought how lucky I was to have a husband like Eden, the childless ones who would have done almost anything for a daughter. And then there was the restaurant, Little Italy, that my father spent his life building up and gave to me when he retired. Anyone who struggles with an awful job or boss would envy that.

All I can say is that lives look different from the outside. Take Little Italy. For as long as I can remember, it has stood on a corner in Clerkenwell beside the street market. It is much bigger nowadays than it was when Papa started it and I've made a few changes: replaced the old canopy sheltering the tables outside, removed the stucco from the walls, exchanged the red chequered tablecloths for stylish plain ones. Still, you can rely on the food we serve. There are the same deep dishes of risotto, creamy and comforting, the peasant soups of pasta and beans, the rich Neapolitan ragu we simmer for hours. There is minestrone in winter, courgette flowers in spring. And there is always tiramisu, made fresh every day. You can definitely rely on that.

The problem is, people today want more than reliability. They're looking for the latest thing: gourmet burger joints, Southern barbecue, raw food, small plates, pop-up this and that. Then there are the ones who used to lunch weekly with their clients before they lost their expense accounts, or worse, their jobs. And the customers that moved away or died or simply stopped eating out.

We still had enough regulars to keep us afloat, so I wasn't making a loss, but the thought of it was what interrupted my sleep. Who would I let go? The sous chef whose girlfriend had just had a baby? The waiter who had been with me for years? The young cook short on experience but bursting with talent? So many of them depending on me . . . and I'm just one person.

Yes, I'm only one person, but since Eden hurt his back and had to take time off work, I'd been keeping up the mortgage, paying the bills. And then there was our daughter Katia, just turned twelve and already more like a teenager, full of small rebellions and big ideas. And the menagerie she insisted we have: the mice, the goldfish and the bloody terrapins. It was me that had to feed them all, deal with dirty cages and tanks.

That was the life I'd made for myself, so I'd been gritting my teeth and getting on with it. Hoping the restaurant would survive without lay-offs. Hoping somebody would fix Eden's back. Really hoping the terrapins wouldn't bite off one of Katia's fingers.

I didn't talk about it really. Better to swallow the words, try to be the old Addolorata on the outside, full of clamour and bounce. Wine helped; it was always a relief when it was time to pour the first glass. Half a bottle softened the edges; finish it off and I was almost me again.

No, I didn't go for counselling or therapy; I hate that kind of thing. Besides, this wasn't proper depression, just a lack of happiness. It wasn't as if I was crying all the time, or struggling to do my job, or thinking of ending it all. I've known people who've suffered from depression. My last sous chef had a terrible time until her doctor got her on the proper medication. I remember once she said her life felt like a steep mountain she didn't have the strength to climb. Things weren't that bad for me, nowhere near. My problem was that I felt numb, stuck somewhere in a no-man's-land of feelings, permanently dull. And I wasn't sure I liked who I'd become. Still, I was getting through the days and weeks all right; I was managing. Right up until the day of Guy Rochester's review.

Possibly you've read his column in the *Sunday Herald*. It's terribly clever and not very nice. I've heard that lots of places have a photo of him tacked up where the waiters can see it. Him, Jay Rayner, Fay Maschler: a gallery of all the influential food critics so they can spring into action if one of them is spotted in the dining room; give them flawless food and service, and hope for a positive review. Not that it ever works with Guy Rochester. No matter how well he eats, he twists the knife afterwards. The man is famously savage.

It had been a long time since any of the major food critics bothered with Little Italy. The place was such an institution and there were plenty of flashy new joints with celebrity chefs to grab their attention. Now and then a customer might mention us on a website, but mostly they were kind. Bad publicity was one thing I wasn't worried about at that point.

I guess he must have come in on a day when Frederico wasn't working. Frederico is our head waiter and has been almost since Papa started the place. He's way past retirement age but refuses to go, and I haven't the heart to make him. Frederico loves Little Italy; it's home to him. He still takes care of all the meeting and greeting, he wields the giant peppermill over your dish and lays a napkin in your lap. But what he does best is roam the dining room keeping his sharp eyes on everything. If Frederico had been here he would have recognised Guy Rochester and come straight to the kitchen to warn me.

And what could I have done? Possibly nothing at all. I like to think every customer gets the finest food and attention. There are off days in any kitchen but I would never send a plate over the pass unless I was happy with it. My father, Beppi, taught me to eat my way through every lunch and dinner service, tasting the sauces, testing the bite of the pasta and the Arborio rice, the tenderness of a side of beef or cut of lamb. He was rigorous and I've followed him in that if nothing else. Had I realised there was a critic in the house, perhaps I might have been able to lift my game a little, but not much. Had I known it was Guy Rochester . . . well, other chefs have thrown him off the premises, and I don't blame them.

Somehow he managed to come and go without any of us noticing. The first we knew of it was when the review appeared one Sunday in spring.

In my house, Sundays are as tyrannical as any other day. There is no time for lazing round in bed with coffee and newspapers like other people do. Instead I'm up at the usual time, boiling eggs for Katia, shoving down a couple of rounds of Marmite toast to keep me going, and then I'm out the door for work.

Little Italy has its noisiest, happiest dining room on Sunday lunchtimes. Lots of the old regulars come in to eat after they've been to the Sung Mass at St Peter's. That's the day they like to bring in their children and grandkids to celebrate birthdays, name days or anniversaries and order their old favourites.

That particular Sunday I was running late. Katia was having a tantrum over her maths homework and needed help. Eden was claiming he'd had a bad night and had to catch up on sleep. I didn't have a chance to flick through to the Eating Out section of the *Herald* to check who Guy Rochester had eviscerated this time.

I arrived at Little Italy to find things behind schedule there too. The atmosphere was tense and Frederico frowned at me as I came through the door. The sous chef and a couple of the others darted nervous sidelong glances in my direction as they worked their knives and chopping boards.

"I know, I know, I'm late and we've got a heap of reservations and it's all a mess." I plucked my apron from the hook and trapped my curls beneath a black cap. "Still, I'm here now, so let's get on with it, shall we?"

Frederico gave me another look, this one more uncertain. "Are you OK?" he asked.

"Yeah, just the usual family dramas, nothing to worry about."

At the start of every working day, I look at the reservations. At Little Italy we still use a big leather-bound book — mainly because Frederico is distrustful of computers — and it's my routine to open it and check how busy we expect to be.

That Sunday, to my surprise, several of the names on the list had been scored out with a thick black line. "So many cancellations today; that's a bit odd, isn't it?"

Frederico stared at me and frowned again, but said nothing.

"Maybe there's an outbreak of flu or something. Oh well, I expect we'll fill up with walk-ins."

8

Only we didn't. In fact it was the quietest Sunday I remembered having for years. There was even time for me to leave the kitchen and do the rounds of the tables. Many of the customers were familiar faces, people who had known me since I was a girl, and it was a pleasure to stop and chat with them.

"Are you OK, dear?" a couple of the old-timers asked, patting my arm, smiling sympathetically.

"Yes, just fine," I replied, wondering if I was looking paler or more run-down than usual.

Towards the end of lunch, as the portions of tiramisu were lining up along the pass, my phone rang. One of the rules I'm adamant about is absolutely no phones in the kitchen. I can't have my team texting while they're cooking; I need them to concentrate. But I must have shoved mine in a pocket as I was racing out the door at home and then forgotten about it.

"Shit," I said, pulling it out. "Sorry."

I had to answer because I saw it was my sister Pieta, and she knows better than to call me in the middle of a meal service unless it's for something really urgent.

"Hey, what's up?" I asked, pushing open the door that leads to the scrappy bit of back yard where we keep a few pots of flat-leaved parsley and woody rosemary.

"Just ringing to check you're OK," she replied.

"Yeah, I'm completely fine. Why does everyone keep asking me that today?"

There was a moment's silence.

"Pieta?"

"Oh hell, you haven't seen it yet, have you?" she said.

I patted down my pockets for cigarettes, then remembered I'd given up again. "Seen what? Pieta, what are you on about?" I asked, irritated.

"Where are you?"

"At the restaurant, of course. It's Sunday."

"But where exactly?"

"Outside, wishing I was having a smoke."

"No one has said anything to you?"

"For the love of God, Pieta, get to the point."

"OK, OK, but you're not going to like it," she told me. "I mean you're *really* not going to like it."

"Hang on a sec, then." I opened the back door and rifled through the pockets of the jackets on the hooks behind it until I found someone's packet of Benson & Hedges. They were Lights but they would have to do.

"Right, what's happened?" I asked my sister once I'd lit it and had my first gasp.

"Guy Rochester has reviewed Little Italy in today's paper," Pieta told me quickly. "Honestly, the man is a jerk. Has he ever said anything good about a place? I don't think so. That's the last time I buy the *Sunday Herald*. I'm boycotting it. Hey, Dolly, are you OK? You mustn't take him seriously; everyone knows what he's like . . ."

I think Pieta said other stuff, lots and lots, her voice going on, but I'd stopped listening. Dropping the cigarette, I catapulted back into the kitchen.

"Who's got it?"

Waiters froze and stared; the kitchen staff tried to seem busy. "Come on, you know what I'm talking about. The damn newspaper, one of you must have it."

10

Nino, the sous chef, looked like he was going to be sick. "We thought you'd seen it and were just being really cool," he muttered.

"No."

He nodded towards his satchel, slung up on a hook beside his jacket. "In there," he said.

I took the newspaper outside, retrieved the cigarette, stuck it in my mouth and managed to revive it. Then I turned to Guy Rochester's page and began to read.

They say you should never try to go back, that the past is another country. I should have listened. For in the cosy fug of my memories, one of the warmest places has been reserved for Little Italy. As a boy, this is where I was taken for supper the evening before I was driven back to boarding school. I was allowed to have whatever I liked — extra Parmesan, two desserts, even a little wine mixed with my water — and the owner, Beppi, always gave me paper packets of breadsticks to take away. As a boy, I loved that place. The food was smothered in tomato sauce as in any good neighbourhood trattoria; the stucco walls were covered in family photographs from the old days, the diners at the next table often chatting in Italian.

I should have been content with remembering. But something drew me back and my heart was broken. For Little Italy is like an old friend who has had a bad facelift everyone is too polite to mention.

Beppi's daughter Addolorata Martinelli took over from him some years ago, and since then it seems she has been busy stamping her lack of character on the place. I might have allowed her the whitewashed walls, snowy tablecloths and standard-issue porcelain. Pared-back style is ubiquitous but hardly offensive. If only she had taken the same approach to the food — kept it simple and honest, the way it was in her father's day.

But no, Ms Martinelli has done quite the opposite. She has taken beautiful ingredients and dressed them up with frills and furbelows. It's as if she has travelled Italy snapping up food bling and now is tossing it about indiscriminately — a salmoriglio here, there and everywhere, a spray of breadcrumbs or crushed pistachios or both, an odd crunch in a roasted pumpkin risotto that may have been walnut. More is more at Little Italy. Every dish has an extra accessory or two that ought to have been removed. It is a stark place full of muddled flavours.

There are remnants of the glory years. I'm certain I recognised the giant peppermill that showered chunks of grit over my companion's spaghetti with clams, and there were photos on the wall of Beppi as a young man. Sadly the new broom has swept away all the rest.

I could have forgiven Little Italy for not being the same. All of us change as we age. But I can't forgive this thing that it's become. If only I hadn't gone back.

I finished reading and what did I do? None of the things you might expect. I didn't shout or scream, dissolve into tears or storm out. For a moment I stood there, holding Nino's copy of the *Sunday Herald*, then I went back inside and returned it to his satchel. I didn't mention the review and no one said a word to me. We got on with the clean-up and prep for dinner service, mostly in silence.

In the dining room our customers were ordering coffee. The old Gaggia was screaming and whistling, handfuls of biscotti were clattering on to side plates, and waiters were ferrying back dishes scraped clean of tiramisu. Everything was exactly the same as every other Sunday. And yet it was entirely different.

"Addolorata, your sister is here to see you." Poor old Frederico; he looked like someone had died. "Shall I bring her through, or will you go to her?"

I hesitated. On the rare occasions Pieta popped in, we liked to settle at a table in the dining room and enjoy the chance to catch up. But today I wanted to avoid going back out there.

"Bring her through, thanks, Frederico," I said, marvelling that there wasn't so much as a wobble in my voice.

I suppose Pieta must have dashed out of the house and hailed a cab the moment she'd realised I'd gone silent on the phone. Still she was perfection. A coloured scarf knotted at her throat, her hair sleekly bobbed, red lipstick in place. Who in the world sat about their house looking like that on a Sunday afternoon? No one but my sister, surely?

I rubbed at my own shiny forehead. "Come out the back with me," I told her. "I need some air."

We sat down on the doorstep, side by side, and Pieta handed me a packet of cigarettes.

"I stopped smoking," I told her, opening it.

"Mmm, yes, I know." She passed me a cheap plastic lighter. "You can always stop again tomorrow."

Pieta and I spent much of our childhood sitting together on doorsteps. It was where we made daisy chains and coloured in our picture books. As teenagers, we smoked furtively when we were feeling daring. Then we grew up, and now Pieta led a clean and polished life, leaving the bad habits to me.

"So?" she began.

"So," I agreed, and that's when I let go, crying loudly enough that they might have heard me in the kitchen; so hard I couldn't speak for a while.

Pieta took the cigarette from my hand, had a drag, coughed a bit and gave it back.

"You know, Dolly, it seems hideous now, but it's just a review," she said, all good sense and reason. "No one who loves Little Italy will pay the slightest attention to it, because, like I said on the phone, everybody knows what he's like."

I didn't tell her about the morning's cancellations, just like I hadn't bothered to mention how often nowadays we had more empty tables than full ones. Pieta is such a success. She's a top bridal designer,

14

owns a chain of coffee bars and roasteries with her husband Michele, has two sporty kids and a shelf full of their trophies. I'm painfully aware I can't match up.

"Perhaps he's right and I have ruined the place," I said dully.

"Nonsense. You've changed things, but for the better. And what he said about the food . . . well that idiot doesn't know what he's talking about. I don't believe he ever did come here as a boy." Pieta was as angry as I'd ever known her. "It's all complete rubbish."

"Yes, but what is Papa going to say when he sees it? It'll be posted online. He may have read it already."

My parents had kept a small place in London but spent most of the time at their villa beside the sea in southern Italy. I had thought my father would be bored living there, but he'd discovered what he referred to as "the interweb", and, to my mother's dismay, fast become obsessed.

"There's every chance he won't, you know. Don't you have to pay to look at the *Sunday Herald*'s site? Papa is far too thrifty for that."

"Someone will tell him about it, show him. And then he'll be devastated."

"He'll be angry," Pieta said thoughtfully. "He hates it when anything upsets us. But I'm sure he'll think it's as dumb as I do."

"He was beside himself when I had the stucco taken off the walls," I reminded her. "And he's never really thought I cook as well as he does."

Pieta laughed. "No one cooks as well as Papa; you know that. He'd be furious if they did."

I stubbed out the cigarette and put my head in my hands. "I just want to run away," I moaned.

"Yeah, me too sometimes."

That surprised me. "Really?"

Pieta shrugged. "Everyone does, don't they? We all have fantasies about escaping the rat race and living in a simple beach hut or a cottage in France. Michele and I talk about it all the time. We'd never do it, though."

"Why not? If you sold all your businesses, you could afford to. And if it's your dream . . ."

"Yeah, but would I want it to become reality? I can't imagine walking away from everything we've got. Like you with the restaurant — it's too precious. There's too much of us all gone into it."

"I suppose."

"I know you feel rubbish right now, but . . ."

"Stamping my lack of character on the place," I said, quoting the review bitterly. "Lack of bloody character."

"Clearly the man hasn't met you," Pieta said.

"He'd better hope he doesn't. I'll thump his ugly face if I ever see it."

"Ah good, you've already moved from grief to anger."

"What comes after that?"

"I'm not sure," she admitted. "But I imagine I'm about to find out."

I leaned into her. "Thanks for coming over so quickly. I bet you were in the middle of something."

"Actually I was making a cake. It's your nephew's birthday," she said brightly.

Birthdays are one thing I love; I've always made a fuss over them. I bake treats, wrap gifts madly in layers and layers of paper so there's not a hope of guessing what's inside, organise games and costumes for the kids, cocktails for the parents. Lately I'd got so busy, all that had been scaled down quite a bit, but still I couldn't believe I'd managed to forget this birthday altogether

"Oh shit," I said to my sister. "I'm sorry. I've been flat out and it completely slipped my mind. I must be losing it."

"That's OK. I quite enjoyed the cake-making. It's a red velvet," she told me proudly. "Michele promised to take it out of the oven, and I've already done the buttercream icing. So I don't have to rush off. Perhaps we could go somewhere for a glass of wine?"

Pulling off my cap, I fluffed up my hair with my fingers. "I'd love to, but I ought to get home as soon as I can. Katia was messing up her homework when I left, and Eden isn't in good shape."

"Is his back no better then?"

I shook my head. "Nope," I said shortly.

Eden is a builder. He's always been super-careful on sites and projects, never had silly accidents like some of the other guys do. Then he spends money we can't really afford on a snowboarding holiday with his mates and comes home with a buggered back. Despite months of physio, it's never come right. In my bleaker moments I wondered if it was a useful excuse for him to avoid all the stuff he'd prefer not to do: working, washing dishes, cleaning toilets.

"Come on, Dolly, just one drink," Pieta said. "Half an hour max. Those two can wait a little longer, surely?"

"I guess so," I agreed. "But only if we go right now."

Normally I'm happy to linger at Little Italy, playing about with new ideas in the kitchen or pottering round the dining room. But that afternoon I couldn't wait to hand over to the evening shift and get away from the place and the doleful expressions of everyone in there.

"Let's head down to Soho," I suggested. "There's a bar I've been meaning to check out."

It's not an especially long walk from Little Italy to Soho: twenty minutes at a brisk pace. But on the way we passed two of my brother-in-law's cafés. They're all fitted out in exactly the same way, with industrial concrete floors covered in jute, sacks of coffee and mismatched metal furniture. The smell of roasting beans hits you ten paces away, and they seem to be open and busy at all hours.

It's difficult to believe that ten years ago Michele started out with just his father's old shop. He and Pieta have worked so hard since then. Now there are people lining up for their cappuccinos and sugar-dusted pastries all over London.

My sister never talks about the money they've made, but there's an ease to the way she spends it these days. She's always suggesting mini breaks or lovely little places in the south of France. She means well — I guess she's forgotten what it's like to live on credit cards or borrow on the house to pay your staff's wages. If she knew how things were for me she'd offer to help, clear my overdraft or give me a loan. But I don't want that, just like I don't want her paying our taxi fares or picking up the tab in restaurants.

"So where are you taking me?" she asked as we strolled down Old Compton Street.

"A new hole-in-the-wall place that does small plates of northern Italian food — it's had great reviews." I tried to sound ironic and failed.

Pieta took my arm and gave it a comforting squeeze. "I'd prefer it if we were celebrating rather than commiserating, but still, it's good to be out with you. Hasn't it been ages?"

"Mmm, I guess."

"And I'm sure I'll like northern Italian small plates, whatever they are."

Pieta doesn't get food. She missed out on whatever gene my father passed to me. She'll skip a meal without noticing, and would live off egg on toast if it weren't for Michele and the kids. As a result she is at least two sizes smaller than I am and looks great in whatever she puts on.

On balance, I think I'd rather eat. For me it's always been the best reason I can think of to get out of bed in the morning. Even as a teenager I lived for the pork and fennel dumplings from my favourite dim sum place; for Vietnamese noodle soups fresh with herbs, foil cartons of oily Middle Eastern salads, and dense almond croissants from the French bakery up the road. I'd steal Pieta's perfume, borrow her lipstick, cadge cigarettes from friends, and spend all my cash on delicious things. Often I'd bunk off school and go alone to eat in grubby places in Chinatown, or walk east to the bagel bakes and the Jewish delis where they sold lox and latkes. I even gave the eel-and-pie houses of Hoxton a go.

Food has filled my world ever since. I can't explain why, but I feel edgy if I don't eat well. Pieta would say I'm obsessed; I expect my mother would too. Only Papa understands, because he's the same as me. Mostly. Where we differ is that he is a traditional man, happy with the way he's always cooked and eaten, while I'm always keen to try the latest thing. And that's why I'd brought my sister to this tiny, trendy place where the door was unmarked, the bartender liberally tattooed and the counter groaning with scuffed enamel plates filled with Mediterranean snack food.

"You're going to over-order, aren't you?" Pieta sounded resigned.

"Probably . . . Here, you choose the drinks." I passed her the wine list.

She ordered some Prosecco, while I picked out what I wanted to taste from the counter food. A couple of *pizzette* topped with thin slices of marinated raw courgette; deep-fried olives stuffed with anchovy and sage; some sort of salami spiked with chilli; a plate of meatballs; a small bowl of marinated green chilli peppers.

"Enough," said Pieta. "I have to go home for Carlo's birthday supper later, remember."

I felt another pang of guilt. "I'll drop off a gift for him tomorrow," I promised. "Something lovely."

"Oh he's got plenty of stuff, don't worry about it. We can't stop his grandparents from spending on him."

"Still, he's my nephew, I want to spoil him," I insisted as we watched the bartender filling two flutes with sparkling wine.

Pieta took her glass and raised it. "To you and Little Italy," she said.

"To eating and drinking my way through the pain," I replied, clinking my glass against hers before taking a gulp of the light, citrusy wine.

Even though I wasn't especially hungry, I ate most of what I'd ordered, my hand moving from the plate to my mouth and back automatically. A lot of it was very good, and I was feeling full by the time I'd finished.

"Time for another glass?" Pieta asked, glancing at the expensive-looking watch Michele had bought her for Christmas.

"Go on then," I agreed.

Outside, it was a dull, blustery day. People were rushing past the window, coat-tails flying, chins pushed into scarves, and I was glad to be inside, sitting in a fuzzy pool of light while a bartender with whorls and swirls inked up his arms poured me more Prosecco.

"You may as well leave us the bottle," I told him.

In the old days Pieta might have tried to match me drink for drink. Now my sister thinks ahead to headaches and hangovers and rarely breaks her two-glass limit. If I'm making her sound like a prig then I'm sorry, because really she isn't. But we're different; I guess we always have been.

"Dolly," she said now. "When did you last take time off work?"

"We're closed on Mondays," I reminded her.

"Yes, but I mean a decent amount of time, not just a day."

I shrugged. "I don't know."

"It's not healthy. Everyone needs a break."

"Yes, but everyone doesn't run a struggling restaurant, do they?"

"Oh . . . is it struggling?" Pieta sounded concerned.

I swirled the Prosecco round my glass. "No more than lots of other places are right now, I expect."

"Well then I think you have to work out how to organise things so you can take some leave. It has to be possible. A couple of weeks won't make that big a difference, surely. Can't you leave Frederico in charge? And that sous chef — Nino, is it? He's been there long enough to look after the kitchen."

"Great, so now you know all about running my restaurant."

She looked hurt. "Don't be like that."

"I can't go swanning off on holiday, especially after today. Isn't that obvious?"

"Actually I'd say the timing is perfect. Get some distance between yourself and Little Italy, relax and free up your mind. I promise you'll come home better for it."

"Lovely idea, won't happen."

"It could if you wanted it to," she insisted.

Pieta topped up my glass, then splashed a little more in her own, breaking her personal limit.

"Where would I even go?" I asked wearily.

"There's a whole world out there you haven't seen. You'd love Asia, or what about Morocco? Obviously it would have to be somewhere with amazing food and lots of life and colour. You're not the cycling-through-France type, are you?"

"Definitely not," I agreed.

"Just think about it. Keep an eye out for cheap deals."

"I suppose I could talk to Eden . . . although whether he could sit on a plane for any length of time with his back the way it is . . ."

"In that case just take Katia," she suggested. "Do a mother/daughter trip. Wouldn't it be fun?"

"Maybe . . ."

Pieta has two noisy, uncomplicated sons. She has no idea what Katia can be like when she's in one of her witchy girl moods. Still, perhaps she was right and time away together was exactly what was needed.

"A holiday right now would be so lovely," Pieta enthused. "I'd come with you if we weren't about to hit wedding season."

"Ditch your brides and I'll ditch my restaurant," I suggested.

"Not that easy," my sister said regretfully. "And Michele and I have a big trip planned over Christmas, the Galapagos Islands. It's a surprise for the boys, so don't say anything."

Somehow my sister always managed to make me feel like a bad mother. Where had poor Katia been? Beyond a couple of soggy camping trips to Cornwall, days out to the pebbly seaside in Brighton, and time with her grandparents in Italy, she'd seen nothing of the world. Her cousins had her beaten in every way, it seemed.

"I should get home," I told Pieta, finishing my drink. "I expect Eden's seen that review by now. He may even be worried about me."

"OK then. But let's catch up soon. Family dinner at our place later in the week, perhaps? Don't worry, Michele will cook."

"You made a red velvet cake today," I reminded her.

"Well you never know: if it turns out OK, perhaps I'll try another one."

Pieta paid the bill; she insisted, and for once I couldn't bring myself to argue. Out on the street she embraced me. "Love you, Dolly," she breathed into my ear.

"Love you too, hon."

I watched her walk away in her little ankle boots and short skirt, slim legs in patterned tights, looking like she'd stepped straight out of some French art-house film. For a moment I considered rushing after her. On the corner of Wardour Street Pieta was going to hail a taxi that would take her back to her well-ordered house and husband. There would be birthday treats for Carlo, a supper table set with bright serviettes, gifts wrapped beautifully. Meanwhile at my place all would be chaos as always. Standing outside that funny little bar in Soho, wind-blown and softened by alcohol, I could have broken down at the thought of it.

Instead I walked to Oxford Circus and caught a tube home. As we rattled along the Victoria Line, I thought about what my sister had said. It was ridiculous; I was much too busy to take time off. Still I shut my eyes against the bright train lights and thought about the

24

sound of the sea and the feel of the sun, about cocktails in tall glasses, Katia and I lying in a hotel bed together watching movies in the evenings, and whole stretches of blue-sky days drifting lazily into each other. I could almost smell the tanning lotion.

Years ago I had this group of friends I used to go on holiday with. They were girls from school I'd stayed in touch with, and we'd meet up in villas beside some part of the Mediterranean with nothing on our minds but a good time. I still hear from them now and then. We exchange emails and cards for birthdays and Christmas, but it's ages since we've all been away. Everyone is busy marrying, divorcing, working or having babies, and we can't settle on a time, never mind a place. Now we've pretty much given up pretending it might happen.

I trudged home from the tube station feeling dejected. What little light the day had managed was starting to fade, and the wind was chilling. Would it be warm in Spain by now, or Morocco like Pieta had suggested? Surely it wouldn't be so flat and grey, so smelling of exhaust fumes, so utterly empty of anything to look forward to.

For a moment I considered booking a flight to someplace sunny, sticking it on my credit card and worrying about paying for it later. Then I reminded myself how impossible that was, and turned up the pathway to home.

CHAPTER
TWO

Eden and I still have the two-bedroom flat we bought just after we got married. It was a cheap house conversion and you can hear every squeak and footfall from the couple upstairs but it has a garden — one I kept meaning to plant up properly with shrubs and trees — and the street is quieter than any that surround it.

Not that it was ever peaceful behind my front door. Pushing it open that Sunday afternoon, all I could hear was the sound of motor racing. Eden was watching the Formula One, lying flat on his back in front of the television, probably still wearing the track pants he'd slept in last night.

"Turn it down," I roared as I went through to the kitchen. The dirty breakfast dishes were piled in the sink and some from lunch had joined them. Katia must have been painting pictures with her friends then got bored and left her stuff cluttering the table alongside the pile of bills I'd abandoned there.

Opening the fridge, I grabbed a half-empty bottle of Chardonnay, unscrewed the cap and poured myself a generous glass. "Did you hear me? I said to turn the damn TV down," I yelled again.

"What?" I heard Eden call back. "Dolly, is that you?"

"Yes, it's me. Who else do you think?" Glass in hand, I marched into the living room. "Where's Katia?"

"Um . . ." He shifted and winced. "In her room, playing on the computer."

"Playing what?"

"I don't know, whatever it is she plays."

"Eden, we've talked about this. You're supposed to be monitoring her. She could be looking at anything — porn . . . violence . . ."

"Why would she want to look at porn?" Very gingerly Eden pulled himself up. "I'll go and check, but I bet you anything she's not."

Throwing myself on the sofa, I noticed the *Sunday Herald* spread out on the floor near where Eden had been lying. Generally the restaurant reviews didn't interest him much, but if he'd read today's, it was odd that he hadn't bothered phoning me.

"Yep, playing games," he told me, coming back. "Nothing to worry about."

He settled on the sofa beside me, cushions braced against his back, engrossed again in the racing.

"So? Did you see it?" I asked.

"Hmm, see what?" He sounded vague.

"Guy Rochester's review of Little Italy in the paper."

"Oh that, yeah, I did. Pieta rang and told me about it."

"And?"

"Bit of a bugger," he said, still staring at the television.

"Is that all you've got to say about it?"

He spared a glance for me. "What else do you want me to say?"

Sometimes I look at Eden and remember why I fell for him right at the beginning. He has the most amazing profile, strong like a statue. His skin is the colour of milk chocolate, and although he's trimmed his dreadlocks shorter so they barely skim his shoulders now, still they're sexy. When I get close enough to smell that deep muskiness his warm skin gives off, when he touches me or smiles for no reason, when I see him again after we've spent a few days apart . . . but this was not one of those times. No, it wasn't.

"You could start by asking if I'm OK," I told him.

"Why wouldn't you be?" He looked perplexed.

"You're kidding, right? Guy Rochester just tore me apart. Obviously I'm devastated."

"It's one bloke's opinion, that's all."

"It's been published in a national newspaper. It's humiliating and . . . I work so hard and this is what I get . . . It's heartbreaking."

"Come on, Dolly, it's not like you've lost a leg or someone's died. Don't overreact."

"Overreact? Really?"

"You know what I mean. If you turn it into a big thing, that's what it'll become."

I gulped some Chardonnay. "Of course it's a big thing. If you can't see that, then you don't know me at all."

Eden surprised me by turning off the television. Without the scream of car engines the room seemed awkwardly quiet.

"So you want to talk about yourself again?" he asked. "Fine, I'm listening. Get on with it."

Eden and I have always fought. Usually we shout, on occasion even throw things. But he had never used that tone with me before: so cold and resigned.

"It's always about you, isn't it?" he continued steadily. "Your restaurant, your staff problems, your tiredness, your busyness. You never think of asking about my day — I assume that's because you're not interested in listening. Even Katia always comes second to whatever's going on with you."

"That's not true." I was outraged.

"You've been home ten minutes, but have you bothered to stick your head round her bedroom door and say hello? No, you're drinking wine and talking about your own issues as usual."

I stared at him, too shocked to respond.

"You use up all the oxygen when you're around, Addolorata; do you know that?"

"I've come home upset so you decide to pick a fight? What's wrong with you?" I asked.

"It needed to be said."

Eden was still speaking in that weirdly detached way, and it dawned on me that this was different from all the arguments we'd had before.

"I am what I am," was all I managed to say.

"Of course you are. So shall I top up your glass? And then you can keep drinking till you get all slurry and pass out on the sofa like you do every Sunday evening. Then tomorrow, on your day off, you'll be terse and impatient with everyone. Katia and me, we're used to it. That doesn't mean we like it, though."

The unfairness of this was breathtaking. So what if I needed a few drinks to relax me?

"Sorry for not being perfect like you," I sniped.

Eden ignored me. "We could carry on like this, I suppose. I'm sure lots of couples do. But is that really what we want?"

Suddenly I felt very cold. "What are you saying?"

"That something has to change sooner or later." Eden sounded sad. "I read that review this morning and you know what I thought? Here we go. Here we bloody well go."

"My restaurant supports us, Eden. It's what's paying the mortgage and putting food on the table right now . . ."

"Yeah, I know. You remind me constantly. But haven't there been plenty of times over the years when I've earned good money, paid for more than my share. You never mention that. Surely you don't think I like this situation. I can't do my job, play sport; it hurts to get in and out of a car, for God's sake. Then on top of that, you have to make me feel like . . ."

"Like what?"

He looked away from me. "Like a loser."

This was the man I slept beside every night. I knew his body like my own, even better perhaps. The scars on his hands, the moles on his back, the sprinkling of wiry black hairs on his chest. Still I'd had no idea this had been going on inside his head.

30

"Do you want to take a break from me?" I said in a low voice. "Is that it?"

He shrugged.

"Eden?"

"I don't want to upset Katia."

"So yes, then?"

He pressed his lips together and nodded.

"Oh God." I was stunned.

Suddenly it seemed ridiculous how upset I'd been earlier about a restaurant review: words on paper, cruel perhaps, but still only words.

Hoarsely, hesitantly, I said, "You want us to split up?"

"We just need some time apart so I can breathe properly . . . and think. If we can manage it without Katia being hurt, that is."

"Do you still love me?" I had to ask it.

Eden was silent for just a moment too long. "I'll always love you."

"But?"

"Like I said, neither of us is happy with the way things are right now."

I crossed my arms and hunched my shoulders. "Oh God," I said again.

Katia must have realised we were fighting even though we'd barely raised our voices. She abandoned her computer games and came to sit between us on the sofa, snuggling like she used to as a small child, begging me to tie up her hair in a French plait, shrieking when Eden pretended to tickle her.

My daughter is a scarily beautiful creature, a perfect combination of all the best parts of Eden and me. She has his full lips, my shiny curls, his cafe au lait skin, my heart-shaped face, his athletic body. She's one of those kids that people are always wanting to photograph or paint — I've even had model agents pass me their cards. Eden wouldn't hear of that, of course. He's as protective as he is proud of his little girl.

Now she lay on her back across our knees and kicked her legs in the air.

"What's got into you?" Eden said fondly.

"The devil," she told him, giggling.

"Uh-oh, that's what I was afraid of." Eden rubbed his face into her curls and dropped a kiss on her forehead.

"Don't tickle me again," she warned.

"I might not be able to help it." He wiggled his hands. "My fingers might just be in a tickling sort of mood."

Katia was at such a tricky age, like a teenager one minute and a little girl the next. Eden seemed to keep up with the quicksilver changes in her personality far better than I ever managed to.

I love my daughter, of course, to her very bones. Still, now and then I imagine what life might have been like without her. You're not supposed to admit that, are you? Not if you're a good mother. But what if she'd never been born? What if we'd never had those months of bath time, nap time, lunch time; the same routine on high rotation? If I hadn't spent the next years feeling overwhelmed and overworked? If my life still belonged just to me . . .

"What's for supper, Mum?" Katia sat up. "I'm starving. Did you bring me something from the restaurant?"

"No, sorry," I mumbled.

"Can we have burgers and fries, then? Please?"

As a rule, I was dead against junk food, but this evening I couldn't be bothered to fight her.

"Yeah, OK."

"And a thick shake?"

"Why not?"

Katia sprang off the sofa, throwing her arms in the air like an ecstatic football fan. "Yessss!"

I thought of all the special meals I'd prepared that never got that sort of reaction. "Just this once, though," I warned. "Don't think we'll be having it every Sunday night."

She didn't let that spoil her moment. "Can we go get it now? Shall I put on my shoes and jacket?"

Eden seemed surprised. "You're lowering your standards," he said as she raced out of the room.

Shrugging, I threw back the last of my wine.

The next morning, I couldn't get out of bed. Eden must have made sure Katia had some breakfast then walked her to school while I lay in the downstairs bedroom with the curtains drawn and the duvet pulled up to my chin, dozing on and off. This was something I never did, even on Mondays, my single day off in the week. I kept thinking of all the things that needed to be sorted, but my limbs felt too weak and my head heavy.

At one point I heard my phone ringing somewhere upstairs and pulled the duvet higher so it covered my ears. I thought of all the people who weren't me, all the Londoners rushing round out there doing their regular Monday things, and felt so separate from them, so cocooned. Just as I had decided it might be possible to spend the whole day barely moving, Eden pushed open the bedroom door.

"Dolly, are you awake?"

I rolled on to my back and grunted.

"Your sister has called three times."

"What does she want?" My voice sounded thick with sleep.

"Something about a dinner later in the week and a holiday plan; she seemed to think I'd know what she was talking about."

"Oh, OK."

He tossed my phone on to the bed. "Here . . . in case you want to call her back."

"Right, thanks."

"Dolly, about last night . . ."

"Do we have to talk about this now?" I said quickly. "My head hurts; I think I'm coming down with something."

"We have to talk about it at some point. But no, not right now, I suppose."

I waited until I could hear the thump of his footsteps in the living room above me, then dialled my sister's number.

"Hey," she said, answering on the second ring. "Are you OK?"

"How was the red velvet cake?" I asked.

"Oh, it sank a bit in the middle, but I filled the crater with buttercream and Carlo didn't seem to notice. By the way, I wrapped an extra little gift and said it was from you."

I shut my eyes, ducked my head beneath the covers and pressed the phone to my ear. "You didn't have to. I said I wanted to get something nice for him, didn't I?"

"Yes, but I know you're stressed and busy and I didn't want you to worry about it . . ."

Just that was enough to upset me. "Too stressed to buy a birthday gift? Do I really seem that selfish?" I asked her.

"Dolly, what —"

"Do you think I don't care about your children? Or their special days? Or anything but myself?"

"Sweetheart, what's going on? No one thinks you're selfish. Why would you say that? Oh, wait. Did you have a fight with Eden or something?"

"Mmm."

"Right." She didn't sound surprised. "I was ringing with some news I hoped would cheer you up."

"What news?"

"After our conversation yesterday I found this amazing bargain. And I know it was impulsive but I thought it would be the perfect mother/daughter trip so I booked the tickets for you."

I sat up in bed, shaking free of the covers. "Tickets? To where?"

"Venice. It's a package deal: flights, a week in a hotel near the Rialto bridge, a food tour included . . . it sounds so cool."

"But I can't. For a start, I don't have the cash to pay you back."

"I don't want paying back. It's a gift."

"Then it's too much; I can't accept it."

"I knew you'd say that, but the tickets are booked and paid for in your names, and they're non-refundable. Are you going to waste them?"

I sat there for a moment, phone still against my ear, saying nothing.

"Dolly, I can hear you breathing. I know you haven't hung up."

I thought of Eden and his need for time away from me. Imagined Katia's first gondola ride, or sitting in Piazza San Marco listening to a café orchestra with her.

"But I can't . . ." I said again.

"Don't decide right this minute; just think about it," Pieta advised. "And remember, you're not indispensable. Little Italy will survive without you for a week."

I felt tearful. "OK," I said huskily.

What Pieta didn't say until later was that it was a last-minute deal and we were meant to be flying out in a fortnight's time.

By then I'd already talked things through with Eden.

"I know we've been getting on each other's nerves a bit lately," I told him. "Perhaps this is the break we need to sort things out."

"Yeah, maybe," he replied, non-committal.

"We'll talk properly when I get back," I promised, although of course I was hoping that by then everything would be smoothed over, that a week apart was all that was needed to give Eden a chance to calm down and we'd be back to normal.

There were other potential obstacles to the break besides my husband. I wasn't sure how was I going to get permission for my daughter to take the time off school, never mind how best to organise cover for myself at the restaurant. Still, it seemed one way or another we were flying to Venice. We were going to have a holiday together, my daughter and me.

Unexpectedly, it was Katia who created the biggest fuss. She couldn't go away that week, she told me, because she'd be missing a school trip to the Natural History Museum, a rehearsal for the play she had only the tiniest role in, and most importantly, Saffron Cooper's birthday party, which lots of the other girls hadn't even been invited to.

That took me by surprise. I'd been picturing us doing all sorts of fun stuff and assumed Katia was getting as excited about it as me. When I tried to insist on her coming, she treated us to one of her more spectacular meltdowns. Piercing screams, stamping feet, slamming doors, the lot.

Eden managed to calm her a little, but even he couldn't seem to talk her into it.

"Venice will be amazing," he said as she clung to him. "Much better than a party. And you can go to the Natural History Museum any time, can't you? I'll take you when you get back."

She pressed her face into him. "I want to go with my class," she said, her voice muffled by the fabric of his shirt.

"Katia, there's no need for this." I was dismayed by the whole performance. "No one is going to make you go on holiday if you really hate the idea."

She turned her tear-soaked face towards me.

"Lots of your friends would love a chance to visit Venice," I reminded her.

"I want to stay here with Dad," she said solemnly.

I was crushed. It seemed no one wanted to be around me, not even my own child. "OK, I'll go on my own then. And I'll have a lovely time and show you the photos when I get back."

Eden had one more try at reasoning with her. "Your mum will be really sad and lonely. She hates being on her own."

"I'll be fine," I insisted. "I'm perfectly happy with my own company."

That made Eden laugh. "No you're not," he told me.

Oddly enough, everyone else said the same thing when they heard, including Pieta. She didn't think I'd make it through a couple of hours in Venice by myself, never mind a whole week, and kept coming up with ideas of people I could ask to go with me.

I did try a few of them. But my journalist friend Toni was in the middle of some big investigative story she'd been working on; Lou was mad about the latest man she was seeing and didn't want to leave him at this crucial point, and Rosie would have loved to come but her mother-in-law hadn't been well and needed her.

"I'll go by myself; it'll be great," I insisted.

Pieta pulled a face. "You'll loathe it, you know you will. There must be someone else you can try."

We were over at her place for a family dinner. Katia was upstairs playing a game with her cousins, Eden was advising Michele on some construction work he wanted done, and we were in the kitchen, me cooking and Pieta clearing up behind me.

"I don't know why you think I'm so pathetic," I said, mildly affronted. "It's only a week."

"You're a people person, that's all," my sister told me. "You're social."

"I always used to do stuff on my own, remember? I'd go off for dim sum all the time, and to lots of other places I liked to eat at."

"So you'll be fine at mealtimes, but what about the hours in between?"

"Pieta, you booked this trip for me," I reminded her. "Do you think I should cancel if there's no one who'll go with me?"

"Yes . . . no . . . oh I don't know. I suppose you might meet some people," she said hopefully.

"I'd rather be alone," I insisted, trying to convince myself. "A week in a city where I don't know a soul will be like heaven. I can't wait."

CHAPTER
THREE

Dark water lapping on old stone, gondolas slicing through it, graceful bridges and grand palazzos, secret gardens: unfortunately from where I was staying I couldn't view any of that. Pieta would have been horrified to see my supposedly four-star hotel room, with its hairy wallpaper, deafening air-conditioning and a bed that sagged in the middle. If I opened the window a crack, there was the distinct smell of drains and the sound of the chef from the restaurant next door yelling into his phone as he paced back and forth along the narrow alleyway beneath me.

This was no one's dream of romantic Venice, but still I was here, entirely free for the week and determined to enjoy it. I told myself I was going to do all the things there was never time for at home: shop, read novels, take long walks and afternoon naps. I even jotted down a quick to-do list on a blank page in the back of the guidebook I'd bought at the airport.

It had been strange travelling to Italy on my own. On the flight I kept very nearly making comments about the grumpy service, then remembering there was no one to comment to. Pieta had been right: I was surrounded most of the time, used to a crowded restaurant kitchen and a noisy home where people came and went. I kept telling myself it would be a relief to have a break from all of that. I needed time to breathe and think just as much as Eden did — far more, actually. It might take a couple of days to adjust to being on my own, but I would start enjoying it eventually.

I switched on the television so the empty hotel room didn't feel so deathly quiet and busied myself unpacking and hanging up clothes that at home only ever lived in a big heap in the corner of the room. I arranged my hairbrush, lotions and potions on the desk, stacked the books I'd brought with me on the side table, tested the creaky bed, then wondered what to do next.

It was only 3p.m., so strictly speaking too early to begin drinking and right between mealtimes. I decided to take a stroll round the surrounding streets and get my bearings.

Outside, the sun was shining and instantly my spirits lifted. I walked down a narrow street then out into a square lined with buildings the colour of spun sugar. Strada Nuova was only a little way beyond it, filled with street hawkers and tourists, supermarkets and boutiques, shops selling leather handbags and glass jewellery.

I ducked down beside the first canal I found, and within a few steps had left the tourists behind. This little *fondamenta* was almost deserted but its houses had laundry drying in the breeze outside their open windows, and I heard snatches of music and the sound of people's televisions as I passed along. I crossed a bridge, followed a shadowy tunnel beneath an old building, twisted in and out of a few back streets, crossed another bridge and realised I was lost.

Frowning over my map, I tried to work out where I was, but it was too confusing so I walked on further until I found a bar with a bench seat by its window and a couple of old wine barrels to serve as tables. Inside were two old men holding small glasses of wine; perhaps it wasn't too early for a drink after all. Ordering myself a Pinot Grigio, I took a seat by the door.

Up till then I had managed to leave my phone alone, but now I couldn't resist the urge to pull it from my bag. There were no messages, so I sent a quick text to Pieta to let her know I'd arrived, and then tried Eden but went straight to his voicemail. My last call was to Little Italy. Frederico picked up.

"*Ciao, bella*, you are in Venezia?" he asked. "How is it?"

"Oh . . . it's sunny, beautiful. What about things there?"

"Fine, fine, don't worry."

"Have you had many people in for lunch? And has Nino been OK with the specials menu?"

"Yes, it's fine," he repeated. "Have a nice holiday, don't worry about us."

"What about reservations for this evening?"

In the background I could hear people laughing. Loudest was a deep male voice that sounded familiar.

"Who's that?" I asked.

"Ah . . . just some customers enjoying a long lunch at table four."

"Anyone I know?"

He hesitated. "No."

I had the weirdest feeling Frederico was lying to me.

"Are you sure everything is OK?" I asked suspiciously.

"Yes, yes, but *cara*, don't waste your holiday time talking to me. Enjoy the sunshine. Enjoy Venezia. *Ciao, ciao*." And he hung up.

It niggled at me as I drank my wine. Surely I knew the owner of that deep laugh? And why had Frederico hurried me off the phone?

I considered calling back but didn't want my staff thinking I didn't trust them. So instead I ordered more wine, chose a few crostini from the display set out on the bar and had another attempt at deciphering my map. Maybe I wasn't quite as lost as I had thought. If I could make my way back to Strada Nuova, I'd be able to find my hotel from there.

Reassured, I nibbled my crostini, simple slices of crusty baguette with toppings of prosciutto, cheese and grilled vegetables held on by a toothpick. The last time I'd been in Venice had been years ago with a girlfriend and we'd lived off these *cicchetti*, little bites to enjoy with a glass of wine. At this bar the choice was pretty limited, but I knew that in other places I would find crisp morsels of fried seafood, moist meatballs, marinated artichokes, and best of all, *baccalà mantecato*, dried salt cod that had been soaked and poached then whipped up into rich, creamy deliciousness.

On this visit I knew that I ought to explore beyond the *cicchetti*, taste as many dishes as I could and head home armed with new ideas to freshen up Little Italy's specials menu. But for some reason, what should have been an idea to excite me instead felt like a duty.

Cooking has always been my only real talent. I understand food instinctively; or at least I thought I did. Ever since that newspaper review I'd been questioning myself, doubting every flavour. Was the ragu still as good as it had been in my father's day? Was the marriage of walnuts and roasted pumpkin in the risotto really such a happy one? I had asked Nino and Frederico, even Eden, trusting everyone's opinion but my own. It was an exhausting way to work, never mind eat.

What I should have done before I came to Venice was research the top *osterie* and plan the dishes I might try and the ingredients to look out for. There had been enough time, yet still I hadn't bothered. And now here I was, and the whole process of finding the right places and ordering the best things, of isolating flavours and taking notes, of working out how I might approach cooking the dishes myself . . . even thinking about it killed my appetite.

Sitting there with my wine and *cicchetti*, I realised that food didn't make me as happy as it once had. Perhaps I was falling out of love with it a little.

Other people have different passions. I have friends who are into sport or culture or fashion. Some have collections of things, or they like to surf, to play table tennis, ride horses, plant gardens or write poetry. My life had been so filled up with cooking and eating, there hadn't been space for any of that. Now I wondered if I was really so one-sided. Surely there had to be plenty of other things I was capable of enjoying, if only there was time to discover them.

Here in Venice, this was my chance. Yes, I had to eat, but I could do so quickly, standing in wine bars like the old men in this one, with a taste of something in one hand, a glass in the other. Then I would be free for the rest of the time to explore the city and myself. There would be galleries, exhibitions, museums, architecture, so much to see. I pulled out my guidebook to make a proper list of the must-dos, then changed my mind and decided instead to take each day as it came. Tomorrow I'd catch a *vaporetto*, a water bus down the Grand Canal, and find someplace interesting to explore, be spontaneous like I used to be before I had a family and job to juggle.

Feeling buoyed, I ordered a third glass of wine and occupied myself people-watching as I sipped it. Many of those passing the door were tourists; I could tell not only from the maps they were carrying but by their sensible clothes and sturdy footwear, the daypacks on their backs, the aimless trudge of their pace and the semi-lost expressions on their faces.

The few locals were just as easy to pick out, briskly swerving through the crowds, many pulling shopping trolleys loaded with the day's groceries, greeting each other with a quick *"Salve, come va?"*

A middle-aged Venetian couple stopped in at the bar, walking through its low doorway without a glance at me. I suppose they must have sensed I was just another visitor; that they were pretty sick of us clogging up their *calli* and canals even if they did need the money we spent in their city. I heard them striking up a conversation with one of the men inside, laughing at something he was saying, and I wished I was a part of it. I do speak a fair bit of Italian but suspected that here in this city of tourists it would take more than that for the locals to notice me. This was going to be a lonely week; I could no longer pretend to myself otherwise.

I was about to settle my bill when I spotted the woman. She stood out from the throng of passers-by, dressed from head to toe in red with orange bangles up one arm, yellow on the other, and at her feet three very cute fluffy dogs on leashes. She was old — in her early seventies was my guess — but she walked with confidence, head held high, and nodded a greeting at me as she went by dragging her laden shopping trolley behind her.

"*Salve.*"

"*Salve, signora,*" I replied, watching her walk on. Viewed from behind she was straight-backed enough to seem younger. Her hair was pure white and worn in a pixie cut; her skirt showed off how shapely her legs were. Idly I wondered who she was and where she was going.

Inside, the bartender took my cash while the old men avoided my glance and the couple continued to behave as if I wasn't there. It was like being invisible, as though

46

the old woman in red was the only one with the power to see me, and that felt unsettling. Perhaps that's why I set off in the direction I'd seen her heading. I wasn't following her, not really, but her pace had been fairly stately so it wasn't long before I caught up.

She was on a bridge, one hand on the balustrade, straining to lift her shopping trolley up the steps, the adorable dogs in a swarm in front of her. As I drew level, she turned her head and peered at me through the tinted lenses of her large round sunglasses.

"There are four more of these bridges before my apartment," she said almost accusingly, her English heavily accented. Only from the lines etched on her face could I tell she was easily as old as I'd first thought.

"Can I help you with your trolley?" I offered, feeling sorry for her.

"How very kind." With a clinking of bangles she moved aside. "I'm afraid it's rather heavy."

Picking up the smallest of the fluffy dogs and cradling it to her chest, the woman weaved along ahead of me, her bangles creating a rhythmic percussion and a sweet scent trailing in her wake. It was quite a long walk and the trolley weighed a ton. I heaved it up and down the steps of all four bridges wondering how she might have managed if I hadn't come along.

"So very kind," she murmured again as we reached her front door.

Fumbling with her keys, she managed to unlock it. Then, assessing me one last time, she frowned. "You should cut your hair shorter and wear a little make-up," she declared, before disappearing inside and closing the door.

I was left standing on the narrow *fondamenta*, astonished and even more lost than I had been before. Turning, I attempted to retrace my steps, but took a left at the second bridge when perhaps it ought to have been a right, and instead of passing the bar, I found myself walking alongside a wider canal past a row of restaurants with outdoor tables and coloured parasols to shade them.

Cut my hair? Wear make-up? Clearly the old woman was nuts. Still, checking my reflection in a restaurant window, I couldn't help worrying she might be right.

Alert to my glance, a waiter darted out of the restaurant, menu in hand. "You want to eat, *signora?*" he called, hurrying to my side and walking with me. "I serve you beautiful pizza or pasta, fish fresh from the lagoon."

Shaking my head, I kept going and he gave up. Further on there were more waiters touting for trade, shouting about their cuttlefish in squid-ink sauce and their sweet-and-sour sardines. It made me glad we didn't have to do that at Little Italy: hound potential customers and chase them down the street . . . at least not so far anyway.

Thinking of my restaurant drew my thoughts back to home. I wondered what Eden was doing. Had he picked Katia up from school or sent her to play with a friend? Sorted her dinner? Checked if she had homework? Often he forgot about the little things, expecting me to remember them. I think that's what I'd begun to resent most of all.

I was fresh out of school when I first met Eden. Back then we were similar in many ways. Both of us were people who didn't let much worry us, who spent what we earned and did as we pleased. Our attitude to life was the same. We liked to be fun, easy-going, impulsive, and weren't going to let being married change things. As for having babies, well, they would fit in. We'd take them to parties and restaurants, to pub gigs and Eden's steel drum band practice. It all seemed so simple that I couldn't understand why other parents made such a fuss.

Here's what happens if you don't stick to proper nap and snack times. Babies grow cranky and start to cry, get louder and louder until everyone in the restaurant or café is staring at you balefully. You feed them in the hope it'll keep them quiet, and to reward you they throw most of it back up on your shoulder so you smell of your own soured breast milk. Then they scream for half the night.

Katia wasn't even especially difficult. Other couples had infants with colic or bad reflux; kids who appeared never to sleep; who were always red-faced and leaking snot and tears. In comparison she was perfect; nevertheless, we struggled.

Perhaps we were too young. If we had given ourselves a few more years might it have been easier? Or perhaps I was just a bad mother, one of those women who should never have had kids.

Anyway, that's when Eden and I started fighting. I thought he should do more to help me keep the household chaos at bay; he said he did plenty. It was an argument we never settled and one we had so often it became almost a routine. Once, to make my point, I made a list of all the things I was in charge of — the laundry-sorting, the grocery-buying, the appointment-making, the bill-paying, the babysitter-booking — but Eden barely glanced at it before telling me I was being ridiculous and he wasn't buying into my stupid lists.

I'm whining, I know it. Don't imagine for a second that I like that about myself. My mind gets stuck on one track and I can't seem to shift it. There I was in beautiful Venice and still I was doing it: brooding on all the little unfairnesses, the stuff that made me bitter and angry.

I had to pull myself out of it. Looking at myself — a chef in her kitchen, a mum in her home, a friend, a sister, a woman with a week's holiday ahead of her — it seemed like I ought to be able to take a measure of happiness from all those things. That was my life. Why couldn't I be satisfied with it?

CHAPTER
FOUR

The odd thing about Venice is that you see the same people everywhere you go. You might notice a couple of tourists because they're badly dressed or especially loud, and then they'll crop up again and again. There they are on a gondola ride, in the queue for a tour of the Doge's Palace, buying water from a street vendor, crushed into the crowd on a *vaporetto*, sipping coffee in a piazza.

That's what happened with the old woman. Early the next morning I saw her at the Rialto market. She was wearing a white trouser suit that was cinched at the waist with a thin metallic belt, and her sunglasses were even rounder and larger than the ones she'd had on the day before.

I was in the fish market when I bumped into her, literally. There I was photographing the displays of tentacled sea creatures, scallops nestled in shells, blush-pink prawns and silvery scabbard fish, and I stepped back without looking.

"Ouf," she said. "Watch out."

"I'm so sorry, *signora*."

She looked me up and down. "You need to drink a coffee and wake yourself up."

"Yes, probably," I agreed.

"Don't go there." She pointed at a place on the opposite corner. "Further on is better."

That afternoon at the Peggy Guggenheim Collection I saw her again. She was sitting in the garden near a Henry Moore sculpture, wearing a floaty green dress with several strings of blue glass beads round her neck and her pets on the bench beside her (although I'm sure I'd seen a sign that said dogs weren't allowed). She looked very peaceful and I found a seat opposite where I could watch her surreptitiously. By then I'd trekked through the art galleries dutifully looking at cubists and surrealists and American abstract impressionists, and drunk a glass of sparkling water in the café.

If she noticed me staring she didn't show it. Now and then she patted one of her dogs but mostly she sat still, gazing at the sculpture beside her. I might have said something to her but couldn't seem to catch her eye.

After half an hour, I left my bench to walk back through the white stone palazzo and out on to the terrace beside the Grand Canal. There were plenty more galleries in Venice, churches filled with art, museums galore, but the thought of touring them wasn't appealing. I was starting to suspect that culture didn't interest me as much as I'd hoped it might; that it wasn't my thing at all. This old Venetian lady, though, there was something intriguing about her.

By the time I returned to the garden she had moved on. A Japanese couple were sitting where she had been, photographing each other. I stopped and offered to take some shots of them together. They smiled and nodded as they passed over their camera, smiling more widely as I snapped them linking arms, heads tilted together.

Everyone here seemed to be part of a pair or a group. The old lady was the only person I'd seen who, like me, was always on her own. If I spotted her again I'd try to strike up a conversation and find out more about her.

For lunch I ate *cicchetti* in a traditional *bacaro* tucked down a narrow alley. Inside old water carriers hung from the ceiling and the tables were covered with yellowing antique linen. I ate sparingly and fast. Just a couple of fried meatballs and some grilled vegetables washed down with a small glass of wine while standing at the bar, elbow to elbow with other people yet still alone.

I checked my phone again and saw that Eden had texted to say everything was fine. There was still no word from Pieta and that seemed strange. I sent them both messages to say I was having a blast. They would suspect it was a lie but I didn't care.

For want of anything else to do I walked through a maze of alleyways and watery lanes and, crossing the Rialto bridge, let myself be washed along in a river of tourists heading towards the Piazza San Marco. The shops I passed were overpriced, the shadows chilly and the sunny spots too warm. About halfway there I decided I was sick of walking and turned to fight my way back to the hotel. As I went, I kept an eye out for the old woman and her sweet little dogs, but there was no sign of them.

The next time I saw her she was wearing an orange turban and dancing the tango. But I'm getting ahead of myself. A lot happened before that; a surprising amount.

First there was the deliciousness of a guilt-free nap, sliding between cool sheets, closing my eyes and sleeping away the warmest part of the day. When I woke, I felt disoriented. It took a moment to recognise the cut-price chandelier hanging from the ceiling and realise where I was. I had slept for more than an hour, deeply and dreamlessly, in a way I rarely managed at home, where worries woke me in the night, buzzing round my head till morning.

The first thing I did when I opened my eyes was to check my phone. Again nothing from Pieta, but my friend Rosie had sent a message to say how she hated not getting to see me when we were in the same country. Rosie lives miles away from Venice, right down in the south of Italy, not far from my parents. She's one of my oldest mates and I miss her. But it's difficult enough keeping up with friends who live in the same city, never mind in a whole other country, so in recent years we haven't had much to do with another. She's drifted out of my life like so many other people who used to matter. Lying there brooding, staring at the cracks in the ceiling and the dust on the chandelier, I realised how sad I felt about that.

There was no need to get up — not yet anyway — and it struck me that I wasn't used to having so much empty time and looking for ways to fill it. At home it was difficult to find a moment to think. There was always someone ready to interrupt me with a question; my mind was forced to hop around from one thing to another, never settling. But here, with no decisions to make and no one else's problems to solve, I felt different in a way that's difficult to describe. It was as if I was inside my own head like I hadn't been for years . . . as though, without knowing it, at some point I'd lost touch with myself along the way just as I had with old friends like Rosie.

Rolling out of bed, I took a shower to freshen up and changed into clean clothes: loose cotton pants and a baggy linen top. Pieta had booked me on to a food walking tour as part of my package and I was due to meet up with the guide in the Campo della Maddalena in an hour. Judging by the map, it was only a short way away, but since I had little else to do, I headed off.

Outside, the sun was still bright and crowds of tourists seethed down the Strada Nuova clutching sugar cones filled with *gelato* and fingering the cheap leather bags that hung round the shop doorways; they moved slowly, stopped for no reason and generally got in the way. I was one of them, of course, but I didn't much like the idea. So tucking my map out of sight in my bag, I picked up my pace, tacking around the islands of visitors as I'd seen the locals do, telling myself that with my dark hair and olive skin I might pass as Venetian (although even I could see my clothes were all wrong: much too plain and practical).

I reached the Campo della Maddalena far too early, so sat on the steps of the old church to wait for the guide. A food and wine tour wasn't going to do much to further my aim of finding new passions, but still I was looking forward to it. If nothing else it meant I'd have company for the next few hours. And I hoped the things I tasted might inspire me somehow.

Other people joined me on the church steps. First a couple who looked to be in their fifties, then three northern English women and a young guy with startling blue eyes, and finally another couple, hand in hand like honeymooners.

"Are you here for the tour?" asked the young guy, his accent American.

"That's right," I told him.

"Yeah, me too." He held out his hand. "Name's Matt."

We had one of those standard travellers' conversations . . . where are you from and where are you going. It turned out he had been to a friend's wedding in Amalfi and was flying home first thing next morning. I felt a jolt of disappointment; it wasn't that I found him attractive, but it would have been nice if he'd been someone to hang out with for a day or two.

Our guide was the last to arrive. She looked like a local, her dark hair worn in a fat plait that hung over one shoulder, her eyes deep brown beneath a heavy fringe. Her clothes were casual but they hugged her curves. Taking our tickets, she checked our names off on a list and had us stand in a circle around her before launching into a patter she must have delivered countless times.

"*Buona sera*, everyone, I am Valentina, welcome to my tour," she said briskly. "Don't worry, we won't have to walk too far. It's only necessary to go a couple of

56

streets back from the main ones to find the places where the locals eat and drink."

The husband of the honeymoon couple interrupted. "Can you show us on our map exactly where we'll be going?" he asked.

She shook her head. "On this tour I will be your map. All you need to do is come with me and listen."

Swinging her plait over her shoulder, she turned and motioned for us to follow. The American guy hurried to walk beside her. I fell in right behind the gaggle of women, with the two couples bringing up the rear.

We followed in the same direction I'd gone the night before, passing the little bar with the wine barrel tables. Valentina stopped and pointed it out as a favourite with locals but didn't bother to enter. After showing us a church that was famous for its Tintorettos, and a few restaurants where we should be sure to eat if we had the time, she looped back and led us across the Strada Nuova once again then down a side street to a gondola stop.

Gondolas may be pretty but I can't say I've ever had a desperate urge to ride in one. Bobbing between the ferries and water taxis as some gondolier smokes or, even worse, chats loudly on his phone while he punts — well it's not my idea of a fun time.

The honeymooners clearly didn't agree. "I didn't realise this was a part of the tour," said the wife, sounding thrilled.

Her husband was scanning a flyer and frowning. "It doesn't say anything about it here. I hope it doesn't cost extra."

Valentina herded us into a tidy line so we wouldn't get in anyone's way. "Not a gondola ride, I'm sorry," she told the honeymooners. "This is the *traghetto*, the way we Venetians cross the Grand Canal. You will see there are two gondoliers on it rather than only one, and it is customary for passengers to stand up, although you can sit down if you want to."

I opted to sit down. Well I didn't want to be the tourist they had to fish out of the canal, particularly as the water looked none too clean. The rest of the group swayed and wobbled as the *traghetto* made its way towards the Rialto marketplace.

"I don't know if I'll manage this once I've had a couple of glasses," laughed one of the English women.

In the old days I wouldn't have hesitated: I'd have introduced myself to them, fallen in with the group, become an instant friend. But now I held back; not shy exactly, just not as convinced as I used to be that everyone would like me.

The Rialto market had closed for the day and so had the little *osteria* Valentina led us to. She knocked on the door anyway.

"He will unlock it for me," she promised, and sure enough, after a moment or two the door opened a narrow crack.

"*Salve*, Angelo," she called.

The door was pulled open wider and I glimpsed a man with dark glossy curls tied back in a red kerchief. He had a neat beard, long-lashed eyes and heavy brows.

"*Salve*," he said, stepping aside to let us through.

The space inside was all chrome and glass, very modern and not like the other Venetian places I'd visited. On the bar were two glass cases for food to be displayed; both of them were empty.

"Here fish is the speciality, but first of all we will taste some wine," Valentina told us. "I expect you have been drinking a lot of Pinot Grigio, yes?"

All of us nodded.

"We will forget about that this evening, because there are many other wines in the Veneto to discover."

She ordered a bottle of Verduzzo and the good-looking man in the kerchief poured us all a taste. As I took my first couple of mouthfuls I felt the knots in my neck loosen and my shoulders begin to lower and relax a little.

"Lovely, isn't it," one of the English women said. "I'm going to take a photo of the label and see if they have it in Waitrose."

"They never will. You'll need to go to a wine merchant," her friend told her.

"And pay through the nose most likely," the other added.

It struck me that I didn't seem to fit in here and it was difficult to pinpoint why; I just felt different to them, the outsider in this group and awkward about it too. Still, there was no point in sitting in silence for an entire evening, so I made an effort.

"I know a place where you might find it," I offered. "It's in London but you could order it online. I'll write the name down if you like."

"Oh, thanks. I'm Jennifer, by the way. We're from Manchester."

There were more introductions, followed by that search for common ground we English like to have when we meet each other overseas.

"Jennifer, Kim and Vicky," I repeated, hoping I'd remember who was who.

"You're here on your own, that's brave," said Jennifer.

I shrugged. "It was a last-minute thing. And it's only a week."

"Still, I don't think I could do it," she admitted. "I'm lucky that me, Kim and Vicky can take our holidays at the same time. Otherwise I'd never travel anywhere."

The *cicchetti* when they appeared were unexpected. Not the standard crostini, but miniature brioche stuffed with smoked tuna, artichoke and horseradish. Jennifer wrinkled her nose when she tasted hers.

"This isn't really Italian food, is it?" she remarked.

Valentina must have heard tourists say this before, because she had an answer ready. "No, it isn't traditional," she agreed. "But Angelo is becoming quite famous for what he does. This little *osteria* is where all the celebrity chefs come when they visit Venice. The food here is exciting, which is why I brought you. If you don't like the tuna, then try the next one; it is filled with swordfish, mascarpone cheese and sun-dried tomato."

Jennifer seemed unconvinced. I suppose she knew what she liked and this wasn't it. But I thought the flavour combinations were interesting.

"So why is the place closed this evening?" I asked.

"It opens only when the fish market is open," Valentina explained. "At lunchtime Angelo makes a risotto, a different one every day and always very good. You should come back if you have the chance."

"Yes, I ought to," I agreed, watching him as he brought out the final platter, this one loaded with crostini smeared with a creamy topping I recognised. Angelo wasn't a tall man, but he had one of those sexy, compact bodies and, toting the platter, he moved with surety and grace.

"*Baccalà mantecato*," he announced. "A signature dish of Venetian cuisine. If someone makes it for you then you will know they like you very much because it takes a lot of effort."

"In that case I'll have to try it." Jennifer's tone was mildly flirtatious, and this time, as she took her first bite, she didn't wrinkle up her nose.

I'm always slow to admit what I do for a living. I find it changes people's attitudes. Chefs are expected to know everything about food and be judgemental about what they eat, or insightful at the least. If you work in a restaurant kitchen, no one wants to cook for you except other chefs, who do it to dazzle, to show they are better, more daring or original. Even the rock-star types like Angelo who seem so laid-back can get competitive. So as we ate and swapped titbits of information about ourselves, I held back, not making much comment beyond asking for another of the crostini spread with *baccalà mantecato*.

As we were picking up our bags and getting ready to leave, Angelo turned to Valentina.

"You are coming to the *milonga* later, yes?" he asked her in Italian.

"Not tonight, sorry, I can't," she replied in English.

"You're never there any more," he complained.

"I know, but I have to work, Angelo." She sounded impatient.

"So you say. Still, I think it's a pity. It's too long since we danced together."

Valentina sighed. "Maybe if I'm not too tired when I finish I'll come along, but it'll be late. And it will only be for one dance."

"One dance is better than no dancing at all," Angelo told her, switching to English.

Jennifer must have been listening in and trying to understand them. Now she interrupted. "Oh, is there a dance?"

Angelo turned to her. "Yes, a *milonga*, tonight in Campo San Giacomo dell'Orio. We will be dancing the tango beside the old church. It's a lovely way to spend a summer evening in Venice."

"I didn't know Venetians danced the tango. It's not an Italian thing, is it?" said Jennifer.

"Not Italian, no, but these days tango is danced in places all over the world. In most cities you will find dance parties, or *milongas* as they are known. Some are large events, others just a few friends gathering to enjoy a social tango. Here in Venice the summer *milongas* are mostly held outdoors in beautiful places, and that's what makes them special."

"The one tonight, can anybody join in?" Jennifer asked.

"Of course . . . it is open to tourists and locals alike," said Angelo. "You can come to dance, or just sit with a drink and observe if you prefer."

Jennifer chirped excitedly to her friends as we followed Valentina through San Polo's narrow lanes. Tango was sexy, she decided, Angelo too.

"What did he say the name of the place was?" she wondered. "Is it far from here?"

"Campo San Giacomo dell'Orio," Valentina told her. "It's quite close. You could walk there easily, or take the *vaporetto* to San Stae."

"I think we should go." Jennifer turned to her friends. "Don't you?"

Both of them said no; their feet were killing them from walking round all day, they were exhausted from the heat, and the last thing they wanted was to dance the night away.

Jennifer seemed disappointed. "Well I can't go by myself." She turned to me. "What about you? Why don't you join me?"

I couldn't remember the last time I'd danced. It must have been ages ago, and even then I'm sure it was just some formless jiggling after too many glasses of bubbles at a wedding.

"I can't really dance," I told her, "and definitely not the tango."

"I learnt a bit when I was taking ballroom dancing, although I'm not sure I remember the steps," she said.

"Still, it might be fun to go and watch, don't you think?"

I shrugged. "Maybe. Let's see how we feel by the end of the tour."

The next place we stopped at was called All'Arco and it had a more traditional feel. Starched white curtains half covered the windows and there was space inside only for a couple of narrow marble counters to rest your plate or glass on. Behind the bar were a father and son who looked very alike except the older one had grey hair and the early signs of a paunch.

Again Valentina told us how celebrated this *bacaro* was; that many famous international chefs visited for inspiration.

"Really? I've never heard of it," I told her, suspecting she was exaggerating.

The snobbery of food — the restaurants that are in or out for reasons that have little to do with the dishes they serve — is one of my biggest gripes. Celebrity chefs are a nonsense, and don't even get me started on Michelin stars or molecular gastronomy or food that looks like one thing but is actually another.

I eyed the *cicchetti* arranged on the bar. There were the usual crostini topped with cured meats, grilled vegetables, cheese or fish; white asparagus wrapped in pancetta; courgette flowers stuffed and fried; little bits of seafood, but nothing that seemed outstandingly different.

Valentina ordered more wine; this time it was a chilled sparkling red called Raboso that I'd always liked. At one point we'd thought about offering it at

Little Italy, but Frederico hadn't thought there would be any demand. At the first sip I thought I shouldn't have listened to him; the stuff was delicious.

Although he was a waiter, Frederico had an influence that reached beyond the dining room. I listened to him when it came to the wine list, sometimes even the specials menu. His was the voice of my father; the pair of them had worked together so long that Frederico knew exactly what Papa was likely to say about anything. He was kind and well meaning, but still, taking another sip of the Raboso, I wished I'd gone with my own instincts.

As I finished the last drop, I noticed Jennifer doing little dance steps at the far end of the bar, tilting her glass in one hand and coming perilously close to a couple of old Italian men who were sharing a platter of grilled vegetables.

"Tango is all in the footwork," she called to me, arching her back then straightening it again and adding doubtfully, "Although I don't know, maybe that was the foxtrot. Oh well, I expect it'll all come back once we're there."

"I'm not dancing even if I do come with you," I told her.

Perhaps it was having company and making new friends, but the food at that *bacaro* tasted better than I'd expected. The ingredients were fresh and had been put together thoughtfully. Crostini were plastered with melting soft gorgonzola or smoked goose breast. There were tiny fried fish, and baby octopus seasoned with salt and lemon, grilled cuttlefish and marinated anchovies.

As we grazed, Valentina fell back into her tourist guide patter.

"Aldo and his son Pietro spend more time in this *bacaro* than they do in their own home," she told us. "It's the same in many of the other family-run places — they're more than bars, they're small communities with the same friends and neighbours stopping by every day to enjoy a little food, some wine and conversation."

"The locals must get sick of the tourists," I remarked.

"We're used to visitors here," she said coolly.

"But there are millions of us and hardly any of you."

"Yes, that's true," she agreed. "Some people are concerned about the cruise ships and the day-trippers; they fear the city will be overwhelmed or that it is turning into a Disneyland. But I don't think there's any point in worrying. Venice has been here for centuries; it will survive."

I looked round the bar. The two old men were finishing their food and preparing to leave. Apart from the patron and his son, everyone else had the look of a tourist about them.

"Were you born here?" I asked Valentina.

"Yes, my family are glassmakers on Murano. They have a small museum that you should visit if you're here for a few days more. Wait, I have some cards." She reached into her bag.

"So all of your family makes a living from tourism?" I observed.

"I suppose we do." She handed me a glossy card with a picture of a blue vase on the front.

"And you like it? You're happy?" I found myself asking.

She seemed surprised by the question. "Venice is beautiful and I live here. What is there to be miserable about?"

Valentina looked to be younger than me, possibly still in her late twenties. She wasn't wearing a wedding ring and I imagined her life as still unformed and full of possibilities. Perhaps in a few years' time she wouldn't be so sure that all it took to be content was attractive surroundings.

"Thanks," I said, putting the card in my pocket. "If I make it to Murano I'll check it out."

The next *bacaro* she took us to was a short walk up the *calle*: a dark, wood-panelled place that she said was famous for its meatballs. Some were the classic recipe of soft minced veal covered in breadcrumbs then fried, some bathed in a spicy tomato sauce, others made from finely chopped tuna and lots of herbs. The red wine was poured from a demijohn and tasted pretty rough, but I finished my glass anyway and accepted another. I was feeling much more relaxed now.

At the final bar we visited we ate *fondi di carciofo*, the grey-green bottom part of the artichoke, trimmed and steeped in olive oil and garlic, as well as skewers loaded with tiny sweet shrimp.

Before long Valentina began glancing at her watch. "I have five or ten minutes, then I must go," she said. "If you get out your maps I'll write down the names of a few more places you should visit before you leave Venice."

The others were faster than me, so I found a narrow ledge to rest against and finished my wine while I waited.

By the time she got round to my map, Valentina only bothered to scrawl down the names of a couple of spots, then gave it back.

"Be sure to go to the Acqua Alta book store; it's a special place," she told me, before saying her goodbyes and leaving the bar, breaking into a trot, her glossy black plait flying. Wherever she was heading, she was in a hurry.

"I think we should all have another drink here," Jennifer suggested.

"Or we could go back and get another bottle of the Raboso, that sparkling red we had in the place where we ate a lot of seafood," I suggested.

The honeymooners had other plans and the older couple thought they'd drunk enough, so our group was half the size as we tried to retrace our steps. Inevitably we took a wrong turn and got lost. It didn't help that none of us could remember the name of the bar we were looking for.

"Al Babbo," Jennifer suggested.

"No, that was the last place, with the meatballs," I told her.

"So it was. Still, if we find that, shouldn't we be able to find the other? They were barely a hundred metres apart after all."

We walked back and forth in confusion for a while. Just when we thought it was hopeless, we rounded a corner and there was the right bar in front of us, looking busier than earlier, with people spilling from the doorway and out into the *calle*. There was a hum of Venetian voices and the smell of something frying.

"It's too full. We'll never fight our way to the bar now," said Matt.

"Oh, I will, trust me," I promised him.

One thing I'm really good at is getting served in bars. I'm not sure if there is something about my appearance that catches attention, or if I'm pushier than other people, but it's always been this way; it's like my superpower. And this place was easy, because as I shoved myself into the crush and pressed towards the counter, I recognised the man standing in front of me from the red kerchief tying up his black curls.

"Hello, you're Angelo, aren't you?" I said. "Can you let me in?"

Turning, he moved to make a small space for me. "Signora," he replied politely.

"I was at your bar earlier with Valentina's tour," I reminded him.

"Of course . . . You are the one who enjoyed the *mantecato*; you took a second piece of it."

"It was very good."

"And now you need a drink, but this place is madness at this hour. Here, let me help you. Pietro, Aldo," he called. "There is a very thirsty woman here; you must look after her right away."

Pietro shouted something that sounded like a complaint, although he was speaking quickly and in Venetian dialect so I couldn't understand him. There was a lot of laughter and more shouting as he opened a bottle of Raboso with a gentle pop and set it on a tray with some glasses.

Angelo insisted on helping bring the drinks outside, walking behind me carrying the loaded tray. The others looked pleased to see him, Jennifer especially. Perhaps she was hoping for romance while she was in Venice. If so, she was heading for disappointment. Angelo may have been charming, pouring our wine and accepting a glass for himself, but I didn't think he'd noticed her. If anything, it was me he was interested in.

Men like me; they always have. It sounds arrogant, but it's true. I don't think it's to do with the way I look. I'm ten kilos overweight, my hair is so curly it's always a mess and I'm not elegant like my sister Pieta. My theory is it's because I'm relaxed with them; I don't try too hard and they appreciate that. Eden would say I'm a flirt, that I love the admiration and come alive when I'm getting it, but that's only because he gets jealous. The times I've seen him glaring at me from the other side of a room because I've let some guy light my cigarette or simply been standing too close in his opinion. And maybe I am flirting just a tiny bit. But it makes life more interesting, it's fun, and don't we all need more of that? I've never meant for it to lead anywhere.

Anyway, Eden wasn't there now to get all bent out of shape, so I could chat to Angelo for as long as I wanted without it being an issue.

"When did you start ballroom dancing?" I asked him.

"No, not ballroom, Argentine tango," he said.

"They're not the same?"

He shook his head. "Not at all. The two are very different dances."

"But tango is very sexy, right?" put in Jennifer.

"Sexy?" Angelo shrugged. "If you want it to be, then I guess so."

"But that's not how you see it?" I guessed.

"No, for me tango is a feeling, a connection, something very deep." As he spoke, Angelo held my gaze with his chocolate-brown eyes. "When you dance, it changes you. Come and watch us in Campo San Giacomo dell'Orio tonight, then perhaps you'll begin to understand."

"You make it sound very romantic," put in Jennifer

He turned to her. "Tango can be many things," he said gravely. "You have to see what it becomes for you."

I imagined myself trying to dance, tripping over my own feet or standing on his.

"For me I expect it would become humiliating mostly. I'd need a lot more wine before I'd want to attempt it."

"In the tango the woman must be nimble and move with finesse. I believe wine wouldn't help so much." Angelo was smiling now.

"Really?" I volleyed back at him. "I've always thought wine helps everything."

Eden likes nothing better than criticising me for drinking the way I do. He makes out I have an issue, and that's total rubbish of course. Some nights I do get the taste for it, but I never let myself get properly drunk. Often there will come a point in the evening when I feel myself start to tip over, and that's when I stop . . . or at least take it easy.

My husband is happy with a couple of cold beers after work on a Friday and thinks I should be too. It's one of the things we've argued about. I hate the feeling that he's watching and counting the glasses. Yes, it's true wine relaxes me, that the first thing I do when I get home from work is open a bottle, and that I look forward to that moment all day. But so what, I always tell him. Loads of people are the same.

Jennifer and the others were powering through their drinks easily as fast as me this evening. We were all having fun.

By the time we set off for Campo San Giacomo dell'Orio I was feeling pretty good. The American guy Matt had decided to join us, and I walked between him and Angelo, my arms linked through theirs, in a holiday mood at last.

It was a longer walk than I'd expected and there was little chance of finding my way back again, but that didn't worry me at all. I was with new friends, full of food and wine and heading to a party. Who knew when the night would end; who even cared? There was nowhere I had to be and nothing on my list to do except have a really good time. The sudden blast of freedom almost made me dizzy.

CHAPTER
FIVE

It was dusk by the time we reached the *campo* and already music was playing and a few couples were up and dancing. I sat down with Jennifer on a bench beside a small patch of garden and reminded everyone I was only there to watch. Angelo laughed and said he hoped so.

Straight away he joined up with a very pretty dark-haired girl and they began to dance. It was beautiful and, yes, sexy, but also full of feeling and actually rather sad. They began slowly, and as the music changed and quickened, so did their footwork. The other couples dancing near them seemed awkward in comparison.

As the light faded, someone put a glass of Prosecco in my hand, and for a long while I couldn't take my eyes off Angelo and the girl. Had they practised this routine? If not, I couldn't understand how they knew when to move forward and back, or when to turn.

Tango seemed a beautiful dance, and I found myself wishing it were something I could do, but I was certain my feet would never move in those neat steps, my body never pivot so freely from the waist or have that much balance and posture.

"Are you going to have a go?" I asked Jennifer, who was still beside me on the bench and seemed equally dazzled.

"I'd like to, but . . ."

"Looks tricky, doesn't it?" remarked Matt, standing beside us swigging beer out of a bottle.

"You said you'd danced it before," I reminded Jennifer.

"Not like this. I don't want to make a fool of myself. No, I think I'll just watch for a while."

Angelo and his partner took a couple of breaks, stopping to drink some water, but their energy never seemed to flag and they didn't falter. In the slow dances they were soulful, But it was when the music turned fast and urgent that the tango was most exciting. That's when I imagined myself dancing it.

It was pretty late when I noticed that Valentina had appeared and was standing on the edge of a group watching the action like us. She had changed from her tour guide clothes and was wearing high-heeled shoes and a purple skirt that flared above her knees. I looked away for a moment, and when I glanced back, she was dancing with a black-clad man and other couples were moving aside to make space for them.

Even I could see this was a different sort of tango, sexier but more aggressive too. As they moved together it was as if they were locked in battle. She lifted her leg in a kick, hooking it round his. He pushed her into a turn.

At first Angelo didn't look over and I wondered if he'd noticed her. Then he dropped his arms and fell back from his own partner. It was too dark for me to see the expression on his face, but his stance seemed angry. He stood for a few moments, hands hanging at his sides, then moved towards Valentina.

What happened next took me by surprise. Suddenly both men had their hands on Valentina's body. She turned to face Angelo, then back to her first partner, and they began to dance together, the three of them, pivoting round each other, feeling the music. The men passed Valentina back and forth between them, roughly at times, lifting her off her feet. They drew close and joined back together, bodies touching. It was an amazing performance but at the same time almost too intimate to watch.

"Oh my God, that is the sexiest thing I've ever seen in my entire life," Jennifer said softly.

When at last the music slowed, Valentina stopped and held up her hands as if to say *enough*. Angelo touched her arm but she shook free of him, backing away. There was still a crowd of onlookers, but she didn't stop to speak to any of them as she pushed her way past and into the darkness.

It was time for me to leave as well. I reached to my feet to pick up my bag, and that's when I saw my old lady dancing into a pool of light cast by one of the street lamps. I could hardly believe she had turned up here, but it was definitely her, looking serene in the arms of a white-haired man. She was wearing an orange turban and a slash of coral lipstick to match, and her partner was leading her in a stately tango.

By then Matt had taken off and I think Jennifer was trying to find some man to teach her a few steps, so I had the bench to myself. I was curious about the old woman and wanted to see her dance, just for a while. I made myself a little more comfortable, stretching out on the hard wooden slats and using my bag as a pillow.

She and her partner were by far the oldest there, and they moved more stiffly than the others. There were no showy kicks or lifts, and after a few minutes I realised that mostly they were repeating the same few steps. It was a modest sort of tango, but they carried themselves proudly and the crowd was clapping them on. As I lay there watching, the whole scene began to feel quite dreamlike.

Eventually I must have drifted off to sleep. When I opened my eyes the music had stopped, all the dancers were gone and the light was a dirty early-morning grey. Groggily I felt inside my bag and was relieved to find that no pickpocket had made off with my cash. My neck had a crick in it, my shoulder was sore and I was chilled to the bone. How long had I been lying there?

"*Buongiorno.*" A woman's voice startled me.

The old lady was sitting at the end of the bench beside my feet. Her eyeliner was smudged and wisps of white hair were escaping the orange turban.

"Is it morning?" I asked her in Italian.

She nodded.

"Have I been asleep here all night?"

"*Si, signora.*"

Slowly I sat up. No wonder I felt like hell.

"You need some hot coffee. Come, I know a good place nearby." Gracefully she slid off the bench and on to her feet.

"Coffee, yes," I agreed, wondering if she had been right there beside me all night.

It felt very early and there was no one else about so I doubted anywhere would be open; still, I got up and trailed after her. Free of her shopping trolley, with no small dogs at her feet, the old woman was surprisingly swift. She walked three steps ahead, leading me along twisting *calli* and over several bridges, only stopping briefly at a shop window to point out a red glass necklace she thought would suit me.

"You need colour," she said, squinting at me.

"Right, but coffee first, OK?"

Just as I was giving up hope, we rounded a corner to be greeted by the sight of a small *pasticceria* beside a canal. Platters of luridly coloured marzipan fruit lay in the window, and inside there was standing room only. Already a couple of customers were at the counter, downing an espresso or two before they hurried to work. We fell in behind them, the old lady glimpsing her reflection in a mirror on the far wall and carefully tucking the stray hairs back into her turban before giving our order.

I added my own requests: a brioche filled with custard, and a lot of water.

"My name is Addolorata, by the way, although lots of people call me Dolly," I told her as we waited.

"I'm Coco, pleased to meet you," she replied in English, and I thought I detected a tiny hint of an American accent.

"Thank you for staying with me last night."

"I wanted to wake you, but Silvio said that we should let you sleep a while. It was such a lovely evening and we were dancing and talking. Then Silvio left and I dozed a little myself and suddenly it was morning."

She spoke quickly, switching back and forth from English to Italian, with that odd lilt to her voice, so I had to concentrate to keep up.

"Who is Silvio?"

"A friend . . . a dance partner."

"Ah, I watched you doing the tango together before I fell asleep. You looked good."

She shrugged. "Yes, of course."

"Do you dance in that *campo* very often?"

"On Tuesday evenings in summertime you can find us there, although Silvio has had difficulty with his knee and isn't the dancer he used to be. On Wednesdays I go with Marcello to a place above the stairs of the church of Santa Maria della Salute. And on Sundays there is a *milonga* on the terrace of a palazzo and I take turns with both of them there. It is one of my passions."

"I can see why," I told her. "Last night in the *campo* I was watching this chef called Angelo dancing. It was dazzling. There were three of them in the end, him and a tour guide called Valentina and another man, all dancing together."

Coco wrinkled her nose. "I know them," she said. "I saw it too."

"Have you ever danced like that?"

She shook her head. "The girl Valentina, look at me, she is saying. She uses the tango only to impress."

"You don't like her?" I was fascinated by this curious little world I had stumbled into.

"I don't like the way she dances."

"I thought it was very sexy," I admitted.

"It is showy and insincere," she said dismissively. "Now my Silvio, when he dances, there isn't anything of a performance about it; he isn't even thinking about how he looks, only of me, the woman in his arms."

Our coffee was served and Coco fussed for a moment, adding a few drops of steamed milk to her espresso from a small jug.

I dug into the still-warm brioche. It was light and dusted with fine sugar. "Mmm, that's good. I may need another."

"I can't stay long," Coco told me. "My little dogs have been on their own and shut indoors all night."

"Oh, OK."

I must have sounded disappointed, because she glanced at me and added, "If you liked the tango, you should come tonight to Santa Maria della Salute. I will be there." She blew on her coffee before drinking it down in a couple of gulps. "Wear some heels and a nice skirt if you do. Maybe go back and buy that necklace I pointed out to you."

The trouble with a night out drinking is the flatness that follows it. I can cope with the headache, the dry mouth, the dodgy stomach, the puffy eyes, even the liverish feeling. It's the way my mood takes a dive that I really hate.

At home when I'm busy with work there is no time to cosset myself. A couple of Cokes, something greasy to eat and I'm swinging into action whether I like it or not. Here, with a whole day yet to unfurl and not a thing to do, I couldn't escape the way I felt. The fact that it was entirely my own fault was no comfort to me at all.

After Coco left, I drank another coffee then set off to see if I could find my way to my hotel. A couple of painkillers might help, and then a lie-down in a proper bed. If I could manage a little more sleep, the day might still be rescued.

The morning was a cool one and dark clouds hung low, threatening rain. I was glad when my walk turned out not to take as long as I'd expected. Ditching my map, I followed the signs to the nearest *vaporetto* stop, and from there it was easy enough to trace a route back to my hotel. I decided I was beginning to get the hang of Venice.

The first thing I did when I reached my room was to swallow down some paracetamol. Then I stood under the shower for ten minutes, sent a good-morning text to Eden and Katia and collapsed on the bed.

As I closed my eyes, images from the night before danced through my mind: the wild and stirring tango, the strong bodies and the memory of music pulsing loudly.

I don't remember if I dreamt of tango, but my head was so full of it that it was the first thing I thought of when I woke. I was still too drowsy to dig myself out of bed. Instead I lay there, dipping in and out of sleep, imagining there were dancers on the ceiling, spinning over the cracks and circling the dusty chandelier; light and free.

Eventually the prospect of food drove me out of bed. I wanted things that had been deep-fried, and plenty of them. After that perhaps I'd take Coco's advice and go shopping. It had been ages since I'd bought myself anything new to wear. All my clothes were black, and I hardly ever bothered with things like jewellery or scarves. I suspected there wasn't a single item spilling out of my suitcase that a woman like Coco would consider elegant enough to wear.

Throwing on my usual stretchy pants and bottom-skimming top, I laced up my Chuck Taylors and grabbed my denim jacket. Outside, the cobbles were shining with rain, the light was gloomy and a sea mist was rolling over the canals. It might be too wet this evening for any dancing to be happening above the steps of Santa Maria della Salute, but I'd go past there anyway and see.

As I turned on to Strada Nuova, my phone beeped with a text message. It was Pieta. *Hi, hope you're having fun. Need to talk to you. When's the best time to call?* she'd written.

All good here. Just heading off for some food. Call any time, I texted back.

Great. Later this afternoon then, she replied.

Briefly I worried that something might be wrong, but then decided that Pieta only wanted to check up on me.

She would be concerned I was getting lonely, which I was, sort of. I missed having Eden beside me in bed, and Katia's rare but lovely cuddles. At times I even missed the rhythm of normal life and its certainties. Here there was no work, no friends, no lists of chores to anchor me. It was unsettling being cut loose, but it was also beginning to feel like an adventure. When Pieta called, I could tell her I'd had fun last night and it wouldn't be a complete lie. Still, I might not mention how I hadn't made it back to my hotel room till morning.

For lunch I ate three different kinds of meatballs and a plate of *bigoli in salsa*. I hadn't intended to have the pasta, but I saw a waiter go by carrying a dish of coarse wholemeal spaghetti, slick with olive oil and littered with gently fried onions and anchovies, and couldn't resist ordering some for myself. It wasn't the lightest of meals, and after I'd wiped the last of it from the plate with a crust of bread, my stomach felt too swollen for the trying-on of clothes. Instead I decided to take a walk and window-shop as I went.

While I was having lunch, the mist had thinned and now there were streaks of blue in the sky. Avoiding the bustling, touristy Strada Nuova was my main aim, so I struck off in a direction I hadn't explored so far and lost myself in a maze of *calli*. Eventually I came upon a wide square with an imposing church, a statue of a horseman on a pedestal and several pavement cafés. Studying my map, I worked out that it had to be Campo Santi Giovanni e Paolo, and realised that the bookshop Valentina had marked as a must-see was not too far away.

I was about to try and find it when my phone rang. Sitting down beside a table at one of the cafés, I answered it.

"Hi, Dolly." My sister sounded upbeat. "How's it going over there?"

"Really great. I'm at a café beside an amazing old church and am about to order a coffee."

"That sounds relaxing. What else have you been doing?"

"Well weirdly, there's this whole tango scene happening here and I've kind of fallen in with some of the dancers." Yes, I was exaggerating, but that's what I do.

"Tango? Isn't that Spanish or South American? Why are they doing it in Venice?" she asked.

"Apparently people have been dancing tango pretty much everywhere, we just haven't noticed. In Venice they dance outside in the squares on warm evenings and it's gorgeous."

"I'm so envious. Here it's pouring with rain and I've done nothing but work."

"I don't suppose you've been near Little Italy, have you?" My restaurant had only been without me for a couple of days; still, I was feeling anxious.

"That's why I'm calling actually." Suddenly Pieta sounded less upbeat.

"What's wrong?"

"Oh nothing really, don't worry. I just wanted to let you know that Papa's back."

"What do you mean, back?" My heart plummeted. I remembered Frederico sounding so awkward on the phone, and the laughter in the background I'd been sure I recognised. Of course, it had been my father. Who else?

"You mean back at Little Italy?" I pressed her. "He saw Guy Rochester's review, right? Has he come back to save the day or something?"

"Calm down, Dolly, he's not trying to take over, he just wants to help."

"Oh please. I expect he's changing the menu, isn't he?"

"No, I don't think so. Well, perhaps he's put on a couple of new specials, but that's all."

"Bloody hell . . . I'd better come back right away."

"No, don't do that," my sister said quickly. "A few more days won't make a difference. And, Dolly, I think he's having fun. I haven't seen him this excited in ages. Just let him run with it till your holiday is over, then you can burst his bubble if you want to."

I imagined my father in my kitchen, loudly finding fault with every change I'd made and criticising my staff. It would be no surprise if half of them had walked out by the time I returned. The trouble was, Little Italy had been his life's work. He had given it to me but never really let it go. Right now he would be reliving the old days and, as Pieta said, only trying to help. I couldn't tell him he wasn't wanted there; he'd be so hurt.

"Is Mum back too?" I asked my sister.

"Yes, they're both staying at my place because their apartment's rented out right now. Eden and Katia are coming over tomorrow night for dinner. It'll feel really weird having everyone together except you."

"I'll call," I promised.

"I hope I haven't ruined your good time," Pieta said anxiously.

I looked round at the wide *campo*, at the tourists trickling over the bridge towards the church, the waiters moving smoothly between the tables of the pavement cafés, the sun breaking through the clouds above us. Surely it was better to be here right now than waging a silent war against Papa for control of Little Italy?

"No, it's fine, I'd prefer to know what's going on. Just try not to let him overdo it. You know what he's like."

"Don't worry, I talked to Frederico and everyone is keeping an eye on him. He'll back off again once you're home, just see."

"Yeah, maybe."

"Try to have fun in the meantime, OK?"

"Will do."

"Better go. Loads to do. Love you, Dolly."

"Yeah, love you too."

After hanging up, I lingered at the café, drank a coffee and ate a couple of sugary biscuits even though I wasn't hungry. Staring into space, I considered the mess my life was tangling itself into.

If you'd spent any time with my father then you'd know he manages to be both infuriating and totally charming. Some people think we're alike, he and I, which is why we tend to clash. But there are big differences between us; at least I believe so.

Papa is a harder person in some ways and softer in others. He is full of shout and bluster, has strong ideas about anything you care to mention and, like most Italian men of his generation, is big on respect. Nothing upsets him more than finding it lacking, especially from his daughters.

In the past I've gone against him in so many ways. He didn't want me to leave school as early as I did, or to marry Eden. There were big scenes, with lots of yelling, then my mother would intervene and eventually he'd relent. Papa has the ability to forget and move on. Sadly, that's not one of his traits that I share.

He also has a bigger heart than I do; a capacity to care that goes beyond what most of us could manage. He's not a saint, of course; he's made mistakes and hurt people. But it's always unthinkable not to forgive him.

So now he was at Little Italy, filling the place with his loud voice and big opinions, and whatever Pieta thought, he wasn't going to back off any time soon. He'd quote Guy Rochester's review at me, point out the empty spaces in the reservation book and name the old regulars whose faces were now missing. Only because he cared, mind you . . . because he wanted the very best for us.

He wouldn't go so far as to tell me I'd failed at running his restaurant, but that's what he'd be thinking. The worst thing was there would be no arguing — not now a food critic had proved him right.

No fighting for the dishes I wanted to see on the menu, or expecting my opinions to be listened to. It would be as if Little Italy was his again, and perhaps it actually should be.

The more I thought about it, the more relieved I felt not to be there. Sooner or later I'd have to face reality, but not yet. If I gave it some time, let him have a chance to run the place alone, then the best I could wish for was that Papa would discover he didn't have the stamina to work the way he used to, or that my mother would intervene and make him slow down. I didn't hold out a lot of hope, though. Not if he was enjoying himself as much as Pieta thought.

It was mid-afternoon by the time I managed to find the Acqua Alta bookshop. With a makeshift sign and a few racks of postcards next to the door, it didn't look like anything special. Inside it smelt musty. The entrance was lined with a few shelves of new books and blocking the middle was an old gondola overflowing with glossy guides to Venice in various languages.

The further in I went, the shabbier and more romantic the shop became. In a warren of small side rooms I came across wooden boats, barrels and bathtubs with tattered second-hand novels spilling out of them. Old copies of magazines were stacked next to volumes on art. I found rooms where there was barely space for me to walk the pathways between the teetering piles, where dusty chandeliers and old typewriters jostled for space and black cats stalked. At one point I discovered a courtyard with a staircase constructed from quietly decomposing leather-bound volumes. And at the very back of the shop was a doorway that opened on to the canal, the milky green water lapping its steps.

Most of the books were in Italian, and although I speak the language well enough to make myself understood, trying to read it is trickier, so there was nothing much for me to buy there. Nevertheless, I was enchanted. It seemed a place that could exist only here in Venice.

This was a shop to get lost in, to stumble over things you never realised you wanted; books that had interesting lives before you picked them up. Most wore tattered covers and were filled with yellowing pages. Spines were creased and corners folded, words scrawled in the margins. Where had they all come from, and would anyone ever buy them? I couldn't seem to find a shop assistant, never mind a cash register.

Finally I came across it hidden in a corner, not far from the entrance of the shop. To my surprise, boxed in behind the counter was a girl I recognised. She had dark hair worn in a fat plait over one shoulder, and brown eyes beneath a heavy fringe.

"Valentina?"

She looked at me blankly.

"Addolorata," I jogged her memory. "I was on your walking tour yesterday evening."

"Oh, OK." Still she showed no sign of recognising me.

"When you marked this place on my map, I didn't realise you worked here."

"It's well worth visiting, yes? Did you want to buy something? The novels in English are over there." She pointed at the shelves of new books beside the door. "We have a lot by Donna Leon if you'd like to read a story set here. Then there are the guidebooks, of course: walking tours, places to eat, history, even ghost stories — we have a wide selection."

"I saw you dancing last night too," I told her. "With Angelo and another man."

"So you did go to the *milonga*." It seemed she had recognised me after all.

"Yes, it was a good night. You guys were amazing to watch."

She nodded and gestured again towards the shelves of English novels. "I think you will like Donna Leon. They are crime stories but not at all gory."

In the end I bought a notebook with a pretty cover, a couple of novels and a handful of vintage postcards, all infused with the musty fragrance of the shop. Valentina seemed a degree warmer as she took my cash, even managing a smile.

"I might see you this evening, then," I said to her.

"This evening, why?" She sounded confused.

"Won't you be dancing at Santa Maria della Salute?"

"Ah, the Wednesday night *milonga*? No, it's unlikely, I have other plans," she said briskly and then turned towards another customer, a foreigner like me, with much the same selection of books and cards clutched in her hands to buy.

As I walked back towards my hotel, battling through the tides of tourists drifting in the opposite direction, I imagined how it must feel to be among those Venetians still living here, trying to go about everyday life. No wonder the locals kept their noses buried in their newspapers on the *vaporetto* and turned their backs on us in the *bacari*. I couldn't blame them for blocking us out. It would be the only way to cope with such an invasion.

My only explanation for Coco's friendliness was that she was eccentric, possibly quite mad. I wondered if she made a habit of singling out visitors for style advice, making helpful little comments on our make-up, clothes and haircuts. From anyone else it might have seemed rude, but she was such a peculiar old thing it was pointless being offended. I hoped I would get to see her later. And if I could find that little shop again, I might even splash out on the red glass necklace she had thought would suit me.

CHAPTER
SIX

Ever since arriving in Venice I'd been expecting a call from Eden, but there had been nothing beyond a couple of brief texts. Even when we're not getting on we never go a day without speaking, and it was the longest I'd gone without hearing my daughter's voice, so on the way back to the hotel I stopped off at a bar, ordered an Aperol Spritz and called our home number.

It rang for a bit, then there was a click and I heard my own voice demanding the caller leave a short message. That wasn't unusual. If Eden's back was hurting and he wasn't close to the phone, he often didn't bother answering it. So I hung up and rang the number again. Then again and again until at last he picked up.

"Dolly, what the hell?" He sounded exasperated.

"I knew you were home," I explained.

"Yeah, but I hate it when you do that. Can't you just leave a message and ask to be called back like a normal person?"

"I wanted to speak to you right now," I said, reasonably I thought.

"So what's so urgent?"

"Well, nothing," I admitted. "I'm just calling to see how you and Katia are doing."

"I texted you back this morning. Did you think something might have changed since then?"

"No, but I wanted to hear your voice. And Katia's too. Is she home yet?"

"No," he said shortly.

"I wish you'd been able to come on holiday with me."

"I wish I could do a lot of things."

Lately I'd been struggling to find enough sympathy for Eden's ongoing back problem, but now, all these miles away, it seemed easier.

"Have you had a bad day? Is it still no better at all? Not even a little bit?"

"You keep asking me that. It's not going to get better all of a sudden just because you want it to," he said gruffly.

"Eden, don't be like that . . . I called because I'm missing you and thought you might be missing me too."

He was silent. As the waiter appeared with my drink, I lowered my voice. "Are you missing me?"

All I could hear was his breathing. "Eden?"

"Oh God, Dolly, I'm sorry." He sounded terribly sad.

I swallowed hard. "What for? What have you done?"

"For not being what you want."

I felt that same sick fear I'd had the last time we'd fought. "What are you talking about? Of course you are."

"No, I never have been, not really. Your father was right, we shouldn't have got married."

"Let's leave Papa out of this. It's got nothing to do with him. Whatever the problem is, we can sort it out, can't we? We'll talk when I get back."

"Dolly . . ." He was tentative. "Here's the thing . . . When you get back, I don't think you should come home."

"What?"

"The apartment above Little Italy is empty at the moment, right? I know you're using it for extra storage and office space, but there's still a bed and stuff, isn't there?"

"You want me to go and stay there?" I couldn't believe it.

"Yes, I do," he said simply.

"But what about Katia?"

"She'll stay with me, though obviously you can see her whenever you like."

"So you've thought about this, have you . . . you've got it all worked out?" There was an edge of anger in my voice.

"I've hardly thought about anything else," Eden said steadily. "I'm not taking it lightly, you know."

Now it was my turn to be silent. There were things I wanted to say, but I didn't have the words for them.

"Dolly?"

"What?" I asked hoarsely.

"This isn't going to be a temporary thing, do you understand?" he said gently.

At that point I hung up. I turned off my phone, put it on the table next to my cocktail and stared at them both for a few minutes. Then I emptied every last drop of liquid from the glass and signalled to the waiter for another. Eden hadn't meant it, surely. I'd caught him at the wrong time. He was having a bad day with the pain and lashing out at me. That's what I told myself.

As I drank my second Spritz, I got more and more scared. What if he'd met someone else? It seemed unlikely given the shape his back was in, but still it was a possibility. I couldn't think of any other explanation for the way he was behaving.

Immediately I regretted coming away. Hadn't I told Pieta a holiday was a bad idea? She had pushed me and this was how it had turned out. Now I had to get home and fix things before it was too late. Surely there would be a last-minute seat on a flight? If all else failed I'd catch the Eurostar. That was the answer, that's what I'd do.

Except I didn't. Instead I sat there clutching a glass with nothing in it apart from melting ice cubes and an olive stone. And when the waitress passed by I nodded that yes, I'd like another Spritz, please.

The scary thing was, I could imagine the life Eden wanted for me. I saw myself moving into the flat above the restaurant with only a suitcase of clothes, working longer and longer hours, growing apart from my daughter until we never knew what to say to each other any more, hearing that my husband was seeing another woman.

Divorces and separations happen all the time, I'm well aware of that, but for some reason I'd thought we were immune. Yes, we fought a lot these days; there were resentments and irritations, nights when we turned our backs on one another in bed: the shine had worn off like in any long relationship. I suspect I can be difficult to live with at times, but this thing now . . . this definitely wasn't my fault. It all came down to Eden's injured back. If his mates hadn't talked him into that stupid snowboarding holiday, we'd be muddling on together as normal. Not perfect, but good enough . . . at least that's what I thought.

At some stage I switched from Aperol to wine. It didn't seem to help. My world was as sharp-edged as before. And I was angry with all of them: Eden, my father, even Pieta a little. They were my family. Weren't they supposed to support me rather than make my life more difficult? I didn't deserve this at all.

I had a bright flash of recollection: standing beside Eden on the steps of St Peter's church on a golden autumn day as our friends showered us with confetti. I remembered the feeling of relief that we were married at last; that our future was decided. And now my husband wanted to end our marriage. He thought his life would be better without me.

What I wanted was to escape. To sleep for a long time; take a break from being me. I sipped my wine and tried to pull myself together, but there didn't seem much point.

There was a parade of couples strolling past the bar, some old, some young, some hand in hand, some smiling, some solemn; all of them together with life going on as normal. I was alone, and apparently that was how it was going to be from now on.

I paid my bill, picked up my bag of books and started to trail back to the hotel. Then I stopped short. What was I thinking? I didn't want to lie in my room staring at the ceiling for hours. At a time like this, company was what I needed: a sympathetic friend or simply another person to hang out with. I couldn't take much more of this being-on-my-own business. I wasn't really suited to it; I was starting to see that now.

The trouble was, everyone I might have called on was miles away and busy working, and the only living being in the whole of Venice who had shown the slightest inclination to be sociable was an oddball old lady. I made up my mind. Better her than no one.

I took the slow *vaporetto* to the Salute stop. It zigzagged down the Grand Canal, past the wedding-cake facades of the palazzos and beneath the bridges, letting passengers on and off as it went. You have to be in the mood for Venice, and right then I wasn't. All I wanted was to get to Santa Maria della Salute, watch a little more tango, be surrounded by lots of people and hopefully find a friendly face among them.

The rain clouds were clearing, and although the evening wasn't an especially warm one, already a few people were dancing beside the entrance to the church. There was a couple I recognised from the night before, but no sign of Coco. I hoped she wasn't too tired or discouraged by the weather; that her partner hadn't let her down. Feeling lonelier than ever, I found a place to sit and look on.

This was a romantic setting for a dance. Above us were the soaring baroque archways of the old church; beneath us views that stretched out over the water. As it grew darker, the gondolas and water taxis became moving dots of light and someone turned the music up a little louder.

That was when Coco made her entrance. There were feathers in her hair; I saw them bobbing up and down as she climbed the steps with her partner. She was with a different man tonight; not Silvio, but a shorter, more dapper version with a moustache that looked as if it had been waxed and hair that must have owed its startling blackness to the dye bottle. As for Coco, she was dressed like a gypsy, in a skirt that flared from her hips, and strappy silver shoes. Diamanté clips held the feathers to her head, and her lipstick was crimson. She nodded when she saw me but didn't stop to say hello. I supposed she was in a hurry to be in her partner's arms, to be gliding across the flagstones and looking amazingly limber for a woman her age.

Tonight she danced a more racy tango than the night before, a flirtier and faster one. Her partner handled her with great care and I thought the pair of them must have been dancing together for a long time.

Standing up, I moved closer, joining a small group of on-lookers milling about on the steps. Glancing at the white-haired man standing beside me, I realised it was Silvio.

"Are you not dancing tonight?" I asked him in Italian.

He turned and seemed to recognise me. "Not tonight, signora, no. On Wednesdays it is Marcello's turn."

"Don't you have another partner to dance with?" I was curious.

"I dance with Coco." He was again intent on watching her. "Always with Coco in the Campo San Giacomo dell'Orio."

"What about wintertime, when it's cold and raining?" I wondered.

"We find places: palazzos, old churches or hotels. We don't need too much space, as you can see. Years ago, when there weren't so many *milongas*, Coco and I would dance our tango together on the top of a bridge if we were in the mood, or even in the Piazza San Marco. We were famous for it. Of course, there was no Marcello in those days. Just her and me." He sounded regretful.

"She said you'd hurt your knee," I remembered.

"Yes, my knee, my shoulder, my hip, all of it hurts. Still, at my age what else can I expect? The truth is, I can't dance night after night any more, no matter how much I want to. That's why I must share her."

Silvio sounded regretful, and I thought how sweet it was that these two elderly men were vying for Coco's attention.

"But, *signora*, do you dance?" he asked me.

"Me? Oh no, I can't. I'd be completely useless, believe me."

98

He extended a hand in invitation. "Coco said that if you came here this evening I should teach you a first few steps."

"That's very kind, but really, no . . ." I looked across at Coco again. She was dancing in silence, a slight smile on her face. I was amazed she had thought of me at all given that I was just one of millions of tourists. "She really said that?"

"Yes, of course. She likes you, I think. You helped her with her shopping trolley, no? Perhaps now she wants to help you."

Still I hesitated, but Silvio didn't wait any longer. Taking my hand, he pulled me towards the edge of the dancers.

"OK then," I agreed weakly.

The old man took me in his arms, placing my hand on his shoulder. "This is your first time, so we will start with the basic steps," he told me. "All you have to do is walk with me."

Naturally I was beyond hopeless, just as I'd known I would be. Still Silvio seemed unperturbed. "One, two, three, four, five, six, seven, eight," he counted patiently as he moved me backwards across the flagstones. "Keep in time to the music, signora."

I held myself rigid as I hung on to the old man, concerned that I was about to trip over his feet and bring us both down.

"I'm not doing it properly, am I?"

"You are not so bad," he reassured me. "Now try again. Don't try to dance; just walk."

I can't say I noticed much improvement. I felt graceless as we stepped our way round the base of the basilica. Our version of the dance hardly seemed the same as the one the others were doing. Nevertheless, as she whirled past, Coco was encouraging.

"*Brava, signora, brava,*" she called.

The sheer effort of concentrating meant there was no space for anything else in my head. As Silvio moved me forwards and backwards, I stopped noticing the view, stopped thinking about the messed-up state my life was in, pretty much forgot I was in Venice altogether. Everything slipped away except the music and my stumbling steps. And perhaps my steps were slightly less clumsy and my death grip on Silvio's shoulder was starting to relax. Still, it was a relief when he suggested it was time to stop.

"Is there anywhere to get a drink?" I asked him.

"I have some mineral water with me." He gestured towards a cooler bag lying on the steps. "You're very welcome to share it."

"Thanks, but I meant a real drink."

"The water will refresh you," he insisted. "Later, when we have finished dancing, perhaps we will drink a glass or two of Prosecco."

"Haven't we finished yet?"

"No, no." Silvio shook his head. "We are only taking a break. You must try some more before the evening is finished."

I was kind of over it. If only I could skip the whole slow process of learning, and be able to do it effortlessly like the others right that instant.

"All I'm doing is walking back and forth," I said. "That's not even proper steps, is it?"

Silvio smiled sympathetically. "Tango isn't easy, signora. But the walk is an important part of it. And we have to start somewhere."

"How long would it take for a beginner to get really good?" I wondered.

"It all depends on the person, on their natural aptitude and determination, but most of all on the passion they have for it."

"What about that couple?" I picked out a pair dancing fluidly but not doing anything especially tricky. "How long to do it like that?"

Silvio watched them for a moment. "I think by the end of the summer perhaps, if you took some lessons, came to all the *milongas* and practised a great deal."

"I don't have the whole summer. I have to get back to London."

"You will find teachers there, I'm sure. And *milongas* too."

"I've never come across any."

"That doesn't mean they aren't happening." Silvio held out his hand. "Are you ready? Shall we?"

I felt sorry for the poor man shuffling around with me when he could have been dancing with a partner who knew what she was doing. I saw him dart the occasional glance at Coco and could tell he was longing to take a turn with her.

"One, two, three, four, five, six, seven, eight," he continued to chant gallantly. "*Brava, signora, brava.*"

I did love the music. It sounded sad but defiant, and it suited my mood. If only I'd been able to step in time to it, but I never found my rhythm. In my head I could dance but my body couldn't seem to catch up, and however encouraging Silvio was, I couldn't imagine being able to execute the tango elegantly if I tried for ten summers, never mind one.

It was Coco who decided it was time for us to stop. She stepped out of Marcello's embrace and raised a hand in the air. Immediately Silvio released me and moved towards her.

There was a short discussion between them about where we should go next. Since it was clear I was to be included in the plans, I suggested Piazza San Marco to listen to the café orchestras, because it's so lovely there even when it's crowded with tourists. Coco dismissed the idea.

"We will go to Caffè Dodo," she declared. "There is a jazz band playing there tonight. Perhaps we can catch them before they finish."

"Will we take the *vaporetto* or share a water taxi?" I asked.

"Marcello has a boat," she told me. "It is big enough for all of us."

I felt even more sorry for Silvio when I saw Marcello's boat. It was a beauty, long and sleek, all varnished wood and white vinyl seats. There was even a small canopy for shelter if it was raining. It was moored in the canal close to Santa Maria della Salute and looked considerably flashier than any of the other speedboats near it.

102

Marcello fussed over Coco as he helped her aboard, and once she'd sat down, he tucked a rug around her legs. "Comfortable?" he asked her.

"Yes thank you, darling." She smiled up at him. "Perfectly comfortable."

I cast a sympathetic look towards Silvio, but the old man's expression was stoic. As soon as Marcello moved to the helm, Silvio sat beside Coco and began to murmur in her ear. She nodded and smiled, even giggled girlishly. Now I felt a little sorry for Marcello.

We nosed into the Grand Canal. It was still busy with boats ploughing up and down and gondolas bobbing. There must have been rules, just like for a road, but to my eyes it was chaos. Marcello seemed to be driving faster than the rest, churning up the water, showing off I suspected.

"Is there a speed limit?" I asked, fearing for the smaller boats, barely visible apart from their navigation lights.

Coco reassured me. "Don't worry, *cara*, my Marcello is an excellent boatman and he knows the canals better than anyone. This used to be a water taxi. He drove it for many years. Now there are no paying passengers; only his friends, and he takes good care of us."

At the helm, Marcello nodded smugly, one hand on the wheel, the other smoothing down long strands of dark hair ruffled up from his scalp by the breeze. He didn't slow the boat at all and in no time we were whizzing beneath the Rialto bridge. Once past Ca' d'Oro, he eased up on the throttle and we turned up into a narrower canal. Here it was quieter and darker, the only sounds the hum of the engine and the water from our wake sloshing up against the old stone buildings.

As the boat carved through the canal, I had a moment of thinking how insane it was to be here in Venice with three people I'd only just met and no idea where they were taking me. It felt like a return to the impulsive Addolorata of the old days, the one who plunged headlong in without thinking of anything but the good time she was going to have. Generally that version of me wasn't hanging out with a bunch of septuagenarians (I have a feeling Silvio may even have been in his eighties), but still, the idea raised my spirits. Maybe I wasn't a lost cause after all.

We turned into another dark canal and I wondered where on earth we were. I had a feeling I wasn't so far from my hotel, but whether I'd manage to get back there before morning I had no idea. The night could take me anywhere as far as I was concerned. Why worry about being sensible? I'd been trying that for years and it hadn't paid off, had it?

Eventually we reached a strip of bars and restaurants, still lit up and noisy. Marcello found a space to moor outside the Caffè Dodo, where, just as Coco had promised, there was a band playing: one man on a double bass, two on guitars and people sitting on stools or gathered along the edge of the canal to listen.

I readied myself to climb out of the boat then noticed that the others showed no sign of moving. Instead Marcello whistled at the waiter and held up four fingers. "Prosecco," he called.

"Will they serve our drinks to us here on the boat?" I asked Coco.

"Yes, of course. And some *cicchetti* too if you're hungry."

I realised that I'd forgotten to have dinner. It's not like me to miss a meal, but the combination of distress and afternoon drinking had chased all thought of food out of my head. Now I was ready to eat.

"Yes please, some *cicchetti* would be great."

"You must have an appetite after the tango," Coco remarked. "It was hard work, yes, but the first time always is. When you come to the *milonga* on Sunday evening you will know how to begin and it will be a little easier."

"I can't come . . . My flight home is booked for Sunday," I told her. "In fact I ought to go back earlier than that."

"What a pity to stay in Venice for so short a time. Tell me, are you here alone and not with your . . ." Coco glanced at my empty ring finger. "Not with a lover?"

I do have a wedding ring; so does Eden. But we both work with our hands and prefer not to wear them, so they live in the top drawer of my bedside table. My rationale has always been that a ring isn't going to keep us faithful if we haven't the mind to be. I realised I might have reason to regret that now, given the circumstances.

"Yes, I'm here alone," I confirmed. "My husband stayed at home in London with our daughter."

At that Coco raised her eyebrows but didn't follow with another question.

"If I was going to spend a few more days here, what would you suggest I do? Is Murano worth a visit?"

Coco shrugged. "If you like glass," she said.

"Burano."

"If you like lace and brightly painted buildings, then yes, it is pretty."

"The Lido?"

"If the day is so hot you really must paddle in the sea."

"What would *you* do?"

"If I were you, I'd shop," Coco said.

"Shop?" I echoed.

She seemed to be assessing my outfit: the practical stretchy black jeans, the flat shoes, the baggy top I wore to hide my bottom. From her expression I could tell she disapproved.

"You're young and lovely," she said. "You could wear anything at all. So tell me, why choose these ugly, depressing clothes? What was going through your head when you put them on this morning; when you bought them in the first place? They do nothing for you."

"They're comfortable," I argued, taken aback.

"Yes, I'm sure they are."

I tried to defend myself. "I'm on my feet a lot, running round. I can't be wearing high heels and little skirts."

"Are there no occasions in your life when you might think it worth looking prettier?"

"I do have some nice things," I protested. "I just didn't bring them with me."

"No? Why not?"

"Well, I . . ." There was no answer to that really. Especially as the truth was I didn't have anything all that special in my wardrobe any more. At some point I'd stopped caring. I wasn't sure why, but Coco was right, it was depressing

"I meant to go shopping this morning but didn't get round to it," I told her.

"Where were you planning to go?"

"The shops near Piazza San Marco."

"Very expensive." Coco made a face. "Myself, I don't see the point in paying high prices for the same designer things you will find in any big city."

Silvio interrupted. "Coco, why don't you take her shopping tomorrow? You know all the best places, don't you?"

Coco gave her head a modest little shake, setting the feathers in her hair quivering. "Well I suppose I could help her. I have no plans for the morning."

What I ought to have said was that I did have plans. I couldn't stay in Venice any longer, I needed to go back and see my family, to sort my life out. But sitting in Marcello's speedboat sipping wine and listening to jazz music felt like being in a little bubble of happiness. And I couldn't find a single reason why it would be a smart idea to burst that bubble and leave.

I told myself that a few more days spent here wouldn't change anything between me and Eden. The ruins of my life would still be waiting when I got back on Sunday and I'd deal with them then. I abandoned all thoughts of trying to get an earlier flight home. Tomorrow I'd go shopping.

CHAPTER
SEVEN

I'm always being blamed for other people's hangovers. I have no idea why; it's not as though I force the drink down their throats. If I open a bottle and offer to pour a few splashes, it's because I like to be a generous host. I'm never insistent. Still, the morning-after texts are always reproachful. I'm blamed for the pies they eat and the litres of cola they down, for their sleepless nights and their paracetamol consumption. "You did it again, Dolly," they complain. "You're lethal."

Anyway, those old Venetians, once they got going, didn't need any encouragement from me. We sat in Marcello's speedboat sipping bubbly long after the band had stopped playing; and no one but me did more than nibble the *cicchetti*. So I wasn't surprised to find that Coco didn't seem her usual self when we met next morning for breakfast as arranged.

I was beginning to look forward to Coco's outfits; her flamboyance brightened the days. But that morning she was pared down to the point of severity: just some slim pencil pants worn with ankle boots, a shirt buttoned to the throat, and a long cardigan, all of it in black. She was wearing no accessories, only those mad oversized sunglasses that covered half her face. Her concession to glamour was a slash of dark purple lipstick and much of that was smeared over the cup she was drinking from.

"Feeling ropy?" I asked sympathetically, joining her at the café's long counter.

"Not at all," she said indignantly. "We only had a few glasses and it wasn't too late. After dropping you off, Marcello took me straight home and I slept like a child."

That wasn't quite how I remembered the evening going, but I didn't contradict her, saying instead, "I had such a lovely time, thanks for inviting me along."

"You're very welcome." She was gracious now. "It was a pleasure for Silvio to teach you. He told me you are a good learner."

"Well I don't know about that, but it was fun I guess."

I ordered myself a cappuccino and a couple of brioches. Apart from needing food, I didn't feel too bad. Often after I've drunk loads of bubbly I'll wake up halfway through the night with my heart hammering. But I'd had a decent enough sleep despite the Prosecco and managed not to lie awake thinking about all the stuff I ought to have been worrying about.

"So, shopping this morning," I said. "Are you still keen?"

"Yes, of course I am."

"Where will we go?" I was imagining all sorts of out-of-the-way boutiques non-Venetians never had a hope of discovering on their own.

"We'll start on Strada Nuova," Coco declared.

"Really? I thought it was mostly tourist stuff there."

"No, no, I have found some beautiful pieces and the prices are very good. Actually I noticed a blue sundress in the window of a store the other day that you should try on."

"OK, I'm in your hands," I told her. "Especially if the prices are good."

Shopping with Coco was a hoot. First of all she announced her arrival in each place with an energetic cry of "*Salve!*", often kissing the proprietor on both cheeks. Most of them seemed enchanted to see her, even though she proceeded to pull clothes off rails, topple piles of T-shirts and issue instructions that kept them running, fetching and carrying for her.

"Yes, yes, the blue dress from the window. And that yellow silk top, and the pretty white cotton one with the embroidery on it. She'll try them all," she told the woman in the Strada Nuova shop where the rails were so crammed I'd never have picked out anything decent. Coco had an eye for colour and shape, and for what would flatter; she swooped on treasures I hadn't noticed.

I think she might have followed me into the tiny changing room if I'd let her (she didn't quite appreciate how much space my hips require). Instead she settled for standing right by the curtain, her hand appearing every now and then clutching another garment.

"Put this on and come out into the light so I can see," she commanded.

The blue sundress was rejected although I rather liked it. The two tops she considered for a moment, rubbing the fabric between her thumb and forefinger.

110

"Yes, they are quite pretty, but they're the very first things we've seen and we may find nicer styles elsewhere. I don't know . . . perhaps if the price were a little better."

It turned out Coco's favourite word was *sconti*. She hated to buy without a discount and favoured a complicated form of haggling.

"If you gave us ten euros off, perhaps we might think about it," she mused. "Or what if we pay you an extra ten euros and you throw in the sundress as well? Yes, that sounds like the best idea."

The sales person, a middle-aged Asian woman, shook her head regretfully. "Ten euros? No, no, too little."

Coco plucked at the dress. "This fabric is so thin you could spit through it."

"Fifteen euros extra, then," the saleswoman suggested.

"Ten," Coco insisted. "And we pay in cash."

"Still I can't do it."

Coco wasn't prepared to give up. "It's been hanging in the window for weeks; is anyone else going to want it?"

Throwing her hands in the air, the saleswoman caved in. "OK, madam," she said, lowering her voice even though we were the only customers in the shop. "But you mustn't tell anyone. This price is only for you."

"Oh thank you, darling. Now, no need to bother wrapping anything. I'll just pop them all in my trolley, see," Coco said brightly.

Back on the street, she seemed quietly satisfied. "The thing to remember, Addolorata, is that you can only spend each euro you have once," she told me. "Five saved in that shop is five to put towards something else you want."

I had to admire her philosophy. I thought of the Visa bill I never seemed to pay off and the debts that were mounting up further while I was in Venice. It wasn't going to stop me shopping, though. Not now I'd set my mind to it.

The next place she took me to was close to the Rialto fish market and more exclusive. This time she hesitated before going in, peering through the window past a display of silky kaftans.

"Is she there . . . the blonde one? Damn, yes, she is." Turning to me, she warned, "The woman who is here, she is very hard. We will be lucky if she makes us a good *sconto*."

Coco pushed open the door and made her usual big entrance. "*Salve*, darling," she called, pecking the frosty saleswoman on both cheeks. "What interesting things you have in the window. Kaftans!"

"Oh yes, they are very fashionable now," the woman replied. "Is there one you'd like to try?"

"No, no, I don't think so," Coco breezed. "But the sale rail, what have you done with that?"

"It's over there, beside the back wall. Prices as marked as always, though," she warned. "I can't go any lower."

Coco didn't make a move towards the rail the woman had pointed out. "We would like to see linen

112

trousers," she instructed. "Preferably white, and in my friend's size not mine."

"We do have some but they're not on sale," the woman told her. "One moment and I'll find them."

"I can't wear white trousers," I hissed at Coco as the saleswoman disappeared into a back room.

"But they will work beautifully with the pieces you just bought," she argued.

"They'll make me look huge and I'll have stains on them in no time. Besides, I won't get any wear out of them in London."

"Have you ever owned a pair of white pants?"

"No," I admitted.

"Well then, how do you know you won't wear them?" Coco asked patiently.

I paid more for those trousers than the other three items had cost together. Coco looked pained when I handed over my credit card but insisted they were a good buy. "You'll wonder how you ever managed without them," she promised.

"Possibly," I agreed, but only to humour her.

Next we went to a lingerie store for the beige bra and knickers required to wear with the white trousers. Then Coco took us helter-skeltering up and down narrow streets, talking me into Pucci-style prints and brightly coloured scarves, wedge-heeled shoes, short flirty skirts, new sunglasses, a couple of glass necklaces, a brace of bangles.

I've never been a woman who loves to shop (unless it's for food), but I followed Coco, spending money I didn't really have and accumulating stuff I didn't really need, and found the thrill in it. It felt like I was shopping for some other version of myself, a fantasy Addolorata who lived a life that matched the colourful things I was buying.

Coco spent much more modestly, choosing only a shirt with a bold geometric pattern and a wide-brimmed sunhat in a searing shade of acid yellow. She haggled ferociously for both and I began to wonder if she might be short of cash.

"Let me pay for that," I said in the hat shop. "To say thank you for helping me."

"Absolutely not." She was adamant.

"Well at least let me buy you lunch."

"Lunch would be lovely. I know the perfect place."

She took me to a *trattoria* where she said the gondoliers liked to eat. Sure enough it was full of men in striped T-shirts with well-muscled arms, eating and talking with gusto. There wasn't any menu. The minute we sat down we were given a basket of bread, some water and a carafe of red wine; two bowls filled with a soupy mix of *casareccia* pasta, chickpeas and clams swiftly followed.

"*Buon appetite*," said Coco, lifting her spoon.

"Mmm," I replied, already tasting it. It was a good combination — the earthiness of the chickpeas played well with the briny sweetness of the clams, and the dish was comforting.

"I had a boyfriend who used to make this for me," Coco confided. "I've always loved to eat it."

"How does this version compare to his?" I wondered.

"Oh, it was so long ago, I couldn't tell you. All I know is that I enjoy it whenever they serve it to me here."

The second course was a generous platter of lagoon fish and a side of green beans and capers. Coco had an appetite. She helped herself to a large fish, several smaller ones and a handful of prawns, then wiped a crust of bread over the slick of oil left on the plate, soaking up as much as she could. "This is always the best bit," she remarked.

I agreed, doing the same.

We ended our lunch with an espresso and a small dish of honey *gelato*. The place was emptying out now as the gondoliers returned to work.

"I have a date tonight," Coco confided as she stirred a generous spoonful of sugar into her coffee. "But I can't wear my new shirt as it's much too casual."

"Where are you going?"

"To the opera."

"With Marcello or Silvio?"

"No, they aren't interested in that sort of thing. With another friend you haven't met. What about you? Do you have plans for this evening?"

"I haven't really decided."

"Come with us to the opera," she suggested. "My friend will get you a ticket."

"But you said it was a date. I can't gatecrash it."

"Roberto won't mind. And, darling, you have so many lovely new things; you must go out to show them off."

"Thanks, but really I won't." I didn't want to cling like a limpet to the old lady.

"You don't like opera?"

"I've never been. I don't know anything about it."

"So just like tango, then . . . You've been missing out, I think."

"I suppose I have," I agreed.

"It's not too late to learn about both of them, of course."

"Some day perhaps I will . . . but my life is really complicated right now, and, well . . ."

"Life is always complicated," Coco pointed out. "And there are always reasons not to do things."

"Yes, but my reasons are good ones. I shouldn't still be here at all, to be honest. I ought to have flown home this morning."

Then, while the waiters cleared the tables around us, I did what I'd been longing to do and told her pretty much everything. My broken marriage, my ruined business and even the way I felt like such a drone most of the time. She listened without saying a word as I went on and on. Then finally she spoke.

"I don't like giving advice," she told me. "In the past I've found people haven't always wanted to hear the things I've told them. But you seem like you need it."

I nodded. "Yes, definitely, I do."

"I think you must ask yourself what will make you happy. Not anyone else. You."

I stared at her.

"I suppose you think that sounds selfish, but it's how I've lived my own life. Each morning I wake up and the first thing I think is what can I do today to make myself happy. You'd be surprised how hardly anyone else does that."

"Actually I wouldn't."

"Most people think only about what they have to do. They don't stop to ask if they really want to. Me, I dance the tango to be happy, I make love to be happy, look at art, listen to music, wear beautiful clothes, enjoy all my passions as often as I can. I make happiness the thing that matters most." She reached across the table, took my hand and squeezed it. "Now, are you coming to the opera?"

"Yes," I decided.

"Wonderful. Wear the wrap dress with the Pucci print. I'll make sure we look good together."

CHAPTER
EIGHT

A late-afternoon nap turned out to be among the things that made Coco happy. So while she headed home, I took my new outfits back to my hotel room to play dress-up. Trying them on and peering at myself in the small bathroom mirror, I had that same sense I'd felt in the shops that there had been a shift in the person I was. Boring old Dolly had been lent some vibrancy by the coloured tops and dresses. She looked like she was ready to have a good time.

As I was wriggling in and out of the various outfits and throwing them over the bed, I thought about what Coco had said about happiness. It was obvious really, wasn't it? All of us deserve some. But how many days and weeks had I let slip by in a fug of greyness and dejection? How often even did I notice whether I was happy or not?

It struck me that I had been wasting my life, getting it badly wrong. I'd filled it up with other feelings: frustration, guilt, anger, worry and regret. Somehow joy had been forgotten.

That's when I decided to make a list, just like I do when I've got a million things to remember. But this time not a list of things to pick up at the supermarket or bills that needed to be paid or people I had to email. I wanted to come up with the ten things that made me happy. Simple, right?

It turned out it was easier to decide what to leave off the list. Some stuff makes almost everyone happy — family, friends, time off work, unexpected gifts, sunny days. I wanted to discover things that were particular to me; the ingredients for my own personal recipe for happiness. So how to begin? Food had always been my passion, but lately that had dulled. What else was there?

I searched my mind but the page in my notebook remained blank. I couldn't come up with a single thing guaranteed to lift my mood. Oh, except wine. Yes, definitely wine, but I had a feeling Coco would tell me that didn't count. She had mentioned tango, art, music; things that took her into the world and made her life richer. Slumping on the sofa with a bottle of Chardonnay and channel-surfing the evening away didn't compare. And besides, if I were really honest with myself, drinking made me listless rather than happy.

I did the only sensible thing: gave up and went out. It was Aperol Spritz hour after all, and being cooped up in that ugly hotel room wasn't going to make me feel better. I took one of the novels I'd bought the day before and decided to find a shady café table and make a start on it.

The Spritz was good, refreshing and sweetly sour; the book I couldn't get into at all. My concentration was shot. I kept thinking back to that empty page and how

I ought to be able to think of things to fill it, a couple at least. For it to be entirely blank was tragic.

It was easier for Coco, I reassured myself. She was retired and had all day to please herself. My position was different. With a family and a business to run, my time didn't belong to me.

I gave up trying to read and turned to people-watching instead. The bar I had chosen was in a small *campo* with the usual wellhead at the centre and a chocolate shop opposite. There was a trickle of customers going in and out of the shop, and while a few must have been tourists, most seemed like regulars. They called greetings as they walked through the door and left holding purchases, small bags of sweet treats, little doses of happiness to help them through the rest of the day. For a moment I considered putting chocolate on my list, then decided that, just like wine, it didn't really belong there.

A church bell started to ring and I counted it up to seven o'clock. Eden and Katia would be at my sister's place by now and I had promised to call. I fiddled with my phone for a few moments, flagged down the waiter for another drink and hit Pieta's number as soon as he set the glass on the table.

As I listened to it ring, I thought of my sister's house: the kitchen filled with barely used Le Creuset in pastel shades, the living room a riot of Designer Guild fabrics, the conservatory littered with scented candles in storm lanterns. My family was gathered there, most likely in the kitchen. They were together without me.

"Hello?" A male voice answered, energetic and strongly accented. It was my father, Beppi.

"Papa, hi, it's me."

"Addolorata, cara, we thought you might call. How good to hear your voice. Tell me, how is Venice? Is it still sinking?"

I took a sip of my drink, hoping he wouldn't hear the ice cubes clinking. "So they say, but it looks OK to me."

"Good, good." He sounded distracted. "Eden is here, but before I pass you over to him, I need to have a quick word. Wait a moment." I heard the sound of a door being shut. "That's better. Now your sister has told you I'm helping out at Little Italy, yes? Don't worry, I'm not taking over. I would never do that. It is still your restaurant, cara. But with you on holiday and things a little difficult . . . and your mother and I were due for a trip home anyway. So it's all worked out for the best."

"Right," I muttered, not trusting myself to say more.

"And that man from the newspaper, that reviewer. What is his name?"

"Guy Rochester," I said flatly.

"Don't worry, I have come up with a plan. I emailed and told him he must come back and eat with us again. I said I am here now and the food is just as good as it was in the old days, better even. That I can prove it."

I lifted my glass and took a couple of good gulps, this time no longer concerned about the clinking ice cubes giving me away.

"Addolorata, are you still there?" My father raised his voice. "Did you hear what I just said?"

"Yes, I heard," I said dully.

"Good, good, I will pass you to Eden now." Papa was still shouting, although the line was completely clear. "No, wait, he is saying you should talk to Katia. Here she is, *cara*. Enjoy your holiday. See you soon."

"Mum?" my daughter said hesitantly. It was so good to hear her voice.

"Hi, baby, are you OK?"

"Nonno Beppi is cooking *pasta e fagioli* and I'm really hungry but he won't let me have a piece of bread and honey because he says it will spoil my appetite." There was a whining note in her voice.

"He always says that, remember? Whisper to Daddy that you want a little piece and eat it out in the garden."

"OK, Mum, bye then."

"No, wait, don't go yet. I'm missing you. I want to know how Saffron's birthday party went. Did you have fun?"

"Yes."

"Was there cake?"

"Yes."

"What kind?"

"Chocolate and banana."

"And what else is happening? Have you been on your school trip yet?"

"No."

"Remind me what day that's happening?"

"Tomorrow."

"Are you looking forward to it?"

"Yes."

"What part the most?"

"Dunno."

Katia is never exactly chatty on the phone, but this was desperate. I told myself she was grouchy and hungry and there was no point in trying to push her if she didn't feel like talking.

"OK then, baby, you be a good girl for Daddy and I'll see you soon. Love you."

"Right, bye, Mum."

Instead of passing the phone to Pieta or Eden, my daughter hung up. Perhaps I was overreacting, but it felt as if she'd got rid of me. Sitting alone and all those miles away, I started to worry that something had upset her. What if she had picked up on the tension in our family? What if Eden had spoken to her already, told her what was happening? Surely he wouldn't do that. He knew I was due to fly back on Sunday. It was only a few days away. I reassured myself he wouldn't say anything before then; that Katia was just distracted and eager to play with her cousins or be fussed over by her grandparents; that nothing at all had changed and with any luck it wouldn't. I ordered another drink and kept reassuring myself.

If it wasn't for Coco, I might have stayed at that café and lost myself in Aperol. But we had an arrangement, her friend was buying me an opera ticket, and after all her kindness I didn't like to let her down. And actually I had enjoyed her company on our shopping trip and was looking forward to seeing her again. So I drained my glass, paid my bill and went to get ready for our evening out.

As instructed, I wore the Pucci-style dress I'd just bought. My hair went into a messy topknot, I smoked up my eyes, painted my lips and hoped I would do. At the last minute I chucked on a couple of bangles, then hurried out the door, wondering how Coco would be dressed. I was hoping for an extra-special outfit for the opera, something striking and glamorous.

It was an easy ten-minute walk to the concert hall, and Coco had circled it on my map just to be sure I found it. The building stood on a corner close to the Rialto bridge. It was narrow-fronted, with columns, arched windows, and a brace of angelic statues peering down from the rooftop. People were milling about on the steps, Coco among them, and yes, she was looking striking. The effect was so extraordinary, I had to stop for a moment and take it all in. Her skirt was a confection of pink ruffles that fell to her ankles, her top a darker cerise with puff sleeves and spangles, and on her head she wore a fascinator covered in giant fabric poppies that was going to seriously interfere with the view of anyone seated behind her.

She saw me and waved. "Darling," she called.

"Hi, Coco, you look . . . amazing."

"Thank you, my dear. I was in the mood for pink. You look lovely too."

"Is your friend here yet?" I asked.

"Roberto is inside picking up the tickets. This evening's performance is called Baroque and Opera. I have seen it before, of course, but I always enjoy it."

124

Roberto was a tall, slender man and he was wearing a cloak and white gloves. He passed over my ticket with a flourish.

"Enchanted," he said.

Coco giggled. "Roberto is very excited to have two dates for the evening. He's hopelessly vain, aren't you, darling?"

He smiled at her. "Perhaps a little," he agreed.

"But I forgive him because he's so *simpatico*."

He gave a little half-bow and she tilted her head flirtatiously in return. There was a real frisson between them and I thought of Silvio and was glad the poor man wasn't there to witness it.

"Shall we go inside?" Roberto suggested. He took Coco's arm, hooping it through his, and the three of us shuffled along in a queue that snaked through the foyer and up a flight of steps. No one else had bothered dressing up, so we must have made quite an impression in our peacock clothes. People were staring and smiling.

We took seats at the very back of the concert chamber so the fascinator wouldn't get us into any trouble. It was a large hall and not an especially plush one. The stage was low, with no curtain or scenery, the fresco on the ceiling faded. It wasn't what I'd expected at all. I turned to Roberto, who was sitting between us.

"I thought opera was meant to be rather grand?"

"This is more of a recital than a proper opera performance," he explained. "But there is an orchestra and they wear the costumes of the period, so it is very nice. I hope you're not disappointed."

"No, of course not," I said politely, although I'd been imagining a big distracting spectacle and this seemed as if it was to be small and rather shabby.

The orchestra took their seats and tuned up their instruments. There was a ripple of clapping as the first singers emerged from a doorway set into the wall beside us and walked down the rows of seats to the stage. When the applause finished, they broke into song.

I recognised the aria. It was one of those catchy ones used on pop opera albums all the time. The singers had pleasant enough voices but I couldn't concentrate on their performance. My mind kept drifting back to my family, all gathered at Pieta's house. What were they doing? Saying? Deciding on without me?

If I'd taken a morning flight I might be with them by now, but I'd stayed in Venice and gone shopping instead. It's not like me to run away from reality, and I was surprised at myself yet at the same time relieved to be here instead of there dealing with Eden and my father. In fact the more I thought about them both, the less I wanted to go home any earlier than I had to. I needed this time for me, this break from all the madness. I told myself I ought to make the most of it.

The aria finished and the singers began on a new one. Both Roberto and Coco seemed captivated: she was listening with her eyes closed and a smile on her lips and he was mouthing the words silently. I had to stop myself fidgeting. Would there be an interval and a bar to have a drink at? I hadn't thought to ask.

From the corner of my eye I noticed a latecomer trying to sneak in. The young woman opened the door to the chamber very slowly. She was wearing sweatpants and a vest top, and although the lighting was fairly dim, I could make out a tattoo of daisies running over her shoulder. I recognised her as she tiptoed towards the back of the room. That thick black plait and the heavy fringe gave her away. Valentina again. I could hardly believe it. The girl seemed to crop up everywhere.

She slipped through the performers' door and out of sight. On stage the singers had launched into another duet. I only half listened. What on earth was Valentina doing here? Surely it wasn't possible for her to be working in this place too?

The duet finished and the singers left the stage. After a few moments the performers' door opened again and I saw a woman on the threshold who was still familiar despite her dark hair being tucked up into an eighteenth-century-style wig.

"Coco," I hissed. "Look, it's that girl Valentina from the tango night."

The old woman didn't bother turning. "Late again I see," she muttered.

As Valentina stepped up to the stage, the orchestra played the first few notes.

"I didn't realise she was a singer."

Roberto shushed me. "She will give us the Mozart first," he whispered. "'Porgi Amor'. It is beautiful . . . listen."

Valentina had a lovely voice; not one of those screechy sopranos that sounds like a sick cat. She sang sweetly and strongly, filling the room with the most heartfelt lament. It was a song that matched my mood, and I closed my eyes and let it fill me up.

"Yes, beautiful," I said softly as she finished.

The audience began clapping and Roberto leaned towards me, speaking into my ear. "She is Coco's god-daughter. Very talented, but troubled."

"Really?" I was surprised.

Valentina looked flushed and pretty. As she waited for the applause to subside, the performers' door opened once again and a man joined her. Together they sang a coy, flirty number, and after it Valentina left the stage while the male singer stayed to perform a couple of solos.

"Is she finished?" I hissed at Roberto.

"Until the end," he whispered back. "She will close the evening with the same tenor."

Sure enough, the finale belonged to her. This song I recognised too: another pop opera hit. The tenor sang the first part, then she joined in and they finished together with a rousing, foot-stamping anthem. It was bloody good actually. The audience surged up for a standing ovation, and they deserved it.

Joining in with the cries of "Bravo!" I glanced down at Coco. She was still seated, clapping politely, her expression unreadable.

As we filed out of the theatre, I suggested a nightcap, reluctant to have the evening end and be on my own again. Coco refused at first, citing tiredness, but Roberto talked her into it.

128

"You can't go home yet," he insisted. "More of Venice should be allowed to appreciate you tonight, cara. You are magnificent."

She smiled at him, her skin a collage of wrinkles. "Oh, Roberto, you are so good for me. Just one drink, then I must go home and rest. It has been a long day."

We walked together across the Rialto bridge and beyond the deserted marketplace, past a few bars with music pulsating from them and through a doorway set into a scarred stone wall. Inside was a wood-panelled room with a bar running down one side. The two old men leaning on it greeted Roberto by name, and he introduced us as his dates for the evening. "My darling Coco and my new friend Addolorata," he said with a flourish.

We ordered our drinks and some *cicchetti*, although the best of the food was finished. One of the old Venetian men insisted on paying and we stayed at the bar with them, swapping conversation.

They talked of a gondola accident on the Grand Canal, some scandal with a politician, a cruise ship that had sailed into the Giudecca with half the passengers and crew sick with stomach bugs. It was a local conversation scattered with Venetian phrases I struggled to understand, and while it was difficult for me to join in, I was happy sitting there and listening. This was what I'd longed for, to be part of things rather than just another invisible tourist. It had happened thanks to Coco.

She did look tired this evening. Roberto had found her a stool to sit on, and she seemed grateful for it. The

Prosecco restored a little of her sparkle, but still she was quieter than usual.

"Valentina has a great voice," I said to her. "Roberto says she's your god-daughter?"

"Yes indeed," Coco agreed.

"I was surprised to see her. She seems to work everywhere: the walking tour, the opera, the Acqua Alta bookstore."

"She is working there now too?" Her lips formed a thin line.

"You don't approve?"

Coco stared down at her glass then back at me. "The girl is killing herself and there's no need for it. But she won't listen. Some people don't want my advice, as I said earlier."

"Roberto says she's talented but troubled."

"He does?" She took a delicate sip of her drink. "Her problems are very different to those you're facing. Tell me, did you think any more about what I said?"

I was sorry that Coco had turned the conversation back to me. I'd have preferred to talk about someone else's messy life.

"Yes, I've thought about it. I'm no closer to knowing what to do, though."

She rubbed at her face, smudging blue eyeshadow into its creases. "Do the things that will make you happy."

"What if I don't know what they are?"

She shrugged. "Then I think you really do have a problem."

130

Putting her glass on the bar, Coco turned from me and touched Roberto's arm very lightly.

"Yes, my love?" He dropped a kiss on her head.

"Take me home now."

"Of course, of course." He fussed about her. "Are you too tired to walk? Shall we take a water taxi? Will you be warm enough?"

She said good night and grasped Roberto's arm, leaning on him as they left. In the doorway she paused to look back at me. "I've been meaning to tell you, there's an apartment above mine that has come up for rent; just short-term for the summer. It's much nicer than that hotel you're staying in."

I wasn't sure why she'd bothered to mention it. Even if I stuck with my original plan to fly home on Sunday, I only had a handful more days in Venice and could put up with my hotel for that long, surely. Still, Coco was an eccentric, I reminded myself. There was no rational explanation for half the things she said and did. I dismissed her talk of the apartment as just another example of her quirkiness . . . at least at first I did.

CHAPTER
NINE

Coco had planted a seed. She had done it on purpose, of course, although at first I didn't realise it. Also I got very drunk so it slipped my mind for a while.

After she and Roberto left the bar, the two old men had been pleased to stay and share a few more glasses with me. Eventually the patron had locked the door and joined us, pulling out a bottle or two of the Veneto's best for us to taste. The three of them told me stories of growing up in Venice. How there were no skyscraper-sized cruise ships washing up the Giudecca canal back then, how the tourists were fewer and richer, how the water at the Lido was better to swim in, how the place was going to the dogs now and nothing could be done. They seemed to enjoy complaining and I enjoyed drinking, so all of us were entertained for hours.

I'm not sure what time it was when I left, but there was hardly anyone about. Venice was silent and shadowy. A chill wind blew off the Grand Canal and I shivered in my flimsy dress as I hurried back over the Rialto bridge, trying not to weave as I went. Those last couple of glasses had pushed me from pleasantly intoxicated to smashed.

Thankfully I made it safely back to the hotel, where I collapsed into bed without taking off my make-up. When I woke a couple of hours later it was with a raging thirst and I had to get up to fetch some water. After that I tossed and turned until the morning light crept through the cracks in my shutters. Just as I was beginning to drift off to sleep again, my phone rang.

"Yes?" I said fuzzily.

"Hey, it's me," said Pieta. "Did I wake you?"

"Um, yeah, hang on." I groped for my glass of water and swigged the last few drops. "What's up?"

"I talked to Eden last night. He told me about you two . . . you know."

"What did he tell you exactly?"

"That you're splitting up," she said, sounding awkward. "Dolly, I can't believe it."

I was awake now and furious. "I can't bloody believe it either. We've had one conversation and nothing has been decided. Has he told Katia too?"

"I don't know . . . I don't think so."

Even without the hangover I'd have felt sick. "What about Papa?"

"Eden told me not to say anything to him and Mum yet."

"Shit," I said. "I don't know what sort of game he's playing."

Pieta hesitated for a moment. "He seems really sad."

I felt a proper wave of nausea and decided to go and sit on the floor next to the toilet just in case. When I stood up, my head swam. "What else did he say?"

"Just that he's felt like this for a while and you going away gave him a chance to think about it properly."

"And?"

"He's decided there's no point in carrying on together if neither of you is happy." Her voice was soft and sorry.

I leaned my head against the bathroom wall. "OK," I said. "Thanks for letting me know."

Pieta was repeating my name as I hung up. Turning my phone on to silent, I lay on the cold tiles and tried to think clearly. I guess I was down there for a while, because I fell asleep, and when I came round my neck was sore and I felt freezing.

The first thing I thought of was Coco telling me about the apartment for rent. Was she actually suggesting I should stay in Venice for the whole summer? I pulled myself to my feet, stared at the wreck of my face in the bathroom mirror and splashed some water on it. Perhaps she was.

Snuggling back beneath the bedcovers, I indulged in a fantasy: me living in Venice, shopping at the Rialto market for fresh produce every morning, a basket over my arm; taking the *traghetto* back across the Grand Canal, stopping for a cappuccino and a brioche at my regular café, wandering the narrow *calli* and always knowing my way. I imagined evenings dancing the tango until the steps came easily; late mornings and lazy afternoons; sudden mists and sunny skies, me with bangles on my arms, coloured skirts and pretty tops. It was a really nice fantasy.

134

Only when I'd decided I could stomach food did I bother to get up. My room was in chaos. I'd thrown the Pucci-style dress on the floor and it lay in a tangle with my shoes, bra and yesterday's knickers. Stepping over them, I rummaged through my new clothes to find something clean to wear. Why not the white linen trousers? I'd pair them with the embroidered top and take my denim jacket in case it was still chilly.

After a long shower, I put on some make-up — not just a lick of tinted moisturiser, but blusher to freshen my cheeks and colour on my lips. I still had glassy hangover-eyes with dark shadows beneath them, but I looked and felt better by the time I'd finished.

Out on the street, I slipped on my sunglasses against the glare of the day. There was no point going far, so I stopped at the nearest tourist place and ordered a pizza with prosciutto and a couple of Cokes to wash it down.

The pizza wasn't especially good. I had to throw salt, olive oil and most of a rocket salad over it to pep up the flavour. But I worked my way through the whole thing, even the crust. Too liverish still for coffee, I paid my bill and tried to decide what to do with the rest of the day. Whatever happened, I was in no state to get on a plane. That Sunday flight home was looking more likely.

It hadn't been my intention to look for Coco's apartment, but I started walking and that's the direction my feet took me in. I didn't bother with my map, just wandered on, recognising the bar where I'd had a drink that first afternoon and the steps I'd lugged her shopping trolley up and down. It was a pretty part of Venice this, with bridges criss-crossing narrow canals, window boxes of flowers, and drying laundry fluttering. I took a wrong turn or two but enjoyed the places they led me to and eventually found myself walking up a *fondamenta* that seemed familiar. This was where Coco lived. Still I might not have picked out her building if not for the sign saying "Apartment to rent" tacked up on the wall.

She must have been doing housework, because when she answered the door, small dogs yipping around her feet, Coco's cheeks were flushed and on her head was a yellow kerchief.

"Addolorata," she said, sounding pleased. "Ah, so you have come to see the apartment?"

"Yes, I suppose I have," I said, surprised at myself.

"Good, good, the key is with me. Come in for a moment while I find it."

It was the art I noticed first, brightly painted canvases covering every inch of her walls. Her furniture was shabby, but wherever my eye fell, there were extra touches: rugs thrown, scarves draped, beads hung. The result was cheerful and cluttered, the home of a woman who had lived a long life and held on to things to remember it by.

"Here we are." Coco returned with the key and I saw she had taken a moment to powder her face and put on lipstick. "It's upstairs, the door on the first landing. Take a look around and bring it back when you've finished."

The rental apartment looked bare and basic in comparison to Coco's place. There wasn't much furniture, only a battered chaise in the living area, a high double bed with a carved wooden headboard, and a small dining table. The kitchen was set against one wall, the bathroom attached to the bedroom, and neither was remarkable. What made the place special were the soaring ceilings and the shuttered glass doors that opened on to a balcony overlooking the canal. There was space for no more than a couple of chairs and some pots of geraniums, and the buildings opposite were close enough for me to see into their windows. I stood for a while enjoying the silky pond smell of the water, and imagined making a temporary home here. Arranging flowers in a vase on the table, fruit in a bowl. Stacking books beside the bed, buying good linen to put on it. Cooking a simple meal, inviting Coco to eat with me. Yes, it was still a nice fantasy.

"So what do you think?" Coco asked when I went to return the key.

"You're right, it's much nicer than my hotel. I wish I was staying there."

"The landlord is an old friend. He will do you a good deal on the rent if I talk to him."

"Thanks, but there's no point. I'm only here for another couple of days at most."

"Why rush to go back home if it's making you miserable? Stay in Venice a little longer," she suggested.

"I can't do that."

"Why not?"

"I have a family, a job; people are expecting me. I have responsibilities."

"Oh, responsibilities." Coco rolled her eyes.

"Well it's true," I said defensively. "I can't just please myself."

The old lady didn't seem to understand that not all of us could lead lives centred on ourselves like she did; other things had to come first.

"I would love to spend a whole summer here," I admitted. "But even this holiday was a mistake as it turns out. I shouldn't have come at all."

"Yet still you wanted to see the apartment. Why?"

"I was dreaming, I suppose, being ridiculous. I've wasted your time, I'm sorry."

"There's nothing wrong with dreams," said Coco, "and I have plenty of time. I was about to make coffee and enjoy it in my garden. Why don't you join me?"

Coco's garden was a beautiful secret, walled in and over-grown with plants that climbed and entwined. Glossy leaves of ivy tangled with flowering wisteria vines, oleander crowded out palms, lavender sprang from crumbling urns and broken pots. In one corner, beneath an old fig tree, was a table that Coco had covered with a cloth in the same yellow as her kerchief. She brought out a pot of coffee, a plate of polenta biscuits, a jug of chilled water, napkins, vividly painted espresso cups, coloured glasses.

"I like to set a nice table," she told me, sitting down.

The dogs had arranged themselves on the ground beside her and Coco bent to stroke them. "My darlings," she said fondly. "They like to be out here with me."

I crunched on a buttery biscuit and sipped the coffee, patted the silky head of the dog nearest to me, enjoyed my view of the garden. "It's a lovely place. Have you lived here for long?"

"Yes, for many years, and I will never leave now. The darling dogs I have lost are buried here, you see. I visit their little graves every day."

"That's sad," I remarked, not sure what else to say.

"Yes, it's always sad to lose a friend." She smiled brightly at me. "But much better than never having made the friend in the first place."

I realised it was time for me to thank her. "Coco, you've been so kind —" I began.

"It made me happy to be," she interrupted. "I wouldn't have done it otherwise. Unlike you, I don't believe in selflessness."

I laughed. "No one would describe me as selfless, really they wouldn't."

Coco carried on as if she hadn't heard. "To my mind it's the most overrated of virtues. Selfless people spend their lives putting others' needs before their own and waiting to be thanked; to be told they are marvellous. That almost never happens, of course, so then they get twisted and bitter. Selfless people are unbearable, I think."

"Really I'm not selfless at all," I promised.

"If you say so," she murmured.

It was peaceful in Coco's garden, with a cool breeze teasing the wisteria blossoms and no sound but the birdsong. I imagined her spending long afternoons out here in the height of the summer, whiling away the time and suiting herself. I envied her a little. Being old might mean she had creaky joints and wrinkles, but it also brought such freedom, the relief of letting go ambitions and goals, a lot less wanting and striving in general. Coco was at a stage in life when it was easier to be happy; or at least that's how it seemed to me.

"I'll come back to Venice some day when I have more time," I told her. "Some day when I've got my life back."

"And what if some day never comes?"

I looked at her, still in her bright kerchief, one of the dogs pulled up on to her knee now. She was sitting in a pool of spring sunshine, its golden light dappling her face, and I could see the make-up she'd applied so hastily sitting on her skin and the lines she'd been trying to mask with it scoring her face like scars.

"Oh I'm sure it will," I told her. "If I want it to."

"Ah, I see . . . You haven't heard the slamming of the doors yet, have you?"

I was confused. "Sorry? What do you mean? What slamming?"

There was something in Coco's expression that made me suspect she felt sorry for me. "I suppose you're not old enough for that yet," she said. "But soon enough you'll realise those doors are closing on all the lives you might have lived, the children you could have had, the lovers too, the places you might have visited."

"You're talking about regrets?" I guessed.

"Not exactly. What I'm trying to say is that if you're unhappy, then now is the time to shake yourself free. Don't wait for some day. Trust me, that is a mistake."

"You sound as if you're speaking from experience."

140

Coco shrugged and turned her face away. If there was some personal story behind her words, she wasn't going to share it. Instead, putting the dog back on the ground, she began loading cups and glasses on to the tray.

"Thanks for the coffee," I told her, helping to carry it all back to the kitchen. "And for letting me see upstairs."

"Don't wait too long to change your mind," she warned me. "It's a very good apartment. Someone else will want it."

On the way back to the hotel, I stopped at a newsstand and bought a couple of English magazines. Then I treated myself to a *gelato* and found a bench to sit on while I ate it.

Flicking through the pages of one of the magazines, a self-help article caught my eye. It was written by a life coach and was all about managing your time. She'd done a pie chart dividing up the hours in the day for work, sleep, exercise, housework, kids, relationship, etc. The slimmest segment was the bit left over for "time entirely for you". Just fifteen minutes a day, and the life coach said few people managed that. The thought made me feel incredibly bleak. Fifteen minutes? Was that it?

I appreciate that there are people with bigger problems; starving, sick, war-torn people who would say I've got nothing to complain about. But really, fifteen minutes per day of your own life is all you can lay claim to? And that makes you among the fortunate ones? I could imagine what Coco would have to say about it.

Then I remembered that my phone had been on silent all day, most likely vibrating away in my bag. I grabbed it and checked the screen. Four missed calls from Pieta and two messages; nothing at all from Eden. I felt even bleaker.

I listened to Pieta's messages, then deleted them. She'd said the things I knew she would: that she was worried, that I should call, that we should talk. My sister is such a good person. She always does the right thing. I'm not like that at all. I'm the one who drinks and eats too much. I live in a messy house, go to bed with my make-up on, smoke even when I've given up and let my child eat junk food. Perfect I've never been, never even wanted to be.

I dialled Pieta's number.

"Eden's right: neither of us is happy," I said when she answered.

"OK," she said slowly. "But does that mean you have to rush into anything? I mean, you haven't even tried counselling yet."

"I'm not planning to rush," I told her.

"That's good, because I'm sure this is just a rough patch, what with his back injury and work being tricky and everything." She sounded relieved.

"I'm thinking about staying in Venice for the summer." As soon the words were out, I knew it was exactly what I wanted to do.

"Sorry . . . you're what?"

142

"I haven't gone crazy," I promised. "But like Eden I've had time to think, and I've realised a few things."

"What things?"

I tried to explain the whole happiness business but she didn't get it at all. I think she thought I was being self-indulgent.

"That's the whole point," I said. "This is about me."

"What about Little Italy?"

"Papa has the restaurant under control, doesn't he?"

"He does," she agreed. "Actually he seems to be loving being back, so if you need a longer holiday, perhaps you ought to take one."

I looked at the tourists passing to and fro, clutching their guidebooks and maps, all intent on touring the Doge's Palace or taking a gondola ride.

"It's not going to be a holiday," I insisted. "If I stay on here it has to be much more than that."

"Look, you needn't feel guilty about taking more time off —" Pieta began.

"Do you know what really makes you happy?" I interrupted. "Don't say the obvious things that everyone would choose, like family and friends; I mean the things particular to you, Pieta's own ingredients for happiness."

"I've never thought about it," she admitted.

"Exactly. Me neither. So that's what I'd be busy doing here. Thinking about it."

"And then what?"

"I don't know yet," I told her. "It will just be a summer, that's all. Hopefully by the end of it I'll have a better idea."

CHAPTER
TEN

It's amazing how difficult it is to free yourself from your own life for a few months. Everyone came up with obstacles, reasons why I should go home, and most were entirely valid, but once I'd made up my mind, I wasn't going to be talked out of it. If we had to load more debt on to the mortgage, take on another chef at the restaurant, reorganise and reshuffle a few things, then we'd do it. Nothing I was asking was impossible.

Of all of them Eden was the least surprised. He used words like "typical" and "selfish" but didn't try to talk me out of staying in Venice. Our conversation was terse, and mostly focused on Katia, but he let slip that my sister and her husband had hired him to project-manage the construction work they were doing on a new building they had leased. "So I'm going to have a busy summer," he told me.

"Yes, me too," I replied.

At that he laughed and said he hoped it all worked out, whatever I was up to.

I felt a little sad when the call ended. And guilty too. I was deserting my child for the summer, and Eden was right, it was a selfish thing to do. But we could talk, Skype, email; I hoped she might come over to visit once the school holidays began. So talking myself round wasn't too difficult. And I had Coco to buoy me up, which helped.

That evening, after I'd made my decision, I walked back over to Coco's place to tell her. Beyond the barking of dogs, there was no answer to my knocking on her door, so I had to wait until the next day.

I tracked her down very early at the café where she liked to drink her morning coffee.

"I'm doing it, I'm staying," I said the moment I reached her side.

"Ah, Addolorata, good morning."

"Yes, yes, good morning," I said impatiently. "Can you talk to your landlord about the apartment? I want to take it."

She smiled. "Of course, but first you will drink a coffee with me?"

"You don't seem surprised."

"No," she agreed. "But I am glad you are the person I thought you were. Now, a cappuccino, *si?* And a brioche? Then we will begin to get things organised."

I thought she must have haggled fiercely, because the rent was very reasonable. And then she lent me what I needed to move in straight away: bed linen and towels, some pots and pans, mismatched plates, old cutlery.

I was more than pleased to pack my suitcase and check out of the hotel. Coco gave me the key to my new apartment and I let myself in, then sat on the balcony for a while with my notebook on my knee. There was still an empty page where my happiness list was meant to be, but now I had a whole summer ahead to fill it.

I felt elated in some ways but also a little anxious. What if the time passed and nothing had changed? What if happiness was something I was bad at, like tango?

"Take your time. Don't try too hard," was Coco's advice. "Happiness will sneak up on you. You only have to notice it's there."

I looked down at the quiet stretch of canal beneath me. There were fewer gondolas in this part of Venice, as tourists rarely strayed this far from the main attractions. But I wasn't one of them now and it was time to start making myself at home.

First I wanted to fill my fridge and cupboards with food. Cooking a meal might help settle me in. The rhythm of chopping onions, the sizzle as they fell into a hot pan, the savoury scent as they bubbled in a tomato sauce; I needed that familiarity.

Heading out to the Rialto market, I stopped at Coco's door. "Are you busy tonight? Would you like to come for dinner?"

"I have a date," she told me.

"Another one? Who with this time?"

"My darling Silvio. I said I'd have an *ombra* with him later."

An *ombra* was one of the few Venetian phrases I did understand. It's the word they use for a small glass of wine drunk standing at a bar, often while enjoying a few *cicchetti*.

146

"Bring him back here to eat after you've had your *ombra*," I suggested. "I'm going to make pasta and then perhaps some fish."

"Silvio would love that, I'm sure. He has given up hoping I will ever cook for him."

I took a *traghetto* across the Grand Canal, this time paying the residents' rate rather than the tourist charge. Earlier there had been a mist hanging over the water but now the sun had burned it away and the sky was clear and blue. I felt a rush of pure delight. This was it: my Venice fantasy come true. I was really living it.

In the vegetable market I managed to restrain myself, but passing through the archways to the fish stalls I bought soft-shelled spider crabs and a pile of the sweet, plump prawns they call *canoce*, razor clams, baby octopus, tiny fish and a silver-skinned branzino, with no idea how we would manage to eat it all. My parcels of food went into the shopping trolley I'd borrowed from Coco, along with cheeses, olive oil, pasta and garlicky *sopressa* salami I found in the shops surrounding the market. Finally there was space only for some last-minute wild strawberries, tiny purple-leaved artichokes and bunches of fresh herbs.

By then my head was full of food. I was putting together ingredients and dreaming up flavour combinations, the way I have since Papa first taught me to cook.

Before I could deal with what I'd bought, I needed to eat, and not a slice of bland tourist pizza either. I was hungry for dishes that had been made with care, flavours to surprise and inspire, a proper meal to eat slowly and remember.

We'd visited several decent places near the market on Valentina's *cicchetti* tour. The one that had appealed to me most had been Angelo's small *osteria*, and I recalled how she'd mentioned him serving up a different risotto each day. Hopefully it wasn't too late for me to get a plateful.

His little place was only a few steps from the fish stalls, and it was packed. I managed to find a free stool at the end of a long shared table and, parking my shopping trolley next to it, went to order a portion of risotto. The *cicchetti* in the cabinet weren't the usual run-of-the-mill meatballs and crostini, and I couldn't resist getting a few of the more interesting to nibble while I waited. A scallop in its shell flavoured with fennel seeds, a little tart of creamed cod with the crunch of celery and a hint of ginger. Eating them only made me hungrier. It struck me that I'd been skipping meals and snacking my way through the days since arriving in Venice. Now I planned to make up for it.

There is no dish I yearn for more than risotto. I love its creaminess, the way it ripples from the wooden spoon you stir it with. I like folding in handfuls of grated Parmesan cheese and hunks of salted butter, the comfort of eating it, the warm, solid feeling of it sitting in my stomach.

This risotto was a soupy one, tasting of salt water and lemons. It was cheered with flecks of green parsley and filled with tender clams to be prised from their shells. Briefly I closed my eyes so I could focus on its flavours.

148

When I opened them again, Angelo had emerged from the kitchen. He was busy clearing plates, greeting regular customers by name, pausing to share a joke with one and take a compliment from another. He might have walked right past my table and not noticed me if I hadn't stopped him.

"Hi, this is really good. What did you use in the stock?" I asked.

"I make it with the goby fish," he told me. "Do you know it?"

I shook my head.

"It's a small fish that lives in the lagoon. Its flesh is no good to eat but its flavour can be captured in a risotto. I'm happy you're enjoying it."

"I'm Dolly," I told him in case he hadn't remembered. "We met the other night and I came to watch you dance tango in the square."

"Ah yes, you are the one we left asleep on the bench. I'm glad to see you're OK. Coco said she'd look after you."

"And she did — she has been ever since really. I'm cooking dinner for her tonight to say thank you. I've just leased the apartment above hers."

"That place, yes, I know it. I lived there myself for a while a couple of years ago."

"You did?" I was surprised.

"Coco is my aunt," he explained. "My mother's eldest sister."

"Really? She seems to be related to everyone I meet in some way or other."

Angelo laughed. "She's lived in Venice her whole life. Most local people know who she is, even if they aren't family."

I could see that he was about to move off to share a few words with another customer and pick up more scraped-clean plates. I stopped him again.

"Would you like to come for dinner?" I asked impulsively. "One of Coco's friends is coming as well, but I've bought so much from the market that it's going to be a feast."

"Tonight?" He sounded taken aback.

"Yes, if you're free. It'll be very casual as I'm pretty much camping in the apartment. And I can't promise anything as good as this risotto."

Angelo treated me to another smile. "You do realise that no one ever offers to cook a meal for a chef?"

I nodded. "Well I'm offering."

"What are you planning to make?"

I listed the ingredients I'd bought and the dishes I was considering, and as I talked, Angelo nodded, making several suggestions then describing where to find a nearby spice shop he thought I should visit.

"So will you come?" I hoped he'd say yes.

"It would be a pleasure."

I was delighted by the idea of Angelo joining us for dinner. Much as I enjoyed Coco's company, if I was going to spend an entire summer here it would be good to meet some people who were more my own generation. Also I was interested to know what he would think of the food I made. My confidence had been given a huge knock by Guy Rochester's review, and to have a Venetian chef approve of the things I did with the fish from his lagoon might help steady it again.

Sure, Angelo was a very good-looking guy, but let me be clear, I wasn't flirting; that's not why I'd invited him at all. I was interested in getting to know another one of the locals. Really that's all, I swear it.

I took the *traghetto* back across the Grand Canal, then walked towards my new temporary home trundling my shopping trolley, returning a *salve* every now and then from other women doing the same. Many of them would be planning dinner for their friends or families, just like I was.

Back at the apartment Coco was waiting for me. She must have had a spare key because she'd let herself in and was hanging a painting on the wall with help from a man I hadn't met before.

"It's one of Pegeen's," she said. "Something to brighten the place up."

"This is Pegeen?" I asked, pointing at the man.

She knitted her brow. "No, of course not, this is Lorenzo, come to help me like the good friend he is."

"So who is Pegeen?"

"She was my friend too. She died a long time ago, poor girl."

I stared at the picture. A child might have painted it. The canvas was covered in big daisies, and dotted among them were yellow-haired naked women holding striped parasols.

"This is one of her earlier works; quite valuable I expect, but I would never sell because she gave it to me."

"Is she famous? Should I have heard of her?" I asked.

"She was Peggy Guggenheim's daughter. You were at the gallery; I saw you there. But perhaps you didn't notice her paintings since they are hidden in a small side room all on their own."

"You're talking about the Peggy Guggenheim Collection?" I was still confused. "You were friends with her?"

"Not Peggy; I met her, of course, but I wasn't important enough to be noticed. It was her daughter I knew." Coco looked from the painting to me. "What do you think of it?"

"Very bright and happy," I managed.

"No, it's trying to be happy; just like you. That's why I decided it would be good to hang it here."

"Thanks, that's so thoughtful," I said, remembering my manners. "Would you and Lorenzo like coffee? I could make some."

We both glanced at Lorenzo to see him shake his head.

"He has to go," said Coco. "I think his wife is expecting him."

Lorenzo was quite a handsome old guy, and when he kissed Coco goodbye it was on the lips, with one hand cradling the curve of her bottom and the other on her waist. It wasn't a quick kiss either, but long enough to make me feel I shouldn't be there and watching.

"Well," she said, once he'd gone. "That was an unexpected visit."

She was dressed in a long robe in soft shades of blue and green; her cheeks were pink and her make-up was smudged. "So kind of him to carry the painting up for me; I wanted to surprise you but couldn't manage it myself. Lorenzo is very strong," she added. "He lifts weights."

"Have you known him long?" I asked.

"Oh yes," Coco said so very lightly that I could tell I wasn't going to get any more out of her.

She helped me unpack my shopping, exclaiming at how extravagant I must have been and how we'd never eat it all. When I told her I'd invited Angelo along to help us, she seemed pleased.

"Such a talented boy," she said. "But like Valentina, he works too hard. All the young ones seem to."

Once Coco had headed downstairs to resume the nap Lorenzo had interrupted, I began to do things with food. Often people say they find cooking relaxing, meditative even. That's not the way it is with me. When I'm trying a new dish I start out tense, worried it won't taste the way I'd imagined. Pieta reckons she can tell how I'm feeling just by the way I hold my shoulders. As things progress I get faster. I fire through the chopping of onions, flipping things in pans, setting hot fat spitting. The adrenalin is flowing and I'm having fun.

When the meal is plated up, there is always a moment of doubt. Is this the best I could have done? Is every single ingredient working as hard as it should be?

153

I don't have my father's blithe confidence that each dish created is a masterpiece.

Here in Venice, with borrowed pans and barely enough of them, I was forced to slow down. My knife was blunt and its handle loose, my chopping board pathetically small and the burners on the gas stove in need of attention.

I began with a fisherman's *ragu*, flavouring it with cinnamon, *peperoncino* and cloves, letting it simmer on the stove, sloshing in white wine every now and then, and tasting, always tasting. When everyone was ready to eat I would slip in the prawns, the baby octopus and the smaller fish and we would enjoy it with a few slender strands of spaghetti.

For the crabs I made the lightest of batters so I could serve them deep-fried along with buttery razor clams; the branzino was to be stuffed with herbs and covered in a rock-salt crust, the artichokes cut into paper-thin slices and eaten raw with a thread or two of olive oil. This was my first attempt at a Venetian meal, based on half-remembered recipes and Angelo's advice; I hoped it would measure up.

The final thing I prepared was myself. Mindful of Coco and her disapproval if she turned up to find me in flour-dusted clothes and no make-up, I picked out a bright top and skirt I hadn't yet worn. Hopefully they would survive the evening unscathed by splashes of fisherman's *ragu* and cooking oil. Finally I dashed round tidying, plumping up cushions Coco had lent me and polishing the wine glasses that had also come from her apartment.

154

Angelo was the first to arrive. He brought flowers and a vase to put them in and went straight to the kitchen, lifting the lids of pans, smelling and tasting, adding more wine to the sauce I'd thought was perfect.

"You can cook," he said, sounding pleased. "This isn't bad at all."

I poured us both a drink and we sat out on the balcony talking about his *osteria*. He told me how he'd set it up with no money at all, borrowing from friends and family, buying up mismatched furniture cheaply from places that had closed down, running up debts he wasn't sure he could ever repay.

"Coco helped," he said. "She let me stay here for as long as I was struggling. She never asked for rent."

"Didn't the landlord mind?"

"What landlord? She owns the place."

I gaped at him. "Really?"

"You didn't know that?"

"I don't know anything much about her," I admitted.

"My aunt is a very private woman. Possibly even I haven't been told half the things worth knowing about her."

"She has a lot of boyfriends," I confided. "I mean loads."

"Ah now that I did know." He laughed. "She scandalises my mother, but then she always has."

"Coco and all these men . . . they're just friends, right?" I asked, even though I was beginning to suspect otherwise.

Again Angelo was amused. "She is who she is," he told me. "Don't think she's changed just because she's old."

Coco was half an hour late and most apologetic. "We lost track of the time," she told me.

"And perhaps we had more than one *ombra*," confessed Silvio, who was holding a couple of bottles of wine.

They were appreciative guests and all had an appetite; even Coco put away a surprising amount for someone with such a birdlike frame. She was wearing a black dress with a hemline that barely grazed her knees, and tangled round her neck were several strings of glossy pearls. "Very chic, yes?" she said when I complimented her.

Silvio draped an arm along the back of Coco's chair. Every now and then he stroked her shoulder with his fingers. I watched the two of them for a moment, then caught Angelo's eye. Yes, more than a friend, I wanted to say. I see that now.

We made our way through the courses, giving the entire evening over to eating. Everyone praised the dishes I served, and Silvio was especially fulsome.

"I hear you are staying in Venice. This is excellent news," he declared. "Not only can we enjoy your wonderful cooking, but now you will be able to continue to learn the tango."

I wasn't at all sure about letting myself in for another evening spent stumbling backwards as Silvio counted out my steps. Still, I didn't want to be rude. "Oh yes . . . maybe."

"You enjoyed our little lesson at Santa Maria della Salute the other night, didn't you?" he asked.

156

I laughed. "Enjoy isn't entirely the right word, but I did appreciate you trying to help. Perhaps tango just isn't for me."

"Tango is for everyone," Silvio argued.

Angelo interrupted. "That's not true. You must be a certain sort of woman to dance the tango. You need to have self-respect and awareness, balance and coordination, but most of all you must be prepared to follow a man. If you can't do that then you should try another dance."

"I'm not sure I'm the kind of woman who's designed to follow a man," I told him.

"Because you're a feminist?" he guessed.

"Not just that. I kept getting in the way of Silvio's feet. I couldn't understand how I was supposed to know he was about to move sideways or backwards. No matter how closely I watched the other dancers, I couldn't work that out. I guess I should try something else."

"Tango is a conversation," Angelo explained, "except we communicate through our hands and our muscles. But in my opinion a *milonga* isn't the best place for a beginner to learn. It is better to start somewhere not so public. If I were to teach you, we would work together in my home, and the very first thing you'd be shown is the change of weight, because that's how to find a rhythm."

Silvio nodded. "I should have started with that; you're right. I've been dancing with Coco so long that I forgot what it is to be a beginner."

Angelo seemed convinced that by the end of the summer if I took private lessons and put in enough practice I could be a dancer. He had such a passion when he talked about the tango, it was impossible not to get caught up in it.

"It feels like pure happiness, an almost chemical high," he said and then offered to give me a few lessons.

Curiously it was Coco who discouraged us. "It will use up too much of your time, Addolorata, and distract you from the real reason you're in Venice. And Angelo, I'm sure you have enough to do with your work. Don't take on more commitments."

Angelo looked at me. "But we might enjoy it, Dolly and I."

"You would need far longer than one summer to teach her properly," Coco insisted. "Nobody can learn enough in that time."

"I disagree. It would be possible to reach a threshold we are happy with. I could make a social dancer of her . . . maybe even more than that."

"Such vanity." Coco tutted. "You are an arrogant boy, Angelo."

The criticism only seemed to amuse him. "Confidence is not the same thing as arrogance," he pointed out. "Not at all."

"So you keep telling me," Coco said. "I'm not convinced, however."

"In that case I'm going to accept the challenge," he declared.

"But there has been no challenge," she protested.

158

"Yes there has," Angelo told her. "You've said I can't do something. I believe I can and I'm prepared to prove it to you."

Coco continued trying to dissuade us; she even grew quite mulish on the subject, but Angelo persisted. With all his talk of pure happiness I was tempted to give it a try. In the end he went downstairs and came back with an old-fashioned ghetto blaster and a few CDs of tango music.

"We will begin this evening," he declared.

He spent a while fussing about finding the right track, something not too fast, but not slow either. I threw back another glass of wine for courage. And then we stood in the middle of the living room, face to face, with Silvio and Coco looking on.

First Angelo showed me how to shift my weight from foot to foot, and that seemed easy enough. Then he came closer and took my hands, placing them flat against his shoulders.

"Now we will walk," he said. "And you must try to follow."

He pushed me backwards, gently at first and then more powerfully so I had to use my hands to resist him. Every now and then he issued an instruction. "Lengthen your stride. Don't lean in but don't hollow your back like that either. Feel with your hands where my body is going. Stay in time to the music."

It seemed to go on for ever, this backwards walking, with a pause every now and then for some weight shifting.

"Her posture is good," Angelo called to Coco.

"Not too bad I suppose," came the response.

Once or twice Angelo took me by surprise by pausing or changing direction and I lost my balance or my leg shot out behind me. "Don't go without me," he said, laughing.

"It's impossible not to," I complained. "I'm still struggling with this whole following business."

"Come closer to me then," he instructed. "It will make it easier for you to feel which way I want you to move."

Putting his arms around me, Angelo drew me in so we were standing heart to heart, my hands on his shoulder blades, our bodies touching. It was incredibly intimate — essentially a hug — and I felt myself stiffen in surprise.

"Just relax, Dolly. You are OK with this, yes? We can stop if you want to," said Angelo.

I could smell the musky warmth of his skin and the wine on his breath. "No, it's fine," I said in a half-whisper, although I wasn't entirely sure yet if I was OK with it or not.

"Shut your eyes like you did when you were eating my risotto this afternoon," he told me. "Don't try to dance; just be with me, trust me."

I did what he asked and together we moved around the room again. This felt entirely different to dancing with Silvio. Angelo's body was firm and strong rather than failing; he led more forcefully, and with my eyes tightly shut, it almost seemed as if there was nothing to do but follow.

160

"Good, good," he muttered now and then. "Better."

To me this seemed like something more than just a dance. Our faces were almost touching, the warmth of each other's skin was beneath our fingers and our embrace was a close one. As Angelo's body asked, mine began to respond, and it felt almost natural and powerfully physical. If it hadn't been for the music playing and the people watching us, it would have seemed exactly like foreplay.

I was beginning to understand why everyone was so keen on the tango.

Addolorata's Happiness List

1. Parties. Noisy dinners with friends, chaotic family gatherings, dressy events, impromptu celebrations, I love them all. I like being surrounded by lots of people who are their very best selves and having a great time. I like it when the noise level creeps up and everyone is talking at once, shouting over the music. I like when I'm the host, or the guest so long as I'm the last to leave. There haven't been enough parties, not lately, nowhere near . . .

CHAPTER
ELEVEN

I woke late to dirty dishes, to a sink filled with prawn shells and fish heads, and a row of empty wine bottles. I woke to the knowledge that I'd thrown a great party and that always pleases me.

As I washed dishes, I remembered the tango lesson and how unnerving it had been.

I filled a rubbish sack with fishy detritus and tied it tightly at the top. I got rid of the empty bottles and wiped down surfaces. I don't think I've ever tidied anywhere like I did that apartment. The place belonged to Coco and it seemed bad manners to live in my usual chaos. Also I had this shivery, restless energy and it was the only thing I could think of to burn it up. Clothes were taken from where I'd dropped them and placed on hangers, the floor and balcony swept, even the toilet given a once-over.

The thing about cleaning is it uses only the tiniest part of your brain, leaving the rest free for other thoughts. Mine was seething with them. Mostly I thought about Angelo and the prospect of more dance lessons. I imagined us alone in his apartment, my eyes closed and his arms round me. I visualised us dancing except in my head I moved like Valentina at the *milonga*. I could even sense how it might feel: amazingly freeing, a little wild and abandoned; and I thought how good it would be to feel like that, even if only for a few dances.

For some reason Coco had remained unenthusiastic about our plan. When the lesson ended, I'd opened my eyes to see that her expression was pinched. She hadn't joined in when Silvio praised my efforts. She hadn't said very much at all.

My mind flitted from tango and settled on Coco. She was such an enigma. We'd spent so much time together over the past week, talked about all sorts of things, yet the details of her life remained a mystery, and not because I wasn't interested. She had a knack for sidestepping questions, for turning the conversation back to me. She was one of those rare things, a good listener.

So I had no idea whether she had been married or had children, how she'd found the money to pay for a place like this, what the story was behind the endless stream of men flowing through her life.

The one real clue she'd given me was the name Peggy Guggenheim. It hinted at a glamorous, racy past. I didn't know much about the American heiress except that she'd lived in the amazing palazzo on the Grand Canal that now housed her collection of splodge-covered canvases, so she must have been pretty interesting. And Coco was connected to her.

If only I'd paid more attention when I'd visited the place, but I'd been thrown by the exhibition. It had left me feeling excluded, as if art was for other, more polished people who understood what they were seeing. I glanced over at the painting Coco had hung on my wall. It wasn't one I'd have chosen myself. The women in it had unnatural elongated bodies, breasts like poached eggs and no features on their faces. A child could have done it.

I hadn't planned to go back to the Peggy Guggenheim Collection again, but if there was a whole room of paintings by Coco's friend that I'd somehow managed to miss, then perhaps it was worth another visit to see if they were any better than this one.

The day was springtime fresh and I walked there in the Venetian manner, stopping off for a quick coffee here and a small snack there, so it was a pleasant way to spend a Sunday morning. I paid my entrance fee, bought a guidebook this time, and moved about Peggy Guggenheim's one-time home looking for things I hadn't noticed before.

The framed photographs caught my eye. They were dotted about the walls. In some the heiress was sitting in the same rooms I was walking through, beside furniture that was still there. I examined them more closely and realised that Peggy Guggenheim reminded me a bit of Coco: the same small dogs, similar crazy sunglasses. Still, it wasn't this woman who had been Coco's friend but her daughter Pegeen. So I kept looking until I found the room lined with her bright canvases.

All of them reminded me of the painting in my apartment: lots of flowers, seaside scenes and parks, the same long-limbed women and bright colours. Hung together in such a small space, they were dazzling, and I spent a long time walking from canvas to canvas, standing and looking. Finally I read a plaque on the wall that gave the bare bones of Pegeen's life. It seemed she'd been a typical poor-little-rich-girl, with failed relationships, depression and an early death. No mention at all of Coco, but it did say Pegeen had lived in Venice for a time in the 1950s.

In the gallery café there were more photographs that I hadn't bothered with on my first visit. They hinted at what life had been like back then, at least for the wealthy. Everything was stylishly bohemian, from Peggy Guggenheim's outfits to the glimpses of her home and the boats that whisked her down the Grand Canal; if Coco was telling the truth, then she had been on the fringes of all this.

Sitting in the palazzo's sheltered garden, I read the guidebook from cover to cover. I found lots about the art and nowhere near enough about the family, but there was one photograph captioned with Pegeen's name. In it she was standing next to a woman who was unmistakably a younger Coco. My friend's hair was long and dark, and her figure fuller than now. She was holding a glass and laughing, her head tilted back. It was a stance I'd seen her in myself.

I rubbed my finger over the photograph as if it would bring the scene to life. One of these women was gone now, the other old and grey; but here they were lovely. Pegeen's frock was very simple, Coco's encrusted with silvery diamanté. They must have been at a party and the photographer had caught them sharing a joke. They seemed to know he was there, although neither was looking directly at the camera. Coco was the one who stood out, the more beautiful of the two.

"Who are you?" I whispered at the picture.

By then it was afternoon, and I decided to return home for a rest before heading out to the *milonga* later. Angelo might have told me it was no place to learn, but still I could watch the dancing and see if I could pick out a few more steps.

Walking back, I stopped every now and then to take photographs of small things that caught my eye: wisteria spilling over an ochre-coloured wall, a statue of a Madonna and child, a shop window filled with cellophane-wrapped biscotti, a woman in a red straw hat sitting on the steps of a church with an adorable-looking Irish wolfhound at her side.

The dog was so striking I stopped to take another shot of it. As I raised the camera, the woman looked up and caught me at it. "No pictures," she called angrily in Italian. "Leave me in peace, for God's sake."

Then I realised who it was.

"Valentina?"

"You again." She sounded sour. "Why were you photographing me?"

"You looked so great sitting there," I told her, a little embarrassed. "Like an image from a fashion magazine. And your dog is beautiful."

"This is Boris." She transferred her sullen gaze to the animal. "Although why you would give an Irish dog a Russian name — why you would even own such a creature in a city like this — it makes no sense. It's like everything my mother does."

"May I stroke him?" I said, moving closer.

She gave me the leash. "Here, you can have him."

"You don't mean that," I said, fondling his head.

"No, I don't," she admitted. "My mother loves the thing. Not that she can exercise him, of course; it's me who has to do that. As if I wasn't busy enough."

Boris was sitting on his haunches and leaning into me as I stroked him. I've always liked big dogs, but living in London and working such long hours I'd never thought it fair to have one.

"I'll walk him for you," I offered impulsively. "I'm staying here for the whole summer. He can come with me when I go exploring."

She looked dubious. "I'm not sure . . . My mother doesn't know you and she can be difficult . . ."

"It's no big deal. Just tell her I offered."

"If she met you, perhaps . . ."

"Say that I'm a friend of Coco's," I suggested. "I'm living at her place."

"In the apartment upstairs?" Valentina said sharply.

"Yes, I'm renting it from her."

"Really? She wouldn't let me stay there when I asked to."

"It's only a short-term thing," I said quickly, fearing I'd put my foot in it.

"Oh don't worry, it's not your fault. Coco doesn't approve of me; not any more."

"I'm not entirely sure why she approves of me," I told her.

Valentina laughed. "I can tell you. It will be because you say yes; you do the things she tells you to."

I thought back over the past few days — the shopping trip and the opera, the tango — and how I'd fallen into line at every stage.

"You may be right," I admitted. "I have been letting her boss me round a bit."

"Of course I'm right. She is my mother's oldest friend. I've known her my whole life."

"So what's her story?" I asked. "Her past, she hardly talks about it."

"Even if she did, she would tell you one thing, my mother quite another, and both would believe what they were saying was completely true."

I went to hand the dog's leash back to her but Valentina shook her head. "You're truly willing to take him for walks? Then I suppose you should come to meet Mamma. Her place is on the Strada Nuova; walk there with me."

Valentina knew the most direct route. It was one that took us down *calli* so narrow we could touch the walls on either side of us. She moved briskly, and with Boris loping along beside me, often I was forced to fall a couple of steps behind, making conversation difficult. Still, whenever I could manage to, I slipped in a question.

"Was Coco married?"

Valentina laughed. "She never says much about that."

"Has she got children?"

"Not that anyone knows of."

168

"So what did she do? Did she have a job?"

That brought Valentina to a stop. "A job? Coco? No, I don't think that's very likely."

"Where did she get the money for that beautiful place, then?"

Valentina raised her eyebrows. "From men, of course. Where else?"

I assumed she meant Coco was a kept woman, a mistress.

"Ask her about it after she's had a few glasses of Prosecco,"

Valentina suggested the next time I caught her up. "Ask about her glory days."

When Valentina had told me her mother lived on the Strada Nuova, I'd imagined a tiny apartment above one of the shops. Although I must have walked past its gates several times, I'd never noticed the palazzo. It was half hidden by a drinks stand and there were lots of people milling about flogging fake designer handbags, so perhaps that's why I hadn't seen the wrought-iron railings with the patch of grass beyond them and the stone staircase leading up to the imposing building.

At first I thought the place looked extremely grand. Our footsteps echoed in the lofty hallway as Valentina let us in. There were more stairs, that Boris bounded up energetically, and we followed, past dusty chandeliers and ancient chairs with the stuffing hanging out of them, doors half off their hinges, faded frescoes, fissured walls. Yes, once it must have been grand, but not any more.

"Mamma," Valentina called. "Where are you?"

We passed a large reception room that looked not to have a stick of furniture in it.

"Mamma," Valentina called again.

"She may be out," I suggested.

"I doubt it. She never goes out."

Finally we found her. She was sitting by a window overlooking the street. To me she looked older than Coco, but that might have been because she was clad entirely in black, or because her shoulders were stooped and climbing from her chair seemed to take a great effort.

"Who is this?" she asked worriedly. "Do I know her?"

Valentina glanced at me and I realised she had forgotten my name.

"I'm Addolorata, a friend of Coco's," I told the old lady, holding out my hand. "Pleased to meet you."

She looked at me but didn't touch my hand. "Ah, I see."

"Mamma, please introduce yourself properly," Valentina scolded.

"I am the Contessa Leonarda di Malipiero," she said imperiously.

Valentina gave a despairing shake of her head. "You can call her Nanda," she told me.

"No she can't," the old lady snapped.

"Mamma, please . . ."

"She can call me Contessa if she must. She is a foreigner, *si*? She speaks Italian but not with a good accent."

170

"Mamma, she is going to walk Boris for us."

"We can't pay her."

"She doesn't want money," Valentina assured her.

"Good, good." The old woman returned to the chair she had been occupying and heaved herself back into it. "Take her to the kitchen. See if the cook will feed her."

"OK, Mamma I will," Valentina said, more gently.

I could tell there had been no cook in that kitchen for a very long time. There was a thick layer of dust on the rows of copper pans hanging from racks on the wall. Valentina poured glasses of water from a jug she took from the fridge and invited me to take a seat beside a scuffed marble table.

"Is your mother a little bit . . . well . . . confused?" I tried to find the right words.

"You mean does she have dementia? Perhaps . . . I don't know, she won't see a doctor." Valentina sounded worn down. "Often I wonder if she's playing a game with us. Acting as if life is still the way it was in the old days because it pleases her. The grand title, the staff, the airs and graces . . . then she'll say something and it's clear she knows exactly what's going on."

"I think that's what happens: their memories come and go."

"Of course I've read about it . . . a thousand websites. But Mamma is different. She doesn't forget things exactly, just chooses not to see them. And she still has such strength of will. Sadly I'm the only one who's left here to order round."

"It must be tough," I said.

"Yes, it is," she agreed. "But if you can exercise Boris for me it would help a great deal. It would give me some time for myself, to rest and see friends. And he's a good boy; he won't give you any trouble."

I promised to return the next morning and pick him up. It felt good to have something to structure my day around. Boris could come with me to the Rialto market to shop for food. Together we'd find parks and green spaces, shady outdoor spots to stop for coffee. Having a dog would open up a whole new Venice to me. It would make me look and feel as if I really belonged.

"Tell Coco I said hello," Valentina said as she showed me out of a side entrance. "Tell her to come and see Mamma very soon. Don't forget that."

"Won't we see you this evening at the *milonga*?" I asked.

"If I'm not too tired I may come along when I've finished working." Valentina frowned. "These days I'm always tired, though, so I doubt it."

I wondered about the Contessa and her run-down palazzo as I walked home. It seemed a pity to let such an incredible old building go to ruin. And where had all the furniture gone? There was no art on the walls, rugs on the floors or curtains at the windows; no shelves of books; not much at all besides a few uncomfortable-looking chairs. Living there, just the two of them, with all those empty rooms, must have been spooky, but if the old lady was losing her mind then I supposed Valentina had no choice. She was a spiky little thing and I was beginning to see why.

On my way up to my apartment I knocked on Coco's door, but softly in case she was sleeping. There was no reply so I headed to my own bed with plans to do the same.

There is such decadence about an afternoon nap. Closing the shutters against the light and sinking down between the sheets, letting sleep take over even though the day is far from finished. If I'm tired I can doze off within minutes, but that afternoon it wasn't so easy. My mind was full of new people and places; it was chugging along with thoughts. Then I remembered the people I'd left at home — my daughter and husband carrying on without me. Maybe it was witnessing Valentina's dedication to her mother, but suddenly I felt totally self-indulgent. I'd been worried about my own happiness. What about everyone else's?

I really didn't want to feel guilty, but even I could see that what I was doing was pretty outrageous. Most of the women I knew would never have dreamed of anything like it. They were devoted to their families, used to putting themselves second, accepting of their busy lives filled with small sacrifices. For a long time I'd been trying to be like that, and in the end everyone had been made unhappy — me, Eden, possibly even Katia too. There had to be a way to change things, for all of us to feel better and find more joy in life. But as hard as I thought about it, tossing and turning in the unfamiliar bed, I couldn't begin to see how.

Sadly this was one afternoon nap that wasn't working its magic. Giving up on sleep, I put on my wrap and went to sit on the balcony. The day was warming; late spring was giving way to early summer. Ahead of me were days filled with sunshine. Here there were endless possibilities, at home only problems. I might have felt guilty, but I wasn't going back. Not yet.

Below me I heard the creaking of shutters opening.

"Coco, is that you?" I called, leaning over the railing.

"*Si, cara,*" her voice floated back.

"Do you want to come up for a late lunch? I have some bits of cheese and salad here."

"Bring them down to the garden. It's lovely this afternoon. We can have a picnic"

I took a platter of Asiago cheese, peppery *sopressa*, crusty bread and olives and found she had set a pretty table with mismatched old china and a crystal vase of fresh-picked flowers. We sat together: me still in my wrap with my hair in a knot on my head, Coco in her robe and drowsy. I poured glasses of chilled sparkling water flavoured with a dash of bitters and she sipped at hers as she fed slivers of the salami to her little dogs.

"This morning I went back to the Guggenheim Collection to look at your friend Pegeen's paintings," I told her.

"Ah yes," Coco said.

"I found a picture of you in the guidebook I bought. You were at a party with her."

"There were so many parties."

"At this one you were wearing a dress covered in sparkles."

"A white dress?" Now she seemed more alert. "Cut quite low over my décolletage?"

"Yes, that's right."

174

"It was one of my favourites. I wonder what became of it."

"Do you remember the party?"

She frowned. "I wore that gown once to a very smart reception at the Gritti Palace. I think Pegeen was there but maybe she was in Paris . . . or London . . . I can't be sure."

"How did you meet her?"

"Through a friend."

"A man?" I guessed.

She was staring into the middle distance, half lost in the memory. "I think he thought I could help her. And I did try, but she needed more than me."

"It sounds like she had a sad time of it."

"Life can be sad if you let it." Coco glanced at me. Nibbled at a square of cheese, broke it in half and offered some to her dogs. I waited, hoping to hear more, but her silence continued.

"I met another of your friends today," I told her. "Valentina's mother."

Coco seemed surprised. "Poor Nanda, how is she? Last time I saw her she looked so tired."

"She's not great, I don't think. Valentina said you should visit soon."

Coco sighed but didn't reply.

"Was she at the parties with you and Pegeen?" I asked.

She shook her head. "Not those parties, no. Nanda was part of a different world."

"Her family were rich, though, weren't they?" I persisted. "She's a genuine contessa?"

"The title means very little these days, but she comes from a noble family. Not rich, though, not for a long time. What money there was belonged to her husband."

"What did he do?"

"He was a glassmaker."

"Oh yes, I seem to remember Valentina saying her family runs a glass museum on Murano. That's right, isn't it?"

Coco nodded. She was staring into space again. After a few moments she turned to me. "I hate going to see her. Everything about it makes me sad: the run-down palazzo, the hopeless state Nanda is in, the mess they've made of everything. That's why I've been staying away."

"Valentina thinks it's because you don't approve of her."

"She told you that?" Coco sounded dismayed. "I should go there, I know it, but there is never a day when I wake up and decide it's the thing I want to do."

"I offered to walk their dog," I told her. "I'm starting tomorrow morning. You could come with me and sit with the Contessa while I'm out . . . Well, if you can find something to sit on. Where is all their furniture anyway?"

"Sold, I expect, like everything else that was worth anything."

"Are they broke?"

"If not now, then soon they will be."

Coco closed her eyes, seeming deep in thought.

"Poor Valentina," I said. "No wonder she has to have all those jobs."

Opening her eyes again, Coco declared, "I will come. Not tomorrow, but soon, very soon. Just promise me we will do something very lovely to cheer me up afterwards. We will drink cocktails on the terrace of the Gritti Palace, yes? Wear beautiful clothes and watch the rich Americans. Perhaps then I'll remember the party and what I did with that gown."

Most people can't wait to tell you about themselves or gossip about their friends; they need no encouragement. Coco was frustratingly discreet. Snippets, that's all she had given me, entirely fascinating but not enough to stitch into a proper story.

I tried to think of ways to tease more information out of her. Perhaps if I plied her with cocktails on the terrace of the Gritti Palace and got her talking about those parties, maybe then she'd tell me about her glory days.

Addolorata's Happiness List

2. Afternoon naps (really good ones). Forgetting all the dreary things that need to be done, closing my eyes and letting drowsiness take me, even if it's only for twenty stolen minutes, then waking to a quiet house and a cup of tea. Bliss.

CHAPTER
TWELVE

The Sunday night *milonga* was held on the terrace of an old palazzo that had been turned into a guest house. Although we were among the first to arrive, Silvio had beaten us to it, and he greeted me like an old friend, pressing his cheeks to mine and showering me with compliments.

"Such a wonderful evening . . . and the food! A home-cooked meal is a rarity for me. I have been thinking about it all day long."

"Really, it was a pleasure," I murmured. "We must do it again soon."

He continued to enthuse about what we had eaten but I was distracted, wondering if Angelo were there half hidden by the loggia at the far end of the terrace. I had spent a lot of time thinking about our impromptu dance lesson, trying to make sense of the way it made me feel. There was so much closeness in the tango, so much power and tenderness too. It had been unsettling, exciting and new.

You have to understand, I hadn't had much experience. I was an innocent when I met Eden. Sure, there had been a few teenage fumbles, but he was the only man I'd ever actually been with. That never bothered me at all. I'd watched my girlfriends run through lovers without feeling envious or tempted to follow suit, because I belonged to him. Now Eden was threatening to change that, not me. I was angry and hurt, of course, but most of all lonely. Who would I be without him?

Tango had helped me forget, if only temporarily. Perhaps it was the having to concentrate so damn hard, but it seemed more than that. Something about the connection, the struggling to sense with the palms of my hands which way my partner wanted me to move, the being with another person so completely, the comfort of our contact. If he was really serious about teaching me, then I might take Angelo up on his offer no matter how discouraging Coco had been.

Casting round, I found several other familiar faces but not his. Coco's friend Marcello arrived; two couples I recalled from that first *milonga* in the *campo* began to dance together and others joined them. I stayed on the edges, watching and waiting.

It had been a long time since I'd felt a prickle of anticipation at the thought of seeing a man. When I first met Eden he was renovating my friend Rosie's new apartment and I turned up regularly for visits with the frailest of excuses. I was there to check the progress, celebrate each milestone with her, or simply keep her company.

Not that I fooled Rosie: she knew exactly why I was there. But Eden, in his work-scuffed denim dungarees, with his swinging dreadlocks and the tool belt round his waist — beautiful, sexy Eden — took ages to even notice me. Walls were finished, rotten window frames rebuilt, the place took shape and still he showed no sign of interest.

In the end I could see the renovation was nearly finished, and panicking, I asked him out for a drink. That's how it was from then on: I made the running and he was happy to let me. The feeling I'd always had, the anticipation, waiting for him in bars, standing in the foyers of theatres and cinemas, lingering at the entrance to tube stations and looking for his face in the crowds . . . I couldn't remember when I'd stopped being that way about him. But I knew there were times now when I paused at our front gate and dreaded going in. Times he called my phone and I didn't pick up.

If you listen to tango music then you'll discover it matches your mood. When you want to find it gloomy then you will, but it can as easily be soulful, passionate or uplifting. For me that evening the music wasn't beautiful at all. It nagged me, reminded me that time was passing; it set me on edge; it was relentless. I watched the dancing, waited for Angelo to come, and felt nothing but sadness.

It was almost dark by then and candles had been lit on the tables set up around the dance floor. I moved back into the shadows of the loggia and saw Coco step into Marcello's arms. Their tango was a playful one; he pivoted her and she laughed. They seemed so relaxed together.

I watched how Coco shaped her body to the music. To dance like that, almost carelessly, not having to think about every step; to have such balance and posture, such control and yet passion too — that seemed to me what tango was about. I longed to be able to do it myself.

Then I felt a light touch on my shoulder. "Dolly," Angelo said in a quiet voice.

"Hey." I turned round. "How long have you been here?"

"Not so long."

It was far too dark beneath the loggia to see the expression on his face.

"Are you OK?" I asked.

"Yes, but this evening I can't be bothered with this place. It's boring; every Sunday the same music, the same people. Let's go somewhere else."

"Now?"

"Yes, right now. Just you and me."

"OK, I'll say goodbye to Coco."

"No." He caught my hand in his. "Don't bother her. Just follow me. She won't care; she's busy dancing."

"But —"

"Follow."

He pulled me through the shadows, away from the dancers and the music, out of the palazzo. He moved fast, even along the crowded *calli*. He didn't turn back or speak; just held my hand and tugged me after him.

We were almost running now, weaving between the tourists, up and down bridges, past shops and churches and places selling pizza by the slice.

"Angelo, where are we going?" I asked but he didn't respond.

We hurried beneath another loggia and out into the wide span of the Piazza San Marco. It was full of people and noisy with café orchestras competing for their attention.

"Angelo, stop." I was breathless. "Where are you taking me?"

He turned and his expression seemed stern. "Dolly, you have to learn to follow me. We won't get anywhere together otherwise."

I stared at him uncertainly. At last he smiled. "We're going to Caffè Florian. My friend's band is playing tango music there and we are dancing."

"But, Angelo, I can't, not here in front of all these people; I'm a complete beginner."

"Then I will dance for you. *Vieni, vieni,* we don't want to miss them."

Between the tall pillars hung with swags of white curtains there was a stage where a band was playing. Only half of the tables surrounding it were occupied, but beyond them a crowd of people had gathered to listen to the music for free. To me the sound was instantly familiar: the soaring of strings and the call of the clarinet, the unique tones of the accordion-like instrument they call the bandoneon. I'd only been in Venice a week but already it was feeling like the soundtrack of my life there.

"Ready?" Angelo caught and held me.

"No," I protested.

"But you know what you have to do?"

"Follow," I said. "Just follow."

Angelo laughed. "See, there is hope for you."

He put his arms around me and pressed his cheek to mine, making me shift my weight from foot to foot until I relaxed against him. Then he instructed me to put one hand round his shoulder and press the other palm-to-palm to his. There at the edge of a semicircle of tables we began to step together. He didn't appear to care about the bystanders; he must have known they would fall back and out of our way. He walked, he pivoted me and I followed. On the stage someone was singing in Spanish but I could feel Angelo's attention focused entirely on me. It was intimidating and kind of amazing too.

That's when I forgot myself. I wasn't Addolorata any more, worn-out chef, mother of one, solver of problems, picker-up of dropped items. I wasn't a sister or someone's child or wife. I was in a piazza flooded with light. I was following Angelo, we were touching, and it felt so good.

Piazza San Marco might seem like the one place in Venice that is always busy, but I can tell you it's not so. As it grows later, the crowds thin and the cafés empty; the tourists go back to their hotels, footsore after a day of walking the *calli*; the street hawkers disappear too, the music stops, the chairs and tables are packed away. That doesn't stop you dancing, however, not if that's the mood you're in and your partner won't admit to tiring.

It wasn't a warm night but our bodies had heat in them. We made our own music, like Coco and Silvio once had, dancing past the bell tower and beside the

183

Doge's Palace right to the banks of the Grand Canal. We stepped together until my feet felt bruised and my shoulders ached. We danced when everyone else was sleeping and there wasn't a soul to see it. We continued until Angelo decided it was time to be still.

He took my face and held it in his hands. "Good," he said. "Much better. You have some talent for this, I think."

I lowered my eyelids and rested my forehead against his. "Thank you."

For a few minutes we stood together, breathing in rhythm, until Angelo released me and stepped away. "Tonight what I wanted was for you to get a feel for what tango can be. That's why I brought you here. So now do you want to learn properly?"

I hugged my arms around my body. There was no doubt in my mind. "Yes."

"It will be hard work, frustrating at times, and I may be tough on you," he warned. "You have to be sure."

"I'm sure," I promised him.

"OK, then tomorrow evening, come to my place." He gave me the address and touched his forehead in a mock salute. "Until then, *buona notte*."

Left standing alone in the dark, I was kind of shocked. I had thought Angelo would take me back to my apartment, but instead he turned and walked away, not expecting me to follow him this time.

Eventually I managed to find a water taxi to get me home. It cut through the dark water of the Grand Canal, through the lights of the palazzos reflected in it, past gondolas tethered and covered for the night bobbing in our wake.

I didn't feel like sleeping, tired though I was. Instead, back at the apartment I wrapped myself in rugs and sat out on the balcony, listening to the silence. I dozed on and off until I heard a gentle chorus of birdsong. Fetching a cup of coffee, I took it back out on to the balcony and wound the rugs round me again for warmth.

A fine rain was drizzling into the canal and the morning light was misty. If I hadn't made my rash promise to walk the Contessa's dog, I might have taken to bed with a book and avoided the day completely.

Instead I finished my coffee and went to do battle with the unpredictable temperature of the shower. I dressed in jeans and flat shoes, covered my hair with a cap, shrugged on my denim jacket and headed downstairs. There was no sign of life from Coco's apartment so I didn't bother knocking on her door to say good morning. I hoped she wouldn't be too upset with me for leaving the *milonga* the night before without saying goodbye.

I stopped along the way to fuel up on brioche and coffee, and by the time I reached the palazzo the drizzle had become proper rain. Running up the steps, I knocked on the door, and after a few minutes Valentina answered.

"I wasn't sure if you'd come," she said, staring out at the grim weather.

"Getting wet doesn't bother me too much so long as Boris doesn't mind."

She fetched a leash and an old towel to dry the dog with later, then gave me the key to let myself back in. "I'm working a shift at the Acqua Alta bookshop this morning. Come by and say hello if you're passing that way."

"I'm not sure where I'll go. Maybe not far this first morning."

The dog wagged his long tail and looked from Valentina to me as if he understood what we were saying.

"Any walk is a good one as far as Boris is concerned," she told me.

As we left, I looked back and thought I saw the Contessa staring down from an upstairs window, a dark shadow behind the leaded glass. It was difficult to imagine her being Coco's close friend. The two women seemed as different as it was possible to be.

Boris tugged me down the Strada Nuova, apparently certain where he was going. I let him take the lead for a while. Rain was soaking into my jacket and I envied the tourists their ugly plastic capes. Just as I was considering turning back, Boris changed direction, pulling me alongside a canal then down a passageway that led to a hidden park fringed by palazzos.

It was a surprisingly big space filled with tall trees and clipped hedges, wooden benches and a small children's playground. On a stretch of wet grass there were people throwing balls for dogs of all shapes and sizes. I unclipped Boris, hoping he would come back when I called, and he trotted over to join them. Several people seemed to know him. They said his name and stroked his big grey head; called out *buongiorno* to me. I suppose they must have been wondering what had happened to Valentina.

I stood beneath a tree while Boris found a broken branch and set up a game with a Labrador then ran round excitedly for a bit with a bunch of other dogs. Finally he came and sat at my feet, panting, so I guessed he'd had enough and was ready to go.

As we headed back to the palazzo, the grey flagstones of the Strada Nuova were slick with rain and the tourists were still wrapped in their plastic capes. The weather showed no sign of improving and even Boris's tail was drooping low between his legs. Tomorrow if it was dry we might go further, but this was turning out to be a day to take cover.

The Contessa was there, standing by the window waiting for us. She moved away as I was hurrying along the path to her front door. Unlocking it, I called out a polite *buongiorno*, but there was no response. Then, while I was rubbing down the dripping dog with the towel Valentina had left, I heard a voice coming from somewhere upstairs.

"Signora, you are terribly wet. Come up and bring my Boris."

I might have preferred to go home and change out of my soggy denim but I didn't want the Contessa to think me impolite, so instead I climbed the stairs and walked through the empty rooms and hallways till I found her.

Again she was dressed from head to toe in black, but today she was also wearing a pendant, a long silver chain with a stunning chunk of hand-blown coloured glass hanging from it.

"This rain, this awful rain," she complained. "Take off your jacket, come and get warm."

The draughty old palazzo seemed to offer little chance of warmth but still I smiled and thanked her.

"I would offer you some tea but I don't know where all the staff have gone," she said querulously.

I looked into the Contessa's muddy grey eyes and thought she looked anxious.

"I can make tea," I told her. "I know where the kitchen is."

"How kind," she murmured. "We will drink it up in my little salon. It's cosier there, I think."

I watched as she climbed another flight of stairs, Boris at her heels, then headed to the kitchen, where I rummaged through cupboards packed with antiquated cookware until I managed to assemble a teapot, cups and a tray to carry them on. In the absence of a kettle I boiled water in a pan, found tea in a cupboard above the sink and fresh milk in the fridge. I even managed to track down a packet of biscotti.

I took the whole lot upstairs, peering into each vast room until I found a smaller one filled with high-backed chairs and gently lit by standard lamps.

"Contessa?"

"Yes, over here. Put the tea things down on the table. That's right. And will you pour?"

She drank the tea thirstily, and when I offered her the plate of biscotti, she scooped up several. "No one brought me breakfast this morning." She sounded resigned. "I'm expected to get my own, you know."

The first time I had met the Contessa I'd thought she might almost have passed for Valentina's grandmother, but now I saw it was the clothes she wore and the way she moved that aged her. Her body was trunk-like, her ankles swollen and her hair steely, yet her skin looked soft and her face unlined. She was younger than Coco certainly.

"Would you like more tea?" I asked, and she held out her cup eagerly.

"You make it well. But then you are English, aren't you? My daughter told me that. She said you know Coco."

"I'm living at her place," I told her.

The Contessa nodded. "Yes, so I hear. Does she still keep a pretty garden? And all the art on the walls, is it there still? It is so long since I've been to visit, years and years."

"Coco is planning to come here and see you. One morning very soon, I think."

"She promises but she never comes." The Contessa sounded matter-of-fact. "We argued the last time I saw her, perhaps that's why."

"She didn't mention that . . ."

"Coco thinks she knows best about everything. She gets impatient, then we fight." Her grey eyes widened and stared into mine. "It's not fair at all. I never judged her like others did. Why must she judge me now?"

"I don't know," I said, hoping for more.

The Contessa stared into her empty teacup. "I'm still very hungry," she grumbled. "Will you go down and ask how long I must wait for lunch? This isn't satisfactory, tell them that."

"OK." Gently I took the cup from her hand and put it back on the tray. "I'll see what I can do."

There were bits and pieces of food in the house. I discovered eggs, pancetta and a heel of Parmesan cheese in the fridge, pasta and olive oil in the cupboard, enough for a plate of *spaghetti alla carbonara*. Dusting off a couple of pans, I set to work.

Clearly this was a kitchen where once big feasts had been prepared. There were stashes of wine glasses, multiple platters and dishes, massive stock pans and deep-sided oven trays. It must have been bustling in the days when they'd had staff, but it felt lonely now, cooking there in silence.

Still, the Contessa was grateful for the meal. She bent her head over her bowl and sucked up the spaghetti hungrily. "This is very good, perfectly al dente, and the pancetta is crispy. Is there a new cook?"

"Yes, I think so."

"No one mentioned it to me," she complained.

"You were telling me about Coco," I reminded her.

"Really, what was I saying?"

"How people judged her."

"Ah yes, that was a bad time, poor Coco. Still, what else could she expect?"

"What did she do?"

The Contessa twirled spaghetti round her fork and sighed.

190

"Poor Coco," she repeated.

She fell silent as she finished her pasta. Once the plate was nearly empty, she held it out to Boris, who licked up the last traces of food then laid his head in her lap to be patted. She smiled down at him fondly. I think she might have forgotten I was there, because when she looked up, she appeared startled to see me sitting in the armchair opposite.

"Ah, it's you," she said, recovering. "Before you leave, please tell the cook how much I enjoyed my lunch. Tell her . . . tell her . . . It is a woman, yes?"

I nodded.

"Tell her I would like to discuss menus for the week. That is how I like to do things here."

"Right," I said, not sure quite how to handle that.

"And I will see you tomorrow for Boris's walk? Good, good. Thank God my daughter has found some help. It has been so difficult lately."

The rain was a softer drizzle as I left the palazzo and there was another great flood of plastic-wrapped tourists pouring down the Strada Nuova. My jeans were still damp and I needed to go home and change. As I walked, I saw dogs everywhere. Lots of small fluffy ones, a few long-legged and loping, pedigrees and mongrels; strolling along the *calli*, sitting proudly on the sterns of boats, trotting over bridges or staring down from the balconies of terraced gardens. I hadn't really noticed them before; now, thanks to Boris, my eyes had been opened. It made me smile to see them:

191

citizens of Venice as much as any of the people who lived here, running free without fear of speeding cars.

As a child I pestered for a dog every Christmas but my parents said no and stood firm. We lived in London, in a house tightly packed into a Clerkenwell terrace, its small garden entirely given over to Papa's vegetable-growing. There was no space for a dog, no time to exercise it, no tolerance for the mess it might make. My mother offered me smaller pets: a gerbil, a tank of goldfish, eventually even a cat, but I was stubborn. If I couldn't have a dog then I didn't want anything.

When I left home and moved in with Eden I could have got my own dog. But London isn't a place where they're welcome to sleep in shop doorways or curl up under café tables. And I got busy and forgot about the idea. It stayed in my childhood, along with pink princess dresses and felt-tip pens, lemon sherbet bonbons and Disney cartoons. I might have got a little one for Katia but she never asked. She was happy with her terrapins and mice. It had been no one's dream but mine, and I had let it go.

Now I passed long-haired Jack Russells with tufty mutton chops, smartly clipped toy poodles, white dogs with black spots, smaller ones with pushed-in faces. And each time I felt a little burst of love, a lifting of spirits that was almost physical, a big soppy *aaah* moment.

Addolorata's Happiness List

3. Dogs — ideally big ones like Boris: Great Danes,

192

New-foundlands. But little ones with cheeky faces, spaniels that look like slippers, even those teensy things you can carry in your handbag . . . they all make me happy. So long as they don't yap . . . I can't be doing with yapping.

CHAPTER
THIRTEEN

Coco was shitty with me. I should have realised she might be when I disappeared from the *milonga* with Angelo the night before without saying goodbye. Now she was making me suffer.

At first she ignored my knocking on her apartment door. When I persisted, nipping downstairs every fifteen minutes or so to try again, she relented enough to let me in but went on to punish me with stilted conversation. Every question I asked received barely more than a monosyllable in response. How was she today? Fine. Did she have fun last night? Yes. What was she doing today? Nothing. It was like dealing with my daughter at her sulkiest.

When Katia is behaving that way it's pointless trying to jolly her out of it. Finding a distraction is the only thing that works. Coco was an old woman but I suspected she might be the same. I gazed at her, wondering what would make her forget her bad mood.

She was dressed stylishly again today, in a different robe, this one deep blue and shot with silver. On her feet were faded embroidered silk slippers I'd never seen before. Who knew how many more pairs of shoes and

194

extraordinary outfits she had tucked away in that small apartment?

"Coco," I said, suddenly inspired. "Will you show me your wardrobe?"

"What?"

"Your clothes, I'd like to look at them all. I always love seeing what you've chosen to put on each day. And it would be a fun way to spend a wet afternoon."

"Well I don't know . . ." She glanced at the window. Outside the light was soft and grey; the panes of glass raindrop-spattered. "I suppose it could be interesting for you. All my clothes have a story, you see. Some I've owned for a very long time."

"Do you still fit into everything?"

"Yes, of course, I've looked after my figure."

"So you can still wear every single thing?" I was envious.

"Every one." She preened a little. "Actually I'm much slimmer now than I was when I was a young woman."

"I wish I could say the same."

"You're a cook; it's more difficult for you," she said generously. "For me, clothes are more important than food. The way I dress sets me up for the day. My mood is affected by the length of my hem or the colours and styles I'm wearing; they change everything."

"Really? How?"

"Well, in trousers I feel efficient, for instance. In a pink dress I'm feminine, in a silky fabric glamorous, in bright colours I'm happy. When I'm wearing the right clothes I feel I have no age. I can still make heads turn. At least I think so."

So it had worked then. Coco's bad mood was forgotten. I couldn't stop myself smiling.

"You think that's amusing?" she asked

"No, I think it's wonderful," I admitted. "I hadn't realised an outfit could be that powerful."

"It has to be the right outfit. Come, I'll show you."

Coco's wardrobe filled an entire room. Against one wall was a single bed, which I assumed was where she slept, but it was jammed beside racks of gowns, shelves stacked with hats, handbags and scarves, rows of shoes, boxes of jewellery.

"You're just like my sister Pieta," I exclaimed. "She used to have a whole room full of clothes too. But none of her stuff was like this."

"This is not stuff; it's treasure," Coco corrected me. "I've been collecting it for years. If I love something, I never throw it away. That's why I can't understand what happened to the dress I'm wearing in that photograph with Pegeen. It must be around somewhere."

She began rifling through a rack of gowns, most of them musty and dusty, clearly not worn for years. The younger Coco must have loved shiny things: sequins and sparkles. Plus there were feathered frocks and velvet capes, chic black dresses, ruffles and ruching, silks in gaudy colours.

"What about this?" I pointed to an evening jacket covered in copper sequins. "Does it have a story?"

"Oh yes. This was a gift from a man I was very fond of. He used to take me for drinks at Harry's Bar and to the opera at La Fenice." Coco touched the jacket and smiled. "One evening he proposed marriage to me while I was dressed in it. I turned him down, of course."

Reaching to the very back of the rack, she pulled out a white dress with an embroidered shawl collar. "Now this one is from Pegeen's time. Pretty, isn't it? I used to cinch in the waist with a narrow belt. That was the look then."

"Where did you wear it? To parties?"

"No, this was for lunch at a hotel or a summer picnic in the gardens at Sant'Elena. If a young man wanted to take me for a gondola ride I might wear it. Once Pegeen invited me to afternoon tea in the garden of her mother's house and it was perfect for that."

Coco held up the dress against me. "You would look pretty in this."

"If it fitted me."

"I'm sure it would. I was curvier myself back then, as I told you. You should borrow it."

I was reluctant. "What if I spill something and it gets stained?"

"This dress has survived for a long time. Take it; give it a new life. Be beautiful in it and stop worrying."

"OK, I'll try it on," I agreed.

"No need. I promise it will fit perfectly. In fact there must be other pieces from then that I could lend you."

She browsed around, pulling out full-skirted halter dresses and little suits with peplum jackets. "No, not right at all," she muttered. "But this might do, or this."

"You were telling me stories, not finding me clothes," I reminded her.

"I can do both." Coco moved to another rack, skimming through the garments and settling on an exquisite dress, pale peach and softly draped in lace. "Now this I wore to Nanda's wedding."

"It's lovely."

"That was after Pegeen's time. The wedding was beautiful and Nanda was very happy. Lorenzo Viadro had the money to give her the life she wanted. With him she could be a proper contessa." Coco moved along the shelves, reaching up for a hat with a wide brim. "This is what I wore with the dress. There's a photograph of me standing with the newly-weds on the steps of the church. Wait there and I'll fetch it."

She disappeared for a moment, returning with a leather-bound album, one of the old-fashioned ones with crisp leaves of paper to protect each page of photographs.

"Here we are." Coco flicked through to the right shot. "Me, Lorenzo and Nanda. Don't we look pleased with ourselves?"

I looked at the photograph. Aside from those familiar grey eyes, I would never have recognised the bride with the cherubic face as the Contessa. She was holding a bouquet of white flowers low against her belly, her white lace veil was billowing in the breeze and her smile had given her dimples. Beside her was her groom, a slightly older man with the dark eyes and the fine, straight nose his daughter Valentina had inherited.

198

Of the three, the one that drew most of my attention was Coco. In this wedding day photograph she wasn't so very young any more and her beauty seemed more delicate. The brim of her hat was drooping over one brow; her hair was cut to her shoulders, her eyes were blackened with kohl. She was standing on Lorenzo's other side, her body half turned towards him, and smiling.

"You do look quite pleased with yourself," I agreed.

"I had played matchmaker, introduced them to one another, made sure they had opportunities to meet again. They married thanks to me." Coco smoothed down the leaf of slippery paper and folded the album shut.

"Did they only have the one child?"

"No, there were two sons as well."

"And Lorenzo died?"

"Lorenzo . . . yes, he's gone now." Coco opened up the album again and studied the picture. "Of course, he was my lover before he ever met her. It was he who proposed to me the evening I was wearing the sequinned jacket. Lorenzo was looking for a wife. And there was my friend Nanda who wanted nothing more than a wealthy husband. So I put them together. They seemed the perfect match."

"You gave him to her?" I was taken aback.

"Yes, I suppose I did."

"But why didn't you want to marry him?"

She closed the album again, with much less care this time. "I was already married."

After that Coco seemed flustered, as if she'd said more than she meant to. Gathering together the outfits she thought might suit me, she insisted I try them all on straight away.

"Take them upstairs and keep the ones you'd like to wear over the summer. It can be terribly hot here in Venice. You'll be needing some lighter, cooler clothes."

I tried to say thank you as Coco, with her armful of outfits, almost pushed me from the room and down the hallway.

"Wait a minute, I need to get Angelo's address from you," I said. "He told me last night but I've forgotten it already, of course."

She narrowed her eyes. "Why do you need his address?"

"He's promised to give me more tango lessons. I want to learn to dance, not just stumble along."

"It takes a long time to learn properly," Coco warned.

"I know that. Angelo told me. He's going to teach me in the evenings and on his days off."

"I see."

"You don't approve?"

Coco sighed. "I think you should be careful who you choose to be your partner. Tango is a dance that opens you up; it forces you to share yourself. Are you sure you want that with Angelo?"

"It's only a few lessons," I insisted.

"There are other people who could teach you if you want to learn that much."

"Yes, but Angelo is the one who has offered. And I think it will be fun."

With a resigned shrug of her shoulders, Coco passed over the jumble of clothes still on their hangers. "He lives in Santa Croce, not far from Campo San Giacomo dell'Orio. Wait one moment and I'll write down his address for you."

Shaped to the waist and flaring out over the hips, the clothes Coco had lent me might have been designed with my body in mind. Most fitted, just as she'd promised. An old-fashioned powdery fragrance clung to some of the fabrics, and trying them on, I could almost imagine the idyllic picnics and tea parties, the afternoon gondola rides and all of Coco's many suitors clustering round. Which one had she married? And what had happened to him? Her reticence only made me more curious.

Wearing Coco's vintage outfits felt a little like impersonating her. They were in styles and shades I'd never have chosen myself, and from what I could tell from my reflection in the small square of bathroom mirror, I didn't look like me in them at all. Still, it was fun, like being a child again and playing dress-up in my mother's things. The final outfit I tried was a turquoise dress with a gauzy skirt. I thought it suited me well enough so decided to leave it on even if it was a little fancy for a dance lesson.

Before leaving, I rang home to check up on Eden and Katia. There was no reply, so I tried Eden's mobile but he didn't answer that either. Pieta was next on my list, and I called her at work because wedding season was coming up and chances were she'd be there still, finishing bridal gowns.

"Hi, Dolly." It was a good line and my sister's voice sounded clear and close. "Do you want me to call you back? Your phone bill is going to be horrendous."

"No, it's fine. I know you have lots on so I won't keep you long. I just wanted to see how everyone is doing."

"They're all great," she promised.

"Are you sure? You're the only one I can rely on to tell me the truth right now."

"Hmm, OK then, the truth is, Papa is working too hard at the restaurant and Mum's tetchy about it."

"He doesn't need to be there all the time." I was irritated. "They can manage without him."

"Yes, I know, but try telling him that. He won't listen to any of us. Anyway, Mum's not too lonely. Katia has been spending lots of time with her. They've been going on outings together."

"That's nice," I said, a little flatly. It's not that I wasn't pleased to hear that my daughter was happy with her grandmother, but it made me feel guilty for not being there . . . and envious too, if I'm entirely honest. It ought to have been me taking Katia on those outings and enjoying having time with her. But even if I had been at home, I'd have thought myself too busy. And that made me feel even guiltier.

"Yeah, I think they're both really enjoying it," Pieta said.

"And what about you? How's it going over there?"

"Good," I told her.

"That's it, good? You're not going to give me anything more?"

I didn't tell her about my night dancing in Piazza San Marco, about the Contessa issuing orders to imaginary staff in her bare palazzo, about the opera-singing tour guide Valentina. These things were part of Venice. They weren't exactly secrets, but I wasn't ready to share them.

"Oh, there's one thing that's new," I said, knowing that Pieta would be interested. "The old lady downstairs has lent me all these amazing vintage clothes to wear; stuff she's had since the 1950s. Some of it's like nothing I've ever seen before."

"Really? What sort of thing?" she asked keenly. Pieta is mad about clothes. They've always been her great passion, just like food has been mine.

I described the embroidered shawl-collar dress and went on to tell her about the gowns hanging from Coco's racks downstairs, my sister letting out little moans as I spoke.

"Oh God, it sounds amazing. I wish I was there. Take photographs of everything. Email them to me," she begged.

"As soon as she lets me back in there, I will."

"I'm so jealous. Perhaps I could come over for a couple of nights." Pieta sounded tempted. "Surely I can get away."

To my surprise, I realised this wasn't what I wanted at all. Much as I love my sister, Venice was starting to feel like it was mine, and I couldn't envisage her here, having the experience with me.

"Who am I kidding, work is insane," she decided. "Sorry, Dolly, but I really can't do it."

Immediately I felt relieved, even though I shouldn't have been. "That's fine, I understand."

"Hey, I'd better go," Pieta told me. "I've got a client coming in now. But we'll talk soon, right? I'll call you in a day or so."

Armed with my map and the scrap of paper with Angelo's address scrawled on it, I took a *vaporetto* across to San Stae and wandered towards the wide *campo* where only a week earlier I'd seen tango being danced for the very first time.

You might think I was playing a dangerous game; that I ought to have listened to Coco's warning. But it's not as if I was some young girl, giddy at the first sign of a little male attention. I knew how to handle myself, and in my mind I was very clear what I wanted from Angelo. A little flirtation to distract me from that hum of worry and guilt that always seemed to be with me. A few dance lessons, some pleasant evenings; just some fun, for God's sake.

On one corner of the *campo* there was a nice-looking bar, so I stopped for a glass of Prosecco and a few *cicchetti* to keep me going. The rain had finally finished, and I sat outside with a view of the old basilica. This place had a neighbourhood feel to it. Old men gathered on the benches beneath the trees to smoke a few cigarettes, passers-by greeted each other with a friendly nod or *buona sera*. If Angelo wasn't home, if he had forgotten his promise to teach me, this would be a good spot to return to, drink more Prosecco and while away the evening.

Angelo's apartment was in an old warehouse building a ten-minute walk from the *campo*. When he answered the door, he was still damp from the shower, a towel wrapped round his waist, chest bare. "It's my day off," he said, slightly shamefaced. "I like to spend most of it sleeping."

"Me too if I get the chance," I told him, trying not to check out his body too obviously.

He poured me a glass of white wine then went to get dressed, leaving me to look around. The high ceilings were beamed and the windows tiny. The main room was a large one, with a mirror along one wall and an old leather sofa against the other. The stretch of empty floor between them was perfect for dancing. It was difficult to tell much about Angelo from the way he'd furnished his home. Things were pretty minimal. Next to the sofa was a stack of tattered old paperbacks, all novels by Italian writers I hadn't heard of. On one wall were three rows of framed black-and-white photographs that showed him dancing. In some he was dressed in a suit, his curls flowing free; in others he was more casual, in dark jeans and a loose shirt. Among his dance partners was Valentina, and she appeared more often than the others. The pair seemed to be performing for an audience and their expressions were serious.

"Ah, those old photographs," Angelo said, coming back into the room. "I keep meaning to take them down and put up some art instead."

"Why? They're very cool."

He screwed up his face. "They are images from the past. I don't know if I should keep them where I see them every day. Better to live for now, I think."

"Weren't they good times?"

"Yes, but they are over." His tone was unsentimental.

"You still dance," I pointed out.

"Only socially now; not to perform." He came and stood beside me. "We were very good, Valentina and I. My dream was for us to go to Buenos Aires and compete at the world championships. There's no doubt we could have done it."

"So why didn't you?"

"Valentina wouldn't come. In the end her family were more important to her."

"She's very talented, isn't she?" It was hard not to feel envious. "Her dancing, her lovely voice."

"But what does she do with all that talent?"

"She works really hard. She seems to have three jobs," I said.

"Four," he told me. "I hear she's started as a gondola singer now. Valentina is always working, and that was part of our problem."

"Is she so desperate for the money?"

"She needs it to prop up her family," he explained.

"You mean her mother and the palazzo?"

"No, it's her brother Giacomo that she's helping. From what I understand, there was some problem with

206

the glass museum on Murano, and Giacomo ran up debts that Valentina is helping to pay. They'd have been better selling the place, breaking free of it, but they wouldn't hear of that."

"Why not?" I wondered.

"Because it's part of the family history and Valentina believes that she and Giacomo are guardians who must preserve it for the next generation ... even if that means no chance of seeing Buenos Aires, and a career singing for tourists instead of on a stage at the Arena di Verona."

"You really think she's that good?"

Angelo shrugged. "Possibly she is, but I expect no one will ever know now."

"And so you never went to Buenos Aires and you became a chef instead of a dancer?"

He didn't respond. "I should take them down," he repeated, staring at the photographs. "Not right now, though, because this evening I'm going to give you a proper tango lesson. We will go right back to the basics."

I had thought the lesson might last for an hour or so and then we would repair to the Prosecco bar for drinks and *cicchetti*. But Angelo had really meant it when he'd said he would be tough on me. I was there learning to walk with him, trapped in the space between the sofa and the mirrored wall, until well past midnight, and there were moments I wanted to cry in frustration it was so difficult.

"No, no, do it again," Angelo insisted over and over. "Forget that you are dancing and just walk normally.

We have to get this right before we can progress any further."

"It seemed so much easier when we were in Piazza San Marco," I protested.

"That's because you emptied your head and let me take care of everything," he told me. "Good things can happen when you do that. But technique is still important."

"It's too difficult," I insisted. "I'll never be any good."

"Your posture is fine and you're beginning to feel the music," he encouraged me. "This is a good start. And we mustn't expect too much too quickly. I can teach you many things; still it would take years of study for you to become the partner who would give me what I want from the tango."

I stepped away from Angelo's embrace. "I only have the summer."

Addolorata's Happiness List

4. A glass of chilled Prosecco. Preferably drunk outdoors, at a table with a view. Just one glass . . . at most maybe two . . . taken in the early evening before the sun goes down, with a little dish of olives or some salty pistachios. A civilised, quiet drink at the end of a day of work, maybe with a friend but even on my own.

CHAPTER
FOURTEEN

The days fell into a lovely routine. They began with breakfast at the small café round the corner, where very soon the owner knew my name, as well as how I liked my coffee and the brioche I preferred. If Coco joined me, then we settled at a table outside, her three small dogs attached to our chairs by their leashes, and he served the cappuccino on a silver tray with a lace cloth laid on it.

Once breakfast was finished, most mornings I walked to the palazzo. Usually Valentina had left already, so I let myself in with the key she'd given me and made tea to serve to the Contessa in her little salon. Then it was time to explore Venice with Boris at my heels. On fine days we walked for miles, and I began to piece together the *calli* and canals until I could go without my map and not get lost too often.

On the way back to the palazzo I'd do some shopping at the supermarket or the stalls at the Rialto, then cook lunch for the Contessa. I tried to make Venetian food: sardines stuffed with parsley and Parmesan then fried until their breadcrumb crust turned gold; squid simmered in its own black ink and lots of white wine; salt cod baked in milk.

Afternoons were for resting. I'd take a book down to Coco's garden or sit out on my balcony unless it was raining. In the early evenings it became part of my routine to make a couple of phone calls home. I talked to my daughter most days and Pieta whenever she had time, but Eden and I were avoiding each other. If he did answer the phone he was quick to pass it over to Katia.

Later, if a lesson had been arranged, I'd walk to Angelo's place, usually stopping at the bar on the corner for a couple of glasses of Prosecco. They got to know me there too. It was surprising how quickly they separated me from the temporary people.

The days passed and the weather warmed; spring met high summer. Occasionally I added to my happiness list, but there were whole stretches of time when I was too absorbed in this new life to focus on it.

Once, after a session with Angelo where I felt as if I was starting to make real progress, I wrote down the word "tango". But the next lesson was discouraging — I seemed to get worse again rather than improve — and as soon as I got home I crossed it out again.

Often I thought about giving up. The trouble was, as soon as it seemed I had mastered one element, Angelo would introduce some new sequence and the struggle began again. The rock step, the salida, the ocho, the little embellishments that make the dance special . . . There were evenings when both of us grew impatient: me because I couldn't understand what he was trying to tell me; him as he thought I wasn't trying. Other times the mood was lighter and we laughed at my mistakes.

No lesson ever lasted as long as that first one had. Most evenings after a couple of hours we would go to the bar on the corner or put a simple supper together in his tiny kitchen. Angelo might bring home a few ingredients from his *osteria*: thin slivers of smoked tuna, creamed horseradish, a head of red chicory, a brace of tiny fish or soft-shelled crabs. Since he had been cooking all day he was happy to let me take care of things. He may have guessed by then that I was a chef; but I hadn't told him and he'd never asked.

There were all sorts of things we didn't talk about. My London existence, my husband and child, what I'd done with my life until now. Angelo wasn't a man to ask lots of questions; in fact he seemed happier with silence. That didn't bother me. As we ate together, I'd think about my lesson and try to fix its key points in my mind so we wouldn't have to go back over them the next time.

I offered to pay for his teaching but he laughed and wouldn't hear of it.

"I'm not doing it for financial reward," he said.

"Why then?"

"For my own satisfaction; for the challenge, I guess, to prove Coco wrong." He dug through his risotto with his fork, pulling out the thin strands of wild asparagus to taste first.

I have to admit, the way Angelo ate irritated me. He was so intense about food. He had this habit of dissecting a dish and chewing slowly, considering every mouthful and almost always leaving something on the plate. I preferred to watch the Contessa, who was lusty for every meal I cooked, abandoning herself to it, not caring if she flicked broth on her blouse with the tail of her spaghetti, not above wiping a finger round the bottom of her bowl to catch the last of a particularly delicious sauce.

"There's a tango festival on in Venice this year, just after the Festa del Redentore," Angelo told me, setting his unfinished meal aside.

"Are you planning to get tickets?" I asked.

"No, they've asked me to perform and I'm considering the idea. But it's a matter of choosing a partner. Valentina has turned me down, of course. I have been thinking about asking you."

"You've gone mad, then. I won't be ready to perform in public"

"I don't expect you to dance like a professional, but I want to prove to Coco and all the others that you don't need to study for so long a time to find the joy in tango."

"I'm not taking part in a show," I insisted. "And anyway, I thought you'd given up performance."

"That's not true."

"It's what you told me."

"You misunderstood, then. I said one thing and you heard another, like you do in our lessons. If we're going to perform together, you'll have to try harder."

"We're not going to perform together."

Angelo shrugged. "You'll change your mind."

Coco was being difficult. She had promised to visit the Contessa, but every time I suggested a time for her to come, she found an excuse. She was tired, had clothes that needed laundering or had promised Silvio she'd meet him for an *ombra* at some bar or other. It was starting to seem like it would never happen; which wouldn't have mattered except the Contessa kept mentioning it.

"How is Coco? If you see her, tell her how much I'm missing my old friend," she said nearly every time I saw her.

They had parted on an argument. Neither was young any more and I kept thinking how sad it would be if one were to die without them meeting again. The thought dogged me so much, I had another go at talking Coco round.

"Weren't we planning to drink posh cocktails on the terrace of the Gritti Palace?" I reminded her one morning over breakfast.

"You're right, we were." She tilted her head and smiled. "Let's go today."

"What would we wear?"

Coco considered the question. "For afternoon cocktails at the Gritti we want to look expensive but not like we're trying too hard. So perhaps a pretty tea dress and a single piece of jewellery."

"I think it's hot enough now for me to wear that white frock with the embroidered shawl collar that you lent me."

"Yes, that would be perfect," she agreed.

"We'd better go and get ready, then."

"But, darling, it's still much too early. Even I wouldn't be seen drinking cocktails at this hour."

"But we have to visit the Contessa first. The Gritti Palace was going to be your treat for afterwards. Don't you remember? It was your idea in the first place."

"It was?" For a moment Coco looked sulky. "I suppose you think you've tricked me now?"

"I wouldn't dare," I promised her, laughing.

"Nanda isn't coming to the Gritti with us for cocktails?"

"No, of course not, just you and me."

"And you won't make me stay in that dreary palazzo the whole day?"

"We'll have lunch there and then we'll leave."

Coco sighed rather heavily. "*Va bene*, you win, but just this one time and then I won't hear talk of me going again."

She fluffed about for ages trying on different outfits, finally settling on a tea dress in a vibrant shade of blueberry, teamed with a bright pink turban with a large brooch she claimed was real diamonds fixed to the front.

I wore the white frock and Coco produced pashminas in vivid orange and pink, just in case the breeze got up while we were sitting out on the terrace.

On our way to the palazzo she talked of nothing but cocktails, weighing up their relative merits.

"There are times when you need a proper drink and then a Bellini really won't do," she told me. "That's when you want a Negroni, or perhaps a Cardinale with a good slug of gin. Those are meant to be sipped as an *aperitivo* before dinner, but at my age I can break the rules."

"If I make a good lunch for you and the Contessa, there'll be something in your stomach to soak up the gin."

"I do wish you'd stop calling her that." Coco sounded impatient. "Her name is Nanda."

"But she asked me to," I protested. Then a thought struck me. "Coco, how long is it since you've seen her?"

"A year, maybe two." She sounded doubtful. "Surely not any longer than that, although time passes so fast, who can be sure."

"You may find she's changed," I warned her.

"In what way?"

"She's confused. Often she seems to believe she still has staff, for instance. And there is this act she puts on where she gets very grand."

Coco made a tutting noise and shook her head. Almost certainly her eyes were rolling behind the dark lenses of her oversized sunglasses.

"Don't be too hard on her," I said. "I really don't think she can help it."

Boris was waiting by the door and went into his usual bouncing and leaping routine when we arrived. Anxiously Coco scooped up all three of her small dogs and clutched them against her thin chest.

"No, you big brute, get down," she said, backing away. "This isn't going to work. He'll hurt my babies. I have to go."

"He's fine, just excited," I told her. "Stay there a minute while I put him in the kitchen."

Boris was devastated. His tail was rammed firmly between his legs and he looked like he'd been beaten as I closed the kitchen door on him. "Give me a minute," I told him. "Let me sort the old women, then I'll come and take you out."

I had been concerned that Coco might take the chance to flee, but she was still there when I returned, hovering on the doorstep, holding her fluffy dogs tightly.

"Why in the world would Nanda want to keep an animal that size?" she asked querulously. "Has she completely lost her mind?"

"I don't know. Perhaps he makes her feel safe. And actually he's a lovely boy."

"If you say so." She edged forward. "Are you sure you shut him away properly? He can't escape?"

As we walked through the palazzo, Coco was clearly shocked at the state she found things in: the crumbling walls, the empty rooms, the cobwebs and the grimy layers of dust.

"It's as if no one lives here," she whispered.

"Was it not this bad last time you visited?"

"No." Her voice was still hushed. "Maybe there was still a housekeeper back then. I remember all the art had gone, but this room had a dining table in it, and

216

chairs. And there were flowers; Nanda always loved flowers. I should have thought to bring some."

"She seems to spend all her time in a little salon upstairs. That's where the furniture is."

Coco nodded. "Lorenzo's old room, I expect. Years ago it used to be his study. Poor Nanda."

"What did her husband die of?" I asked.

She lowered her voice to its softest whisper. "He killed himself."

"Oh." I was shocked. "Poor Nanda. And poor Valentina."

The meeting between the two women was very touching. As they hugged, there were tears in Nanda's eyes. Neither seemed able to speak for a while.

"My old friend, my old friend," Nanda repeated. "You came at last."

"Of course I came." There was a wobble in Coco's voice.

"I thought you'd forgotten me."

"Never. I couldn't do that."

"My dear old friend," Nanda said again, sadly.

Coco took her arm and led her to a chair. "Now, darling, we're going to sit down and Addolorata will make us coffee, then we can talk and tell each other everything like we always used to."

"Tea," Nanda corrected her. "She always makes me tea. She is English, you see, although she cooks Italian food very well indeed."

I gave the Contessa a sharp look. Up till now I'd played along with the pretence that there were staff in the kitchen. How long had she been aware that I was the one cooking for her?

"Tea will be fine," said Coco. "And she's promised us lunch later, which will be lovely too. So we have all morning together."

"You'll come back, won't you?" Nanda sounded anxious.

"I'm not leaving yet, darling. I've only just arrived," Coco told her.

"Yes, I know." Now she seemed frustrated. "But you won't go later and then not come back like last time? I couldn't bear it again."

Coco looked stricken. "My dear friend, I'm so sorry. I didn't mean for it to be so long."

"Lorenzo used to say that you were fickle," Nanda told her. "That you moved on from people, forgot about them too easily. Still, I never thought you'd do it to me."

That silenced Coco completely. She looked from Nanda to me. The atmosphere seemed strained and the room too small for three of us.

"Right," I said briskly. "I'll go and get the tea and take Boris out, shall I?"

"Lovely, darling," Coco murmured, and the Contessa nodded her thanks.

I took my time getting the tea things together, and when I got back, the women were talking, although they stopped the moment I entered the room.

"I'll leave you to pour," I told Coco. "Boris is beside himself for his walk."

"How long will you be?"

"I'm just taking him for a quick stroll," I promised, "then I'll pick up some things for lunch on the way home."

We went to Boris's favourite spot: the park he'd dragged me to on our first outing. It was a place we'd returned to fairly often since, and the other regulars were friendly now, engaging me in conversation. I knew the names of their dogs, how old they were, what they liked to eat, all sorts of little inconsequential things. Sometimes I bumped into these people while I was elsewhere, perhaps out shopping or waiting for a *vaporetto*, and we'd nod at each other and say, "*Salve*." I liked having these casual acquaintances; they threaded me into Venice a little more firmly. It was why I stopped for drinks at the same *bacaro*, frequented a handful of cafés and restaurants. A smile, a greeting, a short snatch of conversation seasoned my day. They made me feel connected.

That morning there were plenty of dogs for Boris to play with, so I stayed for longer than I'd intended, chatting to their owners. As I stood and watched, I wondered if Katia would enjoy coming with me to walk him. I was still hoping she would come over for the school holidays and getting excited at the prospect. I'd even started making a list of all the things we'd do together — the *gelato* shops we'd visit, the boat rides we'd take, the tours she might like, the places where I'd treat her to a grown-up lunch, the pretty things we'd buy. With me feeling so much more relaxed, and plenty of empty days to lavish on her, I was certain we were going to have a great time.

Boris was sniffing round the hedges for tennis balls now. I clipped him back on the leash and turned to go. We still had to walk right back along the Strada Nuova to a shop I'd spotted that sold fresh pasta, because I wanted to make *bigoli in salsa*, the traditional Venetian dish I'd eaten several times in restaurants. It's so simple: just coarse whole-wheat spaghetti tossed in a slick of slowly fried onions, anchovies and a little white wine vinegar. It's a dish that sits heavy on the stomach but has a nutty, savoury quality that keeps you eating anyway. The salty anchovies dissolve into the sweet onion sauce, the *bigoli* are thick and chewy, the chef uses a heavy hand with the olive oil and a fine confetti of parsley is sprinkled on the top. It's not much, but it's perfect.

So I had to buy the *bigoli* even though I was running late. There were a few other bits I needed too: cheese and a little salad to serve afterwards, some of the S-shaped buttery biscuits that are good eaten dunked into sweet wine. When finally I arrived back at the palazzo, weighed down by shopping, it was with a certain amount of trepidation. I hoped the old women hadn't clashed over some silly thing that had happened years ago.

Locking Boris in the kitchen, I went to check on them. The salon was empty. All the tea had been drunk and I stacked the empty cups and saucers back on the tray and carried them downstairs, calling as I went. "Coco, Contessa . . . where are you?"

There was no reply, so I set out in search of them. The place was huge and it took me a while. I found more bare rooms, one with a faded frieze painted round its walls, others hung with dusty chandeliers. Uneasily I poked my head round the bedroom doors. Valentina's was messy, with shoes tossed about the floor and a dressing table covered in cosmetics. Nanda's room had a high double bed in the middle and a crucifix on the wall above it. There was a standard lamp with a tasselled shade and an ornate wardrobe made of dark wood, its doors carved with curlicues. Both rooms were unoccupied, and feeling bad for prying, I headed back downstairs.

When I heard the front door open and the sound of Boris barking in the kitchen, I quickened my pace. "Coco?" I shouted again.

"Darling, you're back!"

They were in fine form, the pair of them. The Contessa had changed into a blouse in a soft shade of green that took years off her. She climbed the stairs ahead of Coco and smiled when she saw me.

"We were hungry," she explained. "So we went to Alia Vedova for a little snack. Just some meatballs and an *ombra* or two; don't worry, we haven't spoiled our appetite for lunch."

"We were fading away," Coco added. "And Nanda hadn't been to Alia Vedova for so long. It used to be a favourite."

"I was going to make pasta," I told them. "*Bigoli in salsa.*"

"Ah, that used to be a favourite too." The Contessa smiled again.

She seemed a different woman. All her grandness had disappeared, the pretence of having staff, the sense that she was scared of something. It was almost disorienting.

They came down to the kitchen to keep me company. There was a fuss from Coco over her dogs, but, tired from his walk, Boris merely sniffed their noses then curled up on the floor beneath the table at Nanda's feet. I listened to the two women talking as I prepared our lunch. Mostly their conversation was about people I'd never heard of and I tuned in and out. Hearing Valentina's name, I paid more attention.

"She and Giacomo, they have a plan," Nanda was saying. "Once the debt has been reduced, things will be easier for everyone."

"But she's giving up so much in the meantime," Coco argued.

"It's her choice. No one has forced her."

"Your daughter's talent is going to waste."

Nanda held up her hands. "Stop, please. On this we will never agree. And I don't want an argument, not again."

Coco hesitated. "It's not easy for me to stand by watching this happen and say nothing. Not when there is such an easy solution."

"It isn't easy at all." Nanda sounded vexed. "Not for any of us. But Valentina and Giacomo, they care about who we are."

"Who you used to be," Coco said softly.

The pasta water was boiling, the kitchen filling with the smell of onions gently frying. I could see our lunch being spoiled before I'd finished cooking it.

"Can someone please set the table?" I interrupted. "The cutlery is in that drawer over there, Coco. And Nanda, would you mind stirring the onions, as they're in danger of catching."

They surprised me by doing as they were told. Coco found some yellowed linen napkins for each place setting, then went down to the garden to pick greenery for a vase. Nanda wielded a wooden spoon as I splashed vinegar into the pan to stop the onions colouring up.

"Coco is a good woman but she can be difficult," she murmured, and I wasn't sure if she was talking to me or thinking aloud.

The *bigoli in salsa* was good, but not as delicious as the one I'd had in a neighbourhood *osteria* the week before. Perhaps I had used too many anchovies or not enough olive oil. I decided to ask Angelo and see what he thought. I might even make it for him one night after a lesson.

Nanda looked tired by the time we left. It had been a big day for her, I suppose. She was smiling, though, and she hugged me almost as tightly as she did Coco.

"You will come again tomorrow," she called as we walked down the front steps.

"Not tomorrow, darling, not me at least, but soon, I promise," Coco sang back gaily.

The moment the front door was closed behind us, she seemed to slump. Walking along the Strada Nuova together, she was so dazed she didn't bother trying to stop her little dogs winding their leashes round each other.

"Are you OK?" I asked, stopping to untangle them.

"Not really," she admitted. "I'm very shaken, to tell the truth. The terrible state that place is in, and God only knows when poor Nanda last left it. I had to force her to come to Alia Vedova, and even then she walked so slowly it took an age to get there. She has become an old, old woman."

"Actually she was much better today. I couldn't believe the difference."

"Dear God, really?" Coco shuddered. "I'm not going to be like that, not even when I can see death coming. I won't allow it."

"You need a cocktail," I told her. "Let's catch a water taxi; I'll pay."

"Certainly you will," she agreed. "And for the drinks, too."

The speedboat whisked us down the Grand Canal and delivered us directly to the terrace of the Gritti Palace. A uniformed man was blocking our way, and at first I thought he was going to refuse us entry because of the dogs, but Coco held her head high and smiled graciously, stalking up the gangplank as though she was at home, and he seemed to realise there was no point in resisting and moved aside.

We were shown to a table and left with the menu and the view. This was a front-row seat to the spectacle of the Grand Canal. There were flotillas of gondolas

224

bobbing in the wake of a crowded *vaporetto*, palazzos with Gothic arched windows and painted facades, the domes of Santa Maria della Salute, all within sight. The prices on the cocktail menu were just as impressive; still, this was a treat, I reasoned, and only a small extravagance.

I ordered my favourite Aperol Spritz and Coco asked for a Negroni. Stern-looking waiters ferried out the drinks on silver trays and laid them on squares of crisp white linen with dishes of olives, nuts and crispy snacks. They left us there to enjoy them for as long as we wanted. It was perfect . . . and yet . . .

I looked at the people around me. The man in the mustard polo shirt at the next table was smoking a fat cigar; his expensive-looking wife and daughters were marooned in a sea of designer shopping bags. Beyond them were two middle-aged couples wearing walking shorts and demolishing club sandwiches. There was a suited businessman with an attaché case, a bored-looking woman with a shiny Botoxed forehead, a group of German tourists. No one looked up and met my eyes; certainly no one smiled. They were strangers and happy to remain that way. They were only passing through.

Impressive as it was, I realised that the Gritti Palace wasn't really my kind of place. I preferred my usual haunts: the local *bacaro* with the same old men propping up the bar at all hours, the Prosecco bar I went to with Angelo, the little places I stopped at for coffee several times a week. I liked friendliness rather than opulence, a sense of people's lives touching, of community, of neighbourhood. That's what made me happy.

I pulled the notebook from my bag.

Addolorata's Happiness List

5. Neighbourhoods — familiar places and faces, small greetings and meetings, a sense of being part of my own little corner of the world. Belonging.

CHAPTER
FIFTEEN

Coco was staring out at the view, so deep in thought she hadn't noticed me scribbling in my notebook. I think she was lost somewhere in the past, perhaps with Nanda when they were younger and Lorenzo was still alive.

I left her with her memories for a while and watched the passing gondolas. Some had singers on board, and I kept an eye out for Valentina, but she wasn't among them. Most likely she was busy at one of her other jobs, trying desperately to scrape together some cash. What a mess her family seemed to be in.

"Coco, how did the Contessa's family end up in such debt?"

I asked. "Was it Lorenzo's fault?"

Coco turned from the view and looked at me blankly for a moment. Then she lifted her glass to her lips and took a sip. "He called me fickle," she said reproachfully. "He was hardly perfect himself."

"He wasn't?"

She shook her head. "No, but Lorenzo Viadro was a wonderful artist. If you're interested, you should go to their museum on Murano and see his work. It was exhibited around the world and won many prizes. There's no one like him today in my opinion."

"So he was successful."

"Artistically, yes, but he wasn't such a good businessman. He took risks and failed. There was a shop he opened in London that lost a lot of money, and the museum itself, of course, which was expensive to run. Then there was the way Nanda insisted on living. In those days the palazzo was full of people and parties. They had so many staff: people to cook and clean, a boat and a driver. Lorenzo paid for it all."

"Is that why he killed himself? Because it all got too much and he couldn't cope?"

"Partly I suppose." Coco's gaze followed a gondola as it went past. "Also the shop failing so publicly, the humiliation of it, no man likes that. Lorenzo had low moods and took his life during one of them. Such a waste."

"And his family were left to pay the business debts?"

"Things were tight but there were no debts, not then. The problems came after Lorenzo's death. Remember I told you there were two sons? Giacomo and his elder brother Teodoro. Even when he was a little boy I didn't like Teodoro Viadro. He used to steal things and hide them. He had rages when he'd try to hurt whoever happened to be around; even his mother, who adored him. He was a nasty child and didn't improve. The real problems began when the two boys inherited the glass museum with the understanding that they would run it together."

"What about Valentina?" I asked.

228

"The male children inherited the business, that is the tradition. I think they thought that once they turned things round they'd settle some money on her. That didn't happen, of course. It wasn't Giacomo's fault. He may not have his father's talent but he's a hard worker. It was Teodoro who destroyed them. He lived like a playboy: parties, drink, drugs, everything you can imagine. He borrowed the money to pay for it. Not from the banks, though; from certain individuals, men from the south . . ."

"Criminals?"

Coco nodded as she signalled to the waiter for more cocktails. "With men like that it's a big mistake not to pay them back. When Teodoro couldn't, Nanda was forced to sell paintings and valuable furniture. But the debts were bigger than she knew and the interest was mounting. That's when Teodoro had the accident. He was drunk and in a boat, driving much too fast. It was no loss in my opinion, but poor Nanda was shattered."

"He died?"

She nodded again. "Now they are paying off the debts. Everything is mortgaged: the museum, the palazzo. Meanwhile Giacomo is struggling because cheap glass from China is being sold as genuine Murano and no one wants to pay his prices. And Valentina is missing out on the life she should be living."

"So that's why she refused to go to Buenos Aires with Angelo," I guessed.

"She gave up many things. I have tried to tell them there is an easy way to solve all their problems: they should sell the palazzo and perhaps the Viadro museum and foundry too. But Nanda refuses."

I sipped my Spritz and helped myself to a handful of nuts. "That's why the pair of you fought?"

"It is." Pausing, Coco stared at the boats churning through the Grand Canal. Wearing her bright turban, with the oversized sunglasses on her nose and the dogs on her knees, she looked very like the portraits I'd seen of Peggy Guggenheim.

"My poor old friend won't let go of the past."

"But you've held on to lots from your past: your clothes and Pegeen's paintings," I pointed out.

"Yes, but I knew when it was time to change; to walk away from things even if I loved them."

"What things?" I asked curiously.

From Coco's expression I could tell I'd pushed too far. The corners of her mouth turned down and her eyes grew wary. Her gaze shifted sideways and refused to meet mine. She didn't say anything.

Quickly I changed the subject. "I'd definitely like to visit the Viadro glass museum. Would you come with me?"

"No, I don't think so," she said, still staring out at the water.

"We could make a day of it," I tried to persuade her. "Have lunch somewhere nice."

"I don't want to go back to Murano." Coco sighed. "I will have to return to visit Nanda, though, won't I? You've made sure of that."

The next morning I saw Valentina for the first time in ages. She was waiting for me when I went to pick up the dog, her face bare of make-up, a frizz of loose hair clouding around it. She looked tired, but then I wasn't surprised.

"I owe you a thank you," she said. "Mamma says you've been cooking lunch for her. It's kind but you don't have to. She's more than capable of getting her own."

"It's no bother. I have to eat too," I pointed out.

"She also tells me that Coco came yesterday."

"That's right."

Valentina nodded. "Good. They will argue again sooner or later; they always do. Still, it's nice for her to have the company in the meantime."

I had snapped the leash on to Boris's collar and was about to leave when she stopped me.

"Can I ask you another favour? Would you be able to lead my walking tour for me tonight? It's the same one you came on."

"You want me to be the guide? Why?"

"There's a party of tourists who have asked especially for a female gondola singer to serenade them this evening and I'm the only one available. But the times clash completely. The tips are so good I hate to turn it down and I couldn't think who else to ask."

I wasn't keen on the idea. "It's a few weeks since I did that tour with you and I don't remember it well enough. How would I know where to go or what to say?"

"That's no problem. I have it all written down in the information pack. And it's simple really. The owners of the *bacari* know what to serve and will help if you get stuck. Won't you consider it? Please?"

I couldn't really say no, especially as I had nothing else to do. "OK, I suppose so, but just this once."

She smiled. "Thank you so much. I'll find some way to repay you, I promise."

Fetching a plastic folder full of instructions, Valentina showed me a map with each *bacaro* marked on it. "See how close they are? Angelo's place is first, and then the others are only a couple of minutes' walk from each other. It's impossible to get lost."

"What if people ask me questions about Venetian food?"

"Mamma says that's what you've been cooking for her. You can answer a few questions, I'm sure."

The prospect of being a tour guide for the evening had me nervous. So while Boris was sniffing round the park, I sat on a bench and read through the information. Afterwards the dog and I walked the streets behind the Rialto market, trying to locate each *bacaro* I would be visiting.

When they're not open, many of these little bars can be difficult to find. They close the shutters on their windows, pull in their awnings and seem to disappear. So it took a while before I knew exactly where I was supposed to be going and the best route to take.

On my way back to the palazzo, I stopped at the market for fresh peas to make a *risi e bisi* for the Contessa. It was a dish she seemed especially fond of and it's easy to cook. All you do is make a broth from the pods and simmer the rice in it. Add the peas and a pinch of sugar. Finish with butter, parsley and Parmesan. The flavours are fresh and the meal is satisfying without weighing you down.

We ate together in her salon, bowls on our laps and both of us too busy enjoying our food to talk. Conversations with Nanda tended to be disorienting anyway. I'd tried several times to ask questions about Coco but never got far. She had a way of answering without really telling me anything.

"What happened to Coco's husband?" I might wonder.

"Once he rubbed jam in her hair. Wasn't that awful?" she would reply.

I found it difficult to tell if she was doing it on purpose. Some days I was certain her confusion was an act, a thing she did to escape the truth of her life. Other times I wasn't so sure. That afternoon, as she ate her rice and peas with obvious enjoyment, she seemed in good spirits.

"This dish is a part of Venetian history," she told me, running a spoon round the bowl to find a final mouthful. "They used to serve it to the Doge on the feast day of San Marco. There had to be a pea for every grain of rice in his bowl. Myself I prefer it like this, with plenty of broth."

"I'll let the cook know," I said, and Nanda laughed.

"What a pity Coco isn't here," she said. "She loves *risi e bisi* as much as I do. Have you made it for her?"

"Not yet, and I was lucky to find peas at the market today. The season is finished, I think."

"What a pity for Coco."

"Summer brings other good things," I pointed out. "Like beautiful tomatoes, aubergines, fresh corn, herbs. I'll be able to cook delicious lunches for you both, I promise."

"Do you think she'll come back?" She sounded hopeful.

"She promised to, didn't she?"

"Yes, but with Coco that might mean nothing." Nanda frowned.

"I haven't known her for long," I reminded her. "I don't understand her like you do."

Nanda looked at me. "No one understands her like me," she said steadily.

The rest of the afternoon I spent swotting up on the tour, memorising as much as I could. Then I had a small crisis over what to wear. Normally I would have slung on a pair of jeans without giving it much thought, but Coco must have got to me, because I tried on several options before settling on the blue dress I'd bought on our first shopping trip, and a Murano glass necklace I thought must be genuine given what I'd paid for it.

Still nervous, I had a quick cigarette out on the balcony, hoping Coco had her window closed and wouldn't notice the smell. She didn't approve of my smoking; had made that clear when she'd found me having a sneaky one down in her garden. There had been a long lecture about what it would do to my looks, even though I was only having the occasional puff when I was feeling stressed. That particular day I'd had a tense phone conversation with Eden. He had refused to send Katia over to me in the school holidays and we'd argued until I'd realised we weren't getting anywhere and had hung up the phone. Later, calming down over a glass of wine, I'd decided to try again in a day or so; perhaps get Pieta to talk to him, possibly even my father. Eden was being completely unreasonable and that wasn't really like him. Surely one of us could make him see it?

I set off to the meeting point in Campo della Maddalena in plenty of time. There was a full tour group this evening, and a few were already waiting for me on the steps. They were very like I'd been that first week: dazed by Venice and its crowded *calli*, clutching maps that confused them, wanting to be sure they saw everything they ought to.

I introduced myself and began fielding questions. Which tour would I recommend to take to see the Doge's Palace? Where was the best place for a gondola ride? Could they visit Murano and Burano in just one day?

I took a deep breath. "Other people will tell you about the tourist attractions. I'm here to show you the real Venice that the locals enjoy; the places where they eat and drink."

That seemed to placate them. Then I remembered how on her tour Valentina had told us to put away our maps, so I did the same. When the entire group had assembled, I guided them towards the *traghetto* stop, talking about the way Venetians liked to socialise.

I made it sound as if I belonged because in some ways it felt like I did. The rhythm of life here suited me; it felt civilised, the way people are supposed to live.

"We drop into a *bacaro*, perhaps meet a friend and stand at the bar with them, an *ombra* in one hand and a *cicchetto* in the other," I explained. "It's a small pause in our day, a social moment before we go home or back to work."

"That sounds lovely," an American woman said enviously.

"You're so lucky to live here."

"Yes," I agreed. "Very lucky."

Our first stop was Angelo's *osteria*. The shutters were tightly closed and the door locked, but when I knocked he answered straight away.

"*Buona sera*, Dolly." He kissed me on both cheeks. "You've found a job at last."

"Only for this evening," I said, adding more quietly, "And you have to help me out."

Angelo welcomed my group inside, invited them to take stools at the counter and poured out glasses of wine. He spoke about food, how he opened his *osteria* every morning with the market and found his inspiration in the sea creatures for sale there. He talked of twisting tradition, creating something new from the way things used to be done.

He served the same things we'd eaten when I had come as a tourist: smoked tuna brioche spread with a cream of artichoke and mustard; crostini covered in creamed salt cod. But he talked for much longer, telling us about the seafood to be found on the lagoon's

236

muddy floor and in the valleys of water covering its swampy land: the brill and the bass, the red goatfish and grey mullet, the molluscs to be teased from their shells. It was the first time I'd heard him sound so passionate about food, and I was nearly as enchanted by him as the rest of them seemed to be.

This wasn't our night for a tango lesson, but as my group were climbing down from their stools and finding bags and hats, Angelo came over and asked if I'd like to meet up later.

"I'll be round the corner at All'Arco. Come when you've finished. There's someone who wants to meet you. A good friend of mine."

"Sure, I'd love to," I told him, wondering who it was.

As we walked towards the next *bacaro*, I overheard two women in my group talking about Angelo. One of them thought he was hot; the other didn't agree.

"He's got that arrogant chef thing going on," she was saying. "They all think they're God's gift."

I wanted to tell her she'd missed the point. The very best chefs are artists, concerned with colour, shape and texture but working with flavour too. It takes courage to create. It takes imagination and tenacity, plenty of hubris and perhaps even obsession. That's the chef all of us want to be, the sort I thought I was before I lost my confidence and allowed my father to take his restaurant back. I didn't speak up, however. Instead I tried to remember what I was meant to be saying about the next *bacaro*.

I think the tour was a success. Everyone was happy with what they'd tasted. The woman who didn't like fish still had enough to eat; the keen drinkers ordered more wine and stayed on at the final *bacaro* we visited. Before leaving, I scribbled on their maps, suggesting places to visit, just like Valentina had for me. The bar in Cannaregio with a barge moored beside it where you could stretch out while you enjoyed your Spritz; the Acqua Alta bookstore; and the best places for a cheap lunch or a good dinner.

They seemed like nice people; even so, it was a relief to get away. As I headed to All'Arco to meet Angelo, I felt shattered. Just one drink, I decided, then I'd head home and collapse into bed with my book.

The bar was busy as usual. At first it seemed Angelo was part of a group gathered out on the pavement, but as I drew closer, I realised he was with only one of the women surrounding him. She was what my sister Pieta likes to call "pulled together". Her fair hair was sleek, her clothes expensive, her figure slim. She was laughing at something Angelo was saying and I hesitated for a moment, unsure whether I should interrupt.

"Hey, Dolly, you made it." Angelo was beckoning me over. "Let me go and get you a drink. Spritz, yes?"

There was an awkward moment as he turned to push his way through to the bar, leaving me behind with his friend.

"I guess I'll just have to introduce myself." She held out a hand. "Marie-Ann Billens."

"Addolorata Martinelli. Nice to meet you."

"Good, that's the formalities over with." She smiled. "I told Angelo I was keen for us to meet. We're both foreigners living in Venice. It can be so hard to get to know people here, right?"

Her accent had a lilt in it that I couldn't quite place. South Africa? Australia?

"Where are you from?" I asked.

"Originally New Zealand but I haven't lived there for years. I work in the hotel business so I move around a lot. It can be great, of course, but the down side is that just as you settle into one place, you're moving on again."

By the time Angelo returned with my drink, I knew quite a lot about Marie-Ann. She was a manager at the Molino Stucky Hilton and had been there a couple of years. She lived on the Giudecca, which was so much less frenetic than the rest of Venice, and she didn't dance the tango.

"It's not really my thing," she said. "I've never been a dancer. I hear he's teaching you, though. How's that going?"

"Oh, you know, we have good days and bad."

Angelo had my drink in his hand but he'd been distracted by someone on his way out of the bar and stopped to chat.

"Tell me, aside from the dance lessons, what exactly is going on between the pair of you?" Marie-Ann asked coolly.

She had taken me by surprise. "Sorry?"

"You and Angelo, what's the story?"

"There is no story."

"Really?" It sounded like she didn't believe me.

Angelo chose that moment to rejoin us and there was a discomforting pause before we rearranged the conversation. Marie-Ann asked a question about my necklace and we talked about shopping in Venice for a while until I downed my drink.

I meant to leave but Marie-Ann fetched me another Spritz and I stayed to finish it. After that Angelo suggested we head over to Campo San Giacomo dell'Orio for the *milonga*. Again I tried to say my goodbyes and go home. Ever since our lessons had begun I'd avoided dancing in public. I think I'd had some mad idea that once I got really good I'd turn up and wow them all, but the more I learnt, the more I realised I didn't know, so it had never happened.

"Come," Angelo urged me. "If we're going to perform this summer, then you should take every chance to practise."

Marie-Ann turned to me. "You're performing in a show together?"

"Apparently," I said drily. "At least that's what Angelo keeps telling me."

"I'll have to get a ticket."

"Come along with us now and you can watch for free," Angelo suggested.

"No, I ought to go home. I have some emails to deal with and a big day at work tomorrow."

Angelo slung a casual arm round my shoulders. "OK then. I'll call you soon," he told her.

I saw Marie-Ann's expression change. Her eyes seemed harder, her mouth a firm line. Then she forced a smile. "Oh, stuff the work, I'll come," she declared.

240

I felt a little rush of pleasure when I heard the tango music playing. I knew the song; it was one Angelo and I had practised to. Full of wine and high spirits, I danced a few steps with an imaginary partner. Angelo did the same. Then he took my hand and, leaving Marie-Ann behind, pulled me towards the dancing.

Coco was there with Silvio and I saw them stop to watch us. My heart bumped a little, then I moved into Angelo's embrace and any unease was soon gone. Closing my eyes, I let myself be swept around the *campo*. My steps were controlled, perhaps even rather graceful. It felt like I was in my own body, following Angelo but still sure of myself. We danced for three slow songs, and when the last one ended, we stopped.

"I should give someone else a turn," said Angelo.

"But I thought I was doing so well."

"You are. But tonight there aren't enough men and all these women are waiting for partners." He gestured towards some girls in high-heeled tango shoes and pretty dresses. "We will dance together again later, though, OK?"

"Sure," I said, trying not to sound disappointed.

Marie-Ann was waiting by a stand of trees close to where we'd left her, her arms folded, her smile gone. I left Angelo and walked over.

"Do you want to get a drink?" I asked her. "The bar over there has a fabulous Prosecco menu."

She dipped her head. "Yes, if you like."

I found a table where we could watch the dancing, but Marie-Ann chose to sit with her back to it. Leaning her elbows on the table, she rested her chin on her hands.

"Shall we continue where we left off?" she said. "I think Angelo is seeing someone else. All I'm asking is if it's you."

I sat back in my chair. "Are you and him together?"

"We have been for a year on and off."

I was surprised: he'd never mentioned a girlfriend. But then Angelo rarely gave away much about himself.

"What makes you suspect there's someone else?" I asked.

She chewed at a manicured thumbnail, as if unsure how to respond. "When you've been messed around by enough men, you get to know the signs," she said eventually. "Angelo blows hot and cold. We'll be spending all our free time together, then suddenly he'll go a week without calling. Lately he's mentioned your name a lot. That's why I suggested we meet up. I need to know what's going on."

"I have a family back in England," I told her. "Me and Angelo are about nothing but the dancing, I promise."

She was working at her thumbnail with her teeth again.

"Who, then?"

"Have you asked him?"

Marie-Ann gave a harsh laugh. "Men don't like to be pressured that way. In my experience it makes them run."

Through the trees I watched Angelo dancing with a girl in a short black dress. I could see how it would be

242

difficult to be his girlfriend if you didn't trust him completely.

Marie-Ann leaned in closer. "Here's the thing," she said. "I'm almost thirty-two. If I want to have kids, I need to get on with it. There's an opportunity for me to transfer back to the Hilton in Auckland, but before I make a decision, I need to know if this thing with Angelo is going anywhere."

"If he's cheating, maybe it's better to end things," I suggested.

"But I'm not sure he is," she pointed out. "Look, he's a great guy — smart, successful, gorgeous — and I'd be crazy to throw all that away if there's a chance of making it work."

"Would you rather live here or in New Zealand?"

"If I go home, there's a promotion in it for me."

"Yes, but which place would make you happiest?" I asked.

"Happiest?" She sounded puzzled. "I don't know really. I mean, it would depend on lots of things."

"What things?"

She thought about it. "Relationships, friends, the place I lived . . . I can't say exactly, I've never thought about it like that."

That's when I told Marie-Ann about my happiness list. She seemed intrigued, although she did laugh when I told her I'd only managed to come up with five things so far.

"It's not like I'm just jotting stuff down," I explained. "It involves a lot of thinking. I have to be pretty certain before I add something to it."

She slid her seat sideways so the dancing was in view. "I have a list too," she said, her eyes on Angelo. "It's of the things I want — a family, a house with a garden, maybe even a holiday place by a beach. I have goals for my career and my finances. It's the same thing, I guess."

"The same as a happiness list? Actually, I don't think so."

"Why not?"

"Just because you want these things doesn't mean they'll make you happy."

Angelo was leaving the dance floor now. He seemed to be looking for us. Glancing towards the bar, he smiled and made to come over.

"There is someone he might be involved with," I said quickly. "A woman called Valentina who used to be his dance partner."

"I think I know who you mean. She's in some of those photographs he has on the wall."

I nodded, and as Angelo pulled an extra chair over to our table, Marie-Ann touched my hand. "Thank you," she said quietly.

Angelo and I had one more dance that evening. It was late and most of the others had gone home. It felt as if the *campo* was ours and I relaxed into his hold and closed my eyes. His hair had the burnt butter smell of a day in the kitchen, of simmering broths and onions slowly caramelised. His skin was moist and warm. I think he must have been tired because his movements were looser-limbed and more languid than usual. For the first time we were truly moving together, our bodies connected, our tango sincere. It was a magical thing and I felt sorry for Marie-Ann. She wouldn't ever know the whole of the man if she didn't touch this part of him.

Addolorata's Happiness List

6. Tango — the music and the mood, the way it feels. The sheer pleasure of it, the close embrace, most of all the being in total harmony with another human being.

CHAPTER
SIXTEEN

Coco couldn't be persuaded to change her mind about Murano. So the next day, once I'd taken Boris for a quick outing, I caught the *vaporetto* on my own. There was a welcome breeze out on the lagoon as we cruised away. It felt like proper summer now: the tourists were stripped down to shorts and T-shirts, the locals wearing linen or floaty dresses. Coco had told me it would get much hotter than this, warning that there might be days when she would refuse to move from the shady spots in her garden. Still, it was better than the endless greys of winter, she said, and the chilling mists that stayed for days. Better than the flooding of the *acqua alta* or the freezing rain.

I would miss all of that. By the end of summer I'd be gone. Staring back towards the greenness of Sant'Elena, I tried to put the thought out of my mind. There were weeks to go till then, and so much still to happen. The Festa del Redentore, which everyone talked about; lazy days of sunbathing and swimming on the Lido; the tango performance I had not quite promised to take part in. And I would add more things to my happiness list; I had to do that.

I'd started out with no idea it would be such a challenge. In fact it still seemed far easier to come up with a list of the things that *didn't* make me happy: like sport, celebrity gossip, designer handbags, blaring televisions, gyms, facials, fancy lingerie. That was just off the top of my head. If I thought about it properly I reckoned I could fill pages of my notebook with stuff I didn't care about. And that made me sad. I didn't want to be a person who focused on the negatives.

On Murano there was a man standing by the landing calling out to those of us disembarking, trying to interest us in a free display at a glass furnace. Some people followed him, but glancing at my map, I saw that the Viadro museum was in the opposite direction, so I stayed with my original plan.

It's only a small island so it wasn't difficult to find the palazzo that housed the museum. I paid my entrance fee and climbed the stairs, wandered round the shelves of vases, statues and bowls, stopping to read an information tag or two. The colours and shapes were stunning but I didn't think I'd ever want to own something so perfect and so easily broken.

Beside each display case there were black-and-white photographs of stern-looking moustached Viadro men and a little more of their story was told. It seemed every male child had been bound to the family business, either to make glass or to sell it if they had no talent for creating.

Lorenzo's work filled an entire room and to my eyes seemed the most artistic. Luminous vases in amethyst green, goblets with a coarse, smoky finish, glass that looked raw and rough, shapes that curved like a woman's body. I stayed there for the longest time, staring at each piece, trying to imagine the man who had made them all.

"Excuse me, are you Addolorata?" a male voice asked.

"Yes." Startled, I looked up. He was stockily built, with sallow skin and heavy brows. I had the feeling he'd been standing there watching me for a while.

"I'm Giacomo Viadro. My mother asked me to come and find you."

"Really?" This was unexpected. "How did she know I'd be here?"

"I think Coco must have mentioned it. You are friends, yes?"

"That's right."

"Mamma tells me you've been very kind. She asked me to show you around."

Giacomo seemed as solemn as the moustached men in his old family photographs and I wasn't especially excited at the idea of his company.

"That's very thoughtful," I told him, "but I'm sure you're busy, and actually I've had a good look round already."

"It's no trouble. Perhaps you'd like to see some of my work? It's on display down in the shop and the foundry."

"Sure," I said, since it seemed there was no option.

"Come then."

He led me back through the galleries I'd already visited, pointing out hand-made chandeliers designed for doges, a glass owl created for the Venice Biennale, bowls glazed with gold or covered in bubbles.

"Our family has been passing on our glass-making secrets from father to son since 1400," he said, his voice sounding with pride. "Each generation has pushed forward, creating new techniques and possibilities."

I followed him down the stairs and through a door that opened on to a garden. The building that housed the foundry lay beyond a patch of yellowing lawn. Just beside its entrance there was a roped-off viewing area and a display case filled with pendants just like the one Nanda often wore.

"Oh, do you make this jewellery? It's stunning."

Giacomo smiled and it changed his face, made him look younger and sweeter.

"We produce other things here too — chandeliers, vases, ornaments, whatever will sell. But this is what I love to create. Each piece is unique, and when I see a woman wearing one, the glass warming with her skin, it's as if I've created a living thing, not merely a decoration."

"Coco told me there's a lot of fake Murano glass coming in from China. Is that affecting you?"

"Cheap beads, glass animals, tasteless things that have been mass-produced; nothing like this." Giacomo was matter-of-fact. "People will always want to buy genuine art glass."

He asked me to join him for coffee in the small café attached to the shop. The table we sat at offered a view of many more of his pendants, all exhibited in a long cabinet that was lit so that each one seemed to glow.

Fetching the coffee himself, he set it in front of me along with a plate of raisin-filled *zaleti* biscuits still slightly warm from the oven.

"So, Addolorata," he said, taking the chair opposite. "Tell me what you are doing in Venice. Is this a holiday?"

"No, it's more of a sabbatical. I'm a chef and needed time away from my work." It was the easiest explanation.

"Are you enjoying our Venetian cooking?" he asked.

"Yes, of course." I crunched into one of the yellow biscuits and found pine nuts inside as well as raisins. "Mm, these are great."

"We make them here. Often we add in other things, figs or almonds. They are part of Venice's history, these little pastries. If you like, I can ask the cook to give you her recipe. You are here for inspiration, yes?"

"Sort of."

"It must be good to travel and have time to think. Some day I will do that if I can." He sounded wistful. "But right now I have a business to run and three young children at home. I hardly ever step off Murano unless it's for a business meeting or to visit Mamma . . . and truthfully I don't do that often enough. You're seeing much more of her, I think. Tell me, how does she seem?"

I wasn't sure how to answer that. "It's difficult for me to say because I haven't known her long," I pointed out, "but she seems OK. Coco got her to leave the palazzo the other day. They went to Alia Vedova."

250

"Coco almost always makes Mamma do exactly what she wants. That never changes."

"Is she your godmother as well as Valentina's?" I wondered.

Giacomo looked at me sideways. "Coco? Our godmother?" He gave a dry laugh. "I don't think so."

"I'm sure someone told me that." I tried to remember who it had been.

"Well, they got it wrong. My mother has been a loyal friend to Coco but even she wouldn't have chosen her to be a part of her children's spiritual upbringing." He laughed again. "Not Coco."

"Why not?" I asked, reaching for another *zaleto*.

"What do you know about her?"

"Hardly anything, to be honest. I'm aware she was married once and that your father was a friend of hers."

"He was her lover," he said shortly.

"Well, yes."

He rubbed at his eyes tiredly. "Let me get more coffee. I don't know Coco's whole story but I can fill you in on some of it."

Giacomo came back with another plate of biscuits, this time *fugasse*, sweet, yeasty breads dotted with sugar and flavoured with grated lemon rind. I helped myself to one and waited for his story.

"Where to begin," he said, settling into his chair again. "Their history is a long one."

"When did they meet?"

"They were very young. Coco was the daughter of my mother's nursemaid. Since Mamma was an only child, Coco and her sisters were brought to the palazzo to keep her company now and then. The story I have heard is that Coco doted on my mother, but I suspect the truth is she preferred our home to her own. Her family was a humble one. Her father worked on one of the delivery barges."

"So they were childhood friends."

"Inseparable. Growing up, Coco must have practically lived in our palazzo. She appears in many of the family photographs from that time. Birthday parties, outings to the Lido — she accompanied them everywhere. My grandparents may have regretted that later. Perhaps Coco's parents did too."

"Why?"

"She wanted what Mamma had. Oh, I don't mean she stole things from my family, not so far as I know, anyway. But she longed to live like them." Giacomo hesitated. "Tell me, is Coco beautiful even now?"

"Yes, I think she always will be."

"My brother Teodoro had a crush on her for a while. He told me he'd seen her naked once. I expect he was lying, but maybe not." Frowning, Giacomo glanced at his watch. "I'm sorry, Addolorata, but I have to go and check on a delivery, and after that there is a meeting I must attend. Stay here as long as you like, though, enjoy some more of the biscuits. And come back to watch one of our glass-making demonstrations if you have the time."

He stood, half turned away, then seemed to have second thoughts and, looking back at me, said, "You know, even now Coco's behaviour would seem

252

shocking. And back then people were more traditional . . . back then things were different."

I took a stroll around the canals of Murano before catching the *vaporetto* home. Every shop I passed sold glass, many with the same beaded necklaces in their windows. There was nothing else like Giacomo's pendants, though.

As I walked I tried to fill in the blanks of what he'd told me. So Coco had been envious of Nanda and wanted a life like hers. She'd done something scandalous to get it, but what? And why was it almost impossible to make anyone talk about it?

The *vaporetto* I took home followed a different route, navigating the wide Canneregio canal and dropping me at the train station. From there I had a long walk down Strada Nuova that took me past the palazzo. Its gate was closed but through the railings I caught sight of Nanda sitting on a bench, basking in the late-afternoon sun, Boris at her feet.

"*Buona sera, Contessa,*" I called.

She looked up. "Ah, I told my son you were on Murano. Did I get it wrong?"

"No, I was there and I met Giacomo. Thanks for asking him to show me round."

"I am sure he was pleased to." She nodded graciously. "And the truth is I have a small favour to ask of you. Please, come in for a moment."

I pushed open the gate and walked down the path. She didn't ask me to sit down, so I stayed standing.

"I've been wondering what to do about it all day and then I hit on an idea," she said.

"Sorry, wondering about what?"

"My daughter Valentina's birthday, of course. I'm going to throw a party for her, just a small one on a Sunday evening when there is no opera for her to sing in. My son and his family will come, my dear Coco too of course, perhaps one or two other old friends if I can find them. I need you to talk to the kitchen about preparing something special, a few cocktails and an elegant supper. Would you do that? You're so much better at dealing with them than me."

I supposed this was her way of asking me to cook. "Yes, I can talk to them," I agreed, admiring her cheek. "Why don't you let me know the date and the number of people first, though."

"Wonderful. The menu I will trust to you." Nanda smiled warmly. "How lovely to have a party."

The moment I got home, I knocked on Coco's door. She opened it a crack; far enough for me to see that she had a white mask spread thickly all over her face, aside from two clean circles from which her dark eyes were peering. She looked like an old owl.

"Not now, Addolorata, come back in half an hour."

"I thought you'd want to know about the party."

"What party?" She opened the door wider. "Am I invited?"

When I told her, Coco's response was to laugh. "So will we sit on the floor in a circle in one of those empty rooms as if we are children? This will be a disaster unless we do something."

"I'm sure we'll find enough chairs. It's just a family thing."

"No, no, there must others there too," she said firmly. "The days when any of the Viadro family could be counted on to entertain you are long gone. I will draw up a list. Come back later like I told you."

"Not too many people," I tried to warn her. "They can't afford it."

Before I'd finished speaking she had shut the door in my face.

The mask had been removed by the time I went back downstairs and Coco was properly powdered and lipsticked again. I found her sitting at her kitchen table furiously scrawling a long list.

"We will send out written invitations," she declared. "The menu you must decide on. But it needs to be delicate: little bite-sized snacks you can eat while standing or perched on a beautiful chaise longue."

"There aren't any beautiful chaises longues," I pointed out.

"Leave that to me. I have a friend who will bring in a few things. We'll decorate one of the larger rooms, make it look beautiful again."

"Isn't this a bit over the top? It's only a small birthday celebration after all."

"That's no reason not to do things properly."

"Who'll pay for it all?"

"We'll worry about that later. First let us have the dream."

"Coco . . ." I began to remonstrate. "They are in debt, remember."

"But we can do this very cheaply; you will be amazed."

She was so animated, chattering about plans for dancing in the garden, fairy lights in the trees, a fork and bowl supper for those who stayed late. Looking at the guest list, I wondered how many of those who appeared on it were friends of hers rather than Valentina.

"At a lovely party I went to once with Pegeen they had a magician who was very entertaining," Coco was murmuring. "And of course we Venetians love costumes, masks and confetti. But I think this should be a more sophisticated event. No circus tricks or carnival atmosphere. Don't you agree?"

"Ought we to talk to Nanda and Valentina before we go ahead with any of it?" I asked dubiously.

"Oh no, they'll be sure to love it." Coco sounded very certain. "They'll be completely thrilled."

In the morning when we met for breakfast, Coco was still going on about the party. Now she had an idea to bring in tango musicians, friends of hers who would play for free so I didn't need to fret about the expense. She had opinions about the food as well, inspired by little nibbles she'd eaten at celebrations she'd been to. I had serious misgivings about the whole business but it seemed there was no holding her back.

Coco talked on excitedly while I ate my brioche stuffed with sweet custard, drank my cappuccino and

256

ordered another. As always, it appeared elegant on a silver tray decorated with a vintage lace cloth, and the sight gave me a tiny pulse of pleasure.

One of the things I'd grown to love about Venice was how no one walked the streets clutching cardboard takeaway cups, sipping as they went. In Italy coffee is something to stop for, if only for a moment of pleasure. It's an everyday thing but still they make it into an occasion.

A china cup of coffee set on a cloth-covered tray: it was such an ordinary happiness I didn't think it deserved a place on my list. But that morning, as Coco made plans for cocktails and party food, I realised I'd been wrong. Small joys were just as important. If it truly made me happy then I should make a note of it.

Addolorata's Happiness List

7. Good coffee served properly. Not over-roasted and bitter, but strong and fragrant and delivered to me with enough ceremony to make the moment feel just a little bit special.

CHAPTER
SEVENTEEN

I love parties just as much as Coco, so over the next few days I began to get excited with her. I joined in as she debated the merits of coloured lanterns versus fairy lights in the trees. Mustered even more enthusiasm for a cocktail tasting. Went through boxes of Nanda's old photos pulling out pictures of Valentina to turn into a collage she wanted hung on the wall.

Even as a small child Valentina had worn her hair the same way — that heavy fringe and the fat plait falling over one shoulder. It looked as if she'd been chubby until her teens, then her frame had grown more willowy and her face much leaner, and the daisy tattoo had appeared, snaking over her shoulder. There were pictures of her singing in concerts, dancing ballet and tap as well as tango, posing beside a sequence of dogs, raising champagne glasses at celebrations. There were family shots and school portraits, a few with Coco, several with Angelo. In all of them she looked pretty and privileged, not worn down by exhaustion which was how she mostly seemed to be now.

It took ages to sift through them all because every picture sparked some small memory that had to be discussed; and every conversation brought a reminder of more memories. The two old women repeated themselves so often I grew impatient, so whenever I could, I escaped, walking Boris through Venice's gardens and green spaces, stopping off at the Acqua Alta bookstore to say hello to Valentina or at Angelo's *osteria* to pick up ready-made treats for lunch.

Often it was late afternoon by the time Coco and I headed home. Usually by then she had come up with at least a couple of new names to add to the guest list and I'd have to warn her again that it was all getting out of control.

"But, darling, we need some fun people," she insisted. "Valentina used to be vivacious but she's so tired these days. And Giacomo has always been unexciting."

I had no idea why she had taken against Giacomo. He seemed a nice enough guy to me.

"You're too hard on him," I objected.

"But he's dull. I can't pretend otherwise. He's never done anything truly interesting in his life."

"What about those glass pendants he makes; they're exquisite. There was nothing else I saw on Murano to touch them."

"What pendants?" she asked.

"You know, like the blue one Nanda often wears."

"But that is Lorenzo's work. I was there when he gave it to her."

"Are you sure?"

Coco nodded. "Yes, of course. I have one like it too."

"When Giacomo showed them to me he made it sound as if they were his own design," I told her. "There are lots of them on sale at the glass museum."

Coco's face softened. "He copied his father's work. Of course he did, poor boy. He is so like Nanda."

That afternoon we had stopped at a *bacaro* for a few meatballs and an *ombra* or two, drunk standing at the bar. At least I was standing; they had hurried over with a stool for Coco and didn't complain about the three small dogs snuffling below it for anything she dropped.

"Giacomo was very like his mother even as a boy," Coco said, sipping her wine. "Now Nanda was a sweet child but she was never troubled by a great deal of imagination. That was what I brought to our friendship."

"I've heard you two were inseparable when you were young."

"Yes, for a while. Then I grew up and no longer wanted to play hide and seek with her in the palazzo day after day. We've led very different lives since then, she and I. Really we have little in common."

"You've stayed close, though."

"Oh, there were times I was busy with other things and hardly saw her. But Nanda always sought me out sooner or later. I was the sister she'd never had, you see. She tended to cling to me."

Coco peered at the food in the glass cabinet on the bar. Calling the waiter over, she ordered some *sarde en saor*, the traditional cold dish of lightly fried sardines and thinly sliced onions marinated in vinegar then sprinkled with pine nuts and raisins.

"I keep promising to make *sarde en saor* for Nanda," I remarked, tasting a sweetly sour forkful from her plate.

260

Coco nodded. "She will like it because it's one of the old dishes, a part of Venice's history. Eating *sarde en saor* is yet another way for her to live in the past. Poor Nanda. Still, I expect it's too late for her to change now even if she wanted to."

Coco had a date that evening. Some man was taking her to an art exhibition then out to dinner. She complained that her energy was flagging, but when I suggested she might cancel and stay home to rest, she looked at me as if I were crazy. What was the point of resting? she asked. That would be no fun at all.

I had a date too, only mine was with Angelo's girlfriend Marie-Ann. We were meeting for a quick drink at her hotel. I imagined she wanted to ask me more questions about Angelo, although that wasn't what she'd said when she called.

"So nice to meet you the other night," she had enthused. "I loved having the chance to chat in English for a change. Let's catch up very soon and do it again."

So I caught a boat to the Giudecca. It was my first visit to the narrow strip of island divided from the rest of Venice by the deep canal the cruise ships use. I wanted to take a good look around, so instead of going directly to the hotel, I rode the *vaporetto* to the Zitelle stop and strolled up past the waterside bars and restaurants.

It was far more tranquil than elsewhere in the city and I could step out without worrying about treading on the heels of people stopping to take photographs or gawking at shop windows. There was a breeze to cool me as I walked and a view back over the lagoon to admire. I felt lucky to be here. Every day there were times like this one when I forgot about the stress and sadness that had brought me to Venice and was grateful. Lots of other women have to stay in their lives as they fall apart. Without my sister's help I might have done the same. Instead I had this new, half-borrowed existence; I'd made a home here, and friends.

What if I never went back? That was what I asked myself in those moments when the beauty of Venice rushed at me and I knew there wasn't any place in the world I'd rather be. What if I stayed for good?

It wasn't as impossible as it might sound. In my head I listed the steps I'd need to take. Talk to Coco about staying in the apartment, find a job cooking in an *osteria* or waiting tables, take legal advice about regular access to my daughter. Papa could keep Little Italy or try to sell it; I didn't care. Eden could stay on in our place in London until he was ready to go. One life finished, another begun, as easy as that.

The Molino Stucky Hilton is carved from an old brick flour mill that looms over the far end of the Giudecca. Inside it seemed much like every other international hotel I'd ever visited, with plush armchairs and potted palms, a man tinkling on a grand piano, people milling round wearing name tags for a conference.

I'd arranged to meet Marie-Ann in the lobby bar and was the first to arrive, so I ordered a drink and sat down to wait. As I stirred the olive round my Spritz I remembered the first time we'd met and how she'd run through what she wanted from life. A family, a house with a garden, a career . . . all the things I'd had and was considering walking away from.

"Dolly, so sorry I'm late." Marie-Ann was coolly chic in a beige shift dress. Its plainness only emphasised how lovely she was.

"No problem," I told her.

"There's always another email to send and one last person who wants to ask a question, isn't there?" She sounded harassed. "I need a Spritz. Shall I get you another?"

"Sure, why not."

For a while we made small talk: the warmth of the weather, her summer holiday plans, the best places to eat on the Giudecca. Marie-Ann waited until the drinks had arrived before asking me about Angelo.

"Have you seen him at all?"

"We've had our usual dance lessons and I've popped into his *osteria* once or twice."

She fidgeted with her glass, shaking it so the ice hit the sides. "Is there any reason why he's gone so quiet on me, do you think?"

"Has he?"

"Yes." She screwed up her pretty face. "There have been some texts, a few quick phone calls and we had an arrangement to meet but he cancelled at the last minute. I wondered if he'd been seeing that girl, Valentina."

"He hasn't mentioned it. But I'm not so close to him that he'd confide in me."

"You go to his apartment, though, right? Is there any sign of her having been there?"

I shook my head, feeling disloyal. "No, I don't think so."

"Could you have a good look next time you're there?"

"You're asking me to spy on him?"

"No, not to poke about in cupboards and drawers; just to keep your eyes open."

I wondered whether Marie-Ann was in love with Angelo, or if it was just a matter of timing: if he was the man on hand the moment she was ready to settle down.

"You really ought to talk to him," I said.

"I will," she promised. "But I don't want to go head to head with some woman he's got history with. You know what they're like, these Venetians: they stick together."

Marie-Ann had a point; I'd noticed it too. Perhaps it was a reaction to the flood of visitors, but it was as if the people in this city had formed a private inner circle. To truly belong you had to have been born here.

"Where did you meet Angelo anyway?" I asked her.

"At a bar near the Rialto. I was having a drink with a couple of colleagues. We got talking and I gave him my number. It was a week before he called; I'd given up hope by then. He surprised me with the most romantic date, out in a boat for the day, a gourmet picnic, chilled Prosecco . . . and I was hooked."

"I'm envious," I admitted. "If I wanted a romantic date I'd have to organise it myself. It's not my husband's thing at all."

264

Her smile was sympathetic. "Every other man I've been with has been the same. Angelo made me feel special. Then, after the first thrill had passed, I realised I'd never met any of his family or close friends; we stayed over together at my place rather than his. I began to wonder if I was the other woman."

She must have been waiting for someone to confide in. She poured out all sorts of stuff. The more she said, the more convinced I became that this thing between her and Angelo wasn't going anywhere. How could I tell her, though?

"If I take up this job offer and go back to New Zealand, it will mean starting again from the beginning — online dating, getting friends to set me up." Marie-Ann shuddered. "I'm not sure if I can bear it."

"It might be exciting," I suggested, realising that if Eden and I split for good, I'd have to do the same.

"Trust me, it won't." She fidgeted with her glass. "Look, thanks for listening, though. It's helped."

"I could try talking to Valentina, or to my friend Coco." My offer was impulsive. "I can't promise it'll get me anywhere. They're both pretty cagey."

"It's the Venetian character, isn't it? Just one of the things that drives me crazy about the place." Marie-Ann ran through the others: the heavy fogs in winter, the oppressiveness of the dark tunnels and alleyways, the push and shove to get on to a *vaporetto*, the high price of almost everything. "It's a lot to put up with for the lovely views. You haven't been here long enough, but you'll feel the same if you stick around."

"I've been thinking how much I'd like to stay," I admitted. "Venice might turn out to be one of the things I put on my happiness list."

"Oh, right, I'd forgotten about that. What else is on it now?"

I was reluctant to tell her. My list felt very private. But Marie-Ann had shared so much with me, it seemed churlish to hold back, so I reeled off what I'd managed to come up with so far. She didn't seem impressed.

"So parties, naps, dogs, Prosecco, coffee, tango, neighbourhoods . . . does that add up to much? Surely happiness simply comes down to knowing how to enjoy life." She looked at me for a moment; one of those clear-eyed stares that leaves you feeling thoroughly sized-up. "Do you think this list is really going to change your life in any way?"

"I don't know yet."

"I mean, I get the psychology behind it. Focus on the positives not the negatives, make happiness a habit, don't forget to appreciate the little things, blah blah blah. I've read a few self-help books too."

"This isn't something I got out of a self-help book," I said defensively.

"No? What made you do it then?"

"I want to be happier, that's all. You think I'm wasting my time?"

"About as much as you think I'm wasting my time with Angelo."

Oddly enough, that broke the ice. Both of us laughed, we ordered a couple more drinks and for the next hour or so chatted like proper girlfriends.

Marie-Ann wasn't someone I'd have chosen to hang out with in the normal course of things. All the women I'm close to are spikier, funnier and much less controlled. I couldn't see her getting messy after too many wines, for instance. Couldn't imagine her on a Soho bar crawl or coming for a casual dinner in the chaos of my kitchen. We'd never laugh together till we cried or shriek so loudly people asked us to pipe down; I doubted she would do anything to surprise me. Still, I was warming to her.

Then I had one of my brilliant ideas. "You should come to Valentina's birthday party."

"I can't do that. I've never even met her."

"Not as a guest; as a worker."

I explained how I'd been roped in to help and how the guest list had grown as Coco's excitement had mounted.

"We'll need someone to pour drinks and pass round the food. I'll never manage it alone."

She seemed dubious. "How is being a waitress for a night going to help me?"

"Angelo has been invited. It's a chance to see him and Valentina together, make up your own mind if there's anything going on."

"I don't know." She sounded worried. "Won't he think it's weird if I'm there?"

"I'll tell him I asked you . . . which is the truth."

"Still, I'm not sure about putting myself in that position. Let me think about it, OK?"

In her place I'd have jumped at the chance.

"It's up to you, of course," I said. "But I'm not going to go poking about Angelo's apartment. You can do your own spying."

Coco had been scheming too, as I discovered the next morning when Angelo joined us for coffee and brioche. It was a Sunday, so the *osteria* was closed and he was planning to spend his day off relaxing at the Lido. She had demanded he stop by and see us first. It seemed she had come to her senses and realised the party was too big for us to manage.

"It's going to be spectacular," she told Angelo. "An occasion people will talk about and Valentina will never forget. However . . ."

"However what?"

"I'm a little concerned Addolorata has taken on too much offering to do the catering alone. You must help her, Angelo. That is the obvious solution. You can cook together, the pair of you. It will be your birthday gift to Valentina."

Angelo's lips twitched but he didn't quite smile. "I don't suppose I have any choice in the matter, do I?"

"Not at all," Coco agreed.

"Well then, it seems I am to be Dolly's sous chef."

"Perfect." Coco sounded satisfied. "I'll leave Addolorata to tell you what we're planning. I'm going home before this sun gets too hot for me to bear."

Once he'd kissed her goodbye, Angelo ordered more coffee. He seemed tired that morning. It was a tiredness I recognised: the jittery, grey-faced, emptied-out exhaustion of a chef at the end of a working week.

"Don't you love my aunt Coco?" he said. "Never worked a day in her life yet always finding jobs for other people to do."

"When I agreed to cook, it was only a small gathering," I told him.

"I can believe that." He yawned, then sighed. "Let's not worry about it now, though. I'm going to spend the day lying on the beach and I don't want to think about anything."

"Sounds like an excellent plan."

"Why don't you come with me? Coco's right, it's going to be hot. The Lido is the best place to be on days like this."

When I'd decided to stay on in Venice, I'd spent an alarming amount of money on a swimming costume. It was made from a soft Lycra that held me in without squishing the life out of me, and was the most flattering piece of swimwear I'd ever owned. Even so, I wasn't thrilled at the idea of wearing it to lie beside Angelo on a beach.

I found an excuse. "Actually I'm supposed to be walking the Contessa's dog."

Angelo dismissed it. "In an hour's time that dog will be trying to find somewhere cool to lie down and pant. He won't want to go walking. Come to the beach instead."

The day was humid and I could already feel myself heating up uncomfortably. I let myself be persuaded. "All right then, why not."

We walked back to my apartment together. While I ran upstairs, Angelo waited below in the shade of

Coco's garden wall. It took only a moment to stuff a few things into my beach bag — sun lotion, towel, hat, a long kimono top, a book and a magazine. Even so, Angelo was impatient to be off.

"I need to dive into the sea," he told me.

He claimed he knew a short cut to the *vaporetto* stop, so I raced after him down a series of narrow alleys and covered passages. It was a more complicated route than I usually took and I wasn't convinced about it being quicker, but still I followed.

The boat ride to the Lido is not especially long. Something Angelo had said about Coco had piqued my curiosity. Had she really never worked a day in her life? I decided to wait until we were on the beach and there was more time to ask him about it.

From the Lido *vaporetto* stop we joined a parade of locals and tourists walking the stretch of tree-lined street that led to the beaches. Reaching the seafront, the crowd dispersed, heading to separate sections of the long strip of groomed sand, some to the public beaches, others to the more exclusive private ones where you can hire a small wooden cabin or one of a regiment of beach umbrellas spaced along the sand. Some charge extra for showers and toilets, for a locker to put your valuables in, for a second sunlounger. I was shocked at how steep the prices were.

"No wonder Coco never comes. I don't expect they're open to haggling either."

Angelo laughed and insisted on paying. "You can buy me a drink or some pizza at lunchtime."

Once settled on our loungers beneath a yellow sun umbrella, I watched him strip down to a pair of tight Speedos. He had a great body; it was lean and muscled in all the right places, his skin tawny and smooth. I shrank a little further inside my loose kimono.

"Coming for a swim?" he asked.

"Not right now; maybe later."

With a shrug he turned towards the sea, running barefoot over the sand and into the water, stopping knee-deep to splash it over his body until he glistened. He dived beneath the surface, and a moment later I spotted his dark head bobbing back up and he raised an arm to wave at me.

If Marie-Ann could see us here together, she'd be certain something was going on. I wouldn't have blamed her. At times I wasn't sure what was happening myself. When Angelo and I danced, our bodies in harmony, pressed so close I was enfolded in the scent of his skin and hair, it was impossible not to feel an attraction. But outside of the tango he seemed untouchable. Drinking a Prosecco afterwards at the bar in the piazza, it was difficult to believe that moments earlier I'd been in his arms.

He was walking out of the sea now, water streaming from him. Stopping at the tideline, he shook the droplets from his hair and stood there staring at the horizon until the sun had dried the salt on his skin.

"Better?" I asked when he came back and flopped down on his sunlounger.

He grinned. "Yes, much better. You should go in. The water is not especially clean, but it's the perfect temperature."

Lying on a beach is not something I'm good at. Half an hour or so is fine, but after that I start getting fidgety. Do I lie on my stomach with my face pushed into my towel? Or stay on my back with a book held over my eyes to shield them from the sun? Neither position seems entirely comfortable. Then there's the endless smearing of creams, and sand sticking to skin. The creases of the body moistening with sweat. Getting hotter and hotter. Feeling baked by the sun.

Beside me Angelo had fallen asleep sprawled on his back and was making snuffling sounds as his chest rose and fell. I swung my legs off the lounger and slipped off my kimono. This was my chance for a quick dip.

The sand was scorching and I hopscotched over it towards the sea, plunging in as fast as I could, dipping my head beneath the rippling waves. I might not care for beach life, but I love to wallow in salt water.

Around me children shrieked and played. I closed my eyes and tipped my face to the sky. How long was it since Eden and I had taken Katia to the beach? Last summer had passed without a proper holiday, and the one before.

The problem wasn't really taking the time off work. It was the planning: finding places and booking them, packing bags then unpacking again. All of it seemed far too much trouble. I just couldn't be bothered with it.

Now I felt bad. It should be Eden dozing on a sunlounger, Katia shrieking and playing. As I struck off at a slow crawl and swam out deeper, I had a sense of missing my family that was so intense it became physical. My heart raced and I stopped swimming. For a few moments I stayed there treading water, buffeted by the waves, trying to get a grip on myself.

What was wrong with me? One minute I was longing to stay here in Venice and start a new life; the next I was desperate for the old one back. Marie-Ann had been right: my happiness list wasn't getting me anywhere. I was further away than ever from knowing what I really wanted.

Angelo was still sleeping when I got back, and snoring properly now. The woman sitting beneath the next-door beach umbrella gave me a sympathetic smile. She must have assumed he was my husband or boyfriend. Smiling back at her, I towelled myself dry and threw my kimono back on.

As Angelo dozed away the morning, I tried to read. The book I'd brought with me was a murder mystery and my mind kept wandering away from its plot. I found myself thinking about my family and Valentina's; how hard we had to work at our jobs; the sheer effort we put into every day. And then I thought of Coco partying her way through a seemingly charmed life. How had she managed it? Where were the rest of us going wrong?

It was gone lunchtime when Angelo woke. I passed the time watching families clustered round their beach cabins feasting on trays of baked macaroni, veal escalopes sandwiched in crusty bread, garlicky braised chicken legs, salads spiked with crisp radicchio. People were passing tastes of dishes from cabin to cabin, splashing wine in each other's glasses, sating their appetites noisily and with obvious enjoyment.

"Pizza?" I said to Angelo the moment he opened his eyes.

He glanced at his watch. "Did I sleep so long? You should have woken me."

"You seemed like you needed it. Still, I don't think I could have waited much longer. I'm starving."

"Just a quick dip to wake me properly, then we'll eat," he promised.

True to his word, he plunged into the water and came straight out, wrapping a towel round his waist. "OK, pizza," he said. "*Andiamo.*"

We ordered at the beach bar. The pizza they produced was layered with thin slices of prosciutto and tasted surprisingly good.

"I've had food envy," I told Angelo, biting into a slice. "You should see what some of these people have been serving up for their picnics."

"Ah, Sunday lunch at the Lido; it was my family's tradition too when I was a child. Mamma was up at dawn to start cooking."

"Did you help her?"

"No, I was more interested in sleeping back then. Food was something I never thought about. It appeared on the table and I ate it. Then my mother took a job and it became my sister Donatella's task to prepare the evening meal. Donatella is the worst cook in the world. She can't make even a simple soup or pasta. She doesn't care about what she eats. For her a meal is something to get over as quickly as possible. But my parents and I, we do care. And so I learnt to cook a few dishes and took Donatella's place in the kitchen."

"I was hardly ever allowed to cook when I was growing up," I told him. "My father owned our kitchen. He insisted on my sister and me being there every mealtime, and fed us extra garlic on nights when we were going out on a date."

Angelo laughed. "A typical Italian papa, yes?"

"At the time I thought he was a nightmare. Now I realise it was his way of being in control of his family . . . his life. So long as there was plenty of food in the cupboards, a pot of something simmering on the stove, he felt like we were properly looked after."

"But you are a chef, yes? Coco told me so. How did you learn?"

"I cooked as a kind of rebellion, because I knew Papa didn't want me to. Eventually he had to teach me, but reluctantly and often omitting to mention the one ingredient that made a dish special." I smiled at the memory. "I'd see his hand close round something and he'd slip it into the pan. It might take me a while, but in the end I always figured out what it was."

"He sounds like a character," said Angelo.

"Yes, he is . . . in a good way mostly."

"Like my aunt Coco then."

"No, he's not like her at all . . . but I see what you mean. They're both eccentric" I reached for another slice of pizza then hesitated. "Earlier you said that Coco has never worked a day in her life. Is that really true?"

"She might tell you otherwise, I suppose, but that's my mother's version of her story."

"How has she lived, then?"

"On her wits, I think."

It took a few beers drunk in the hot sun to loosen Angelo's tongue properly. Some of Coco's story was what I'd expected to hear. Other parts of it surprised me.

"According to my mother, Coco always wanted the best of everything, even when they were children," he told me. "She was the eldest child and bossy. Mamma recalls being scared of her — I think there was a lot of hair-pulling and pinching of the younger girls."

"That doesn't sound like Coco. I can't imagine it at all."

"My other aunts have said the same, so it must be true. They were relieved when she started spending all her time with the Viadro family. But being with them only gave her grander ideas. You have seen photographs of my aunt when she was younger? She was very beautiful, but Mamma says it was more than that. She speaks of the way Coco held herself, of her confidence, of her absolute faith in the person she was."

"Yes, I see that about her. I suppose it's what makes her beautiful even now she's old."

"Sadly for Coco, it didn't matter how special she believed herself to be. As the eldest girl, she had to leave school at thirteen and stay home to help her mother cook and clean and look after the younger ones."

"She must have hated that."

Angelo sipped his beer. "She put up with it for a few years and then she ran away with a man called Carlo Rizzoli. He was much older than her, someone she had met at the Viadro family's palazzo. Mamma says there was a huge fuss. At first he refused to marry her, until pressure was applied and finally a wedding took place."

"It can't have been a very happy marriage."

"Even if the marriage was a bad one, she'd have been stuck with him. In Italy there was no divorce in those days."

"So the house and all the money she's lived on ever since; that came from him?"

"I'm not sure. It might have been part of a settlement, but for some reason my mother doesn't think so."

"You don't paint a very flattering picture of Coco."

He shrugged. "She is who she is."

I felt as if some of Coco's past had been shaded in. But Angelo was young; he hadn't been there for any of it. Everything I'd learnt from him so far came second-hand.

"Did you see much of her when you were a child?" I asked.

"Not really," he told me. "She would turn up to family gatherings and be the centre of attention for a while, and when she left, everyone would talk about her."

I laughed; I could imagine it.

"I did see more of her as I got older," said Angelo. "She used to take me places: cocktail parties, dances and exhibition openings. She said it was an important part of my education, but Mamma always believed she only did it to make her jealous."

At that I laughed again. "I imagine your mother doesn't like Coco much."

"They're very different women, and no, they don't get on. But I have a lot to be grateful to Coco for. She took me to my first *milonga*, and helped when I was setting up my business, as I've told you."

"And introduced you to Valentina as well?" I guessed.

"She introduced me to many people," he said offhandedly. "Coco knows just about everyone, as you'll have noticed."

Angelo refused another beer and so I bought us each a *gelato* instead and we ate them walking along the tideline, dodging sandy-bottomed children as we splashed through the shallows. We carried on past the boundary of our beach; the colours of the sun umbrellas changed to blue and the cabins were slightly different, but otherwise the scene was the same. People playing ball games on the flat stretch of sand, kids with buckets and spades, bodies baking in the sun and sleeping off lunch.

"This feels like being on holiday," I said.

"You are on holiday, aren't you?" Angelo replied.

"Not exactly, it's more of a hiatus."

Of course then I had to explain about my happiness experiment. Angelo seemed bemused by the idea at first. He shook his head in disbelief.

"So you're taking an entire summer to write a list of what makes you happy." There was laughter in his

278

voice. "Why is it taking so long? I could give you my list right this minute."

"I bet you couldn't."

"It wouldn't be difficult at all."

"Go on then, ten things that make you happy . . . starting now."

Without so much as a pause, he began. "Being on a beach, eating a *gelato*, the bustle of the Rialto market first thing in the morning when I get to work, a drink at my favourite *bacaro* after I've finished for the day. Those are four things; OK, so I need six more . . . Oh, dancing, of course. Tango makes me happy. Travel, although I don't do enough of it. Movies. Friends. Sex. Surprises. How many is it now?"

"Ten." I had been counting.

"See, how easy was that?" He sounded smug. "I can't see why you're having so much trouble."

"I'm trying to reduce everything down to the very essence of what makes me happy . . . not just banging off a quick list," I told him.

"Even if I thought about it all year long, my answers wouldn't be so different," he insisted. "You're overcomplicating things."

We walked in silence after that, tracing the tideline side by side. I was busy doubting myself; wondering if Angelo was right. I have no idea what he was thinking, but when I glanced at him his brow was creased into a frown.

After a couple of kilometres he suggested we turn back. Picking up his pace, he walked slightly ahead of me. That meant I could watch him; see the strength in his thighs, admire the width of his shoulders. I noticed the looks he got from women, even a few of the middle-aged men as he passed them by. And I thought how nice it must feel to be so good-looking and certain of yourself.

Eventually he slowed and let me catch up. "So, Dolly, you will make your list and then you'll go home and change your life? Is that it?"

"Things may pan out that way," I said. "You see, I sort of fell into the life I have."

"Surely everyone does?"

"Yes, but me more so I think. I took over the family business. I married my first real boyfriend. Those were the easy options, the obvious ones. It doesn't mean they were right."

"It takes courage to change direction," Angelo said thoughtfully.

"I know that. I'm not sure if I can do it. Or if I even want to."

"You're confused, then."

"Yes, and the more I think about it, the more confused I get," I admitted. "If I'm overcomplicating things, I'm doing a pretty good job of it."

Angelo took another dip in the sea when we got back to our bit of the long beach. I stood calf-deep and paddled, watching him cut through the water. There weren't many other people swimming and he had enough space to get into a proper rhythm, arms swinging, head turning. He swam like he danced, boldly and freely.

When he'd had enough, he came and stood with me in the shallows.

"I've been thinking about my list," he said, smoothing strands of wet hair from his eyes.

"Do you want to add even more things to it?"

"No, I've decided it's the wrong approach. In your place I would make a different kind of list altogether."

"Of what?"

"My goals, the things I want to achieve and have; the way I want my life to progress."

"Like Marie-Ann then? That's what her list was all about."

"It was? And what did she have on it?"

I laughed. "Sorry, but if I'm to be the keeper of the lists, I have to be discreet."

That evening I called home and had another go at talking Eden into letting Katia fly over for the school holidays, even suggesting he come too.

"We could go to the beach; it's really close by," I told him. "And I'm sure Coco wouldn't mind us all cramming into the apartment for a couple of weeks."

He grunted something, I'm not sure what.

"There's no reason why Katia should miss out on having fun this summer just because you and I aren't getting on," I said.

That was greeted with silence.

"Eden, are you still there? What do you think?"

"Yeah, look, I'm busy with work," he said gruffly.

"Can't you get away for a short while?"

"Nah, there's a few problems with this building Pieta and Michele have leased. This is a really bad time."

"So send Katia over on her own then. You could put her on the plane and I'd meet her at the other end. She'd cope."

I heard him sigh. "Dolly, no . . ."

"Why not?" I tried to keep my voice level.

"Well, for a start, your mother has offered to look after her for the holidays. They've got all sorts of treats planned and they're really looking forward to it."

"What about me? Don't I deserve some time with my own child?"

"You made your choice. You can't have it both ways."

"Oh stuff you, Eden, why do you have to be so stubborn?"

I was furious with him. "What difference does it make if she comes to me for a few days? This is you using our child to hurt me. I can't believe you'd stoop so low. I can't bloody believe it . . ."

I ranted for a while. I'm not sure at what point he hung up, but eventually I realised I was speaking to empty air. I was so angry I carried on shouting anyway.

Once I'd calmed down a little, I poured a glass of wine and started hatching plans. What if I headed home and insisted Katia came for a holiday? Brought her back here myself. How could Eden stop me then? My mother could come too. We'd all three of us explore Venice together. It would be fun.

Several glasses in, I realised it was useless. If I went home, I'd never escape again. In no time I'd be up to my neck in my broken marriage and my business problems. This summer in Venice was a once-in-a-lifetime thing, a precious chance to be clear about what I really wanted. I wasn't ready to give up on that yet.

Finishing my wine, I opened a second bottle.

CHAPTER
EIGHTEEN

It was morning and I was curled up on the sofa. My head ached, my mouth was dry and someone was knocking on the door. I tried to ignore it, but the knocking only grew more insistent.

"Who is it?" I croaked.

"Me, who do you think?" Coco sounded impatient. "Let me in."

"Just a minute."

When I stood up, my head throbbed. I checked the mirror and frowned at my reflection. My clothes were crumpled, my hair was flattened on one side and frizzy on the other. My eyes were pink and watery, the bags beneath them extra puffy.

Coco, of course, looked new-day fresh. She was wearing a wrap dress in a bold floral print and three strands of chunky orange beads round her neck.

"I looked for you at the *milonga* last night but you never appeared," she said, wrinkling her nose as she came into my stuffy apartment. "What happened?"

"I meant to go but I . . . got sidetracked by something."

Coco had spotted the empty bottles. "You had company?"

"No."

She raised her eyebrows. "You must need coffee rather badly then. Shall I make it or will we go out?"

"I need to take a shower, get changed . . ."

"In that case I'll make it. Come and join me when you're ready."

When I made my way down to the garden, freshly showered but still feeling seedy, Coco had pulled the table into a shady corner and set out coffee and warm bread rolls with butter and honey to spread on them. She let me eat before she began plying me with questions. What was wrong? Who had upset me? Was it Angelo?

"No, it's a family thing."

"Ah, I see. Still . . . two bottles and you drank them all by yourself?" She was disapproving.

"Yep." I didn't have to justify myself to her.

"Angelo was surprised you would miss the *milonga*. He thinks you should be taking every chance you have to practise."

Crumbling the remains of the bread roll on my plate, I shrugged.

"You are quite sure Angelo didn't do something to upset you?" she asked.

"No, of course not."

"You were with him all day at the beach, weren't you?"

"Yes, we went to the Lido. We had a nice time."

"Did you discuss the food for my party? Have you finalised the menu?"

"Not yet."

"But why not?" Coco sounded snippy.

"We didn't get round to talking about it."

She tilted her chin at me. "I expected you to take this more seriously." I didn't bother to reply.

"At this rate you're going to let everyone down."

"Look, I don't need this," I told her. "If it's going to turn into a big drama, I'll back out of it."

She glared at me. "You can't do that."

"Yes I bloody well can."

I had raised my voice and Coco seemed taken aback. Then she managed a smile, and reaching over, patted my hand.

"Darling, I think you're overtired. Why don't you go back to bed for a while; take a rest. You'll feel better for it."

The thought of cool sheets and a darkened room was appealing. Boris could wait until later for his walk; everyone and everything could wait till later. Bed was all I could face. "Yes, you're right. I need to lie down . . ."

Pulling the sheets over my head, I dozed fitfully, disturbed now and then by everyday sounds. A workman a couple of doors down using an electric drill; a group of tourists trundling their suitcases down the *fondamenta* below; Coco playing tango music; a gondolier shouting to his friends. It struck me that this was exactly what I'd be doing on a normal Monday morning at home: trying to have a lie-in while London geared up all around me, and Eden got Katia to school.

286

So much for being in a different place; it seemed everything was still the same.

I was impatient with myself. I hated being like this. If only there was something I could do to feel better instantly; a pill I could take, or a tonic. I thought about phoning Pieta. Often a chat with her was enough to cheer me a little.

It was still early at home. I called her mobile number and she answered on the second ring. "Hey, Dolly."

"Hey," I replied.

"Everything OK?"

"Ah, sort of," I told her. "What about you?"

Pieta launched into a monologue. "God no, it's all a nightmare at the moment. Subsidence, rot and who knows what else has been uncovered in that building we've taken on. It hasn't stopped raining here. The kids have been sick with some puking thing we've all caught. And I seem to have all these impossible brides who can't stay the same dress size for a minute." She started telling me about one of them in more detail. I half switched off as she went on about French lace, Chinese silk and beading.

"Oh hell, I have to go," she said just as I was about to interrupt. "I'm having another wave of nausea. I'll talk to you soon . . ."

After she hung up, I stayed in bed, kicking my feet against the wall. Then I decided that the only thing likely to make me feel better was to get up and get going. I sent a text to Angelo asking if he was free to talk about the party menu. *Coco is on the warpath*, I told him.

A few minutes later the reply came back. *Don't worry, I've been thinking about it. Come over earlier if you like.*

On Mondays the fish market was closed so Angelo didn't open his *osteria*. Normally we scheduled a tango lesson for some point in the late afternoon. It was only just past lunchtime by then and I knew he didn't mean for me to arrive quite that early; still, I had to get out of the apartment.

Trying to sort my appearance took a while. I drank a couple of glasses of Coca-Cola as I smoothed on an arsenal of creams and concealers. Both perked me up a little. Once I looked more acceptable, I crept downstairs and past Coco's door.

Angelo seemed surprised to find me on his doorstep, but not displeased. He suggested we go and find a shady spot in the *campo* where we could sit and talk about the party menu. He brought along a list he'd made but started talking excitedly about brioche fillings and crostini toppings before I'd had a chance to read it.

Food hadn't been the most important part of my time in Venice so far. There were the lunches I cooked for Nanda and the odd meal I made in the apartment, but mostly I survived on *cicchetti* or hunks of bread with cheese and salad. It was such a change from my London life, where the greater part of every day was spent cooking, or at least thinking about it. I hadn't missed it really, but now listening to Angelo felt a little like coming home.

288

He shared his ideas for finger food and a more substantial risotto, little sweet treats and a late supper to serve to those who couldn't bear to leave. He favoured a fusion style of cuisine and I wanted to keep things more Venetian. We argued, crossed things off his list and added others. Sitting in the busy *campo*, as women passed with shopping trolleys or toddlers in tow, and tourists stopped to admire the ancient church and bell tower, it felt as if Angelo and I shared a language none of them could understand.

We kept talking even once we'd decided on our menu. We discussed places we'd eaten, dishes we'd tried, things we loved and couldn't live without, ingredients we despised. I remember we grew especially heated on the subject of most flavoured olive oils (disgusting). Angelo had a long rant about molecular gastronomy (playing with food). I might have had a bit of a vent about restaurant critics (know-nothings). Then we got on to difficult customers and psychopathic kitchen staff. And it was fun talking to him like that. He made me laugh. He made me feel better.

"I'm looking forward to cooking with you, Dolly," he told me. "We'll have a good time, I think."

"I hope so. Coco was stressing me out about it earlier."

"Yes, what is wrong with Coco?"

"I don't know. She's gone crazy about this party. She's over-excited."

"I suppose it's been a long time since she's had an occasion like this one to get excited about," he said. "That must be it, I guess."

We talked about food for half the afternoon, and when we'd finished with that, our conversation turned to dancing. Angelo told me about a teacher he'd had, an older and very experienced woman who had changed the tango for him completely.

"She showed me how to dance from my heart rather than my head. I think that is the most difficult thing of all to learn," he said.

"How do you know when you're dancing from the heart?" I asked.

Angelo looked thoughtful. "It's one of those things that's different for everyone. For me it's when I accept myself. I stop worrying about whether I'm boring my partner with the steps I'm repeating; stop focusing on her enjoyment or even my own and stay in the moment, stay in the feeling. That's when I'm dancing from my heart."

He sounded so sincere and serious. Sitting on that bench, his thigh close to mine, leaning back with his hands crossed behind his head, he looked very beautiful;

"Sometimes it's like I'm nearly there," I told him. "Then I'll find myself worrying about the steps I'm dancing or my balance will be all wrong and I'll lose that feeling."

"You'll find it more and more if you keep trying," he promised me. "It's like learning to be a good cook: it takes time, hard work and patience. It can't be rushed."

"We are rushing, though, aren't we?" I pointed out. "If we're going to take part in this tango show in a few weeks, then we have to."

He looked at me. "You don't have to come up on stage with me; I'm not going to force you. There will be other dancers there that evening so no one will miss us. But I think it would be a shame. Performing has such an amazing energy about it; it's a thrill. You ought to feel it."

"I haven't practised enough," I argued. "Coco's right about that."

"Let's dance now, then." Angelo got to his feet. "Right here in broad daylight?"

Angelo nodded. "In Buenos Aires they dance everywhere, day or night. On the street corners and in the plazas, the markets and parks, and although you know it's only for the tourists nowadays, still it is beautiful."

"So you've been, then? You went even though Valentina wouldn't go with you?"

"Yes, I went . . . and I came back." He held out his hand. "Addolorata, please stop talking and dance."

Of all the times I danced the tango with Angelo, before and after, that afternoon in the bright, sun-filled *campo* was when it felt most glorious. There was no music, my footwork wasn't flawless, I still had more dash than true skill, but it didn't seem to matter.

Angelo felt it too, I could tell. When I looked into his face, he was smiling. "You will perform with me. Of course you will," he said. "You want to."

I'm not sure how long we stayed there. I heard the sound of children's voices when the nearby school let out. The shadows lengthened and the tables outside the bar began to fill. People on their way home from work paused to watch us.

Angelo's feet stopped moving but still he didn't release me from the embrace. "You are tired?" he asked.

"Yes," I said.

"Let's go back to my place then and rest."

It seemed natural for us to lie down on his bed together, fully dressed and on top of the sheets. Angelo turned his back to me and quickly fell asleep. Exhausted from so much dancing, I closed my eyes and drifted off too.

I had one of those wonderful afternoon naps, two hours of complete obliteration, and woke to find that Angelo had shifted position. Now his body was spooning mine, his hand resting lightly on my hip, his breath on my neck. It felt so nice that I didn't dare move in case I disturbed him.

Sometimes Eden and I would lie like this, but not very often. Even in the early days it happened only when he wanted it, and it always led to sex. But this wouldn't, I told myself. This was two friends resting together, not so different from being side by side on sunloungers at the Lido or on a bench in the *campo*. Not so different to bodies touching in the tango. It meant nothing at all.

Then Angelo's fingers began to move. They stroked my hip, setting up an easy rhythm, drifted towards my belly and slipped beneath my T-shirt, warm against my skin. They moved in long strokes, exploring further and

292

further. I almost held my breath as I waited for him to say something.

Angelo didn't speak. His face brushed the nape of my neck; his breath felt hot. He covered my legs with one of his and I felt him press into me. I let out a moan.

He half laughed at the sound, as if it was what he had been waiting for, and his movements grew surer. He stroked further and deeper. And then he put me on my back and slid his body over mine. Still fully dressed, we pushed against each other like teenagers.

Angelo began to move me with his hips and with his hands. I went this way and that, just as he wanted. We shucked off our clothes and I forgot to be awkward about myself. Every sensation felt new, but at the same time his touch was familiar.

I almost heard the tango music in my head. Our skin was slick with sweat; our breath ragged. I followed Angelo, just like I'd learnt to and practised over and over, and we made love and it felt just as beautiful as dancing.

Only when it was finished did he speak.

"OK?" he asked.

"Yes." It was all I could manage.

He pushed the hair from my face and smoothed it back. "Are you hungry? I'm going to make a big plate of spaghetti with squid ink and lots of *peperoncino*."

To my surprise, I was starving. Then I realised that all I had eaten all day was Coco's bread rolls and honey.

"I think there is some radicchio," he continued. "I could braise it with olive oil and lemon juice. Or perhaps a few baby artichokes simmered with garlic. Let me go and see exactly what I have."

He climbed out of bed and shrugged on the cotton shorts he'd tossed on to the floor earlier. Taking a silky robe from a hook on the back of the door, he left it on the bed for me.

"Come when you're ready," he said.

The robe smelt of another woman's fragrance; Marie-Ann's perhaps, although she'd said she hardly ever came here, or maybe Valentina's. I put it on anyway and tied the thin belt round my waist. I suppose I was shocked at myself, shocked but not sorry. I felt too good for that . . . I felt amazing.

Angelo emptied the fridge for me. He sliced a lean piece of beef very thinly and served it smothered with olive oil, shaved Parmesan and slivers of mustard fruit. While we were devouring that, he puréed some cooked cauliflower with softly braised leek and covered it in salted fish roe. Then came the spaghetti, and we ate it hungrily without caring about our ink-stained mouths. Finally he produced two elegant stemmed glasses and filled them with crushed amaretti biscuits soaked in vermouth and covered with mascarpone whipped with eggs and sugar. I ran my spoon round the empty glass to catch every last hint of the sweet creaminess.

"That was a feast, thank you," I said when I had finished.

"You're welcome. I like to feed a hungry woman."

294

I wasn't sure what was meant to happen next. Should I leave, or did Angelo intend for us to spend the night together? He was busy clearing up and stacking plates in the dishwasher. I offered to help but he shrugged me away.

"Relax, put some music on, some tango."

"You want to dance again?" I asked him.

He looked at me and smiled. "I want to do it all again. Don't you?"

CHAPTER
NINETEEN

I knew I ought to feel sorry, but somehow that only made it more exciting. When I slipped back to my apartment early the next day, careful not to wake Coco, I was sore and satisfied.

I sat out on the balcony in the morning sunshine, drinking black coffee and smoking a cigarette. Then I took a shower, remembering his touch on my body as the warm water ran over me. Washing off the smell of him, I told myself no one need ever know. I liked having a secret. It made me feel more interesting.

I'll never entirely regret that night; even after all that's happened, even though I shouldn't have done it. I've thought a lot about how angry I'd have been if Eden had done the same. Later, I felt guilty — bad for him and Marie-Ann too. But right then that night seemed the tonic I needed and I wasn't thinking about guilt at all. In a far lighter mood than the day before, I dressed in one of the sweet summer frocks Coco had lent me and went down to knock on her door.

"Oh, it's you," she said a little sourly. "Am I safe to talk to you?"

"I'm sorry about yesterday. Can I buy you breakfast to apologise?"

Coco looked me up and down. "You do seem better. You have a healthier colour and that dress suits you. Put on a little lipstick then I'll let you take me out."

That morning we walked a little further than our usual place, to a touristy spot where the tables were set out along the canal. Coco was wearing a wide-brimmed green hat and a yellow shift dress teamed with a bold acrylic flower necklace. Heads turned as we sat down, and she smiled. She enjoyed attracting attention.

"Did you sleep away all of yesterday?" she asked. "You were very quiet up there."

"I went out to see Angelo."

Hearing that I had spent the afternoon planning menus with him pleased her.

"And so my little party is organised." Coco made an expansive gesture with her hands. "Now all we have to do is decide on our outfits."

"I'll be cooking," I reminded her. "I won't be dressing up."

"Still you must look beautiful. You won't be in the kitchen all night long. I think what you need is a chic black dress you can pop an apron over. We should go shopping. There's a place in Santa Croce where I'm sure they'll have the perfect thing at a very good price."

"OK, but not today. I've been neglecting poor Boris. I haven't walked him for days."

Coco looked at her own small dogs and stroked their silky heads. "How silly of Nanda to have such a big creature when there's no way she can exercise it."

"That's what Valentina says too."

She sighed. "My dear old friend, she doesn't have an ounce of sense. Everything she does seems to make Valentina's life more difficult. Thank goodness we are throwing this party for her. The child deserves to feel special for an evening."

"Coco, have you thought any more about how we're going to pay for the food and wine we'll need? Angelo can get things wholesale, but even so it's going to be a pretty steep bill."

"Leave it to me. Everything is under control."

"It's not far away," I pointed out.

"I know, such a busy time, isn't it exciting? First our party, then a week later the Festa del Redentore. We'll need to decide on different outfits. Something colourful for the Festa, of course, and I think you should buy new shoes, it would be an investment . . ."

I let her talk about the perfect clothes for different occasions without really listening. It was concerning me, this business of paying for the party. While I didn't mind contributing, I couldn't afford to be stuck with a big bill. Coco kept promising to take care of it; still, I wasn't convinced. Often it felt like she lived in a fantasy world. She had a talent for avoiding the things she didn't want to see or know. I really hoped the reality of paying for this party wasn't one of them.

Coco must have guessed what I was thinking. "Stop fretting, Addolorata," she scolded. "Soon I will have more than enough to cover all the bills. You need to trust me. Really, I'm most offended that you don't."

Valentina's party was meant to be a surprise for her, but so much fuss had been made and so many invitations sent out that inevitably word had got back. She was at the palazzo that morning when I arrived, and it was clear she wasn't pleased.

"You are part of this plot, yes?" she asked, holding on to Boris's collar as if I was about to steal him.

"Your mother asked if I'd help."

"And Coco, she is involved?"

"Her and Angelo too."

This only seemed to further agitate her. "Angelo? Surely he's learnt by now that I'm not interested in him interfering in my life."

"It's a party; a nice thing people want to do for you," I reasoned. "Coco and your mother have been excited planning everything. They're getting so much pleasure from it. And it was your mother's idea in the first place. She means it as a treat for you."

Her expression pained, Valentina half closed her eyes. "Oh God, I know. Poor Mamma. To her I'm still a little girl who loves parties."

"And you don't love them?"

"If I'd wanted one I'd have organised it myself." She sounded exasperated. "Now I'm being railroaded. That's what I'm objecting to. Why is it everyone seems to think they know what's best for me? No one bothers to ask. Did I ever say I'd like to have a birthday party? No!"

"Cancel it then. It's not too late. Although Coco will have a meltdown and your mother will be upset."

"I'm not at all concerned about Coco ... but Mamma ..." Valentina's face softened. "I suppose she is looking forward to it; a party like the ones she and Papa used to throw."

"She's been the most animated I've known her. Really sparkling," I told her.

"Yes, I've seen the change in her. But I thought it was having company again, yours and Coco's. If I'd realised what was going on ..." Valentina heaved a sigh. "I can't stop this thing now, can I? I may as well add my friends to the guest list and do my best to enjoy it."

"Yes," I agreed. "You should do that."

"Does Angelo have to be involved?"

"He's helping with the cooking."

"Of course he is." She sighed again. "And I expect he'll take over completely and we'll all have to be grateful for it. That's how it is with Angelo."

It was late when we escaped for our walk and too hot by then for a big shaggy dog like Boris. I went slowly and stuck to the shady side of the street, stopping at a bar to beg a bowl of water for him when he started panting heavily. I had intended to go all the way to the Rialto to buy ingredients for a *sarde en saor* for Nanda's lunch, but giving up on that idea, I turned back earlier.

Boris seemed glad to get home. He lay on the cool marble floor of the kitchen, his head on his paws, watching as I pottered round looking for ingredients. There was no pasta left, so I made dough from eggs and semolina flour and cut it into dusty streamers of *pappardelle*. I soaked dried porcini mushrooms, fried up garlic with lots of pancetta, covered it with a few splashes of a Marsala wine I found in the back of a cupboard and let it simmer down. What I needed was cream, but there was none in the fridge, so I threw in a slab of butter instead. I like cooking this way, making the most of what I have. I suppose it's my father's thriftiness coming through in me. And Nanda would be appreciative, no matter what I served. She was as grateful for the attention as much as the food, I think.

We ate together in the kitchen, since her little sitting room had grown stuffy in the heat of summer. Polishing off the *pappardelle*, she asked if there was more.

"You didn't come to me yesterday, or the day before," she complained as I emptied the pan into her bowl.

"Sorry, I was busy. What did you eat for lunch?"

"No one came and I was so hungry. I telephoned that *bacaro* Coco took me to. They sent over fresh *tramezzini* filled with smoked pork and some excellent meatballs, even a few prawns. It was delicious. Expensive though; I can't afford to do that very often."

I apologised again, explaining that I'd been with Angelo planning the menu for the party.

"Has Coco commanded his help too?" She sounded dismayed.

"He seems fine with it."

"Poor Angelo," she said.

I laughed. "What's so poor about him?"

"He is in love with my daughter, you know. She broke his heart."

I put the bowl in front of her. "Really? What happened?"

"Nobody ever tells me the details of these things." Absentmindedly Nanda forked up a wide ribbon of pasta. "There was a fight; that's all I know. Before that we all thought they were destined to marry."

"Were they together for long?"

"Since they were teenagers. When she was younger, Valentina used to follow the boy round like she was his puppy."

"I wonder what went wrong."

She shrugged. "Who knows? Perhaps she got sick of following him."

Nanda seemed to have said all she was going to for the moment. She concentrated on her food, finishing her second helping of pasta then patting her belly and complaining of being too full.

"I must rest to help my digestion." Pushing away her empty bowl, she stood. "Boris, my boy, come."

The dog fell in behind her as she left the room, abandoning me with the dirty dishes. There was nothing as high-tech as a dishwasher in the palazzo, of course, but I didn't mind washing up by hand. As children, Pieta and I had done it after dinner every evening. No one can trash a kitchen quite like my father. Every pan in the place gets used, and at times tomato sauce literally runs down the walls. Pieta has never been able to bear it unless order is restored completely, and cleaning up together was when we got to have a gossip and a laugh. As we got older, very often we'd sneak a cigarette sitting out on the back step afterwards. So now a sink of soapy water almost seems a reassuring thing to me. It means everyone is fed and all is as it should be.

When I got back to the apartment that afternoon, Coco's door was ajar. I called out a greeting and she told me to come in. I found her sitting at her kitchen table. She'd covered it with a soft cloth on which she had arranged several pieces of jewellery. These were very different to the bangles and beads she wore most days. There were a couple of gold rings, a bracelet, a necklace, a pair of earrings, a large brooch I'd once seen her pin to a turban; all old-fashioned designs and sparkling with what looked like diamonds.

"I'm saying goodbye to them," Coco told me. "I've had them a long time and I've never been tempted to sell even when times were hard. But now I'm going to."

"Why?" I asked, hoping she wasn't going broke.

"To pay for Valentina's party, of course. All of it is real. Don't worry, I know someone who'll pay me what they're worth."

I was shocked. "But, Coco, you can't do that." She looked at me. "You don't understand. I have to." "Valentina wouldn't want it. She doesn't even want a party, to be honest."

Coco held up the necklace. "This was extremely expensive. Lorenzo never should have spent that kind of money on me. It was foolish. But he liked to buy me things then take me to smart places to wear them."

"Valentina's father gave you all of this jewellery?"

"That's right."

"He must have been completely crazy about you."

Coco smiled a little sadly. "I never loved anyone like I loved him. He felt the same. We were extraordinary together."

"You mustn't sell it if it has such sentimental value," I argued.

Coco put down the necklace and slipped on one of the rings, holding out her hand to admire the way the diamonds sparkled. "I'm getting old; I have to think of what will happen to my things when I'm gone. I always meant to leave all this to Valentina, but she refuses to take it. She doesn't even want to come and have a look."

"Even though she needs the money?"

"I suppose she has her reasons." Coco slid the ring from her finger. "I know her well enough to be sure she'll never change her mind. So I will sell it all and use the money to give her the sort of party her father would have thrown if he'd been here."

"If she finds out . . ."

"She would be furious, I know. But she won't. Valentina will think her mother found a few last things to sell off. And perhaps she'll be a little cross with Nanda but the party will be wonderful and she'll forgive her."

I watched as Coco wrapped each piece of jewellery and locked it away in a wooden box. She turned the key with an air of finality.

"I hardly ever wear it anyway," she told me. "I lead a very different sort of life now from the one I had with Lorenzo."

She went to put the box away and on her return announced that she needed a great deal of gaiety to cheer her up. She had tickets for a concert at the famous La Fenice theatre but her friend Roberto had called to say he was unwell and couldn't accompany her.

"He was so upset to let me down. I told him not to worry, that you would be happy to take his place. The orchestra is playing Beethoven's Fifth. You will enjoy it."

I had been planning an early night because I hadn't managed much sleep the night before with Angelo, but Coco seemed genuinely low. And so I agreed to go.

La Fenice is so ridiculously ornate it's like being inside a shining jewel box. Our seats were close to the front; around us the private boxes soared upwards to meet the painted ceiling edged with carved figurines and more of the curlicues of gold that could be seen everywhere you looked. I knew my daughter would go crazy for it if she could see this place. And I was glad Coco had made me change into evening clothes, as I'd have felt completely underdressed in a simple summer frock.

While La Fenice looked impressive, the seats weren't especially comfortable. I expected to be bored by the music and was hoping it wouldn't go on too long. But from the very first note I was swept away.

I loved everything about it. Being in that amazing theatre and listening to the music fill it. Watching the orchestra, and the passion in their expressions. Seeing the violinists shred their bows as they played and the conductor almost dancing on the podium as he urged them onwards, and all of it just for us.

They played something else beside the Beethoven; I've no idea what it was, but I loved it just as much. When they'd finished, I surged up with the rest of the audience, clapping my hands and calling for more. I was almost bursting with the joy of it.

Even as we headed home, it felt as though I was walking more lightly than before. I kept telling Coco how incredible it had been and she laughed, replying several times, "Yes, I know, darling. I know."

When I got home, the first thing I did was find my notebook . . . which took ages because it was buried under a pile of clothes. It had been a while since I'd written in it, but at last I had something new to add.

Addolorata's Happiness List

8. Music. Not jingly-jangly pop tunes coming out of builders' radios. Real music. Sounds that soar and fill you with joy, echoing in your head long after the playing has finished.

CHAPTER
TWENTY

The text came through from Marie-Ann the next morning. Yes, she would love to waitress for the night at Valentina's party; thank you, it was a great idea. It was a heart-sinking moment. Things had changed since I'd made my impulsive offer. Now it seemed like a big mistake.

Quickly I sent back a message to say I'd found someone else to do the job. She replied immediately insisting she would come anyway. *Two will be better than one, surely*, she finished.

So I was in what my mother would call a pickle, and there seemed no way out of it. Angelo was going to think I was playing some sort of strange game. Still, I thought it best to break the news to him as soon as possible, in case Marie-Ann got in touch and mentioned it.

By now he'd be at work. If I passed by on my way to buy fresh sardines for Nanda's lunch, I might be able to catch him.

I slipped a note beneath Coco's door suggesting she join us at the palazzo later for a dish of *sarde en saor*, then set off pulling my empty trolley behind me. It was still early when I got to the market and there were no tourists yet, only locals. Many of the older ones had shopped at the same stalls pretty much for ever, and several times I'd had to wait impatiently while they were served ahead of me and prattled endlessly to the vendors about the ripeness of their peaches and the sweetness of their tomatoes.

I liked to move from stall to stall rather than favour only one. I picked up some *fondi di carciofo*, the tender bottom parts of the artichoke that can be bought all trimmed and ready to prepare. I found salad leaves that looked as if they'd just been harvested, then moved on to the fish market for the sardines.

Angelo was standing outside the door of his *osteria*, sipping an espresso and watching people pass by. He smiled when I caught his eye. We hadn't seen each other since I'd left his place yesterday morning, but there was no trace of awkwardness about him. Possibly he was accustomed to having casual flings and Marie-Ann had been right, there was another woman, or more than one. I remembered that silky robe he'd given me to wear, with the distinctly female scent clinging to it. Poor Marie-Ann.

"You're out early. What's going on?" he called as I drew closer.

"I'm buying fish to cook for the old ladies. And actually I hoped to see you. I have some news."

If anything he seemed amused when I told him. "Marie-Ann a waitress? That will be interesting. I suppose she is curious about Valentina and that's why she agreed."

"I guess so."

"Ah well, this will be their chance to meet." He said it lightly and I wondered if he cared for Marie-Ann at all, and if he realised what she wanted from him.

Finishing his coffee, Angelo turned to return to work. "You are coming tonight to the *milonga*, yes? I'll be at the bar round the corner if you want a quick drink first."

Having an arrangement to meet cast a new light on the rest of the day. Please don't get me wrong, I wasn't naïve enough to expect much from Angelo — certainly I wouldn't be trying to pin my future on him. But there was some adventure back in my days at last, excitement and unpredictability. Those were all the things I'd stopped expecting to find again, the things I'd desperately wanted in my London life, where every day seemed greyer than here and nothing ever changed. Tango was a big part of that; Angelo was part of tango.

Once I'd finished shopping, I took a *traghetto* across the Grand Canal and walked to the palazzo, planning to pick up Boris and take him to the park, then cook a lovely lunch for Coco and Nanda.

As I pushed through the mass of tourists seething down the Strada Nuova, I remembered arriving in Venice and wondering how I was going to fill the empty days of my holiday. Now I was busy. Almost every morning I woke to some sort of plan, but was never deluged like at home, never swept away in a flood of all the things I needed to do, never stressed or overwhelmed or unhappy for no particular reason. If only real life could be that way, there would be no need for lists at all.

Most of that day was spent at the palazzo in preparation for the party. We planned where the bar would be, and the dancing. Coco and Nanda helped me count up tableware and glasses to make sure there was enough of everything for all our guests.

I found some beautiful stuff tucked away in a large cupboard that Nanda unlocked: glass platters, vases, goblets and bowls made by Lorenzo and his family. We pulled them out and held them to the light to admire the rich colours swirling through them. It was all laid out on the kitchen table and we were poring over it when Valentina appeared unexpectedly. The sight stopped her short.

"What are you doing?"

"Just looking . . . and remembering," Nanda told her.

"You're not going to use these things for the party." Valentina sounded stern. "They are too precious, too breakable."

"Your father would have wanted them to be used and admired," Coco told her.

Valentina glared at her. "Don't tell me what my father would have wanted."

"Don't you remember how he always brought out the very best glass for parties?" Coco persisted.

"Yes, I remember everything. Of course I do." Valentina almost hissed the words.

"At any rate, these things belong to your mother," Coco reasoned. "Nanda, what do you think? Wouldn't it be a pity not to have a couple of the bigger pieces out on display?"

310

The Contessa looked from her friend to her daughter, her expression uncertain. She ran a finger round the curving rim of a large green bowl. "I don't know," she said.

"You used to pile oranges in that bowl and have it in the centre of the table," Coco reminded her.

"Yes, that's right, it looked very stylish."

"And at least a couple of the vases would be filled with fresh flowers," added Coco. "We liked to arrange them, you and I."

"That's a long while ago," Nanda said wistfully.

"Wouldn't it be fun to do it together on the morning of the party? I think we might use that red vase . . . or no, perhaps the yellow."

Valentina was still scowling at Coco. She must have realised by then that the argument was lost.

"We'll be very careful. They won't get damaged, I promise," Coco told her. "But if you hate the idea . . ."

"You don't care what I think," said Valentina. "You'll do exactly what you want like always."

"Darling, don't be like that," Coco said coolly. "It was you who asked me to come back here, remember. I can just as easily go away again."

Valentina stared at her. "You know, Coco, sometimes I hate you almost as much as my mother loves you."

The words were delivered without emotion, and when she'd finished, Valentina turned on her heel and stalked out.

"Silly girl . . . and all over a few pieces of Murano glass," said Coco when she was out of earshot, "Never mind, she'll come round, I expect."

Of course it hadn't been simply about the glass. There was something else going on and I was the only one in the room who had no idea what it was. These secretive, shadowy Venetians didn't have any intention of telling me either. Coco and Nanda exchanged a glance then began returning the glassware to the cupboard, leaving out the pieces Coco had chosen.

As they tidied, they talked about the flowers they might buy and how many oranges the bowl would accommodate. They helped me polish glasses and wipe dust from plates. It was as if nothing had happened.

Eventually they went to take a rest in the Contessa's sitting room and I escaped them. What I wanted was to see Valentina again, but I wasn't sure where to find her. Would she be singing on a gondola in some backwater of a canal? Rehearsing with the opera company? Working at the Acqua Alta bookstore? Since she appeared to have no regular schedule, it was impossible to know.

The bookstore was the easiest place to check, so I set off there first. Sure enough, she was sitting behind the till, stroking a black cat that had draped itself over the counter. She nodded when she saw me.

"It's good you came by. I have some English novels that I've been meaning to give you. The pages are loose because of the damp so we can't sell them. It's funny, but the old books seem to survive in here much longer than the new ones do."

"I'm not getting much time to read," I told her. "But thanks, I'll take them. Perhaps after the party I'll have some lazy days."

"The party . . ." Valentina hissed an impatient sigh. "The sooner it's over with the better."

"Do you really mean that? Everyone except you is looking forward to it, which is ironic really since it's your birthday celebration."

"But this isn't my party, it's Coco's; even my mother can see that. Still, Mamma is going along with it like she does with everything that woman wants."

"I don't understand. What have you got against Coco?"

"Ask her."

"She won't tell me. She'll say that I should ask you."

"Well then," Valentina ducked beneath the counter and produced a small stack of paperbacks with curling covers, "ask Angelo. He knows that old story; or most of it."

I presumed this all came back to the fact that Coco had once been her father's lover. "At least tell me this," I said, taking the books from her. "If you don't like Coco, why have me bring her back to the palazzo?"

"For my mother's sake." Valentina stood up and pushed the cat from the counter. "You see, Coco is connected to much of what was good about the past as well as what was bad."

I had resolved to ply Angelo with drinks this evening and see if he could tell me any more of Coco's story. But when I arrived at All'Arco, I was surprised to find Marie-Ann among the crowd of friends surrounding him. She looked sensational. Her hair was tousled with loose curls and she was wearing more make-up than usual. Spotting me, she smiled, and as we hugged hello she whispered in my ear: "Thank you."

I wasn't certain what I was being thanked me for but assumed it must have something to do with Angelo.

"I didn't realise we'd be seeing you this evening," I said.

"I'm coming to the *milonga*," she told me. "Don't say anything to Angelo, but I've been for a couple of tango lessons. You've inspired me, the way you've learnt so quickly, but also what you said the other evening. You're right: if I want him then I need to fight for him."

I didn't remember saying that. In fact I was fairly sure I hadn't.

"So I'm going to take more lessons until I'm good enough to dance with him. And I'm coming along to Valentina's party like you suggested." Marie-Ann gave me a brilliant smile. "Proud of me?"

I felt completely terrible, but what could I say? That I'd slept with her boyfriend. That I was pretty sure some other woman was sleeping with him too? This wasn't the time or place for that . . . and even if it had been, I'm not sure I'd have had enough courage.

"Yes . . . of course," I managed. "What about the job in New Zealand that you've been offered?"

"I've turned it down. I'm good at what I do and there'll be other job offers. But there's only one Angelo, right?"

"Right." I was trying not to think about the night I'd spent with him. Not while I was standing there face to face with her. Still, for some reason the memory of it seemed to fill my whole mind.

"Not a word, though, especially not about the tango," Marie-Ann reminded me. "I want to surprise him when I'm better at it. This evening I'm coming as an observer. My teacher told me it was a good idea."

"Who's teaching you? Surely whoever it is will be a friend of Angelo's; he knows all the tango dancers."

"It's a woman and she knows to be discreet. I talked to her at that first *milonga* I came to with you. And then I bumped into her the other day and suggested that she give me a few basic lessons."

"I'm surprised you didn't start learning sooner," I told her. "What stopped you?"

"I can't have been thinking properly," she admitted. "All this time I've been in total control of my career but I've left my personal life to itself, imagining it would all fall into place. Dumb, hey? And here's you with your happiness list, so focused on your own needs. It made me see where I've been going wrong."

I stared at her. Wild thoughts of admitting the truth danced through my mind. And then I felt someone touch my shoulder and Angelo was there, putting a drink in my hand. My eyes met his, and his crinkled with a smile.

"I'm glad I got you a large glass rather than an *ombre*," he said, watching me gulp down a couple of mouthfuls.

If having us both there made him uneasy, Angelo didn't show it. He was his usual self. We talked for a while, then he went to fetch more drinks and a couple of plates of *cicchetti*. I didn't feel nearly as relaxed as he seemed to be. I'd never dealt with anything like this

315

before. Sure, Eden had ex-girlfriends and women he'd slept with before meeting me, but I'd never been in the same room as them, let alone jammed elbow to elbow. The whole thing was freaking me out. Oblivious to my discomfort, Marie-Ann was still chattering away.

"I think you know the woman who's been teaching me," she said, her mouth close to my ear. "Her name is Coco. She says you're a friend of hers."

"Coco is teaching you?" I repeated stupidly.

"That's right. She seemed pleased to be asked, actually. Those old people like to feel needed. She's quite a character, isn't she?"

Dancing at the *milonga* that night in Campo San Giacomo dell'Orio, I felt Marie-Ann's eyes on me as if she were imagining herself in my shoes, feeling each stretch of my leg and pivot of my hips. She was sitting on one of the benches beneath the trees, and every time I glanced over, she smiled back. I found myself wishing she'd go home and leave me to have the evening as I'd imagined it.

As usual, more women than men had turned up, so I had to share Angelo with other partners. Even Coco was obliged to loan out Silvio. We spent lots of time sitting on the bench beside Marie-Ann, and now and then I heard the pair of them murmuring together. This dancer had good form, while this one was sloppy in her movements and that one too showy. It niggled that Coco had agreed to teach the tango to Marie-Ann but never offered to help me. I couldn't understand it. She was my friend after all.

316

When Silvio asked me to dance a *tanda* with him, I accepted, even though I knew Coco would be itching to be back on her feet with him. It felt odd stepping into the older man's embrace. His touch was lighter than Angelo's, his lead less forceful. His tango was courteous and calm.

"Very good, very good," he purred as we moved together. "You have come such a long way, *cara*, since those first few steps we made together. You are a dancer now."

The *tanda* ended, and the other men released their partners, but I stayed in Silvio's embrace.

"Another?" I asked.

"It would be my pleasure," he replied gallantly.

That was when Valentina arrived. She stalked into the middle of the Campo San Giacomo dell'Orio, everything about her screaming *Look at me!* Her dress was a swingy slash of scarlet and extremely short, the daisy tattoo snaked over her shoulder, her hair was loose and fell in soft waves down her back. But it was the way she walked, head high, ready to take on the world, that awed me.

She paused, and I could see she was searching about for a dance partner. The only man standing alone just at that moment seemed to be Angelo. With a shrug of one bare shoulder, she held out a hand to him. He stared back at her and for a moment I thought he was going to refuse. She raised her eyebrows. He smiled. They stepped together.

"Now we will see a show," said Silvio.

The first time I'd watched them together I'd been impressed but I hadn't really understood what I was looking at. Now I realised they were extraordinary. Valentina and Angelo danced like two animals locked in combat. First she seemed to be leading, then he took over but she didn't stop fighting. The rest of us fell back and let them have the floor.

At one point I glanced over at Marie-Ann. She was open-mouthed and enthralled. Beside her, Coco was pretending not to be impressed in the slightest. But she must have been. All of us were.

I recognised the song that was playing: "Libertango". It builds to a crescendo and so did their dancing. This was what Angelo had wanted for Buenos Aires, to dazzle audiences with their skill and daring, but Valentina had refused to go. Watching them together now, I wondered if she regretted it.

They were breathless by the end. Angelo stepped away from Valentina, made a little bow and began applauding her. The rest of us joined in; there was even some cheering. Then another *tanda* began, but most of us held back, because how could we top that?

Only Coco wasn't daunted. She reclaimed Silvio and they took to the floor to embark on a dignified tango. Gradually others joined them.

Returning to my place on the bench beside Marie-Ann, I told her, "That is Valentina."

"Yes, of course it is," she replied.

"So what do you think?"

Marie-Ann turned to me. "I think I need a drink."

318

We moved to a table at the Prosecco bar and I ordered us a bottle. I'd poured two glasses from it when Valentina strode over, still flushed from the dancing, her skin sheened and eyes all lit up. I saw Marie-Ann stiffen.

"This is what I came for." Valentina flung herself into the remaining seat at the table, crossing her long bare legs. "I'm here to buy you a drink. I owe you one, Addolorata. And an apology too."

"You do?"

She nodded resignedly. "Mamma gave me a long lecture when I got home this evening. I've never heard her so stern. Apparently I'm being ungracious and ungrateful. She is very disappointed in me."

I couldn't help smiling. "Oh dear."

"Yes, I know. Still, she'll forget she's angry with me soon enough, I expect. She always does." Valentina turned to Marie-Ann. "I'm sorry, I don't think we've met."

"No." Marie-Ann held out her hand and introduced herself as a friend of mine. As usual she was agonisingly direct. "And you are Angelo's girlfriend? Or you used to be?"

"That's right, I used to be." Valentina appeared unfazed. "Not for a long while now, though."

"In that case, I'm pleased to meet you. Let me organise another glass."

Once all of us had a drink in front of us, Marie-Ann proposed a toast. "To the future, and whatever it holds," she said as we clinked our glasses together.

"The future?" Valentina sounded doubtful. She put down her glass without drinking. "I try not to look too far ahead. I find it easier."

"The past is finished with," argued Marie-Ann. "There's no point in toasting that."

Valentina was quick to contradict her. "The past is never finished with; at least not here in Venice. It's always with us. Many of us it controls."

"Does it control you?"

"Yes, certainly, in some ways . . . but not my past with Angelo, if that's what you mean. No, that I am happy to be finished with. For me, now, there is more to life than dancing."

Marie-Ann drank a lot of Prosecco that night. I think she sensed a victory. I wasn't sure if she had won much, though. I was fresh from watching her boyfriend and Valentina dance together, and I knew that all that passion must have come from one of them.

After shouting us a bottle of Prosecco, Valentina left without taking a single sip. Coco came and helped drink it instead. The three of us had a little party and she told outrageous stories about the past. The parties at the Guggenheim mansion, the artists she'd known, the gowns she had worn, the men who had courted her. Marie-Ann seemed as seduced as I had been. This was the irresistible side of Coco. The blaze of colour she loved to show the world. I wasn't sure how often any of us got to glimpse the woman she truly was.

As we finished our second bottle, Angelo came over to say goodbye, claiming tiredness. Marie-Ann disappeared shortly afterwards.

320

"I like that girl," said Coco, watching her go. "She has strength."

"You're teaching her to dance," I said.

"Yes, because strength won't seal the deal; she needs help." Coco reached over and patted my hand. "She would be good for Angelo, I think. Perfect, in fact."

"So you're setting them up, matchmaking like you did for Nanda and Lorenzo?"

Coco seemed startled. "Not like that at all. That was very different."

I topped up her glass from what was left in my own and pushed it towards her. "Tell me, then," I said.

"Tell you what?"

"Your story, everything."

"I've been telling you stories all night," she protested.

"But I want to know more, the real story, all of it. I don't understand why you're so secretive."

"I've never told anyone all of it. I wouldn't know where to begin," she said helplessly.

"You were married when you met Lorenzo, weren't you?"

She nodded.

"Start with him, then; tell me about your husband."

This is what I teased from a reluctant Coco as the *campo* emptied of dancers and the barman brought us one last bottle before closing. It was her side of the story, and as she spoke, I imagined how it might have differed if Nanda had been telling it, or the man she'd married, or the one she'd really loved . . .

CHAPTER
TWENTY-ONE

He was an artist, or at least he was trying to be. He wasn't a handsome man and he was much older than me. But he told me I was his muse and it was my destiny to be in his paintings. He said all sorts of flattering things and I loved to hear them.

Eventually I allowed him to paint a nude portrait. It took a long time for him to complete it because he made love to me more than he worked. He said he couldn't resist. And I was very lovely then, you know. So young . . . only just ripening.

He promised I was his secret but he was a vain man. He showed the portrait off to his friends and boasted that he'd had me. The whispers reached my family. They realised I'd been lying, creeping out at night to be with him, sneaking away whenever I could. Those days being what they were, we were forced to marry. It wasn't what either of us wanted. My husband had enjoyed the single life and I had thought I was a muse, not a drudge to cook and clean and scrub the stains from his undergarments.

He carried on painting me. Hours and hours stripped naked and standing still before his easel. If I moved, he'd get angry. If he thought the painting a bad one, I suffered for it. It was a miserable time and it seemed no one could save me.

My family weren't interested; my fate was my own fault, they told me. My only real friend was Nanda, and what could she do?

Then my husband had an exhibition. He made me go to the opening night. There I was naked on every wall, and parading around on his arm. I didn't let anyone see how I felt, even though it nearly killed me. My God, the effort it took to stay standing, never mind keep the smile on my face. He'd made me look ugly, you see. Horribly ugly.

That was the night I met Lorenzo. My husband was being feted, smoking cigars and getting drunk, and he'd forgotten about me for the moment. I was standing alone in a corner of the gallery, feeling lost, and then this tall, handsome boy came and put a glass of Prosecco in my hand.

"I would like to kill your husband," he said to me, and I was sure he meant it.

Lorenzo knew all about art. He told me everything that was wrong with those paintings. He made it seem they weren't of me but some awful figure my husband had conjured from his imagination.

"People will buy them," I despaired. "They'll hang them on their walls and see me like that every day."

"I'll buy them," he promised. "And I'll destroy them."

Every one of those paintings was sold by the end of the night, and to a single buyer who had asked to remain anonymous. My husband was flushed with triumph. He believed he had found a rich patron at last. For a short while he was charming again because I'd played a part in his success. But when no rich patron came forward, when nothing changed at all for him, he returned to being a monster.

Lorenzo was always in my mind. What he'd said about my husband and his paintings. What he'd done for me. I went to the gallery and begged for his details but they refused to divulge even a surname, just as they had the countless times my husband demanded them.

My husband was drinking too much. He grew sloppy and lazy. He lived in the *bacari* with his friends and hardly ever came home sober. I started escaping whenever I could and spending time with Nanda. He didn't notice. And so I grew bolder. I went to parties, first at the palazzo and then to other places with friends I'd made. Once I went to a party in an artist's studio only to realise my husband was there too. I stayed and drank a glass of Prosecco anyway, then slipped away before he caught me.

I was becoming a woman and naturally other men were paying me attention. After a while I took a secret lover. He too was an older man and he showed me that it wasn't only art my husband made badly. This man had plenty of money and he wanted to look after me. He was married, trapped just like I was, because there was no divorce in Italy back in those days. He begged me to leave my husband. Promised to give me a place to live and as many beautiful things as I wanted.

Fearful of the disgrace, I refused. It seemed wiser to continue as we were. But then my husband realised he was running out of money. He wanted to fill more canvases with warped images of my naked body and hold another exhibition to sell them. He stopped going to the *bacari* and kept me with him in his studio, painting feverishly. I was living through the same nightmare as before.

As the opening of the exhibition approached, I grew panicky. Surely this time there would be no kind stranger like Lorenzo to save me. And so I contacted my lover and told him I would agree to his proposal. And I ran away.

All I had done was swap one man for another. He may not have wanted to paint me, but this one was possessive. He put me in a small apartment in Santa Croce and expected me to be waiting whenever he came. I hardly went anywhere. My husband had threatened violence if he laid eyes on me. My family were scandalised; Nanda was told she mustn't ever see me again. Fortunately my old friend was disobedient. Her visits were rare, but she managed a few.

I had walked into another trap. Desperate to escape, I began to coax my lover to buy me gifts: jewellery, furs, anything I thought I could sell to raise money. I had this idea of leaving Venice, although where I would go I hadn't decided.

Then I saw Lorenzo again. I was in the Rialto market early one morning, hurrying to pick up a few bits and pieces, and I heard his voice calling to me: *"Signora, signora."*

I was afraid to spend too much time talking to him in case my lover arrived to see me and I wasn't home. At the same time I couldn't bear to drag myself away. I'm sure Lorenzo felt the same. He told me he was a glassmaker and he'd created a special piece inspired by me. He was eager for me to see it.

How could I go to Murano to see this special piece without my lover? He was a demanding man and his need for me was frequent. There was never a day when I didn't hear his knock at my door.

I told him I wanted some art glass for my birthday. I knew he would insist on touring Murano with me to choose it. My plan was to leave the Viadro factory until last in the hope that he might have grown bored by then or felt he must return to run his business or attend to his family. But he gave me the whole day and hardly left my side.

At the Viadro factory Lorenzo himself came out to show us his wares. I saw straight away which object he had modelled on me, a figurine of a nude woman with flowing curves in opalescent gold. I admired it so fervently my lover had no choice but to offer to buy it.

Lorenzo insisted the figurine was too fragile for us to carry home. He would arrange to have it properly wrapped and delivered instead. I knew he meant to bring it himself and for the next days was delirious with excitement and fear, waiting for him to come.

He arrived mid-morning on the Monday of the following week. Together we unwrapped the figurine and he placed it on the shelf for me.

"It needs a light behind it to glow as much as you do," he told me.

It broke my heart to think I might never see him again. The figurine was all I would have to remember this beautiful man by. I was so crazy about him that even though I knew it wasn't safe, that my lover could come by at any time, I took Lorenzo to my bed.

Once wasn't going to be enough for either of us. He came back again and again. We took risks to be together. Several times we came so close to being caught. But I couldn't give him up. Truly I'd rather have died.

Lorenzo wanted me as his wife but we both knew it was impossible because I already had a husband. At nights I cried myself to sleep with frustration. Soon his family would expect him to marry and start a family to continue the Viadro line. It seemed certain I would lose him then.

That's how I turned matchmaker. The idea came to me, and the more I considered it, the cleverer it seemed. Lorenzo and Nanda. The two people I loved most in the world would marry, then I wouldn't lose either of them.

Lorenzo wasn't sure at first but Nanda's head was turned more easily. This man I had introduced her to had everything she hoped for in a husband: he was handsome and wealthy, from a good family; he was kind. I didn't feel guilty. Lorenzo would always love me more, but he would care for her. She would have a happy life and need never know he had bought the house in Cannaregio that I moved into when I left my lover.

It was a long time before she found out about us. By then divorce was a possibility, but as she and I both knew, Lorenzo would never do it. He adored me, yes, but he valued his position too much. My Lorenzo was a man who needed to be respected and admired. He was a brilliant artist, a businessman, a prominent member of Venetian society. He loved his children and his home. I think perhaps he had come to love Nanda too.

I was angry that he hadn't put me first so I took up with other men and made sure he knew it. Lorenzo never said anything. Still, I think I broke a little piece of his heart every time I flaunted another lover, until eventually I shattered it like I did his glass figurine.

When he killed himself, Nanda said I must take a share of the blame. I called her a stupid woman, although the truth is she was right. Lorenzo had believed he was losing me. That was just as impossible for him to bear as all the failed investments and the business problems. He was such a beautiful, clever man but he had bleak moods; like all artistic people, I suppose. Still, I never believed he'd take his own life; that he'd choose to leave me. Even today I find it difficult to understand how he could do that.

So that's my story, Addolorata, and it's a sad one. I prefer not to dwell on it. Far better to put on bright clothes and go out to meet the world with a smile. I can't change the past and undo my mistakes. All I can do is get on with life. Keep going and keep trying. It's all any of us can do.

I think Coco expected me to judge her harshly. But how could I, having just slept with another woman's boyfriend? I knew how easy it was to mess up your own life. At the same time I could see why Valentina might find it difficult to like her.

At that point I didn't suspect she hadn't told me everything. I was too drunk on Prosecco and too transported by her words. And I couldn't help drawing parallels with myself. We'd both been so young when we married, we'd both made choices that set our lives in stone.

It wasn't until the night of the party that I heard the rest of Coco's story. Even then I had to piece it together from what other people told me. And now, like them, I have a secret to keep.

328

CHAPTER
TWENTY-TWO

Lights were glittering in the trees and tango music was playing. Marie-Ann was moving through the crowd filling glasses with wine; Angelo and I were in the kitchen covering platters with food. After all the planning and anticipation, this was the party at last.

Coco was up there somewhere wearing a simple black dress made of silk jersey with long sleeves and a high neckline . . . and bangles stacked up both arms, rings on all her fingers, and a multicoloured feathered snood.

"I'm going completely over the top," she'd declared. "I don't care what anyone thinks."

They had all gone over the top. People were costumed in gold and silver; they'd pulled out their best jewels and piled them on. It sounded like they were enjoying themselves. Even from the depths of the kitchen I could hear the hum of conversation growing louder.

I was too busy to go and join in at first. Downstairs in the kitchen Angelo and I had become competitive, pushing out trayloads of *cicchetti* and running Marie-Ann ragged trying to distribute them all.

"Stop, this is ridiculous," she cried. "No one can manage any more. I'm having to force them to keep eating."

She helped us to clean up, then insisted Angelo take her for a dance. I saw him showing her a few tango steps and imagined what he'd be saying. "Follow, Marie-Ann, just follow."

For so long tango had been our thing; his and mine. I'd been the one in his arms, stumbling over his toes as Marie-Ann was now, struggling to read the language he spoke with his body, frowning with the effort.

I expect you think I was jealous; that it gave me a pang. But men like Angelo — you may be able to hold on to them in the dance, but once the music stops it's not going to be so easy. I was almost glad not to be in Marie-Ann's shoes . . . even if they were dancing the tango.

Leaving them to it, I went in search of someone I knew. Nanda was the first person I spotted. She was sitting alone on a white leather chaise that one of Coco's boyfriends had procured from somewhere. She looked anxious, as if she was struggling to recall what all these people were doing in her palazzo. At her feet there was a half-full bottle of Prosecco and an empty glass.

Sitting down next to her, I took her hand. "Is everything OK?"

She held on to me, squeezing my fingers.

"Nanda, do you want me to take you upstairs? Is this all too much for you?"

"No."

"Are you sure?"

"Yes."

She was staring at someone. I followed her line of sight and realised it was her daughter. Valentina must have decided to enjoy the party after all. Dressed in a loose silky black dress and glowing from the dancing, she was talking to a man I didn't recognise.

"It looks like she's having a good time," I said.

Nanda didn't reply.

"Can I get you a drink?" I offered. "Some water."

"Nobody knows," Nanda said. She was still watching Valentina.

"I'm sorry?"

"Nobody knows," she repeated.

"What do you mean? What does nobody know?" I asked.

She looked at me, her expression quite desolate. "I can't ever tell. I promised."

It occurred to me that Nanda was having some sort of episode. Perhaps the stress of the party had been too much. Or she'd drunk too much of the Prosecco.

"I think it's time for your rest now," I said. "You look very tired."

"My rest?" She looked at me doubtfully. "Do I need one?"

"Yes, let's go to your sitting room. It will be quieter there."

She allowed me to help her up and manoeuvre her out of the room. Upstairs, she was happy to settle into her armchair. "You're right, I do feel tired," she said. "I might close my eyes for a few moments. No one will miss me. It's always Coco that everyone wants to talk to at parties anyway."

Knowing what I did about their past, I felt sorry for her. "I'm sure that's not true."

"Oh yes it is. I was always the dull one and she was exciting. We never knew what wild thing she'd do next."

"I can imagine that."

"There were times when Coco's whole life was a party," Nanda told me.

"Was that when she was married?"

"No, much later, after Valentina was born. Who could blame her, though . . ." Nanda shook her head. "But still . . . nobody knows."

She seemed so sad, I thought I should fetch someone. First I opened the shutters to let some air into the room and turned off all but a single lamp. By then her eyes were closed and her breathing had deepened.

Downstairs, I looked for her son, Giacomo. I pushed my way through hordes of dancers and knots of people partying in the hallways, finding him at last out in the garden drinking brandy with a pretty woman who turned out to be his wife. He wasn't slurring his words but his cheeks were flushed and his face was shiny. To me he seemed a little drunk.

"Poor Mamma," he said when I told him. "This party, these people . . . Sometimes it doesn't do to be reminded so much of the past."

"She's sleeping at the moment, but perhaps you should go and check on her later. She did seem upset."

"If she is, I'm not surprised," he replied. "As I have said to my sister many times, it wasn't a good idea of hers to have Coco come back here. She always brings trouble."

Naturally I sprang to my friend's defence. "That's not very fair. Coco cares for your family; she must do. She organised this party and sold off all her good jewellery to pay for it."

"Was it jewellery that my father gave her?"

"Yes," I admitted.

"Ah, then I suppose she's trying to make amends at long last."

"She certainly wasn't trying to upset anyone," I told him.

"I should hope not. Coco has done enough to upset us in the past."

"Because she had a love affair with your father?"

"A love affair?" He gave me a distinctly withering look. "It was much more than that. Did you know that he once brought Coco here to live beneath the same roof as my mother?"

This shocked me. "No, I didn't."

"Oh yes, she lived with us for several months. It was around the time Valentina was born. I was a little boy but still I remember it. Mamma crying so much, and voices raised. What kind of man brings his mistress to live with his pregnant wife?"

"Why did your mother put up with it?"

"I suppose she felt there was no choice. What I've never understood is why she's stayed so loyal to Coco.

Mamma has been bound to that woman her whole life."

"They fell out for a bit," I reminded him.

"Yes, over Valentina; she's the one thing they argue about, for some reason."

"Really? I thought it was because your mother won't sell the palazzo and Coco thinks she should."

"No, the fight was about Valentina." He sounded very certain. "She works too hard, she wastes her talent, she does this, she needs that . . . Coco always has an opinion about my sister."

That's when it all fell into place for me. Actually the signs had been there earlier but I'd missed them: lots of little things adding up to one big truth that now seemed so obvious. "Oh my God," I said, without meaning to.

"What's wrong?"

"I've just realised I might have left a candle burning in your mother's room," I lied. "I'd better go and blow it out. I'd hate it to start a fire."

Excusing myself, I raced back upstairs so fast you'd have thought the curtains were already alight. There was no candle burning, of course, and Nanda was sleeping peacefully. Crouching down beside her, I gently shook her arm.

"Contessa."

"What is it?" Her eyes flickered and blinked open. "Oh, it's the foreigner. What are you doing here at this hour?"

I came straight out with my suspicion while she was still only half awake. "Valentina is Coco's daughter, isn't she? But she doesn't know it."

"Nobody knows," she said quickly. "Nobody must ever know."

"I guessed."

"I don't believe you." Her eyes were wide now.

"It's true," I promised.

Nanda looked frightened. "All these years, no one has known. Only Coco and me, and my late husband."

"Why have you never told Valentina?"

"There have been times I've wanted to, but Coco was adamant. She is very kind, my friend. She looks after me." Nanda wrapped a hand round my wrist and her fingernails dug into my skin. "She loves me."

"She loves Valentina too," I said softly.

"Yes, but there has been enough scandal and Coco understands that." Nanda took a deep breath as if to steady herself. "Why should Valentina's life be touched by it too? That's not what Lorenzo wanted for her. When he convinced Coco to let her go, when he asked me to raise her as my own, scandal was what he was trying to avoid. This is why no one must know."

"I won't say anything," I promised.

She loosened her grip a little. "My daughter was brought up in a well-respected family. She learnt to value its traditions. This palazzo, the glass museum, our family name, our place in Venice's history, these things belong to her. Why tell her the truth and destroy so much of that, especially now that she is starting a family of her own."

"A family of her own?" I repeated stupidly. "Valentina is having a baby?"

I was shocked by what I'd learnt that night. This news shocked me again.

Valentina was showing no signs of being pregnant; she hadn't said a word. I hadn't even realised there was a man in her life.

"That's right. Such happy news." Nanda smiled.

"Is it Angelo who's the father?"

"No, of course not. My daughter finished with him long ago, thank goodness. He was never right for her. It wouldn't have done for them to stay together."

I could guess why now. "She and Angelo are cousins but they don't know it?"

Nanda nodded. "Cousins, yes. But that doesn't matter any more. My daughter is with a glassmaker, a young man our family has known for a long time. With him I hope she will have the life Lorenzo would have wanted for his daughter. And Angelo, he has someone else, yes?"

"I think so."

"Coco and I thought that everything was fine at last . . . at least we hoped it was."

"I won't say a word," I promised again. "Not to Valentina or Coco . . . or anyone."

"Secrets can be painful to keep." Resting her head against the high back of the chair, Nanda closed her eyes again. "Secrets can be brutal."

How had I guessed? Coco and Valentina didn't look alike, but there was something in the way they carried themselves, their fierce confidence. Then there was that telltale mix of criticism and pride so many mothers show their daughters. And Coco always had an opinion about her. Giacomo had noticed it but he hadn't understood. Valentina was her daughter and it was hard for Coco to watch her make mistakes in life.

Other things made more sense to me now. This was why Valentina hadn't been allowed to live in the apartment above Coco's place. It would have been painful to have her so close, and upsetting for Nanda too perhaps. This was why my old friend went time and again to hear her sing opera. Why she allowed friends to believe she was her god-daughter.

Seeking some peace from the still noisy party, I went down to the kitchen and sat alone at the long table, thinking and wondering. If I were Valentina, would I want to know? If I were Coco, would I be able to stay quiet?

It was Nanda I thought about most. For so many years' she had shared more than anyone imagined with Coco. The strength it must have taken; the determination to preserve life the way she wanted it to be. I admired the woman almost as much as I felt sorry for her. After all, she had kept everything in the end.

I'm not sure how long I sat there alone, fitting the pieces of the story together as the party continued without me. Finally Angelo came to find me and said that it was time to dance.

It was tempting to go into the garden where the band was still playing, to stand with him heart to heart and let his body move mine where and how he wanted. I almost stood and took the hand he offered. But I stopped myself. Not for Marie-Ann's sake, or my husband's, nothing so noble, but mainly for my own. Angelo wasn't what I wanted.

"I think we've finished with our dancing," I told him.

He seemed puzzled. "Why?"

"Because it's for the best."

He came to stand beside me, resting his hip against the table. "Have I hurt you?"

I shook my head. "No."

"Well if I have, I'm sorry. But you're married, Dolly, and you're only here for the summer. It's never going to be more than it is."

"I didn't expect any more."

He touched my cheek gently.

"Better not to start that again," I said softly.

Angelo took a step back and stared down at my face for a moment, then paced over to the cooker. Shifting lids off pans and lifting the covers from platters, he rattled around.

"We call you *foresti*, did you know that? The outsiders, the ones who don't belong here in Venice, who will leave and go back to their own lives sooner or later."

I'd heard the word before.

"With women like you . . . and Marie-Ann too . . . there's no point in more than what we've had. You'll be going home eventually. It's necessary to be in the same city for a relationship to work. You have to want the same things from life."

"That's why you split from Valentina? Because she wanted different things?"

"Valentina?" He slammed down a pot on the counter. "She's with some *stronzo* from Murano now. They're having a baby."

"So I hear."

"I can't believe it. He is a boring little glassmaker and I know the life she'll have with him — work, family, keeping a nice house, throwing dinner parties at the weekend. With me she might have had so much more."

"Perhaps that's what she wants, though," I said.

"But she can sing, she can dance." He clattered a pan down on to the stovetop angrily.

"Just because you can do something doesn't mean you should," I told him. "Maybe the singing and the dancing isn't what makes her truly happy. Perhaps she wants this life you think is boring."

Angelo dismissed my words with a shake of his head. Moving to the fridge, he started rummaging about, pulling out a bowl of leftover *baccalà mantecato*, some *sarde en saor*, scraps of seafood, some other bits and pieces, and laid it all out on the table along with a few slices of charred white bread.

"We cooked a lot this evening but we didn't eat," he said. "Now we ought to have something."

I watched him spread the creamy salted fish over the *crostini*, carefully topping each one with a cooked prawn and a mini crouton.

"Were you hoping to get back together with Valentina?" I wondered. "Is that why you're so upset?"

"No . . . maybe . . ." Angelo's head was bowed over his task. "It just seems impossible that she's with this man. I don't like to see it."

"She wasn't going to stay single for ever," I pointed out.

He started spooning the sardine mixture on to the remaining slices of bread in precise little mounds. "Valentina and I had a connection. Even after we broke up, it was there. Am I supposed to pretend that means nothing now?"

He looked up and I saw that his eyes were welling. "We belong to each other. That's how it should be. This guy has no right to her."

I felt very sorry for him, just as I did for everyone caught in the wake of Coco's love life. If only I could tell Angelo what his connection with Valentina truly was. But I'd promised. No matter what, I couldn't go back on that.

He pushed a plate of crostini towards me. "Eat. You must be hungry, and all this food will go to waste if someone doesn't finish it."

To my surprise, I did have an appetite. While we were cooking, I'd been too busy to do anything but taste for flavour. Now I ate hungrily, tearing into the crostini. The *baccalà mantecato* was rich and satisfying; the sardines spiked with vinegar were piquant.

Angelo returned to the fridge and brought back more left-overs. A pungent goat's cheese dipped in ash, tender morsels of grilled peppers stripped of their skins, soft meatballs fragrant with rosemary, little tarts filled with savoury custard and topped with zingy *salsa verde*.

"So are you angry with me?" he asked as I made inroads into the food. "Do you think I've treated you badly?"

340

"No, not at all. We had a great time and we're still friends."

"Good." As he chased an oily strip of red pepper round his plate with a crust of bread, Angelo smiled. "I like you a lot, you know."

I liked him too. But I'd spent that night hearing of the sacrifices two women had made for the daughter they loved, and it put my own life in perspective. Nanda's words had made me consider all I'd taken for granted, everything I'd walked away from that summer, and for the first time I couldn't justify it even the tiniest bit. I looked at myself through her eyes . . . and I found myself wanting.

There was only one thing for it: I had to get Katia to Venice. Somehow I'd beg Eden until I wore him down. Then the rest of the summer would be entirely hers. We'd do all the things I'd planned and more — *gelato* tasting, a walk across the Bridge of Sighs, gondola rides. I'd get to know her properly, as a person, not just my child. She'd see another side to me apart from the always busy mother she was usually stuck with. We'd make good memories together.

If that meant no late night dancing at the *milongas*, no tango performance and no more Angelo, well, that was fine. I couldn't entirely regret what I'd done with him . . . but it was time to stop before, like Coco, I lost the things that really mattered.

I did dance that evening, but not with Angelo. First Silvio partnered me, then Coco's other boyfriend Marcello took his turn. After that I got up with a few guys I recognised and some I'd never met before. Each led me in a different sort of tango and I followed them all.

As the night wore on, Angelo and Marie-Ann disappeared, as did many of the other guests. It was the older ones who stayed the longest, the pale-haired women in stiff taffeta and the stooped men with silver-topped canes. Perhaps they understood that there might not be many more parties like this one left for them and were determined to enjoy every moment of it.

Coco was in her element and right at the centre of things. She was flirting with a man dressed in a blue tuxedo with wide lapels edged in velvet that looked like he might have owned it since the seventies. Tossing back her head, she tinkled a laugh. She knew I was watching. She expected me to.

With the soft lights blurring the lines on her skin, it was easy to picture Coco in that same garden decades ago. She would have been all dressed up just like now, partying with artists and glassmakers, treating them to her sharp wit and infectious laughter, loving every moment.

There had been such painful times here too; I knew that now. Hiding a pregnancy behind the palazzo's high walls, giving up a baby. Coco had taken some wrong turns in her life; she'd made a mess of things and paid a high price for it. I hoped that I still had a chance to make sure I didn't do the same.

Even when it was obvious the party had finished, Coco refused to end the night. She found a full bottle of

Prosecco and talked Marcello into cruising round the canals in his water taxi while we drank it.

The night was hot and in the backwaters there was that eggy smell you often hear people complain of. When you live in Venice you get used to it, but right then it must have been especially strong because even Coco noticed. I could hear her, Marcello and Silvio grumbling about the cruise ships clogging their lagoon and the *foresti* filling up their narrow streets; about their city being taken over. This is the conversation Venetians like to have and it always goes the same way. They didn't expect me to join in. I was a foreigner and would be going back to my own world soon enough, just like Angelo had said.

When I left Venice at the end of the summer I would miss all of this, the people and the place. I'd miss the water and the way it changed from nearly grey in the mornings to a glossy green, then entirely black at night. I'd miss that floating feeling I had when I lay down and closed my eyes. I'd miss walking down streets so narrow I almost had to turn sideways. I'd miss the gondolier sitting on the bridge who never seemed to work but who always sighed and said a hopeful *buongiorno*; the graceful bridges and the sun-baked *campi* and the great sweep of the Grand Canal. But most of all I'd miss those moments when, footsore and sick of other people, I'd glimpse the nose of a gondola, with its distinct metal teeth, edging round a corner where I hadn't even realised there was water, and suddenly I'd be lost to Venice completely and all over again.

9. Being surrounded by water. Canals, the sea, lakes, fountains even. The sound of it moving, the way it reflects the light. Being in it and on it.

CHAPTER
TWENTY-THREE

After the party, the days seemed to pass more quickly than I wanted them to. Mostly I did the usual things. Walked Boris, spent time with the Contessa, shopped at the Rialto market. Once I persuaded Coco to come to the Lido with me and she waded into the muddy water dressed from head to toe in Indian cotton. I took her out for lunch and treated her to dinner.

Knowing the truth about her was difficult. The silence was hardest of all. There were so many things I wanted to ask, and so much I wanted say. If I found more similarities between her and Valentina, there was no one to remark on them to. If her mood seemed a little low, I could only guess why. And it was always there on the tip of my tongue ready to blurt out, this great secret she and Nanda had held between them for all these years. But I couldn't tell Coco what I'd learnt. She hadn't wanted me to know or she'd have told me herself, after all. And I feared she'd blame Nanda, that it would spark another fight between them just when they were getting on so well.

Looking for ways to help without Coco realising became my mission. I bought tickets for the opera so we could hear Valentina sing. I made dinners at the palazzo and we ate like family around the kitchen table. The food was often very simple: lagoon fish with fresh herbs and light salads, wooden skewers of meat served over creamy polenta. But I enjoyed preparing those meals. It was cooking with a purpose, not just nourishing people but bringing them together.

I think Nanda may have forgotten what she'd told me. She never referred to it again and even the party seemed hazy in her memory, as if she'd confused it with other celebrations in the past.

One night I was cleaning up after we'd finished eating dinner and Valentina came to help me, the two of us alone in the kitchen together, scrubbing and drying as a team.

"We'll miss you when you leave at the end of the summer," she remarked. "My mother has grown very fond of you. She talks about you a lot."

I was intrigued. "What does she say?"

"Lots about the food you cook for her. She likes to describe what she's eaten that day. At the very beginning I thought she was making it up. It seemed incredible that a stranger would do so much for us."

Valentina was polishing blue goblets from the stash of Murano glass that Nanda now insisted on using every day. "I think you're the first foreigner Mamma has had much to do with. She wonders about your life in England, where you live and why you're here with us instead of with your own family. I tell her I'm not sure and that it confuses me too."

346

The thought of launching into a long explanation was too exhausting to contemplate. Instead I said, "I've been having some time off; just a summer."

"But it seems strange to me. You're so involved with our family and we know very little about you apart from what Coco has told us." Seeing my expression, Valentina added quickly, "Oh don't worry, she hasn't been gossiping. All she said is that you're going through a tricky period in your marriage."

"Yes, that's true."

"So why come here and involve yourself with us when you have problems of your own?" she wondered. "If I took a summer off from everything, I'd want to spend it lying on a beach, not looking after two old women."

If I were being entirely honest, I might have told her that other people's problems are always easier to deal with, that they can be a distraction, even a relief. Instead I said, "I've enjoyed it. They're interesting."

The goblets and plates were put away, the pans resting on the draining board. Valentina hung the damp cloth over the edge of the sink, turning her back on me as she tidied away a few last things.

"You've spent a lot of time with Angelo this summer too," she remarked.

"While he was teaching me the tango, but I've stopped that now."

"Does his new girlfriend not approve?"

"I've had enough of it, that's all."

"That new girl Marie-Ann was at my party, wasn't she? Watching him."

"She came to help out. I asked her to."

"She's worried that he's still in love with me, I suppose." Valentina poured two glasses of water and passed one to me. "And maybe he is but I can't control Angelo's feelings. I never have been able to. That's the thing with him. He goes his own way and expects you to follow in everything, not only the tango."

"But you didn't follow him, did you? At least not to Buenos Aires."

"He thought I'd change my mind; that I wouldn't want to lose him, perhaps, or that I needed to compete and perform as much as he did. But that's not how it was."

"And you don't regret it?"

"Never," she promised. "I've got what I want: a man who loves me and will let me make my own choices, a man who doesn't treat me like I belong to him. We care about the same things and want the same future. That's never how it was with Angelo. You can tell that to your friend if you like. Wish her good luck with him."

Walking home along the Strada Nuova later that night, I decided Valentina had a point. I'd become so caught up in the Viadro family that my own had started to feel like the strangers. Since the party I'd been trying my best to change that. I called home once or twice a day, caught up with my daughter and tried to talk my husband round.

Slowly we were making progress; we'd even started talking dates. Eden had shown signs of agreeing to Katia flying over to me at the very end of July. I was a little disappointed as it meant she'd miss the big celebration of the Festa del Redentore and August really was the wrong time for us to enjoy Venice properly together. Most people would be escaping the heat then and heading to the beach for their holidays. Still, I didn't want to push too hard in case Eden changed his mind.

Perhaps if Venice got too hot then Katia and I would travel to my parents' place on the coast of Basilicata, get my family to meet us there, persuade Coco to come too. I hatched all sorts of plans; I made all sorts of lists. I sweet-talked Eden as if my life depended on it.

Coco didn't seem hugely interested in the news that my daughter might be coming. All she wanted to talk about was the Festa del Redentore. She had chosen her outfit already but didn't have an invitation to any of the parties that would be held on boats in the lagoon. This was the source of much anxiety.

I wondered if Marcello might take us out in his water taxi, but she was quick to dismiss the idea. The boat had to be much bigger, something elegant and not full of rowdy young people.

"Years ago I'd have taken my pick of invitations," she lamented. "Now everyone I used to know is either dead or too boring."

Every day Coco came up with a new plan. Roberto might know of a party we could join, or one of her other boyfriends. She would rush off to make a call and come back dejected. Roberto was planning to be with his family; her old boyfriend hadn't been well; another had sold his boat.

"What if we sat on Riva degli Schiavone?" I suggested. "We could pack a picnic and watch the fireworks from there. Valentina told me that's what lots of people do."

"Not our kind of people." Coco was adamant.

As the day of the Festa came closer, she grew sulky and announced that she wasn't going to bother with it at all. "I've been to enough of them. What's one more?"

"But I'd like to go," I told her. "Everyone's been talking about it. They say the fireworks will be incredible this year."

Coco feigned disinterest. "Go if you want to," she said. "I'm not stopping you."

In the end I called Marie-Ann to see if she could help. She had tickets to an exclusive-sounding party and promised to get a couple more. They weren't cheap but included dinner as well as entrance to one of the after-parties held in a hotel. The expression on Coco's face when I told her made all my extravagance worthwhile.

"That boat . . . really? I know it. They throw a party on it every year. Very glamorous and exclusive; it's impossible to secure tickets, they say."

"If Marie-Ann promises to get them, then she will."

"In that case we must rethink what we're going to wear."

Coco disappeared into the room that held her treasury of clothes, closing the door on me. There was a silence punctuated by the sound of her dropping things and muttering; finally she returned with her arms full of evening dresses, some in bright hues, some beaded, others slippery satin and silk.

"If only I hadn't sold all my diamonds," she said, spilling the clothes on to her kitchen table. "This would have been a chance to wear them. Ah well . . ."

I wasn't convinced the boat party was going to be as formal as she thought but went along with it anyway. I let her dress me in floaty coral-coloured chiffon and choose cocktail rings for my fingers.

As she worked, Coco chatted about the Festa parties she'd been to in the past. They always seemed to involve some man who was in love with her, whose heart she had eventually broken. It was difficult to tell what was true and how much of it a story she liked to tell.

"This Festa won't be like those," she finished with a sigh. "But the boat will be lovely, I'm sure, and in the morning we'll walk across the pontoon bridge they'll build to the Giudecca and buy a ticket to the church tombola and some bags of candied nuts. That's what I did with my parents when I was a child. I used to look forward to it. The Festa del Redentore was my idea of fun, with all of Venice out on the streets and everyone so colourful."

Coco told me the Festa was Venice's way of celebrating the end of plague in the city hundreds of years ago, and that a religious service and a gondola regatta were included in the festivities.

"But the firework display is the part no one wants to miss, so the lagoon will be full of boats and barges on

Saturday night. Everyone will be out partying and the atmosphere will be electric"

I had my doubts about wearing the coral chiffon. It didn't seem my kind of colour at all. But Coco was insistent.

"With the right lipstick, and if you wear your hair piled up on your head, you'll be perfect," she declared. "That dress looks so much better on you than it ever did on me."

"When did you wear it?" I wondered. "Did Lorenzo buy it for you?"

"No, it was another man, a very good friend. I doubt I'll ever put it on again. You should keep it, Addolorata."

"Thanks, but I won't. I'd never wear it at home. It doesn't fit the life I have there."

"Then you should change your life," she said crisply.

"I'm worried it's going to change whether I like it or not," I admitted. "I've been trying not to think about that too much — in denial, I suppose. But I'll have to face reality sooner or later."

"Then make a different reality," Coco told me. "I managed to. All those years ago I turned myself into the person I wanted to be. Since then I've chosen what I want to do, where I go and with whom. I've shaped my own days. It's only in the tango that I follow anyone."

"How have you done it, though? What have you been living on?" It was the one thing I still really didn't understand.

"Lorenzo bought this place and gave me a little money. Since then I've been on my own, an independent woman."

"But surely the money Lorenzo gave you only lasted for so long."

Coco muttered something indistinct.

"No, really, how have you lived all this time?" I pressed her. "I know you're very thrifty, but you must have had bills like everyone else."

She was silent for a moment, and then she said, "There were other men who appreciated me just as much as Lorenzo did."

I was beginning to see it now. "You mean they gave you gifts like he did? Money?"

"I never went short. And I never compromised myself. If a man made love to me it was because I wished him to." She said it with dignity.

I stared at our reflections in the long mirror propped against one wall. We looked as if we'd stepped away from some party in another room and were taking a quiet moment together.

"You've had an extraordinary life, Coco," I said.

"In one way or another, yes, I have. I hope there are more extraordinary times to come."

"I hope so too," I agreed.

They say that Venice is sinking. If that's true, I'm surprised it didn't drop a couple more centimetres under the weight of all the people who crowded into the streets for the Festa del Redentore. Coco had insisted on us setting off early, and now I understood why. Dressed in all our finery, we forced our way through the crush as we made our way to board our party boat at San Marco.

On the banks of the lagoon were crowds of friends and families gathered to picnic. They sat on folding chairs with half the contents of their kitchens at their feet. Pans full of pasta, trays filled with meat and vegetables, plates of fruit and bowls of nuts.

Meanwhile out on the water boats and barges were loaded with young people getting rowdily drunk as music thumped from speakers.

Coco frowned at the sight of them. "They drink so much they jump into the lagoon to cool off, then the police boat comes and they're taken away to spend the night in a cell somewhere. And this is what they call a party."

The tickets Marie-Ann had procured gave us access to a larger boat and a more refined gathering. There were waiters with champagne and trays of bite-sized snacks, and as the day faded, the vessel was lit with fairy lights. We were still a little overdressed but Coco was right, she could have pulled off the diamonds.

Marie-Ann arrived with Angelo and I was pleased to see him. I'd missed catching up with him almost every day. I'd missed our lessons and the dancing and the way it made me feel. Still, I wasn't sorry that I'd backed away. We'd had that one night and managed to keep it a secret. But secrets were difficult things, as I was discovering. I didn't want any more of them.

There was a moment, when he wasn't watching, when I saw Marie-Ann raising her eyebrows at me. I

354

wondered if the pair of them had had that talk at last. If so, I hoped she did have all the strength Coco had seen in her. I thought she was going to need it.

There was no dancing that night; the boat was too full for that. But there was music and conversation, there was the sound of other people's parties and the lights of their vessels bobbing over the water, there were the yellow lanterns hung along the floating bridge and the Giudecca in the distance and the beauty of the lagoon all around us.

At the stroke of midnight the church bells rang and the night was lit by fireworks: great showers of colour sparkling against the black sky, some shaped like hearts, others dragon tails. The sound of them exploding above us went on and on for half an hour or more.

As I watched, head tilted upwards, I thought about Venice, this grand old city with as many bad sides as good. The crowds and tourist tat versus the crumbling grandeur; the often fetid smells of the narrow *calli* against the sweep of the Grand Canal; the beggars lying in the street and the water-taxi drivers with movie-star looks.

You could be happy here or miserable, just as in any other place. Coco was right, I thought as I watched the starbursts in the sky. You decided which way to go; you created yourself.

Too tired for the after-party, we said good night to Marie-Ann and Angelo, then walked back amidst a slow parade of other Festa-goers.

As I climbed into bed, I noticed my phone lying on my bedside table and realised it must have been there all evening. I checked the screen just in case I'd missed any calls. There were ten of them, all from Pieta, and a text to say to contact her as soon as possible, no matter how late; that it was very urgent.

CHAPTER
TWENTY-FOUR

There had been an accident. At first I thought it must be Katia, so it was almost a relief to discover that no, Eden had been hurt. Pieta explained everything to me on the phone. She was trying to seem calm but I could hear her voice shaking.

"We're not sure exactly what happened but we think Eden climbed up some scaffolding once the other guys had gone home. He's been frustrated at how slowly the building work has been going. We told him not to stress too much but still he felt bad. Anyway, he went up there and he fell . . . quite a long way. Michele found him when he stopped by to check on progress."

"Is he going to be OK?" I asked, sure that the answer would be yes, because bad things like that happened to other people, not me.

"We don't know yet. He's pretty bruised and smashed up, but I think from what the doctors have said so far that the head injury is the biggest concern."

I started firing questions at her but Pieta didn't have comforting answers for any of them.

"It's early days yet," she kept saying. "He's still unconscious and we don't know much at all. But you should get home. Michele is booking you on to an early morning flight. You just need to get yourself to the airport, OK?"

I dressed and threw some random things in a bag. Stopping to scribble a short note for Coco, I hurried from the building. Outside, the *calli* were still flooded with people in a party mood. One look at my face seemed to be enough to make them shift aside.

Many were Italian and must have come over from Mestre and beyond to be part of the Festa. Now they'd be heading home, filling the trains, buses and ferries; that's if there even were any running this late. I had a panicky feeling. Stopping a couple who looked like locals, I asked if they could tell me the best place to find a water taxi.

"Maybe try next to the train station." The man looked doubtful. "I'm sorry, signora, but tonight it will be difficult . . . the Festa . . . so many people . . . many routes blocked with boats."

The couple began to move away, and then the lamplight caught my face and I think they must have seen the tears streaking it.

"Do you have far to go, signora?" the woman asked.

"I have to get to the airport. I'm on an early flight. It's an emergency." I heaved a sob. "My husband has been badly hurt. There must be some way I can get out of Venice fast."

The woman looked at the man. He nodded as if she'd asked him a question.

"Come with us, signora. We have a boat. We will get you there."

It was only a small motorboat and we didn't travel especially quickly. Tacking through the canals, seeing how insanely busy they were, I was grateful to be moving at all.

The woman kept me talking, asking about my time in Venice, where I'd stayed and what I'd been doing. I tried to answer her civilly but it was an effort. I just wanted to be at the airport, on a plane, back home again, not sitting on this boat saying that yes, I had been to the Guggenheim and toured the Doge's Palace.

The whole trip back to London seemed to take three times longer than it should have. Waiting at the airport, queuing at check-in and security, empty hours in the air, and all the time in a panic and worrying that the worst would happen, that maybe Eden was going to die.

How would we live in a world without Eden, Katia and I? How could there even be such a thing? All you've heard about him so far are the annoying things. I haven't told you the other side — how soft-hearted he is, and kind, how funny and caring in all sorts of ways. I haven't mentioned any of the little things. Like how he rescues spiders and puts them outside. Or the time a baby bird fell from its nest and he spent an hour building a ramp for it to climb back up to safety. Last summer he sowed the lawn with sunflowers because he knows how much I love them. He does silly stuff to make me and Katia laugh: plays tricks, tells terrible jokes. He is the most generous person I know. If you need someone to help you move house, or check up on your sick mother, or pick you up from the other side of town because you've missed the last bus home and spent your taxi fare, Eden will do it without a word of complaint. He's that guy, really nice. It's why I married him. Somehow I'd been so caught up in my bitterness and resentment, I'd managed to forget it. But on that journey home, it was all I could think of.

Later on I would look back and feel as if I'd been torn out of Venice that night. I'd remember the plane trip, and how alone I'd been, and vulnerable. I'd recall the small kindnesses of strangers; not only the couple with the boat, but the man who gave me a handkerchief for my tears and the woman who fetched me a bottle of water and a cup of coffee laced with sugar. They were hazy figures with sympathetic voices. I'm not sure whether I even managed to thank them.

My brother-in-law Michele was waiting in Arrivals. It was such a relief to see a familiar face, even if it was one that was pinched and pale with anxiety.

"I'm so sorry, Dolly," he said, enveloping me in a hug. "I feel terrible. I wish I'd never asked him to work on that building. It's been a disaster from the start, and now this."

As we drove to the hospital, I looked at Michele hunched miserably over the steering wheel. Over the years I'd known him, I'd watched as his dark hair had greyed and his good looks had been chiselled away by fatigue and hard work. Now he looked a decade older than the last time we'd seen each other. He seemed broken by this.

"I feel so guilty," he kept saying. "I feel like this is my fault."

I had so much guilt of my own, there was nothing I could say to help Michele feel better about his. If I hadn't nagged Eden about work, if I hadn't taken off to Venice on some self-indulgent whim, if I'd come home and sorted things out . . . none of this would have happened.

"At least he's alive," Michele said. "When I found him lying there, I thought it was all over. Thank God I stopped by; he might have been there all night otherwise."

He told me how he'd been frightened to move Eden and had sat on the ground holding his hand as he waited for the ambulance. He said he'd prayed for the first time in years and cried at the sound of the sirens. I could imagine it all, like watching a film in my head. I saw Eden slipping from the scaffolding and falling to the ground; I saw Michele crouching over him, the ambulance with its flashing lights and the paramedics with a stretcher. I wished I could put the pictures out of my mind but they played through it on a loop.

"Katia doesn't know yet," Michele told me. "She's with your parents at our place right now. She's been spending lots of time with them over the summer, so there's no need to worry about her for the moment."

I felt numb, in shock probably. I wanted Michele to hurry up and get me to the hospital, as though once I was there I'd be able to do something; sort out the whole horrible situation.

Of course, there was nothing I could do. Eden was in intensive care, hooked up to machines that monitored his heart rate and his blood pressure; that helped him breathe and stopped him choking; that checked the pressure in his head. His eyes were open but he couldn't see me. I took his hand and squeezed his fingers but he didn't move.

It was bewildering. The person I wanted to call right at that moment was Eden. I needed reassurance, to hear him tell me not to freak out, that everything was going to be fine. I longed for the sound of his voice. But he was lying there silent, and I was helpless beside him.

People came in and out of the room; some of them told me things in soft and patient voices. They talked about a CT scan and a contusion on the brain, about broken ribs and a fractured skull. They explained there wouldn't be any miracle surgery and all we could do was wait, monitor Eden, medicate him, keep his body going and hope he would improve.

Pieta had been at the hospital all night and Eden's brother had rushed over as soon as he'd heard. We were a small group of exhausted, worried people taking it in turns to fetch coffee, to comfort each other in low voices, to murmur on our phones to friends and family, to pass each other boxes of tissues, to cry.

"He's going to be all right," we kept reassuring each other. "He's getting good care and he'll come through this. He'll be fine."

I'm not sure if any of us believed it. Most likely we were all thinking the same thing: what if he didn't . . . what then?

It was something Coco had once said that helped me through that long day of watching and hoping. *I can't change the past and undo my mistakes. All I can do is get on with life. Keep going and keep trying. It's all any of us can do.*

I remembered those words whenever guilt threatened to overwhelm me, when the medics were sounding uncertain and as the day stretched towards evening. It was the one thing that made any difference at all.

Later that night, Eden showed signs of coming round. By then we'd sent the rest of the family home to rest and it was just Pieta and me at his bedside. At first we weren't sure what was happening. Eden's eyes blinked once or twice and he moaned. Then he muttered something I couldn't understand.

"Eden." I grabbed his hand as Pieta leapt from her chair and went running from the room, calling for a nurse. By the time she returned, he was entirely still again and I wondered if we'd imagined it.

For the rest of the night he drifted in and out of consciousness. Now and then he tried to speak but made no sense at all, and once he seemed distressed, trying to thrash around.

It was dawn by the time he said something we understood. "What happened?" His voice was hoarse and sleepy. "Where am I?"

At first I was excited. "You're safe, you're in hospital, you had an accident," I told him. "You're going to be OK."

He seemed to understand. But then a few moments later he repeated the question and I had to give the same answer. We went on that way for an hour or so until he closed his eyes and fell back asleep.

I turned to Pieta, frightened. "Do you think he knows who we are?"

She tried to reassure me, but I heard the worry in her voice. "They said he'd be confused, remember? That it would take time."

"What if he never remembers me? Or Katia?"

"You can't think like that. We've got to stay positive."

"God, I feel so stupid," I told her. "I spent all summer making a list of what makes me happy, and I left all the most important things off it."

My sister hugged me and I cried, but quietly so Eden didn't hear. That's how I did all my crying then. There was plenty of it.

"What if he hates me?" My face was pressed into Pieta's shoulder. "I wouldn't blame him if he did."

She tried to talk sense into me. "This is Eden, remember? He doesn't hate anyone. That's not who he is."

"Yes, but what if he's changed?" I said, and my sister didn't have an answer.

I cried again later that day when I saw my daughter at Pieta's place. After two sleepless nights and so much worry, there was my beautiful girl in a pair of skinny jeans my mother had bought her, looking so grown up and pleased to see me.

I hugged her, my face buried in her shiny hair, trying not to let her see the tears in my eyes, feeling almost soothed by our closeness. I didn't want to break the

364

spell and tell her about Eden's accident. When I did, she cried with me.

"He's going to be all right," I told her, still not quite daring to believe it myself. "He's getting good care. You'll be able to see him soon, when he's feeling stronger."

I held her small warm body and dried her tears. To distract her I talked about Venice: the things I'd done and the people I'd met. I told her stories and showed her photographs I'd taken on my phone of stripy-shirted gondoliers, boats cruising down the Grand Canal, the windows of pastry shops crammed with cakes, Boris running to fetch a stick, Coco and Silvio dancing the tango in the evening sunlight. It was bittersweet to see those pictures again. There was so much guilt mixed in with the nostalgia of it; so much love of Venice and yet so much sorrow now too.

"Can we go there one day?" Katia asked, flicking through the pictures. "Will you take me with you next time?"

"Of course," I said. "That's what I'm planning. I even have a list of the things I want us to see together. Just as soon as your dad is well enough to travel, we'll all go together."

I really hoped that everything was going to work out that way and I could keep the promise. I talked about it to her all the time; and to my parents and Pieta too, in the hope that if I said it often enough, it might actually happen.

Recovering from a head injury is all about small triumphs. First there was the triumph of Eden asking what had happened and remembering my reply; then the triumph of him saying my name and squeezing my hand; the joy of hearing he felt a little better, the relief of him being moved out of intensive care into a recovery ward. Small triumphs but we hung on to them. We kept going and trying, just as Coco had said.

It frustrated us all that Eden had no recall of the accident or what he had been doing on that scaffolding in the first place. Often we talked about it, trying to piece things together and understand why someone so safety-conscious had climbed up there after hours, and how he'd managed to fall. Eden thought that perhaps he was unhappy with the work the builders were doing and had decided to pop up and check it after they'd gone home, but he couldn't be sure.

Aside from those blanks in his memory, he was starting to seem more like himself. Day by day he showed new signs of improvement. The drowsiness began easing, as did the headaches; the broken bones were mending and the doctors seemed pretty pleased with his progress. I spent as much time as I could at the hospital to keep him company, reading aloud from books or magazines or chatting about what Katia was up to. Despite where we were and what had happened, it felt good to be together, just him and me, away from all the clamour of the outside world, with hours to spare and nothing to fill them but our conversation.

"I want to come home," he told me one afternoon. "I'll get better faster there. When are they going to let me?"

I stared at him, not sure what to say. All this time our focus had been on his recovery and nothing else seemed important. The other stuff I'd pushed away, refused to even consider, but we couldn't ignore it for ever.

"Eden?" Reaching over, I took one of his hands. His fingers were work-roughened, his palms calloused; these were strong, practical hands. I'd held on to them at all the most important times: when we'd stood at the altar of St Peter's and exchanged our vows; when I'd given birth to our daughter; when I'd been sad, when I'd been happy.

"Dolly?" He stared back at me. I think he understood what was going through my mind.

"I'd like you to come home too. And I want to be there when you do," I told him.

"To take care of me?"

"Yes, but not just that." I squeezed his fingers. "To be a family like we used to be."

"Things have to change, Dolly. I haven't forgotten." He said it softly. "We weren't happy. We can't forget that just because I got hurt. If anything, it's more important."

"But we can be happy," I whispered back at him. "It's not impossible. We just have to let it happen."

Hospitals aren't the greatest places to discuss your future. But I'd delayed it for long enough and couldn't wait any longer. There, huddled beside Eden's bed, I tried to explain myself, to tell him how I felt and what I'd learnt. It wasn't easy, because he thought I was blaming him like I always used to.

367

"You're right that things have to change," I agreed. "I mean, why have we even been doing what we do? Is it because we want to? Or simply because we feel we've got no other choice?"

Eden looked wary. "This is about you resenting me for getting injured and not being able to work, right?"

"No, this is about being happier. But not just me; all of us."

And so we made a list, a proper one, with bullet points and the more important things underlined. A list of the things we had to change. An action plan, I suppose.

I wanted us to have fewer responsibilities and worries. Eden needed me to drink less and be home more. I wanted adventures, Eden family time. We're different people, so of course we came up with different things, but we decided to find a way to make them work together, or at least to try.

The last thing on our list I underlined three times. I planned for us to make it happen as soon as we possibly could — a trip back to Venice, the three of us. I wanted Katia and Eden to share the world I'd found there, to experience that shadowy, watery city. I hoped it would work its magic on us somehow.

"If we stayed for a while, there's an international school that Katia could go to," I told him. "She might even pick up some Italian, which would thrill my father."

Eden was dubious. "A trip will put us even further into debt," he pointed out, "and make things harder in the long run. Are you sure you want that?"

"Yes, it's worth it," I insisted. "If we go right back to the way things were, nothing will change. It'll be too hard. We'll just get buried in it all again. This is the perfect time to go away. You'll be convalescing and Papa is still happy looking after Little Italy. This is our chance."

"Why Venice? Why not just take a holiday someplace else?"

"I had a whole life there this summer without you and Katia. Now I'd like you both to be part of it for a while. I think I need you to be."

"And what if it doesn't work?" Eden asked. "We might go all that way and spend all the money and still fall apart in the end."

I put down my list and took his hand again. I turned it over so I could see the light dusting of freckles on the back and the way his skin was just beginning to pucker and loosen.

"I can't promise you anything," I said. "There are no guarantees. But I think Venice is our best chance."

CHAPTER
TWENTY-FIVE

So now we're here in Venice, the three of us, staying in the apartment above Coco's place. She seems excited to have us there, in particular Katia, who she loves stealing away and dressing up in beads and feathers. My daughter is entirely fascinated by this glamorous old woman; she keeps asking me questions about her. I can only answer some of them honestly, of course. I'm keeping Coco's secrets.

It is late autumn and Venice is giving us mostly golden days. The light is softer, the leaves of the trees and creepers are turning yellow and red and there is a chill in the shadows that heralds the seasons changing.

Coco keeps warning me that we're going to hate it when the weather turns. She speaks of mists and rain, of floods and days of unrelenting greyness. We're not thinking so far ahead, Eden and I. We're learning to live in the moment.

He is coping far better here than I imagined he would. Enough people speak English for his lack of language skills not to be a problem. And although whenever he ventures out alone he gets completely lost in the maze of *calli*, he always finds his way home again full of excitement at something he's discovered. He likes to strike up conversations with the tourists and has taken up with a group of gondoliers who seem to have adopted him. They go to out-of-the-way *bacari* I've never discovered and often, if they're not busy, give him and Katia gondola rides.

His back still bothers him, of course — the fall didn't help that at all. Some days he gets headaches and is sideswiped by exhaustion. He shocks Katia by snapping at her for nothing much at all, or he's struck by a low mood and it's hard to lift him out of it. That's the legacy of his head injury, we remind each other. It's just a matter of getting through days like those and hoping the next is better.

It helps to be in Venice, as I knew it would. There are so many adventures for us to have together. We're doing all the tourist stuff: the boat trips across the lagoon and the walking tours. We're having fun.

And then there is the tango. I hadn't realised how much I'd been missing it until I returned to the *milonga* in the Piazza San Giacomo dell'Orio. The joy of dancing again, of the movement and the music. It's the thing I've kept on doing just for me: my time, my passion.

I see Angelo at the *milongas*, although I don't dance with him so often. He's split up from Marie-Ann and has some other girl in tow. She's a local, younger than him, dark like Valentina and a very good dancer. He is talking about Buenos Aires again, about show tango and competitions. This time he believes he's found a woman who'll follow him where he needs to go.

The night we spent together hasn't been mentioned by either, of us and hopefully never will. Perhaps you think I should have confessed to Eden, told him everything? Well, I did consider it for a while. In the end it was the thought of so much hurt that stopped me. It was only one night, when I let the passion and excitement of the tango lead me somewhere it shouldn't have, one crazy night that would destroy this fragile new thing growing between Eden and me. Better to stay silent and keep my secret, that's what I decided; to bury it deep inside me. Everyone has secrets, don't they? At least that's what I think now.

Marie-Ann is still around. I see her at the *milongas*, where she complains about the lack of male partners and keeps an eye on Angelo. I tell her to forget about him, that he was never right for her, but I'm not sure she's convinced yet.

I haven't seen so much of Nanda, but we've all been invited to the wedding next spring when Valentina will marry her glassmaker. The pair of them are staying on Murano for the time being and the palazzo is closed up. Coco hopes they will come back to it soon. She misses them more than anyone suspects . . . except perhaps me. She even agreed to accompany us on a day trip to visit them.

We found Nanda installed in a smart house where there really is a housekeeper to cook her meals, make tea and walk Boris. And Valentina, her pregnancy showing, is so much brighter than in the days when she was working all those jobs. She is still guarded with me, careful with what she shares, but I gather money isn't such an issue now that she and her fiancé have decided to combine their family businesses. She doesn't seem to miss her old life much, not even the singing and dancing. As far as I can tell, she is content with the way things are. Perhaps it is what she wanted all along.

The other day I found my notebook in a drawer, the one with my happiness list scrawled in it. Coco must have saved it for me after I disappeared, along with the clothes and bits of jewellery I'd left behind.

1. Parties
2. Afternoon naps
3. Dogs
4. A glass of chilled Prosecco
5. Neighbourhoods
6. Tango
7. Good coffee served properly
8. Music
9. Being surrounded by water

It's an odd mishmash and hardly a recipe for happiness. So much of the most important stuff has been left off for a start — family, friends, love. I thought they were much too obvious to be included. I see now I was wrong.

So I've added them to the very top of my list and I'm holding on to the notebook because I have a feeling I'm not finished with it yet. Why stop at ten things after all? Everyone changes, and so do their dreams. Happiness never stays the same.

In the meantime I've been thinking about that summer and why exactly I wrote down the things I did. I even showed it to Eden, and with his help I've been planning how we might weave some of them through our life when we return to England in a little while.

What I dream of is changing Little Italy, of turning it into a sort of *bacaro*. In the mornings we'd do amazing coffee and pastries served on little trays covered with vintage cloths. We'd get rid of the white tablecloths, all the fancy restaurant stuff. Instead it would be the kind of place you'd feel you could drop into for breakfast and return to later on for a few bites of *cicchetti* and an *ombra* of wine. Casual but stylish, friendly like a club, and if you became a regular we'd make you feel special, greeting you by name and stopping for a chat, offering you small tastes of new things we were trying or the latest wines we'd added to the list.

In summer Papa and Frederico would play cards outside with the other old Italians who still live in the neighbourhood. Eden and I would rent out our flat and move with Katia to live upstairs above the restaurant. Little Italy would be an extension of our home. All of us would be there together, pouring drinks and picking up empty glasses, making our customers into friends. On Sundays we'd still do the old lunchtime favourites for the regulars who have been coming for years. And a couple of nights a week we'd clear the tables away and open up for a tango club to hold a *milonga*.

It's only a dream at this stage, but I've made dreams a reality before. Eden and I plan the details, jotting them in my notebook. Perhaps some day we will do it, or perhaps we won't. I like the not knowing; it makes everything more interesting. I've decided my life is just like the tango now. I won't force it along; I need to let it happen naturally, stay in the moment, stay with the feeling, live with my heart not my head. I'm getting better at it.

When I started that list of mine, it was because I felt like I was wasting my life, letting the years slip by in a fug of so-so-ness. I wanted to be more content. It was naïve of me in some ways and actually quite brilliant in others.

There was a reason I didn't appreciate what I had — I wanted something different. Not a new husband or even a new job, but a life that changed, one where every minute of each day wasn't already accounted for, planned out. And it was possible all along; I was just too stuck to see it.

The trouble with chasing happiness is that it tends to dance away and stay shimmering out of reach somewhere in the distance. The trick is learning to pause, to notice it's there and let it in. Of course, that's far from easy and I'm still no expert, but I'm better now at taking the small pleasures from every day and stitching them together into a bigger joy. Venice taught me a little, Coco even more, and what happened to Eden drove the lesson home.

Happiness is many things for me. Most of all it's doing what I love, being with the people I care about, spending time in the places that make me feel anything is possible.

Right now Venice is my secret to happiness. I'm not saying it's the answer for everyone, or for ever, particularly today as the rain drizzles on to my balcony and I begin to see that Coco may be right about winter.

I'm hoping for a break in the weather. I'm hoping that Katia will come upstairs soon and show me what fabulous gown and make-up my friend has dressed her up in today. I'm hoping Eden will wake from his nap refreshed and all of us will go to the *milonga* this evening and I'll dance a *tanda* while the light fades behind the stark facade of the old church and my daughter hangs out with the local kids and my husband chats to a tourist and tells them about all the places they must be sure to visit before they leave Venice.

Right now we're here in Coco's place, we're together and safe, and that's happiness enough.

Acknowledgements

Tango turns out to be another of the many things I have no natural aptitude for. So thanks are due to Auckland dance teacher Rilind Modigliani for risking his toes and sharing his knowledge of Argentine tango with me. I also took inspiration from Sally Potter's movie *The Tango Lesson*, developed a crush on tango superstar Pablo Veron (he is not unlike Angelo), played the music in my car and danced beautifully in my imagination.

Gretchen Rubin's book *The Happiness Project* helped spark the original idea. Sally Spector's *Venice and Food*, Tessa Kiros's *Venezia: Food and Dreams* and Michela Scibilia's *Venice Osterie* informed and inspired. Ari Seth Cohen's photo blog Advanced Style helped me stock Coco's wardrobe. And Auckland neurologist Dr William E. Wallis talked to me about head injuries.

As ever, thanks to all at Orion and Hachette. Extra thanks to my editor Genevieve Pegg and my agent Caroline Sheldon. And all the other people who make a book happen and put it into readers' hands, from the designer, copy-editor, sales reps and publicists to the booksellers themselves . . . thank you, one and all.

Also thanks to Marie-Ann Billens, whose husband bid for her to have a character in this book named after her at an auction to raise funds for the excellent charity Look Good Feel Better.

Finally, thanks to my husband Carne Bidwill, who put up with me swanning off to Venice for research purposes and insisting on going alone because "that's what my character does". You're coming next time, I promise.